Hunting November

Hunting November

ADRIANA MATHER

ALFRED A. KNOPF
NEW YORK

THIS IS A BORZOI BOOK PUBLISHED BY ALFRED A. KNOPF

Text copyright © 2020 by Adriana Mather
Jacket photograph copyright © 2020 by Robin Macmillan/Trevillion Images

Visit us on the Web! GetUnderlined.com

Educators and librarians, for a variety of teaching tools, visit us at RHTeachersLibrarians.com

Library of Congress Cataloging-in-Publication Data is available upon request.
ISBN 978-0-525-57912-0 (trade) —
ISBN 978-0-525-57913-7 (lib. bdg.) —
ISBN 978-0-525-57914-4 (ebook)

The text of this book is set in 10.75-point Mercury.
Interior design by Ken Crossland

Printed in the United States of America
May 2020
10 9 8 7 6 5 4 3 2 1
First Edition

In loving memory of my cat Charles,

who had a small head and a long tail, flexible

shoulders like a flying squirrel, and two different-

colored eyes. He slept on my pillow every night

and bit my head every morning when he wanted

food. I carried him in my sweatshirt as a kitten, and

he folded his head into the crook of my neck as an

adult. He was my perfect cat, and I was his person;

I will forever miss his snuggles.

One

WHEN I WAS a little kid and people asked me what I wanted to be when I grew up, I gave them all sorts of wild answers. I told a teacher I wanted to be a couch potato so I could spend my days snuggled up under blankets in the living room. I told my best friend Emily's mom I wanted to be a cookie taste-tester because that's what Emily wanted to be. And I told my dad I wanted to be a knife so I could cut my grilled cheese sandwiches in two perfect triangles instead of the four dinky squares he always prepared. Of course this answer earned me raised eyebrows and an explanation about how a *girl* is a living, breathing thing that can be *cut;* and a *knife* is a sharp piece of steel that does the *cutting.* But now that I've discovered most of my childhood was a lie, I'm starting to think my younger self was onto something with the knife answer. Because in the past few weeks at Academy Absconditi, I've come as close to being a knife, or being stabbed by one, as anyone can get.

I shut the door to the infirmary behind me and head down an empty hall that's lit by torches. I roll my sleeve down over the bandage on my forearm, where the nurse slathered my wound with some kind of strong poultice that smells of pine needles and clay. She kept telling me how lucky I was to have survived the fall from the tree in the courtyard, and with no broken bones. She *tsk*ed a lot and said, "You young people take everything for granted." I doubt she would have used the word *lucky*, though, if she knew I was thrown from the tree because the Lion Family wanted me dead.

As I turn the corner into another silent hallway, I notice the torches have burned down, leaving the corridor ahead of me almost completely black. I slow to a stop, eyeing the dying embers on one torch suspiciously. Shouldn't someone have replaced them? And where are the Academy guards? There's usually one posted in every hallway. I frown, wondering if I should head back to the infirmary, when I hear a faint gurgling noise.

I lean forward, reluctant to step into the unlit hallway, as if the dark might bite me. For a beat all is silent and I wonder if I only imagined the sound. Then a gasping cough breaks the quiet and my adrenaline spikes.

"November!" a strangled voice calls, and everything in me sinks. I recognize that voice.

"Ash?!" I shout, and my previous hesitation disappears; I sprint full-speed into the dark.

My boots click rhythmically against the stone and my breathing accelerates with my pace. I run with my hand along the wall to keep my footing as I chase Ash's distressed voice.

Ahead of me on the left I can just make out a strip of light—the sliver of space under a closed door—and the choking sounds get louder as I near it. I grasp at the door latch in the dark, throwing my weight against the heavy wood. The hinges whine as it opens and I burst into the room, only to stop again so fast that I almost lose my balance.

My chest heaves as I fight to regain control over my runaway heartbeat. The room is enormous, with stone walls and a high arched ceiling. It's oddly devoid of furniture—except for the far end, where there are a platform and a large lavish chair that resembles a throne. The walls are hung with fancy portraits and ornate tapestries. But what's stopped me in my tracks isn't the architecture or the decor. It's the *dead bodies*.

My eyes sweep across the expansive floor and my hand flies to my mouth to keep from crying out. Most are people I've never seen, a sea of unknown faces, their features contorted in pain in their last moments. But then I spot him at the far end of the room: Ash, clawing at his throat as his mouth foams. Lying next to him is Layla, and beside her are Ines, Aarya, and Matteo. They're splayed out, unmoving, their backs arched, bloody marks scratched across their throats. And standing in front of them all with his back to me is a tall man with silver hair. He starts to laugh, long and loud.

"Nonono . . . ," I sputter in one fast breath, my pulse battering my temples as I frantically weave around bodies, panic fumbling my footing.

Layla's delicate hand is still clutching at her throat as if she's fighting to get air, but her eyes are closed and she's perfectly still. A cry escapes my lips and I trip over someone's arm, my hands skidding on the cold stone floor. I immediately right myself. Ash's desperate eyes meet mine and he chokes again, reaching out for me.

The man with the silver hair looks down at Ash as he struggles.

3

"What did you do to them?" I shriek, my words fighting their way past the lump in my throat.

He bends down toward Ash, a small blue bottle in his hand. *Poison,* I think, and I yell for him to stop, but my words don't come out right, twisting into a sob.

"You mean, what did *we* do, November," the old man says without turning around. His voice is like the purr of a big cat.

He holds the bottle to Ash's mouth, but Ash isn't looking at him. He's staring at my hand in horror. I follow his gaze, and there in my palm is a small matching blue bottle.

The old man pours the liquid from his bottle into Ash's mouth and I scream.

"November?"

I shoot straight up, my arms flying out to steady myself, and I end up grabbing a handful of gray velvet cushion. The end of a scream escapes my lips, muted and unsure.

Ash grips my shoulders, steadying me.

"I didn't—" I say, and stop short, disoriented and tense, my heart still racing like I was running in that room.

"Look around you, November. Breathe," Ash says calmly, and I cling to his voice.

I do a fast scan of my surroundings to find a lit fireplace, a breakfast table by the window, maroon blackout curtains, and Ash—alive and sitting next to me on the couch in the common room I share with Layla. Everything looks normal, but the feeling of dread is still there. And even though I'm not sure how, the one thing I know—the one thing I'm *certain* of—is that whatever happened in that dream was my fault.

"You were . . . ," I start, my tone unsettled, my voice shaky. "And it was my . . ." But I trail off there, not able to put words to the awfulness I just witnessed. It felt so real, so very real.

Ash gives me a sympathetic look, like he knows all too well the type of thing I might be dreaming about. I take a breath, my shoulders dropping an inch. *It was a nightmare. Just a nightmare. No one is dead,* I reassure myself, but my unease lingers like a bad taste.

"I don't remember falling asleep," I say, and rub at my face, only to discover that I'm sweating.

Ash studies me, letting go of my shoulders but remaining close. His straight black hair falls perfectly around his temples and his eyes are insistent under his long eyelashes. Even though he's got his fair share of cuts and bruises from being attacked yesterday, he looks more poised and elegant than I do on my best days. The longer I look at him, the guiltier I feel. Maybe the dream wasn't real, but what is real is that Ash and I narrowly escaped with our lives—and it was all because of me.

"I was reluctant to wake you, or I would have moved you over to your bed," he says, but he doesn't ask me about my nightmare. Strangely enough, I get the sense that he doesn't want to pry. I've come to understand why Strategia guard their Family secrets, but the way they guard themselves and their emotions is something I'm still not used to. If my best friend, Emily, had seen me wake up in a panic like I did just now, she would not only have insisted I tell her every detail, but would have analyzed the dream with me until the meaning was nothing more than the prediction of a bad hair day.

I glance at Layla's closed bedroom door.

"She went to bed an hour ago," Ash says in response to my unasked question.

I look back at him, taking in his concerned expression. "But you stayed," I say, relieved that he did. Despite our rocky start when I first came to Academy Absconditi and all the suspicion between us, I've grown to truly rely on Ash.

"I was lost in thought," he replies with a small smile, and while I'm sure it's true, I'm also certain it's not the only reason he's next to me on my couch late at night. If he were any other guy and I hadn't just had the most gruesome nightmare of my life, I would tease him about how much he obviously wanted to be near me. But knowing Ash, he had a less romantic reason, such as trying to ensure no one stabbed me while I slept.

"Lost in thought about what?" I ask.

"I was just thinking that we can't be sure who knows about your father," Ash says, directing the conversation right back to my family's conflict and squashing the small amount of comfort I was starting to feel, which I suppose I should be used to by now—comfort isn't an Academy trademark. This school is more about survival than academics, more about carefully planned alliances than friendships, attributes I learned the hard way when I discovered that the most powerful Strategia Family had a vendetta against my dad. And it turns out several of the kids—as well as a professor who happened to be my dad's brother—were prepared to kill me to show their allegiance to that Family. "Obviously Dr. Conner knew *something*," Ash continues, "but what about the Lion Family in

6

general? I think we have to assume they are hunting your family for a specific reason, one we will need to uncover if we have any hope of finding your father."

At the mention of the Lions, my thoughts flash back to the bloodied bodies in my nightmare. I momentarily look away, overcome once again by a wave of guilt for having gotten Ash involved in all of this. I rub my eyes with the heels of my palms. "Are you saying you think the Lions are after me and my dad for a reason *other* than my parents' Romeo and Juliet defiance?"

"I do," he says. "Think about it. Your mother was a member of the Bear Family, and your father was a Lion. Twenty-five years ago, they fell in love and decided to desert their respective Families, abdicate their leadership positions, and go into hiding." He pauses and looks at me gently. "And then the Lion assassins killed your mother when you were . . . ?"

"Six," I say, readjusting my position on the couch.

"So eleven years ago," Ash continues. "But between then and last month, when your aunt was killed and your father sent you here, were you aware of any threats from the Lions?"

I scrunch my forehead, scanning memories of my childhood, looking for any period where my dad seemed stressed or out of sorts, anything that might indicate that the Lions were after us. I shake my head. "Honestly, I don't think so. Dad would have moved us if there were. I mean, we had a rough patch after Mom died, of course, but other than that, we were happy and our life was simple." My voice quiets as I realize I've just put *happy* in past tense.

Ash is nodding, as if I've confirmed his suspicion. "You see, the events are spread out. Your parents' initial disappearance, your mother's death, and your aunt's recent murder," he says.

I watch him for a moment, unsure. "What are you saying, that you don't think the Lions were after us the whole time?"

"I'm not saying it isn't possible, but it would have required committing resources to the effort for twenty-five years straight. It is more likely that each attack was instigated by some other event, something that gave the Lions insight or intel about your family's movements. Correct me if I'm wrong, but from what I've gleaned from our previous conversations, you've lived in the same small town your entire life, somewhere remote, where you weren't in hiding, but well integrated into the community." He waits for me to contradict him, and when I don't, he continues. "To me, that doesn't sound like you were under siege; it sounds like you were *safe*."

I chew on my thumbnail, scouring his theory for fault points and finding none. "Okay, so let's say you're right," I reply. "Then how did they find my aunt Jo? What changed?"

"My point exactly—something changed," Ash says. "And I imagine the reason is directly tied to whatever your father is doing at this very moment."

I exhale loudly, my mind once again reeling with fear for my dad. *At the very least,* I tell myself, *Dr. Conner is gone and I'm finally free to leave the Academy.* But the moment I think it, I feel ill. Dr. Conner isn't gone, he's *dead,* and his death had everything to do with *me.*

Ash's look is almost apologetic. "I know you've been through a great deal, but I can't stress enough how important it is that everything go smoothly tomorrow. We aren't in the clear yet." My stomach drops at the word *we.* Ash offered to go with me to help me find my dad—an offer that is likely to get him killed.

"No one can find out we're leaving," he continues in a calm

8

voice. "You need to go to your classes with Layla as usual, eat in the dining hall, and study in the library as if everything is *normal*."

I meet Ash's gaze, giving him a look that questions the suggestion that this place was ever normal. "'Been through a *great deal*'? Now there's an understatement," I say, making light of how upside down I feel. "It's almost unbelievable to me that only a month ago I had no idea this bizarre boarding school even existed, that Strategia were real." I gesture at the common room. "And despite dodging death a half dozen times and being framed for murder, my troubles are only just beginning because my dad is now being *hunted by an assassin-like secret society* of Families that is so effective it's influenced the course of history for *thousands of years*." I give Ash a please-make-light-of-this-with-me look, seeing as my sleep is already threatened by untold horrors.

"I cannot tell you things will get easier," he says, and I groan. "In fact, they are about to get much worse."

"Nailed it on the comforting."

A small smirk appears on Ash's face. "I'll comfort you when I'm certain we're not going to die."

In spite of myself, I laugh. "That's literally the worst thing you could have . . . Haven't you ever heard of telling someone their outfit looks good when it doesn't? White lies save hearts."

"Your outfit looks good," he replies, playfulness dancing in his eyes.

I look down at my rumpled uniform, which consists of a white button-down, black leggings, and black lace-up boots. "It does, doesn't it?" I say. "I could win a pirate costume contest in this thing."

Ash's mouth pulls up into a smile, but his expression seems more than amused. He's looking at me like I'm the most unusual and interesting person he's ever met.

"Also, when did you get so worried about danger? Aren't you usually the one making light of everything? You're seriously slacking on your duties," I say, blushing slightly under his admiring gaze.

"I started worrying about danger when I started having feelings for the person involved," he says, and his answer catches me off guard.

For a moment we're both silent, sitting only a couple of inches apart, the air between us thick and warm in the firelight. I struggle to come up with a reply; sincerity from Ash is always unexpected.

"Brendan," Ash starts when I don't respond, yanking me out of the moment.

"Huh?" I say, trying to catch up.

"Keep an eye on Brendan tomorrow," he says, his voice low and reasoning. "With Nyx temporarily out of commission and Charles and Dr. Conner dead, I'm not certain what the Lions' next move will be, but Brendan is one of their last weapons here. There's no sense in speeding up his timeline by letting him suspect we're leaving."

I sigh, my head swimming as I recall the incidents of the last week: Charles dead after trying to kill me, Nyx banished to the dungeon for trying to skewer me with her sword. And now Ash is telling me Brendan might try to pick up where they left off. "Isn't there a universal rule somewhere that says it's bad manners to attack people right after they've outmaneuvered you?"

Ash leans back into the pillows. "Not when you're Strategia. In fact, it only makes you a more interesting target."

His answer reminds me of a twisted version of that old saying: If at first you don't succeed, try, try again. I grab a gray velvet throw pillow, hugging it to my chest. As I look at Ash, images from my nightmare fill my head once more. I frown. He survived Conner's poisoning, but only barely. What about the next time? How would I live with myself knowing I got Ash hurt, or even killed? What sounded daring, even romantic, when Ash offered to drop everything to help me find my dad is now tying up my stomach in knots.

I stare at the flames as they get lower in the fireplace. "That's the thing, *I'm* the target. But you don't have to be."

"What are you suggesting?" Ash asks, unsure.

He waits a moment for my response, but I'm too lost in my tangled worries. He looks me up and down. "You're leaning away from me, November, which means you're trying to protect yourself. And you're rubbing your palm with your thumb—a self-soothing gesture," he says. "I can keep reading your body language, but it would be easier if you talked to me."

I shift my gaze from the dancing flames to Layla's bedroom door, which adjoins the common area of our suite. She generously retreated earlier to give me an opportunity to talk to Ash, her twin brother. "The thing is, I'm unbelievably grateful that you want to come with me to find my dad. But think about the cost, Ash. First, you're leaving Layla. If something happens to your sister while you're away, you'll never forgive yourself—or me. And vice versa with Layla, if something happens to you."

"Then we had both better come back in one piece," he says, looking at me curiously.

"Second," I say without acknowledging Ash's flippant response, "what is your Family going to say?" Given the power Brendan and the Lions have, I hate to think what backlash there will be for Ash's Family if he moves against them. "Won't you be putting yourself in a vulnerable position?"

Ash smiles, but I can tell by his eyes that he's concerned about this, too. "None of which is a problem if we succeed."

"I'm serious," I say. "You just finished telling me how risky this all is and that we could die. We have no idea what we're going to find out there. We have no idea if the other Strategia even know that I exist—"

"I suspect more know about you than you might think," he says quietly.

I stare at him, hoping he's joking.

"Some of the students here—Matteo, for example—recognized you the moment you set foot on campus. We have to be prepared that others may do the same," he says, answering my unspoken fear. "Then there's the fact that Aarya told the entire school who your parents are, and even though communication to and from the Academy is monitored and often delayed, it's possible it'll get out before we find your father. Not to mention, suspicions will run high after you and I disappear tomorrow. People might assume Blackwood gave us leave to see our Families after what's happened, but it's just as likely that they will suspect we're out for retaliation after how aggressively the Lion Family tried to kill you. So as I said earlier, we don't want anyone to have information a moment before they absolutely need to."

"See," I say with emphasis. "There is no way you won't be affected by helping me."

"I've already helped you," he says.

"In *here*, yes. But we're insulated, more protected. Out there, you'll be a member of the Wolf Family, actively attempting to thwart the Lions. You've worked your whole life to prove yourself as a potential leader; this crazy mission I'm about to embark on could erode that in a flash," I reply.

Ash sighs like I've completely missed the point. "And if I let you navigate a world you don't know and confront the most powerful Strategia Family by yourself, I might as well give up my future leadership now, because I will always know that I wasn't there when it mattered most."

I stare at him, terrified of what could happen to him and just as desperate to have him with me. "If you join me, you might not live to graduate the Academy, much less lead."

"And I also might never learn to speak French with an undetectable accent. There are just some things one needs to accept about oneself," Ash says, and the smile creeps back onto his face.

"Ash—"

"*November,*" he says, and takes my hand, the warmth of his fingers sending goose bumps up my arm. "I've considered the danger; I know very well what kind of risks we're taking. But my decision remains unchanged. I'm going with you."

Two

THE EARLY-MORNING LIGHT seeps around the edges of the blackout curtains, and I lie awake in my canopied bed, watching the room slowly come into focus. There was a time, not long ago, when the grayness of this school and the lack of electricity unnerved me. I felt so isolated in this castle in the middle of a forest, away from everything I knew and loved. And it strikes me in this moment that I don't know when that changed, when *I* changed, but I don't feel trapped anymore. I don't feel out of place the way I once did.

I pull my curtains open, letting in the hazy light. There is a deep chill in the room and my socks aren't cutting it on the cold stone floor. I make my way over to my antique dresser, which holds a bowl of water and a fresh towel. I splash some water on my face and inspect myself in the mirror. The shadow under my eye where I was punched a couple of weeks ago is barely noticeable anymore, and the cuts on my arms and legs from Felix throwing me out of the tree are red but starting to heal. The bruise along my jawline is darker than it was yesterday and I'm sore, but those seem like infinitesimal worries compared to locating my dad.

I look out the window to the trees; between the branches, the first bits of snow swirl and flutter. "Snow," I breathe, instantly homesick for Pembrook and Emily and our wintertime antics. And then it occurs to me what day it is. "December twentieth," I say, and my chest constricts.

"Deeeecember tweeeentieth!" Emily and I shout out the back windows of my dad's truck. There's six inches of snow on the ground, making the trees sparkle and our town square look like an idyllic scene from a New England holiday card.

"What do you think? Should we go sledding?" Dad asks from the front seat.

"Well . . ." Emily gives me a mischievous look. "We were thinking we could go over to Eastbury Pond and ice-skate if you don't mind the drive."

"Breakfast, ice-skating, hot chocolate, sledding," I say, seconding Emily's enthusiasm. "Then we order a large pizza, maybe two large pizzas, and drive around to look at all the holiday decorations in the rich neighborhoods."

Dad parks his truck in front of Lucille's diner and turns off the engine. "This is your day, Nova. Whatever you girls want to do, I'm game."

The winter after my sixth birthday and a couple of months after Mom died, Dad started the December Twentieth Winter Celebration Day—our own made-up holiday, which had no association or nostalgia to remind us of our loss. Emily's been a part of it every year since. And even though it's fun if the twentieth falls on a weekend, it's a million times better when it falls on a school day and our parents let us take the day off.

15

Emily and I jump out of the truck, our boots crunching the newly fallen snow, with grins on our faces—the particular kind of enthusiasm garnered from knowing we're doing something awesome while everyone else is in math class.

There's a knock on my bedroom door and I wipe my face off with the towel. "Come in."

Pippa, the young maid who attends our suite, walks in with my freshly pressed clothes draped over her arm.

"Good morning," she says, only it sounds more like a question than a statement. She lays my black leggings and white linen shirt over the trunk at the end of my bed.

"Thank you," I say, trying to force life into my words, but I just wind up sounding uncomfortable.

Pippa's eyes drift to my banged-up arms peeking out from the rolled sleeves of my nightgown. Her forehead wrinkles with concern and I quickly pull my sleeves back down, but the gesture only reminds me of my dream last night. I give her what I hope looks like a reassuring smile, but my heart's not in it. If I can't make Pippa think I'm okay and that everything's normal, I've got no chance of convincing my deception-expert classmates.

Pippa stops halfway to the door and makes eye contact with me like she wants to say something, but just then Layla walks in and Pippa excuses herself. I fight the urge to blurt out a goodbye, give her a hug, and tell her thanks for taking such good care of me while I was here. *No one can know we're leaving,* I remind myself.

"I'll tell her," Layla says quietly as the door to the hallway closes. Despite having been locked in the dungeon herself, Layla is as poised and unruffled as always. Her long dark hair is loose and slides over her shoulder in a glossy wave. "While I may find your effusive behavior questionable, Pippa's a nice person and I know she would appreciate a goodbye from you." There's no fanfare in Layla's voice, as though she believes politeness is simply perfunctory.

I nod at her, grateful.

"Also, since you and Ash are leaving tonight, it's time to talk about where you think your father is," she says, and my anxiety comes back full-force. "Is your father the type to go directly after his Family in retribution for killing your aunt? Or will he hide out and gather information, opting for a subtler approach?"

"I want to say he's *not* the revenge type," I say, and bite my thumbnail. "But if there's one thing I've learned at this school, it's how little I actually know about my own father." I look up at Layla. "I can only assume that whatever he's planned is dangerous. Otherwise he wouldn't have sent me here."

"Okay, that's a start," Layla says with her usual studious expression. "If he decided to infiltrate Lion territory, that would certainly qualify as unsafe."

I sit on the edge of my bed. "That conclusion is exactly what kept me up half the night."

Layla tucks her hair behind her ear and sits down on the bed next to me. "If he's going after the Lions, it likely means he's somewhere in the UK. It's the seat of their power, it's where Jag resides, and it's where their allies are the strongest." She readjusts her position on the bed to better face me. "Our Family has contacts in the UK. Everyone's Family does." She pauses. "I'm just concerned that our Wolf Family contacts may not provide assistance to you and Ash. Not all of our Family dislikes the Lions as much as we do." She looks at me like she's just made a decision. "And you're not going to be able to track down your father without some help."

I stare back at her, trying to decipher the secondary meaning of her simple statement. "I agree, Lay. But what are you suggesting?"

"That you use your Bear contacts," she says.

"But I don't know who they are."

"Maybe not, but Matteo does," Layla says, and I wince.

"You don't really expect me to ask Matteo for help, do you? What are the chances that will go well? He hates me," I say.

"I didn't say it would be easy, I said it would be smart," she replies matter-of-factly.

I exhale. Making it through this one last "normal" day just got more complicated.

Three

I TAKE MY seat next to Layla in poisons class, which is set up like a medieval version of a high school chemistry lab. There's a large fireplace that warms the room, the flames of which are used to heat and prepare poisonous substances, and a stone basin filled with water. At Academy Absconditi they don't provide you with safety goggles to protect you from an explosive poisons accident, but they will extinguish you if you set yourself on fire. So that's nice. The truly shocking part, though, isn't the school's lack of safety precautions; it's that I've somehow grown accustomed to its risk-enthusiastic curriculum. I would shake my head at the absurdity of it all, but it wouldn't go unnoticed by my classmates. Ever since I stepped out of my room this morning, watchful eyes of students and teachers have followed my every step.

I'm certain Aarya made a big show of telling everyone that my parents were the rebel Romeo and Juliet of Strategia—the firstborn daughter of the Bear Family running off with the firstborn son of the Lions, only to be chased by Lion assassins. That, combined with Headmaster Blackwood's perfunctory announcement that Dr. Conner is dead, and the fact that Ash and I are covered in unexplained cuts and bruises, has made me the subject of a great deal of side-eyed whispering.

"Sit, my beauties," says Professor Hisakawa, which is the way she addresses us at the beginning of every poisons class. She scans the room from under her blunt-cut bangs, her eyes twinkling. "We have so many wonderful things to discuss. You're not going to want to miss a minute of it."

Aarya and Felix sit at the wooden table across from ours. Aarya spins the glass vials and jars in front of her, which are filled with varied horrors, while she whistles. She keeps directing smug looks to Brendan's back, obviously still gloating about her role in Dr. Conner's demise. The part that strikes me as unsettling, though, is that if everyone assumes Brendan was involved in the plot to kill me, why doesn't he suffer any consequences? Does his status as a head Lion really shield him that well, or is there just no evidence to prove it?

I shift my focus to Felix, who, unlike Aarya, is stiff and tensed, causing the long scar on his cheekbone to pull at the skin around it. He looks as banged up as me and Ash, and by the careful way he sits, I'm certain he's as sore from plummeting through that tree as I am. He's refused to look in my direction since he walked in the room. I guess it's hard to look at me knowing he tried to kill me only to later discover that I'd saved his life.

"*Atropa belladonna,* or deadly nightshade," Hisakawa says with a smile, reveling in her passion for poisons. "The Gothic siren of any good apothecary and one of the most romantic poisons, if I do say so."

Atropa, I think, and begin my usual analysis, *a name that likely pays homage to the Greek goddess Atropos, who was the oldest of the Three Fates and was responsible for choosing the way mortals die—hence the "deadly" bit. And of course* bella donna *means "pretty woman" in Italian.* I glance at Brendan—poison is just about the only thing he and his friends didn't try to use on me, although I'm sure he would have if he'd had the chance.

Brendan sits at a table by himself, his shock of white-blond hair standing out in stark contrast to the dark wood and stone walls. Nyx hasn't returned from the dungeon after attacking me with her sword, and it's obvious Brendan's aware of her absence by the way his brow furrows when he looks at her empty chair. He doesn't make eye contact with me, but his eyes narrow and I'm certain he notices. Layla kicks my boot under the table, which I can only assume means: "Don't be stupid enough to instigate Brendan when all you need to do is make it through one more day."

I adjust my gaze back to Hisakawa, who stands in front of the large fireplace with her hands clasped behind her back, rocking from the balls of her feet to the heels and back again. "The thing about belladonna that's fascinating is that there aren't that many recorded examples of poisoning. However, my personal favorite concerns eighteenth-century poisoner Giulia Tofana. She made Aqua Tofana, a 'cosmetic' sold exclusively to women for more than fifty years to help them kill their husbands. Instead of being applied to the skin, this product was poured into soup. When she was caught and executed, it was believed that Tofana had assisted in the poisoning of over six hundred men throughout Italy." Hisakawa sighs wistfully, the way some people react to a touching poem.

"Now, tell me, why would I be excited about something that has so few examples to teach from?"

Aarya leans back in her chair, the picture of ease. "Because belladonna is readily accessible and grows wild all over the world."

"Which would have us logically conclude that there would be an *excess* of reported cases of belladonna poisoning, not a shortage," Hisakawa interjects.

"Exactly," Aarya says like she just won a prize at a carnival, "which is what is so great about it. Belladonna is *effective*. Combine that with the fact that it's easily acquired and it tells you that the people who use it go undetected."

"Precisely!" Hisakawa says, and goes up on her toes for emphasis. "Now, why do belladonna users go undetected?"

Layla opens her mouth to respond, but Brendan beats her to it. "Because belladonna isn't and wasn't only used to kill. Women used to rub it directly into their eyes to make their pupils dilate, which was fashionable at the time. Mixed with morphine, it was called Twilight Sleep and was used as a painkiller for women giving birth. And we still use it in medicines that treat everything from Parkinson's to bronchitis."

"Well said," Hisakawa replies, and Layla looks disappointed she didn't get an opportunity to answer. "Belladonna is *common*. And in being so, it often gets missed as a cause of death. Instead, the death gets assigned to an overdose or an overextended use of medication. An illegal sleep aid, even."

Brendan soaks in the compliment from Hisakawa and I'm reminded of the scrolls in the library that keep record of the best students in each discipline for the past thousand years. Ash told me that if you can't excel at the Academy, you're seen as unfit to rule your Family. And that even after you're admitted here, you're not done proving yourself.

Hisakawa runs her fingers along the edge of her desk and leans against it. "It's like I was telling you in our lesson last week. Capitalize on what is already in your environment. *Blend.* That's what Giulia Tofana was doing with her husband-killing cosmetics. But this isn't just about poisoners; it's also about poison detection. You will be most vulnerable in a situation where everything seems normal and as it should be." Hisakawa looks at me and I stare back, trying to read her expression and see if maybe she's telling me something I need to hear. It wouldn't be the first time she's gone out of her way to give me a message from Headmaster Blackwood.

As if on cue, the door opens and Blackwood steps through, letting it swing closed behind her. Her hair is pulled back into a severe bun and she wears her uniform, consisting of a white frilled blouse under a black blazer and matching black pants. "Pardon my intrusion, Professor Hisakawa. But there is a matter I would like to settle without delay, if you wouldn't mind."

Layla gives me a concerned look.

"By all means," Hisakawa says, and gestures at the room like she's offering it to the headmaster.

The heavy wooden door opens with a whine and Nyx comes through, followed by two guards. *Oh no.* My stomach drops all the way to my toes and I shrink an inch in my seat. Nyx's curly hair is limp, and even with her permanent eyeliner, the dark circles under her eyes make it seem like she hasn't slept in weeks. Her face is drawn and her shoulders are slumped.

Brendan pushes his chair away from the table with

purpose, like he intends to stand and help her, but Blackwood glances in his direction and he stops midmotion.

The guards aren't restraining Nyx, and all I can think is that the dungeon must be an absolute nightmare to subdue someone as fiery and spiteful as she is.

"November," Blackwood says, and I wish I could crawl under my desk. The only thing more disturbing than the Academy's dungeon is its eye-for-an-eye punishment system. "Come up here."

I push my chair back, and the noise it makes is amplified by the eerie stillness of the room. All eyes are on me.

"Show us your arm," Blackwood says, and I reluctantly pull my white linen shirt off my shoulder, revealing a four-inch cut where my stitches were recently removed.

Blackwood turns to Nyx. "Nyx, you swapped your dull practice sword for a sharp blade in class. As far as I can ascertain from your professor, you intended to kill November with it. For that offense, you have spent time in the dungeon. But there is still the matter of the wound you inflicted. As per our rules, November will now be given a chance to retaliate." Blackwood holds out her palm and one of the guards hands her a rolled-up piece of leather from his belt. As she unfolds it, the firelight reflects off the blade of a knife.

Blackwood gives the weapon to me and I reluctantly take it from her. "An eye for an eye, November. You may cut her arm in the same way she cut yours. No other action will be taken." She gives me a warning look.

I reflexively glance at Layla, hoping something about her expression will tell me how to deal with this nightmare of a situation, but her face is completely neutral and she stares straight ahead at the headmaster.

I study the knife before looking up at Nyx. She meets my eyes, and even though it's obvious she wants nothing more than to collapse, she straightens her posture and wears a proud expression. I can't see how hurting her will change the fact that she tried to kill me. It definitely won't make us even. But I also can't flat-out refuse to retaliate; everyone here will consider it weakness. Beads of sweat form in my hairline.

Blackwood watches me, noticing my hesitation. "I don't imagine you require further clarification, considering this is not the first time I have explained this to you," she says, referring to my second day at the Academy, when Matteo punched me in the face. "You are not above the rules, November."

Aarya sucks in air like this is the best show she's seen in years.

The knife feels foreign in my palm, with none of its usual familiar weightiness. I glance at the door, and when I look back at Nyx, my stomach does a somersault.

"I want to inspect the knife," Nyx says, yanking me out of my thoughts. As weathered as she appears on the outside, it's instantly clear by her tone that her spark hasn't diminished. "This is poisons class. How am I supposed to know she didn't put something on the blade?"

We all look at Blackwood, who doesn't answer right away. She can't really be considering letting Nyx have the knife, can she? I shift my weight from one leg to the other.

"I'll grant that request," Blackwood says, and I nearly drop the knife out of shock.

Aarya slaps her knee and Layla's cheeks drain of their color.

Blackwood retrieves the knife from my hand and gives it to Nyx, who slowly examines the blade and handle. She sniffs it, rubs her finger on it, and holds the metal up to the light. The entire roomful of students sits on the edge of their seats, and it's so quiet that I can hear myself breathe.

Suddenly Nyx darts forward, the knife extended in front of her. I raise my arm in defense and the guards reach for her. But she stops short and laughs.

Brendan snickers behind me.

"I take it you're satisfied?" Blackwood says to Nyx, without reprimanding her for the lunge.

"Almost," Nyx says, but she's not looking at Blackwood, she's looking at me. She makes sure she has my full attention as she raises the knife to her own shoulder. She pulls the blade along her skin without so much as a wince. A smirk appears on her lips. She hands the knife back to Blackwood, handle first, and wipes her now-bloody palm on her shirt, creating a red smear.

"There, it's done," Nyx says, holding my gaze. "We're even. Now you can stop looking at the door like you want to run and cry."

My whole body tenses. *How in the hell did she just beat me at her own punishment?* Now if I do nothing, the damage will be done—everyone will get the message that when it comes to a physical confrontation, I'm afraid to act.

"Aaactually," I say slowly, fighting to keep the uneasiness out of my voice, "you cutting your own shoulder in no way makes us even. In fact, that was one of the worst strategic moves I've seen in a long time."

If Layla looked worried before, she now looks like she might have stopped breathing. Blood drips down Nyx's left arm and she narrows her eyes.

Before Blackwood can say a word, I grab the knife and jab forward, just shy of Nyx's uncut shoulder, grazing the fabric of her shirt with the sharp blade, creating a small tear. Nyx gasps and jumps out of the way.

The class watches with wide eyes. I can tell by Nyx's expression that she's furious not only with me, but also with herself for having jumped like that in front of everyone.

I laugh. "Nah, I guess we're even. Now that *you're* looking at the door like you want to run and cry."

She locks her jaw and glares at me like she wants to tear my head off, and even though I can't see him, I can feel Brendan's eyes boring into my back. So much for having a normal day.

Four

I SIT ON one of the cold moss-covered benches in the garden courtyard. Overhead the oak branches are strung with strands of royal-purple profusion berries, and in the fading light of day they glow like they're lit from within. The last of the blue, purple, and white flowers peek through the grass in intricate patterns around my feet. I look up at the canopy of tall trees, where the flurries from this morning have already melted. When I first got here, Layla explained that a hot spring runs under the school, allowing us to enjoy the flowers nearly all year round, and while it is a bit warmer on the ground than in the trees, I'm still convinced that the head horticulturist here must be something of a genius. I twirl a piece of fresh grass between my fingers, the fast motion mirroring the wound-up tension in my body.

A small group of elemental-level students are clustered at the other side of the courtyard, speaking in hushed voices. It's impossible to know what Families they belong to, since the students come from all over the world and speak multiple languages. But they clearly know who I am, because every once in a while they glance in my direction and lean toward one another, as though to further conceal their words.

There is movement near the arched vine doorway leading into the adjacent courtyard, and I hear cloaks being taken off hooks on the other side of the vine wall, signaling that strategic sparring has just ended. Strategic sparring, knife throwing, mind games—a month ago I would have laughed at the idea that such a curriculum even existed.

Aarya and Felix are the first to come through the vine doorway, and I get up from the bench. Aarya's eyes light up and she brushes back a piece of wavy hair that has fallen out of her loose ponytail.

"Well, if it isn't my favorite circus act at Phantom High," she says loudly enough that the elemental students turn in our direction. She switches from a British accent to an American one, both of them impeccable. In fact I don't think there's an accent that she hasn't mastered, making it impossible to know anything about her upbringing, other than that she's a Jackal and a force to be reckoned with. "After you graduate, well . . . if you live to graduate, you should take your show on the road. I would pay good money to watch stunts like the one you pulled with Nyx."

I exhale audibly. In a normal world, the fact that she helped me escape from Conner would mean that we're now friends, but this is Aarya. "Anything else you want to shout in front of everyone, or did you get enough attention for the day?" I reply.

Just as I'm finishing my sentence, Brendan enters the courtyard and sees me talking to Aarya. We make eye contact and his gaze is openly threatening, like he's broadcasting the fact that he's not done trying to kill me. The sickest part is that he's my cousin, and even though I didn't know that until a couple of days ago, he knew all along—and it didn't faze him in the least.

"Cranky, cranky," Aarya says as she follows my line of sight. "Looks like . . . what's the American saying? Ah yes. It looks like 'someone bit off more than they could chew' this morning."

Felix doesn't leave Aarya's side, but his shoulders are turned away from me and his arms are crossed, like he's guarding himself from having to interact with me or maybe he just doesn't want anything to do with this conversation.

I look away from Aarya as Matteo exits strategic sparring and heads for the door leading inside.

Aarya's eyes twinkle, like she's found something interesting. "Unless maaaybe you're not scared about the consequences of pissing off Nyx and Brendan because, oh, I don't know"—she inspects her nails—"you're leaving us soon?"

"What?" I nearly choke on the word and shift my attention back to her, trying to keep the shock out of my voice. "As much as I'd love to stick around and listen to your crap, I've got to go." Given Aarya's victorious look, it's too late; she already knows the truth. So instead of continuing this disastrous conversation, I follow Matteo.

Aarya growls and slashes her fingers at me like she's a big cat.

There were three things I was supposed to do today—act like everything was normal, not let people know I was leaving, and talk to Matteo. I haven't even finished my classes for the day, and I've already managed to screw two of them up.

I follow Matteo through the heavy wooden door leading into the foyer. Ancient shields adorn the walls; Layla once told me they are symbols of Strategia's roots throughout world history, but to me they're a reminder that I don't know my own Family history the way I should.

"I can go? You're letting me go?" I say more to myself than to Blackwood.

Blackwood hesitates. "Technically, you can go. However, I must advise you that you still have a great deal to learn and your skills are severely lacking in several areas. But more importantly, you know very little about the Strategia world at large."

"Maybe so, but there's no way I can stay here while my dad's out there all alone. Especially knowing what I now know," I say. *"What happened here with Dr. Conner seems to be just a microcosm of what's happening out there."*

"This school doesn't involve itself in outside politics," Blackwood says, *even though we both know that the situation between her and Conner was completely political.* *"I'll just say again that it would be prudent if you made additional alliances here and learned as much as you can before you leave."*

I speed up and fall in step with Matteo's long strides. "Hey, can I talk to you for a minute?" I say, careful to keep my voice low. With the high arched ceilings, sound is amplified in this room.

His broad shoulders tense. "I'd rather not," he says. He doesn't bother turning to face me.

"Look, I know you blame me for Stefano's—" I start as we enter the hallway to the boys' dorm.

Now he does look at me, or rather down at me, with frustrated brown eyes that remind me of my aunt Jo's. He's a good six inches taller than me. "You're damn right I do. And maybe it wasn't directly your fault that he was murdered. But the fact remains that my best friend from the time I could talk is *dead* because you came to this school."

His words stop me in my tracks. I rub my forehead near my eyebrow—a gesture Ash once told me signifies shame, which I suppose is pretty accurate in this moment. "I can't imagine what it would be like if someone killed my best friend," I say, and my voice is gentler. Just the thought of anyone hurting my feisty Emily makes me want to cry. "I'd be hateful till the end of time."

"Yeah, well . . . ," he says in front of his dorm room door.

I stare at him, unsure where to go from here. I can't very well say "Sad about your friend, but I need something, so can we talk about that now?"

"Sorry I bothered you," I say instead. "And I'm sorry about Stefano. Really." My mind spins, trying to come up with something, anything that will make him listen to me, because in three more seconds he's going to disappear into his room and my chance will be gone. "I just came to say goodbye."

Matteo closes his eyes momentarily, like my presence is exhausting. "I'm not in the mood to play games with you."

"No game," I say, and I scan the hall to make sure we're alone. I pause, hoping this gamble doesn't backfire. "I'm leaving the Academy tomorrow."

He exhales and breaks eye contact, looking up at the wall. After three seconds and some head-shaking, he bangs the latch on his door with the side of his fist. The door swings open.

"Well, are you coming in?" he says, clearly displeased.

I don't hesitate. I slip through the doorway and into his common room, where the blackout curtains are already drawn and the fireplace is lit for the evening.

"Speak quickly," he says like he can't get rid of me fast enough.

I move my loose braid over my shoulder and straighten my posture, working up some courage. Ever since he told me he was my cousin, I haven't been able to unsee the resemblance. The last thing I ever thought I would find in this school was family. And now I have two cousins—Matteo and Brendan— one who hates me and the other who wants me dead.

I run through a few approaches in my head, but everything I want to say sounds awkward. So instead of asking him flat-out for help, I simply say, "I'm going to find my dad."

Matteo huffs. "You're here to talk to me about your *Lion* father? I really don't care what happens to him."

I take a step forward, frustration sparking in my chest at the suggestion that my dad is anything other than wonderful. "If you would listen for more than ten seconds you would see why you do care. And I'm sick of these Family lines. You're a Bear. He's a Lion. Who cares? Some people are terrible and some people aren't. My dad is one of the good ones. End of story."

Matteo's fist clenches, and I start talking again before he decides to kick me out.

I take a breath, calming my voice. "After my aunt Jo died— scratch that, after *our* aunt Jo died—my dad sent me here. And as far as I can tell, he went to Europe to do something about it."

"What do you mean by 'do something about it'? What kind

of something?" Matteo says, and I can tell by his insistent tone that this question matters.

"That's exactly what I intend to find out," I say, matching the gravity in Matteo's voice. "I don't know Family politics the way you do, but I know enough to say that Jag is—"

"Jag is your father's father, *your* grandfather," he says judgmentally.

"Do we share some of the same genes? Yes," I say, my defensiveness ratcheting up a notch. "But don't you dare suggest I'm anything like him or the Lions. He killed my mom, and our aunt. The Lions are hunting my dad. They're trying to kill me. And as far as I can tell, they would be happy to take out Layla, Ines, and the rest of the talented students at this school, making all of Strategia bow to their will. Meanwhile everything I've been doing at this school has been aimed at stopping them."

He grunts. "Everything you've done here has been to save your own butt."

For a second, I'm silent. He's not right, but he's also not wrong.

"So your plan is to what? To challenge the Lions by yourself? Or maybe you and your traitor father will team up," he says flippantly, "if they haven't killed him already, that is."

"Geez, Matteo," I say, taken aback. "Can you be any more of an ass? You expect me to understand how deeply your friend's death has affected you, but you can't sympathize with the fact that I'm scared for my dad?" I shake my head at him disapprovingly. "At least he's doing something. At least I am. What are *you* doing?"

Matteo's face falls and he rubs his hand over his forehead.

He takes a few steps away from me. "You're right," he says, and his voice loses its edge. "That was uncalled for."

I watch him. Underneath his temper and his grief, I catch a glimpse of someone decent. And for a few seconds we stand there awkwardly, neither of us sure how to proceed in the absence of our usual ire.

"Where are you going in Europe?" he finally asks.

"I'm starting in the UK," I say.

He nods like he assumed as much. "Who else knows you're leaving?"

"Ash, Layla, and Blackwood," I say.

He watches me with a searching expression. "And Ash is going with you," he says, and I look at him sideways.

Did the way I said Ash's name give that away or was it something in my body language? "He is," I say reluctantly, and as the words leave my mouth, I'm surprised at how easily I'm telling him things. I have no reason to trust Matteo, do I?

"And I'm assuming you're here because you want my help," Matteo continues.

I exhale, relieved by the opening he just gave me. "Yes. Please. Whatever you're willing to tell me," I say. "If I'm going to be in Lion territory, I'll need all the help I can get. And even if you hate me, surely you must hate the Lions more?"

Matteo presses his lips together and looks around the room, like there might be an answer there somewhere. He's silent for a few seconds and then nods like he's come to a decision. "If I agree to help you, there's a condition."

"What kind of a condition?" I say slowly.

Matteo's expression is serious. "You must agree that this information will be used by you and you alone. I need your word. I have absolutely no interest in telling Ash my Family secrets."

I hesitate. I hate the idea of keeping things from Ash, but I can't discredit Matteo's need to protect Family secrets. And in truth, I'm flattered that he's considering trusting me with them.

"Agreed," I say.

Matteo takes a good look at me, reading me again, and when he seems satisfied that I'm telling the truth, he continues. "There's a Bear Family apothecary in London. Her shop is called Arcane Minded; the front is an antiques store. If you need supplies to use against the Lions, you can go to her. Tell her *Aut cum scuto aut in scuto*."

"*Aut cum scuto aut in scuto*," I say, repeating the Latin phrase.

"Either with shield or on shield," Matteo says before I have a chance to work out the meaning. "It roughly means 'Don't surrender; never give up.' It will let her know that you're battling the Lions and you need her assistance."

Secret phrases in secret shops with secret apothecaries. A month ago I would have rolled my eyes and made a comment about how I didn't think apothecaries existed in anything except old stories, but my entire world has shifted since I came here.

"Will it matter that she's never met me before?" I ask.

"Well, that's the thing, you do look like our immediate family. She may just assume you're a second or third cousin she's never met. *But*"—Matteo pauses—"if she realizes who you really are, you may have a problem."

I remember my talk with Ash last night and his warning

that some European Strategia might recognize me. "Do the Bears hate me, too?"

He looks thoughtful for a moment. "My mom might accept you. She loved her sisters a great deal. But our grandfather is head of the Family and I'm not sure he'll want anything to do with you. I can't tell you what to expect out there. You might have Bear support. You might not."

Five

MY BOOTS CLICK against the stone corridor as I speed-walk toward the dining hall. Layla and Ash were in their classes for a good hour longer than I was and so I spent that time stewing in my room. I've had an awful knot in my stomach ever since my encounter with Nyx this morning, and I'm crossing everything I have in the hopes that I can make it through the rest of the day without incident.

I push through the enormous arched door with iron rivets that leads to the dining hall. Maroon velvet chairs, long tables laid with white linen tablecloths, and sparkly silver await me. There are centerpieces made from green ivy and clusters of white flowers, and from the ceiling hang cast-iron chandeliers alight with real candles. On a platform at the end of the room is a table of nineteen teachers presiding over the hall and an empty chair where Conner used to sit. The students speak in polite and quiet voices, exactly what you wouldn't expect from a room full of a hundred teenagers eating dinner.

I walk between the tables, avoiding the probing glances

from the other students. No one has said anything to me about Conner's death, but as I make my way across the room, everyone I pass follows me with their eyes. There were times this happened to me in the cafeteria in Pembrook, once in sixth grade after I scaled the flagpole and strung up a pair of enormous underwear and once in ninth grade when I put all the supplies for a dreaded science practical on the roof of the school. Only, back then I was met with hoots and cheers and pats on the back. But this attention is neither congratulatory nor good-natured, and instead of strutting I find myself wishing I could pull up the hood of my cloak.

I'm halfway to my usual spot, where Ash and Layla are already seated, when Brendan suddenly pushes his chair back. He stands up, still chatting with a group of guys, and takes a wide stance, placing himself and his chair directly in my path. I slow my pace, unsure how to navigate this obvious challenge and aware that everyone is now paying attention. It's not as though I can turn back and go a different way; it'll look like I'm scared of him. Nyx, thankfully, is nowhere to be seen.

I stop in front of Brendan. He makes no effort to move, and by the way his chest is puffed out, I'm certain he has no plan to.

My shoulders tense. "Excuse me," I say with as much civility as I can muster, but he doesn't even look in my direction. "I know you hear me, Brendan. You're not that subtle."

Now he does make eye contact with me. "Go around," he says like he couldn't care less that I'm being inconvenienced. He wears a smug smile and his voice is confident. His platinum hair reflects the candlelight above.

From farther down the table Aarya leans back to get a good view. Ines gives me a sympathetic look.

I stare at Brendan. "Or, you could literally move over a foot and push in your chair so I can get to my dinner," I say. I could try to squeeze past him, but it would be tight and if he shifted his weight and knocked me over, I would fall into the table and probably land on a strategically placed knife.

He considers my suggestion. "Nah, I'm pretty comfortable where I am."

So much for not starting a fight.

I exhale, scanning the room for an alternative solution, and find none. "Since we're going to be here for a minute until you decide eating is more interesting than blocking my path, what should we discuss?" I say in a relaxed voice. "The weather, sports . . . or your friends helping Conner kill other students? Which makes me wonder, how were *you* involved in Stefano's death, Brendan?"

Brendan smirks. "Not bad. Not bad. But I was thinking more friendly chitchat." He glances to the side to make sure the people near us are listening. "Maybe I should wish you well *on your trip.*"

Aarya is practically falling out of her chair to listen.

My heart thuds. *He knows.*

Brendan scans my face. "Oh, you thought that was a secret?" He laughs. "Just another reason you're going to fail."

I'm not sure whether he means I'll fail to find my father in time or fail to retaliate against the Lions or maybe both. And I can't help but wonder if he's right.

"It's odd," I say, outwardly dismissing his comment. "No one in this school saw me coming. No one thought I would be

40

any good. And yet I keep beating you at every turn. Does that mean I'm that good? Or you're that bad?"

His smirk suggests he knows something I don't. "*Maybe you'll last a week . . . if you're lucky.*"

"I'll take that bet," I say, doing my best to convince him and the onlookers that I'm not worried. "You're in the running to be the head of the Lions, right? And technically we're cousins. So does that mean I'm also a contender for the throne? Or whatever you power-obsessed Lions like to call it?"

His chin juts out and his nostrils flare—not one but two indicators that he wants to hurt me. Brendan might not have tried to kill me with his bare hands thus far, but it's obvious he wants me dead, and now I'm wondering if I inadvertently stumbled onto the reason he and his friends went after me so aggressively. I glance at the small gap between him and the table. If I make a move now, it won't end well. But I also can't stand here; he knows I'm leaving and he has every reason to want to incapacitate me, even if it does earn him a punishment.

I make a flash decision and take the only other option available—I slip into his empty chair. I don't dare look back at him. Instead, I scoop some mashed potatoes onto his clean plate.

"How's it going?" I say casually to the guys he was chatting with, who all stare at me, unsure, which I'm fairly certain is the Strategia version of shock.

I keep a close watch on the guy directly across from me as he shifts his attention to Brendan. By the way the guy's eyes move down and the slight pressure I feel on my chair, I'm pretty sure Brendan just gripped the back of it. If he yanks the chair backward, there is no way I won't fall on my butt.

"I wouldn't do that if I were you," I say with a mouth full of garlic mashed potatoes. "There is an entire table of teachers keeping close watch on this room, and if I go flying onto the floor—which I will make sure I do—it will look like you started a fight."

"Do you imagine I care if they think I started a fight?" he says with an arrogant tone, and he's so close to the back of my head that the hair on my neck stands up.

"I do, actually," I say without turning around. "Because the one thing no one's been able to figure out about me is how I did what others couldn't—get into this school at seventeen. Maybe I have more influence than you think. And maybe, just maybe, I'll use that influence to make your stay in the dungeon particularly unpleasant." It's a gamble. I'm banking on the assumption that he's never been sent to the dungeon, considering he's practically catered to at this school. And if I'm right, he probably fears it more than most. "Now as you said, if we get in a fight, I'm out of here. But you?"

I feel his grip on the chair tighten and hear him suck in a deep breath.

"It was lovely meeting you all," I say to the table, and stand up on the other side of Brendan. I immediately start walking toward Ash and Layla, grateful that I got past him without a physical altercation.

"It's a shame what's going to happen to your father," he says, and I stop dead in my tracks. "I would tell you, but I guess you'll know soon enough."

My heart jumps into my throat. I whip around. The look Brendan and I share is pure anger.

Before I take a step in his direction, Ines stands up and blocks my path. Her red braid hangs down her back and her eyes are determined.

"He wants you to attack him," she says, and it's literally the second time I've ever heard her speak. "And if you do, you won't be leaving here anytime soon. He will win." She watches me closely, as though she's looking for a sign that I understand.

I take a breath and unclench my fists. And just like that Ines sits back down and returns to her meal like none of it ever happened.

"Thanks," I say, but she doesn't respond. Both Felix and Aarya stare at her, clearly as surprised that she spoke to me as I am.

I don't waste any time; I walk to my usual spot and sit down across from Ash and Layla, my heart rate elevated. It takes a couple of long breaths before I can relax my rigid posture and lean back in my chair.

Ash smiles at me. "I can't leave you alone for two minutes. Good thing I don't intend to."

Layla raises her eyebrows. "Are you *flirting* right now? That could have turned into a fight."

"But it didn't," he says, as unfazed as usual. "November handled it beautifully. Sitting in Brendan's chair was genius."

Layla frowns. "I seriously don't know what to think about you two. One's more reckless than the other." She pauses. "You're going to be completely lost without me."

Ash nudges her with his shoulder and grins at her in a way that gives me a clear window into what they must have been like as kids. "Is this you looking for an invite? Am I sensing a bit of, I don't know, *jealousy*?"

Layla gives him a hard look. "Jealousy? Not even close. I'm just looking forward to the moment when I can read a book in peace without having to save one of you from your own stupidity."

Ash laughs, but I don't have a laugh in me. "He seemed so certain that I would fail," I say, concern leaking into my voice. They both look at me.

Ash's smile fades, but he doesn't appear worried. "Retaliation against the Lions is no small feat. From Brendan's perspective, it's unthinkable."

There is that word again, *retaliation*. Truth is, I haven't even thought about retaliating. "I just want to find my dad," I say.

"Finding your father will not solve the problem," Layla says as she refills her water glass. "The Lions will not stop hunting you both."

I know she's right, that I haven't properly considered the big picture. "I can't stop thinking about what Brendan said about my dad," I say, looking at them both for reassurance. "Could Brendan actually know something about what's going on with him?"

Ash's lips subtly and momentarily tighten, which I recognize as one of the microexpressions Gupta taught us in deception class. Gupta said that when someone presses their lips together it's often a sign that they're holding back information or refraining from saying something.

"Like I said, communication to and from the Academy is

monitored and often delayed," Ash says. "Brendan was probably just toying with you."

Layla remains silent, which tells me everything I need to know. Brendan might have been toying with me, but that doesn't mean he wasn't also telling *the truth*.

✳ ✳ ✳

The furniture in the common room of our suite, which once seemed lavish and formal, now feels familiar and cozy. I scan every detail, trying to catalogue them all in my mind—the couch where Ash kissed me, the breakfast table near the arched window where Layla coached me for hours on end, and the fireplace, which I often sat in front of contemplating whatever my current mess was. I thought I hated this school, but when faced with leaving it, I realize I've felt more alive here than I ever have.

Layla's bedroom door opens and she joins me in the common room, glancing at the clock. "Almost time," she says with a smile.

I wish I could smile back. "I hate that we're leaving you."

She brushes off my comment. "You'll see me again soon."

"I know, but . . ."

"You'll be fine, November," she says with such assurance that I almost believe her. "Watch out for each other, don't let my brother do anything outrageous, and keep your eyes open. Danger always shows up when you least expect it."

Her words remind me of our lesson in poisons class today and I find myself agreeing with her warning. It reminds me how often Layla called me naïve when I first arrived, how right she probably was, and how much I've changed since I was last in Pembrook. "I'll keep an eye on him. I promise."

Layla gives me a no-nonsense glare. "Now I'm going to give you something, but I swear if you get emotional I will take it right back."

"Okay," I say in a cautious tone.

She pulls something black and shiny out of her pocket and holds it before me.

My eyes widen. "A lock of your hair?" I say, and my voice falters. We've been through some harrowing experiences together over these past few weeks and it's fair to say that we've bonded, but it's also always been clear that I've liked her more than she's liked me.

She holds up the braided lock, which is tied with a piece of thread. "In the Wolf Family we give a lock of hair to someone going on an important journey. It's a show of faith, to tell you that I'm there with you in spirit and to wish you luck-filled travels and a quick trip home." She sighs. "So I expect that you'll bring this back when you both return safely."

I nod at her, at a loss for words.

"Are you crying?" she says, and points a slender finger at me. "You better not be crying."

"Not crying," I say, but my voice cracks.

"Here, turn around," she says, and I do. She tucks the lock of her hair up into my French braid near my scalp. "So they don't take it away from you before you leave."

I turn back to her and wrap my arms around her neck. For a long second she just stands there. Then slowly the tension drops from her shoulders and she hugs me back.

There's a knock on the door and Layla steps away before I get a chance to tell her how much her friendship has meant to me. How I wouldn't have survived without her. And how self-less she's been about her brother, her twin, coming with me.

Layla opens the door and standing on the other side are two of Blackwood's guards with their signature leather arm-bands and belts. I open my mouth, but Layla shakes her head as though to tell me nothing more can be said.

"Good night, November," she says, and her words are heavy.

"See you soon, Layla," I reply.

And just like that I walk away, knowing all too well that this might be the last time I ever see her.

Six

I OPEN THE door to Blackwood's cozy office and Ash is already there, sitting in one of the armchairs in front of her desk. The fireplace fills the room with the familiar scent of burning wood and there is an abundance of candles in sconces on the walls and in silver candleholders on her desk.

Blackwood gestures for me to sit down and I do, remembering the first day I met her. It was before I knew I was Strategia and way before I had any idea about the deal my dad had made—promising Blackwood I would expose Conner for the killer he was in exchange for my admittance to the Academy.

The guards close the door but remain inside.

"As requested, you two will be flown to the airport you departed from, November," Blackwood says, and leans back in her chair. Her relaxed posture doesn't soften her. "You'll be responsible for yourselves from there."

"Thank you," I say, still a little awed that she's letting us go.

Blackwood looks from me to Ash. "Before you travel, you'll receive your clothes and personal effects." She hands us each a thick envelope. "And these."

48

I peek inside to find an enormous stack of hundred-dollar bills. "Holy sh—"

Blackwood gives me a look and I swallow the word, fooling no one. Ash's eyes betray his amusement. Where in the heck did all this money come from? I'm assuming my dad, but this must be half his savings.

"Do you have any logistical questions for me?" Blackwood asks, and I can tell by the way she emphasizes *logistical* that she's discouraging the type of conversation we had two nights ago, when we openly discussed her friendship with my dad. And now I'm regretting not asking her more questions about her time in the Academy with my parents—what they were like when they were my age before they ran away from Europe and their Strategia Families to hide in America.

"How do we get in touch with you if we need to?" I ask, suddenly uncertain that I want to walk away from Academy Absconditi for good.

She nods and the faintest hint of a smile appears in the corners of her eyes. "The usual way—through your Family contacts."

I open my mouth to say that I have no idea who those contacts would be, but since the guards are in the room, I decide against it.

Blackwood looks at Ash, but he makes no effort to ask her anything. He exudes a nonchalant attitude, as though we were doing nothing more than visiting our Families for the holiday.

"Now if that's all," Blackwood continues, "these guards will take you to change into your travel clothes and you'll be off."

Ash and I stand up.

"Safe journey and I'll see you both when you return,"

Blackwood says, and even though her tone is as cold and distant as always, I get the sense that in her own way she's wishing us good luck.

"Thanks," I say, and smile, regretting that I didn't thank her for the various ways she's protected me when I had the chance to speak freely. Our conversation two nights ago was in the wake of being attacked by Conner, and my exhaustion, compounded with the realization that my dad left not one scrap of information about how to find him, made me overwhelmed and cloudy.

I take one last look at Blackwood, aware that even if we survive this crazy mission, I cannot imagine a scenario where I would leave my dad alone to come back here. And I almost can't believe I'm thinking this, but some part of me will miss her severe attitude and her brilliant strategy games. I may never understand everything she tried to teach me, but I know I'm better for it.

Ash and I exit the room, and as the door closes behind me, it feels like the end of another chapter in my life. I didn't realize when I left my house in Pembrook to come here that nothing would ever be the same, but as I prepare to leave the Academy, I know that once again my world is about to shift.

"They're going to sedate us again, aren't they?" I ask Ash as we make our way down the stairwell.

"Oh, definitely," he says, and flashes me a smile that takes the edge off.

The guards lead us to the ground floor and through a dimly lit hallway. The guard next to Ash stops in front of a door adjacent to the teachers' lounge and unlocks it.

"See you in America," Ash says before disappearing into the room.

I follow the second guard to the adjoining door and he, too, unlocks it without explanation. I slip through and it clicks shut behind me. The room is small and cozy, what you might expect if someone transformed a castle into a bed-and-breakfast. It has a colorful tapestry on the wall, a large four-poster canopied bed, and an elegant desk. The fire in the fireplace heats up the room in a pleasant way.

My duffel bag sits by the end of the bed, and the blue plaid pattern and worn straps seem out of place next to the antique furniture. I run my fingers over the familiar textured fabric, and as I undo the black zipper, I realize it still smells like my house.

Inside are bits of home that make my heart ache—my pine tree pillowcase from my bed, an old T-shirt of my dad's that I stole for pajamas a few years back, and a pair of vegan leather fingerless gloves that Emily and I bought last year, convinced we would start a fashion trend. Turns out they weren't warm enough for winter and were too hot for summer, making them useful for only about two weeks in the fall when the air was just turning crisp—which caused us to wear them every day so we could get our money's worth and also caused our friends to make endless remarks about our biker gang. Emily didn't care, insisting that Pembrook just wasn't big enough for any original ideas.

My chest lifts at the memory and a zing of anticipation runs through me. I slip out of my wool cloak, white linen Academy shirt, and black leggings, discarding them on the floor. I trade my uniform for my favorite jeans and a comfy sweater. *Home. I'm headed home.* I sit down on the end of the bed and fish my tall brown boots out of the suitcase.

As I pull them on there is a light knock at the door.

"Come in!" I call, and the guard opens the door, with a glass of cloudy liquid in his hand, which I can only assume is my sedative. And once again I'm painfully aware of my two lives—my gentle one in Pembrook and my deadly one as a Strategia.

I pull on my boots and zip up my bag. I would ask him what happens next, but he wouldn't answer me, so there's no point. He hands me the glass and I scooch back on the bed, not sure how fast this stuff works and not wanting to concuss myself by hitting the floor. I smell the cup, but there's no scent. I look questioningly at the guard, but he just stares at me with the typical detached expression.

I don't know why, maybe I'm just buzzing with excited anticipation that I'm going back to Pembrook, but I sing, *"Put the lime in the coconut and shake it all up."* Then I chug back the slightly briny liquid and hand him the glass. And even though his expression remains cold, I swear I see a glimmer of amusement dance across his eyes.

"Don't worry," I say. "I won't tell anyone that you think I'm funny." For a moment nothing happens, then gradually the world gets fuzzy, as if I were looking at it through a rainy window. "I think I'm funny, tooooo." And as I speak, I fall back onto the cushioned bed. "Wheeee!"

I lift my head off a crisp white pillowcase with a gasp, the world suddenly blinking back into existence. My eyes flit about rapidly, my heart racing, trying to make sense of the disorienting room. I'm in a king-sized bed. There's an armchair near a large curtained window. And there's a desk, above which hangs a large flat-screen TV. I rub my forehead and sit up, frowning at the modern objects. Then I remember the sedative, remember that I left the Academy.

I swing my legs out of bed to find a plush carpet with a pair of white slippers on the floor. *I'm in a hotel?* I almost want to laugh, like when you wake from a strange dream and you're so relieved that you actually feel giddy. But this room, which I would once have found awesome and immediately taken pictures of to send to Emily, now strikes me as foreign after my time at the Academy.

I stand up and stretch my sore body. Everything smells sharp and pungent, like floral laundry detergent and lemon-scented cleaning products, none of which existed in that medieval castle. I'm fairly certain a bar of soap was a fix-all there.

I open the heavy curtains, letting in what appears to be the late-morning sun. I scan the room with its fluffy white linens and spot a row of light switches on the wall. For an instant I'm stunned; it didn't even occur to me that I could flip on the lights instead of opening the curtains. It's baffling that after only a few weeks I would feel this out of place in a world I've existed in my whole life. I've heard of reverse culture shock, but like food poisoning, you don't think it's going to happen to you until you're running full-speed for the bathroom.

I grab the remote on my bedside table, examining it for a moment, and switch on the TV. A local news station appears on the screen and I wince. The sound is jarring and the bright colors make me squint. I turn it off again, feeling relieved when the image disappears. But I love TV, don't I?

"Ash?" My voice cracks with roughness.

"Out here," he says, and I make my way into the attached living room with tall bay windows and oversized couches. I'm instantly struck by how many electronics there are—another TV, a coffeemaker, speakers for music, and *my phone*. A zing of excitement runs through me at the sight of it.

A split second later I'm moving toward the coffee table, but as I get closer, I realize it's not my phone at all, just my empty phone case. I pick up my *Spirited Away* Miyazaki cover, which is cracked in the corner from when I dropped it on my kitchen floor a couple of months ago, and turn it over, frowning at the hole where my phone should be. I run my fingertips over the sparkly star charm that's hanging from it; Emily has a matching moon.

I look up at Ash, confused.

But he seems to have expected this. "Cell phones aren't allowed at the Academy," he says. "If it was on your person when your dad dropped you off, they would have destroyed it."

"*Destroyed* it?" I say, looking up at him in disbelief. "Couldn't they just shut it off or take out the SIM card?"

Ash's dark hair is wet and neatly combed and he's wearing a white button-down with a light gray sweater, a black blazer, and a pair of expensive-looking jeans. I stop dead in my tracks. I've never seen him in anything besides our school uniform and right now he looks like he just stepped out of a magazine.

"With the right technology, your cell phone can be tracked, with or without a SIM card," he says. "It's easier to locate if it's on, but it's not impossible to locate if it's off. It's not worth taking the risk."

My fingers linger over the familiar case. I drooled over that phone for most of the year and bought it for myself for my birthday after painstakingly saving up my babysitting money. It's only four months old.

I frown. "I know it's silly that in the midst of everything that's happened I care about my cell phone," I say, and sigh. "I just . . . do." What I don't tell him is that it feels like it was the last thing linking me to normal teenhood, and I really didn't want to give it up. Missed texts from Emily, pictures from the last two months that I never uploaded to my computer, and notes on the knife and sword tricks I was learning. My old life is being stripped from me piece by piece.

He nods, but instead of silently judging my frivolity, he smiles. "You really are beautiful," he says, and chuckles to himself. "I never thought I would say that to a girl with a *very* sparkly cell phone case. But it couldn't be more true."

I laugh, too, taking the edge off my phone massacre. My braid is messy and strands of it hang around my face. My jeans are worn and cuffed at the bottom, my socks mismatched, and I'm in the same oversized cable-knit sweater as when I arrived at Academy Absconditi.

"You're clearly still feeling the effects of that sedative and your brains are scrambled," I say. "Speaking of sedatives, how did we get to this hotel?"

Ash shrugs like he doesn't think it deserves much thought. "The Academy transportation system is as mysterious as its location. It helps keep the school hidden. Every time Layla and I have returned to Egypt, we've been dropped off and wake up in a different location."

I look around the living room, like there might be an

answer among the couch cushions, but the room is perfectly average for an upscale hotel and lacks any defining features. I'm reminded of the time Ash told me it was futile to try to figure out where the Academy was located, but even so, I couldn't stop analyzing every inch of the grounds.

"So this is just a hotel, then, not something connected with Strategia?" I say, disappointed by the suite's lack of distinguishing characteristics.

"Just an ordinary hotel room," Ash repeats.

When I adjust my gaze back to him, he's still smiling.

"What?" I ask, wondering if I have hair in my mouth or drool on my face. It definitely wouldn't be the first time.

But instead of answering, he walks right up to me. His look gains intensity and my stomach does a quick flip. He touches a loose lock of my wavy hair and places my arms around his neck. He pulls me close.

"If you could see yourself the way I see you, you would know that you're perfect," he says with fresh minty breath, and it suddenly occurs to me that I haven't engaged in any of my morning grooming regime.

He leans in closer, and just as he nears my mouth I turn, give him a fast kiss on the cheek, and step away. "No way I'm kissing you while you're all freshly showered and"—I gesture at him—"dressed like that."

He laughs. "You won't kiss me because of my clothes? Is there an outfit you would prefer? Because I'll gladly change."

"You know what I mean," I say, and I can't help but smile, too. "You're super dressed up and I haven't even brushed my teeth. I'm jumping in the shower and then we need to catch a bus to—" I stop out of habit. At the Academy I trained myself to never reveal anything about my home life. "Pembrook," I continue. "I'm assuming we're in Hartford, given that Blackwood said she would send us to the airport I left from." I walk to the window and pull back the curtain.

Below us I recognize the city streets and the telltale New England architecture, and all of a sudden I'm disoriented again. The cars below seem too fast, the buildings seem too shiny, and the open sky makes me feel exposed. "Definitely Hartford," I say, not finding the comfort I thought I would in this familiar city. "If I remember correctly, the bus we need leaves just about every hour."

I close the curtain instead of leaving it open, finding more solace in turning back to Ash than in soaking in my home state. Just a month ago a trip to Hartford would have been exciting; it would have meant shopping with Em or going to the antiques stores hunting for old knives with my dad. *Have I really changed that much?* While preparing to leave the Academy I wondered the same thing, only the answer seemed to be that I was stronger, smarter, and more discerning. Now I just feel like I don't know who I am.

"I'll order us some breakfast," Ash says as he examines my expression. When I don't answer right away, he adds, "Don't give it too much thought; it takes everyone a little time to adjust after being at the Academy."

I nod, grateful that he understands. "It's like I weirdly got used to living a medieval life. Instead of feeling like I came home, I feel like I time-traveled."

"I used to feel similarly when I was young and our parents took Layla and me to Europe to introduce us to Strategia contacts or to shadow them on a simple mission," he says. "The busy streets in Paris, for instance, were in such stark contrast to our estate that it felt a bit like whiplash."

I pause; while he's relating to my current experience, he's also describing a childhood that couldn't be more different than my own. "Your estate?"

Now he pauses, potentially coming to the same conclusion I just did. "Similar to the Academy in structure, but smaller," he explains. "Every Family has one. They're hidden in plain sight, not tucked away in the forest like our school is, but a non-Strategia would never recognize them for what they are."

I stare at him like he just told me the sky is green instead of blue. "Hang on a second. You grew up in a *castle*?"

"More of a manor house, but yes," he says.

"Please tell me you had electricity," I say with feeling, my face poised for shock.

Ash looks amused by my reaction, and the way his face lights up makes my knees weak. I've dated a fair number of guys, but none of them gave me that stomach-flipping, word-fumbling, drunken feeling that Ash does.

"Yes, we had electricity," he says, his eyes bright, "but we also know how to exist without it. Our parents claimed that Strategia have been effective for thousands of years without modern gadgets, and that reliance on technology would weaken our abilities."

"I thought Layla said that every Family has Strategia technology experts," I say, getting a glimpse into how much I don't know about the larger Strategia world.

"We do," Ash says, "but they are only used sparingly. The point is that if we *didn't* have them we would still be able to complete our missions."

Laid out on my parents' bed are two sets of black gloves, two black knitted hats, and two gray wool scarves.

"I've got a mission for you—a very important one," my mom says like she's letting me in on a secret. "It's a beautiful winter day. There is fresh snow on the ground. Aunt Jo is on her way over."

I hang on her every word.

"Your dad and I were thinking"—she pauses for dramatic effect—"that we should all go sledding."

I bounce on my toes. "Sledding!" I squeal, clasping my hands together and looking up at her. My dad smiles at us from a cozy chair by the window where he's reading the paper.

Mom lifts me up onto the bed. "But we have a problem, you see," she explains. "Dad and I have mixed up our gloves, scarves, and hats, and before we can leave the house, we need your help figuring out which is which."

I look at the black gloves, eager to help my mom. I immediately pick up the set of gloves closest to me. "These are yours," I say. "They're smaller."

My mom smiles encouragingly. "And the hats?" she asks.

"Yours has the pompom," I say, thrilled to have the answers she needs.

"Right," she says, and sits down on the bed next to me to give me a squeeze. "Only one more to go."

I stare at the gray wool scarves, hoping that something will stand out to me, but as far as I can tell, they are identical. I pick them up, turning them over in my hands.

"Do they feel the same?" my mom asks.

I nod.

"Smell the same?" she asks.

I lift each one to my nose, and while they smell familiar, I'm not sure that they smell different from each other. I stare at the scarves in concentration, wondering how I can unlock this mystery so we can go sledding. She doesn't say anything more and I don't ask for help; I know by now that she expects me to do my best.

Then I see it, the answer to my problem. "This one is yours!" I say with enthusiasm, and hold up the scarf in my left hand.

My mother beams. "I told you she would recognize the frayed edge," she says to my dad, victorious.

I shake my head. I hadn't realized hers was frayed at the bottom, but as I focus, I spot the torn bit. "No, Mama, your hair is on it," I say, feeling proud.

She takes a closer look at the scarf and plucks off a long piece of wavy brown hair. She looks at me with a big grin. "My goodness, you are smart," she says, and tackles me onto the bed. "How did I ever wind up with such a smart girl?" She covers me with kisses as I laugh.

"Put down your paper, Christopher!" my mom exclaims. "We have a date with the snow!"

"What kind of missions did you go on with your parents?" I ask, fairly certain that missions in my house were different than in his.

"Mostly espionage," Ash says. "They taught us how to negotiate for information and how to move around undetected."

I nod, wondering if my parents would have done the same if my mom had lived longer. While my dad did train me in his own way, I still don't understand why he didn't tell me the truth about being Strategia.

"Order all the things," I say, motioning to the menu in his hand. "I'm starved."

He grins and I once again get pulled into his inviting look. "All the things it is."

I smile back. "And stop looking at me like that, all attractive and what have you. It's not fair."

Ash laughs. "Got it. Food. Stop being attractive. And start dressing differently."

"Right," I say. "And if that doesn't work we'll just figure out a way to cover your face with something. That way I'll be able to think clearly without wanting to kiss you. Now work on your list. I'm going to get ready so we can get out of here." I walk back into the bedroom and hear Ash chuckling to himself.

I stand in the middle of the modern room for a few seconds, staring at my plaid duffel bag, not yet acclimated to this unfamiliar familiar world. The last time I was in Connecticut, I was at peace. My world was small. My family was small. And I had everything I needed. None of those things are true now.

I touch the back of my head, fish out the lock of hair Layla gave me from my own braid, and hold it to my heart like it might have the answers I'm looking for, or at least help me find my footing.

Seven

THE CLOSER WE get to my hometown, the more my stomach churns. For the past hour, I've been resisting the urge to look over my shoulder at the other passengers, wondering what type of threat might be lurking there. Instead, I fidget in my seat and tap the armrest with my fingers, unable to sit still. Ever since we left the hotel I've had this uneasy, vulnerable feeling, as though something ominous and deadly might spring out of every shadow. Ash insisted it would be unlikely that a fellow Strategia would be on the bus with us, but he also insisted I wear a wig, which he just happened to have in his luggage, like it's common to pack disguises alongside travel-sized deodorant.

I stare out the bus window, watching the familiar tree-lined highway, but the monotony of it only unsettles me more. I pull at the edge of the lopsided scarf Emily knitted for me last winter and glance at Ash, who seems lost in thought himself.

The bus slows, but instead of feeling relieved that the wait is over, I'm even more worried. Worried that I'll find something at my house that will confirm that my dad's in danger. And worried I won't find anything at all.

"Coming?" Ash says, and I realize the bus has stopped and he's already standing. He pulls down our bags from the overhead compartment.

"Right," I say.

I sneak a look at the other passengers on the bus as I stand. They seem like regular people—two families, one with a sleeping baby, a couple of girls in their twenties with headphones on, and so on. But if a Strategia were on this bus, wouldn't they blend in as ordinary, too? How would I ever know if we were being followed?

No one else gets up and I'm grateful; if someone from my town were on this bus, they would likely recognize me, wig or not, and badger me with questions about where I had disappeared to for the last few weeks. The entire town would know I was here within an hour and Sheriff Billy would be knocking on my door.

I follow Ash down the aisle and outside. The trees are bare and the air is freezing, even in the afternoon sun. I pull my hat down farther over my ears and tuck my hands into my gloves. The bus pulls away, revealing Spring Rose Lane, which is aptly named for all the wild roses that grow along it in the warmer months—a street that I've walked down more times than I can count.

"You see these roses," my mom says, *pointing to the bushes covered in pale pink flowers that crowd both sides of the street.* *"These are beach roses. Rosa rugosa."*

"Rosa rugosa," *I repeat.*

"Here, smell," my mom says, *bending down and bringing one*

63

of the pink blooms to my nose. My face lights up and she smiles at my reaction. "Delicious, aren't they? Wild roses always smell the best. You know why?"

I shake my head.

"Because the ones you buy at the florist prioritize their looks over their other properties," she says like it's a shame. "But these? These are hardy. They are strong and bold and even though they love the sun, they aren't afraid of a little frost. They are edible and the leaves and hips have medicinal purposes. When I gave you the middle name Rose, I named you after this kind of rose, not the kind that makes a pretty bouquet but isn't good for much else."

She slips her warm hand back in mine and we continue our walk. As I stare up at her, I can't help but be proud of all she knows.

"We should get off the main road," Ash says, watching me curiously.

I sigh, pulling myself out of my memory. "Town is a block that way," I say, pointing to my right. And an unexpected sadness washes over me. Even though I'm so close, I can't go there, not unless I want all of Pembrook following me down the street like a St. Patrick's Day parade. "But we can't take the streets, even the back streets. I would run into at least ten people I know. We'll have to take the woods." I look down at my scuffed, mud-stained boots and his shiny laced ones. "Will you be okay in those?"

"More than okay," he says. "Since there's no snow, we won't leave much in the way of tracks; the woods are ideal."

I take my duffel bag from his shoulder and lead him through the forest—a route I've taken so many times that I could narrate every twisted trunk and bent limb before we got to it. Our steps are mostly silent, even though I don't anticipate running into anyone. In all the years I've lived here, I've only ever seen hikers in these woods in the summertime.

Our breath billows out in front of us in white clouds and I run my gloved fingers over a gnarled trunk that I nicknamed Mr. Henry as a child because I swore it had a face like my English teacher. As we get closer to my property, I pick up my pace, anticipation fueling my steps. I suddenly have this urge to run to my house, fling open my door, and call for my dad. And as that desire gets more insistent, my chest begins to ache. Will I ever do that again? Will my dad and I ever come back here?

"Do you want to talk about it?" Ash says, and there is none of his usual charm, just a kind offer.

"I don't know," I say, and I'm quiet for a few more steps, trying to figure out how to verbalize feelings that I haven't fully processed myself. "Everything looks and feels so familiar and yet it's all . . . just out of my reach. This is my *home*. I know this place better than anywhere in the world—every porch, the brick sidewalks pushed up by old tree roots, Mr. Martin, who makes the best cakes in all of Connecticut and who's been the reigning champion at the state fair seven years in a row, and Mrs. Bernstein, who has an antiques store and organizes the farmers' market on Sundays. The way you can't park in front of the candy shop for more than an hour, because the owner is the crankiest human alive and will leave you ragey notes. Everything. *Emily.*" My voice catches on her name and I take a breath. "I'm finally home, something I've been dreaming about for weeks, and yet I'm not. My dad's not here, I can't talk to anyone, and I need to sneak around quietly without calling attention to myself. When what I really want to do is march right into the town square and get a big cup of hot cocoa with marshmallows from Lucille's diner." When I stop speaking, my chest deflates, and I realize how many feelings I've been suppressing.

For a split second Ash seems taken aback by the intensity of my emotion for Pembrook, and after a moment of thought he nods. "You'll be able to come back here," he says in a reassuring voice.

I want so badly to believe him. "Will I, though?"

"Yes. We'll find your father and do what we need to in order to stop the Lions from hunting you—even if it means we need to take out the whole group of them." His tone is definite.

I know that what he's saying is highly improbable, but I also know he's reassuring me out of kindness. And I need a little kindness more than I need harsh reality right now. I sigh. "Just take out the most powerful Strategia Family. Sounds like a breeze."

"See? You're getting into the spirit alr—" Ash stops short, and I instantly know why.

"Tires on dirt?" I whisper, and turn toward the noise. "From where we are . . ." I examine the trees around me and my stomach bottoms out. "Oh god, it's coming from my driveway. There's nothing else close enough." I point. "I live just through the trees at the top of that hill."

My heart races and my mind spins, searching for possibilities of who it might be. For a fleeting moment, I get my hopes up that maybe it's my dad returning home to tell me this whole nightmare is over and that I never have to think about it again.

I run for the top of the hill, keeping my steps quiet, and Ash runs by my side. We crouch down behind a patch of brush that has a good view of my small white house with its black shutters, red door, and Victorian trim. My eyes widen. But it's not the longing for my house that shakes me—it's the old silver VW pulling to a stop in my driveway.

"Emily?" I whisper to myself, and I'm flooded with so many emotions that I can't breathe.

I stand up. I need to run to her, hug her, and tell her how incredibly sorry I am for not saying goodbye. I need her to know that I had no choice in going and that I didn't willingly disappear. But before I can take a step, Ash pulls me back down into the brush cover.

"Don't," he whispers, and his eyes hold a warning.

"But that's my best . . . *I have to*," I say, desperation in my voice. I yank my arm, but he has a solid grip on me.

"And what if someone is watching your house? If someone is watching Emily?" he whispers back. "Think, November. I can see by your face how much she means to you. Don't put your friend in danger like I once did."

I shake my head stubbornly, tears forming in my eyes. I can't be this close to Emily and do nothing. "If the Lions already knew about Pembrook, why did Conner threaten to kill us if I didn't tell him where this place was?"

Ash's expression is serious. "Two possibilities: One, the Lions figured it out and because of the communication delay at the Academy, Conner did not know yet. Or two, Conner wasn't privy to all the information his Family had. You have no idea what the Lions know and what they don't know. Are you willing to risk her life on an assumption?"

Emily gets out of her car and I look away from Ash. Her hair is in a high ponytail and she wears red earmuffs, a long peacoat that flares at the waist, and impractical high-heeled winter boots. She rubs her nose with her red-mittened hand and carries a white long-stemmed rose in the other. I clench my jaw, trying to keep my tears at bay.

"These," Emily says, pointing to a cluster of orchids in the flower shop. "Purple orchids are the prettiest flower, don't you think? They just scream elegance."

I glance at the price tag and take a deep breath. "What about roses?" I offer.

"Roses are your *thing," Emily says, like it's obvious.*

"Correction, roses are not my thing. It's just my middle name," I say, and immediately regret it. I love roses, and when my mom was alive she kept vases of them in our house all summer long.

"If this were your birthday, I would get you white roses," Emily says, because even if I claim I don't have an affinity for them, she knows me too well. "But it's not your birthday. It's mine." I can tell by her tone that no amount of reasoning with her is going to change her mind.

I pinch the bridge of my nose. "Let me get this straight. You want me to buy you a bunch of orchids. But then instead of handing them to you like a normal person, you want me to leave them anonymously on your desk and then pretend they weren't from me?" I look at her doubtfully.

Emily clasps her hands together and lets out an excited squeal. "It's going to be perfect."

"It's going to be dramatic," I say with a laugh.

She gives me a mischievous smile. "Same thing."

Emily walks up to my front stoop and places the white rose on a pile of roses in front of my door. Has she been coming here every day since I left, bringing me a rose? The realization hits me hard and it feels like my heart is going to tear straight out of my chest. I had been so concerned with surviving the Academy that I hadn't truly thought about the impact my absence would have on her.

Emily kneels down on my steps and says a few words that I can't decipher before she gets up again. But even from here I can tell that her eyes are red, and she wipes at them with the back of her mittens. And I wipe at mine. More than anything I want to make the grief on her face disappear. As she walks toward her car, I have a desperate desire to call out to her. And as she closes her car door, I feel like I've lost something precious. She turns on her engine and backs up, her silver car jostling on the dips in the dirt driveway. Just like that, Emily pulls out onto the road and disappears behind the tall trees.

I press my fingers into my eyebrows. I take a few deep breaths before I even dare look at Ash because I know I will crumble.

"Would you like a minute alone?" Ash asks, and there is concern in his eyes, but something else is there, too—a question I can't quite make out.

"No," I whisper, and break eye contact with him. "Let's just go." I motion for him to follow me, focusing all my energy on the task at hand.

I take off my wig and shove it in my bag, pulling my coat hood up in its place. Then I zigzag us around the back of my house along a sheltered path that provides maximum coverage. I put out my hand to tell Ash to stop about five feet from the cleared grass of my backyard. We both stand perfectly still and listen, scanning the forest for any sign of other Strategia.

When I'm reasonably certain that there is no immediate threat, I look at Ash and nod.

"Let's make a run for it," Ash says, his breath warm on my ear, and we do.

We sprint full-speed across the grass. I take the steps to my back porch two at a time, an action so familiar that despite the potential danger, a smile appears on my face. I pull my keys out of my coat pocket and without even looking at them I find the right one. I slip it into my back door, turn it, and jiggle the handle so that it doesn't stick. In five seconds flat we're inside my living room, Ash silently closing the door behind us.

I stop dead in my tracks, scouring my living room to be sure that no unknown threats await us. Ash moves to the bathroom, then to my dad's bedroom, and I do the same with the kitchen and my bedroom. After we've opened doors and checked in closets and under the beds, certain that there isn't a Strategia lurking there, we meet silently back in the living room, my shoulders dropping an inch.

Everything is exactly as I left it the night I departed for Academy Absconditi. Dad must have driven me to the airport and never returned. The cushy tan couch still has the red plaid blanket strewn across it, and the bowl with popcorn remnants hasn't been cleaned. The living room smells faintly like fireplace, as it always does, and my dad's snow boots stand on a plastic mat near the front door. For a split second I can almost believe that the Academy wasn't real, that my aunt Jo is still alive, and that my dad is on his way home from work. The hope is so intense that I close my eyes for a second, trying to hold the moment a little longer.

"What weapons do you have here?" Ash asks, and the reality of our situation shatters my train of thought.

"Right. Uh, let's see," I say, reluctantly turning away from the living room. "I have a knife collection in my room."

Ash nods. "Knives work and they're easy to conceal. Let's see them."

I lead him into my bedroom, and as he walks through the door, he pauses to take it in. My bed frame is made from twisty pieces of polished wood that are woven together in an arch, something my dad made for me for my thirteenth birthday. My ceiling is painted blue and speckled with clouds. There are stuffed animals on my dresser, tons of picture collages on my walls, and a pile of messy clothes on my desk chair from deciding what to pack to go to the Academy.

Little did I know that there would be a uniform and that I would have no access to my luggage. But my dad didn't tell me any of that. He didn't tell me a lot of things—like that my aunt Jo wasn't in danger, she was *dead*. In fact, the only thing he said that was true was that we needed to leave our house. I know I shouldn't blame him, that he was only trying to keep me safe, and that if he had told me the truth I never would have gone to the Academy. But in my less mature moments I get angry that he didn't take me with him. Since I was six, we've relied on each other, have done everything together, and now he's somewhere in Europe without me.

I sigh, shaking the thought from my head. I pull open my dresser drawer, run my finger along the edge until I find the familiar groove, and tilt up the false bottom. I grab my favorite boot dagger, which my dad gave me when I was ten, and my Browning Black Label, which I hook to my belt loop under my sweater.

I squeal so loudly that my dad leans back on the couch to protect his hearing. "You're kidding me! This is so so cool!" I exclaim.

"It's—" he starts.

"A boot dagger. I know," I say, thrilled that I can identify the small knife.

My dad smiles. "Well, yes, it's a boot dagger. But it's not like your other knives. This one is different."

I turn the knife around in my hand, examining it. It doesn't look particularly different from my others. It's double-edged and the handle appears to be carved from bone instead of wood, but neither of those things is unusual. I look up at my dad.

"It's different because a boot dagger is a concealed weapon," my dad says.

"Seriously? That's the most obvious—" I start, but he holds up his hand, like he was anticipating my objection.

"And a concealed weapon should bear the element of surprise," he continues. "That may sound obvious, but it won't once you realize that the surprise of a boot dagger shouldn't rely solely on its concealment."

"What do you mean?" I ask.

"Let's say you're in a fight and someone pulls a dagger out of their boot. Surprise! Now, what effect would that have on you?" he asks.

"Do I have a knife?" I ask.

"Maybe," he says.

"Dad, how am I supposed to answer a maybe?" I ask.

"That's exactly my point," he replies with a subtle smile. "The possibility that an opponent will have a knife will always be a maybe. So let's take the possibilities one at a time. Say you don't have a knife, what would you do?"

"Find something to use as a shield, and if there's nothing available, I'd look for something long that I could use as a weapon to keep the knife away from my body. But if both of those fail, then I would use the disarming techniques you showed me," I say, repeating our recent lesson.

"Right," my dad says. "And what if you did have a knife?"

"Then I would just fight," I say.

"So how has the surprise of your opponent's concealed weapon affected you in each of these scenarios?" he continues.

I pause to give it some thought. "Well, I guess I would be surprised if I didn't have a knife, but I would also know what to do. And if I did have a knife . . . I don't know. I might be momentarily surprised, but it wouldn't be a big deal."

"Then what is the point of hiding a dagger in your boot if you barely surprise your opponent? Why not just put it on your belt, where it's easier to access?" he asks, slightly elongating his words the way he always does when he's closing in on his point.

"Because it's awesome," I say with a grin, and my dad smiles.

"Awesomeness aside, think about it, Nova. How can you be certain that you will surprise your opponent with a boot dagger?" he asks.

I consider his question and redirect my focus to the window that looks out on our back porch and the forest beyond. "Hmmm. To surprise someone with a boot dagger . . . ," I say, repeating the question like people on talk shows always do when they're not sure what to say, "I suppose I would . . . do something surprising once I pulled it out?"

"Agreed," he says. "But what?"

I inspect the small knife, turning it over in my palm. "I could do one of my tricks," I say.

"Possible," he says. "But you would have to be sure it was the right moment; you know that with knives the smallest mistake can mean forfeiting your weapon."

"So what's the answer?" I ask, now genuinely curious.

"Don't think like a knife expert," he says.

This time I don't attempt to object because I know he's not finished.

"People who are trained to use knives have expectations for themselves and others. Defy these expectations and you can win," he continues with emphasis. "Most people mistakenly use weapons as though there are invisible boundaries or rules dictating conduct. You don't. You integrate moves you've learned in soccer and secret handshakes you made up with Emily—this way of thinking is the key. Just because there isn't a clear shot doesn't mean you can't win. There is always a work-around and a way to surprise your opponent. It just takes creativity and a lack of self-imposed boundaries."

"Take what you need," I say to Ash, but when I look up from my knife drawer, he isn't standing next to me. "Ash?"

I turn around to find him examining my room, which I'm certain tells him all kinds of personal things about me. His expression is curious, like my things surprise him in some way he wasn't expecting. I follow his eyes toward my picture collages and to my bookshelf, which is covered with knickknacks, my book collection on plants and trees, and my mom's old CDs and movies, most of which are scuffed and imperfect from the countless number of times Emily and I played them. And as I look over my belongings, I realize that a month ago I would have called these things unremarkable, brushed them off as normal or griped about wanting a new iPod. But in this moment, they seem invaluable—a catalogue of my childhood imbued with more memories than I can put into words. And I wonder: Will I ever see these things again? Will I ever sit in my bed, which my dad built, listening to music with Emily and talking about our plans for the weekend?

"Okay, now, let's see," Ash says. He joins me at the dresser and turns his attention to the knives, nodding approvingly. "Not bad," he says.

"You mean awesome," I say, looking back at the drawer and the knife collection I've always been proud of.

He smirks. "Well, not quite as good as mine," he says. "But only because you're missing some collector's pieces."

I lift an eyebrow. "Are you trying to make me jealous? Because it's working."

"Or trying to convince you to come and visit my house in Egypt when this is all over," he says with a sly grin.

I look at him sideways. "You think your parents would be okay with that?"

"With you? The disowned firstborn of the Lion and Bear Families that everyone's hunting . . . what could they possibly object to?" But I can hear in his voice that even though he's making light of it, this mess with my family is a big deal. At present, there is nowhere I belong in the Strategia world.

"We need to avoid the windows," he says, shifting our

conversation. "And don't turn on any lights. Let's get our searching done before the sun sets."

"Definitely," I say, aware of the time restrictions. I drop the false bottom back into place and close my drawer.

"What can you tell me that will help me search?" he asks, and I scan my room, trying to figure out how to explain to him what could qualify as unusual in my house.

"The way you were just looking at my room . . . ," I start. "It seems haphazard and messy to you, doesn't it?"

"It seems lived-in," Ash says, and there is something in his voice that almost sounds like longing.

"But I'm willing to bet it's also not the typical bedroom for a Strategia. You keep your space sparse and meticulous, right?" I ask.

"I do. But how do you know that?"

"Because my dad does the same thing. His room is like walking into a stage set. And after seeing how everyone behaved at the Academy—so structured, so exact—it makes sense. So why don't you start in my dad's bedroom? You'll probably understand it better than any other room in the house. Look for anything that might be a message to me. Dad always had a thing for making me search out my birthday presents. So whatever the message is, it's probably a puzzle."

Ash nods and leaves me to my bedroom. For a second I just stand there, nostalgic for my once-normal life. I move to the silver jewelry box on my dresser, which was my mom's, and pull out her gold ring that looks like knobby bark with delicate leaves. I slip it on my pointer finger and sigh. There is no time for me to go through my special things one by one the way I want to. There is just no time, period.

I begin to pace, focusing on the task at hand and trying to remember everything that happened from the time Dad told me about the school until the moment we walked out the door with my duffel bag. My thoughts immediately go to the popcorn bowl and I move quickly into the living room. He left everything exactly as it was. No one but me would know if something changed ... *no one but me*. I scan the room.

Next to the bowl is the open magazine I was reading, exactly where I plopped it down when my dad said we needed to talk. The blanket is draped haphazardly where I tossed it before packing. The matches he used to light the fire lie open on the mantel. The area rug is in its place. The furniture is the same. There is just as much wood stacked near the fireplace as there was when we left.

I spend the next few hours meticulously scrutinizing every detail of my living room, dining room, kitchen, mudroom, and bathroom. But for the life of me I can't find one thing so much as an inch out of place. If someone did search my house, then I'm impressed, because I would never be able to tell.

"November?" Ash says, and I turn to find him standing in my dad's bedroom door. "I found something."

For a second, I'm confused. "Really?"

"Did you think I wouldn't?" he says, and I follow him into my dad's bedroom.

"Truthfully, no," I admit. "I never spent much time in my dad's room. My dad didn't spend much time in here, either—not since my mom died, anyway."

Ash stands near my dad's neatly made bed and gestures to the folded quilt. "Check the second navy square on the bottom left."

I move around the bed and run my fingers over the square he indicated. The seams are straight and nothing is amiss. I put my hand under the quilt and inspect the other side. Everything feels perfectly as it should be. I give Ash a questioning look.

He directs my hand to the corner where the stitching is almost imperceptibly thicker. He uses my fingers to pinch the seam, and sure enough there's something in there. I pick at it until the threads separate, then use my nails to pull out a tiny piece of tightly rolled paper.

On the inside is written:

Meet me under the city.

I stare up at Ash, confused, trying to figure out why in the heck my dad would leave me a message in a place I would never find it. "This doesn't . . ."

"This doesn't what?" Ash asks, reading my expression.

"Honestly? I want to be excited that you found something, but if this wasn't written in my dad's handwriting, I wouldn't believe it was from him."

Ash's eyebrows push together. "Are you *positive* it's his handwriting? Because the seam was repaired where the note was and it looks like it wasn't the first time. If you ask me, another Strategia already found it."

"I'm positive," I say, and I stare at it like it's going to sprout teeth. *A Strategia was in my house.* My stomach does a quick flip and I'm suddenly immensely grateful Ash stopped me from running up to Emily. If someone was watching, I could have gotten us all killed.

I hold the note up to the light, but the paper is thick, with no watermarks and no indentations from previous writing. "The thing is, it's not like Dad's usual clues. I don't have any idea what this means. We mostly never leave Pembrook, much less the state of Connecticut, and we certainly never went underground anywhere."

Ash looks at me like I just said something odd. "And he never talked to you about a city that had underground meeting spots?"

I shake my head and stare back at him, trying to decipher his expression. "You know what this means, don't you?" I say, and I don't need to wait for his answer because I recognize the confirmation in his eyes. "Why do you know what this note means and I don't? That doesn't make sense."

"It does if this note wasn't intended for you," Ash says with confidence. "And if it wasn't intended for you, then it was meant for the Strategia who searched this place." He rolls it up and puts it back where it was.

I chew on my thumbnail as I try to sort out his logic. "I know I'm the one saying this note doesn't make sense, but how can you be so sure? Scratch that. I need you to be without-a-doubt positive, because it would be a complete and total mess if we disregarded a message we shouldn't have."

Ash nods, like he understands my objection perfectly. "There are series of underground crypts, catacombs, and streets all over Europe that Strategia use to meet. But your father wrote *the* city, and given the fact that he's a Lion, that most likely indicates London. And in London there's an underground pub that's used by all the Families—a popular spot for trading information and meetings. You don't know that, but any other Strategia would know what it meant instantly."

I consider his explanation. "Okay, I see your point: Why would he bother leaving me a note that everyone *but me* would understand?"

"Exactly," Ash says.

I exhale. "Even though it's not for me, I'm relieved you found it. If my dad left a decoy note, then there's definitely a real one. And if you're correct that someone has already searched my house, then we need to find it fast."

"Agreed," Ash says. "Have you found anything?" He glances at my dad's bedroom window and he doesn't need to say what he's thinking. This late in December, the light's already dimming.

My stomach knots up as our opportunity to search fades with the sun. And I'm not willing to risk another day here, not with my dad in who knows what kind of danger in Europe and with a potential Strategia lingering around my property.

I shake my head. "No clues yet."

"Let's think about this," Ash says. "If the note was a decoy, then whatever he left for you has to be drastically different in order to avoid the possibility of another Strategia finding it."

I nod. "Right. And if it's drastically different, then it's probably not going to be a hidden object—a hidden object could be found by anyone with the proper searching skills. So maybe . . ." I stop and chew on my lip as I think. "Maybe it's something that's hidden in plain view."

"Potentially something symbolic?" Ash offers.

I walk back into the living room, turning in a full circle and reexamining the room. "And if the message is in plain view, then it has to be something I would know how to decipher but that wouldn't mean anything to anyone else. . . ." My voice trails off as the realization dawns on me. I run to my room with Ash at my heels.

I immediately scour my picture collages.

"What are you thinking?" Ash asks. "Can I help in any way?"

"What I'm thinking is that Dad always said I logged our entire lives in these collages," I reply. "I've been making them since I was eight. I used to spend weeks on them, picking a theme, cutting out the pictures so they fit together exactly the way I wanted them to. I'd take over the whole living room floor with photos from our trips and school dances. Dad used to come along and move a couple of the pictures on me as a joke and I would get super annoyed," I say, scanning every inch of the collages.

Ash stands next to me, noting the details of the pictures with interest. "I always assumed you were missing something because you weren't raised like a typical Strategia, but now I'm thinking it's the exact opposite. It's me and Layla who lost out."

I hear the personal admission in his words, but I'm too focused and we're under too much pressure to give that opening the attention it deserves.

"This!" I practically jump in the air as I poke my finger at a collage from when I was thirteen. "He switched these two pictures. I can't believe I didn't think to look here before."

"What do they mean?" Ash asks.

"Good question," I say, and trade my enthusiasm for concentration. "Let me think this one out for a second." I point to one of the changed pictures. "So this is from the camping trip we went on with Aunt Jo as my middle school graduation present. And this one is Emily and me laughing over the ridiculous things we were thinking of putting in our seventh-grade time capsule."

"What's the—"

"Hold on," I say, not to be rude, but because I feel like the message is at the edge of my thoughts. I just need a moment to pluck it out. "Time capsules preserve memories, personal items that have meanings within specific time frames. And this trip was a celebration. We made our own tent. Dad taught me his favorite sword trick. . . . Oh my god, Aunt Jo taught me how to camouflage my camping gear so that it blended with the woods." I look at Ash, the memories flooding back. "I thought it was the coolest thing at the time. And when I came home, I decided to make a time capsule of my own, a smaller version of these picture collages, in order to commemorate my year. I talked about it for a month." My voice is faster and more animated. "But I didn't want to bury it like the time capsule at school where it would eventually decay. Instead, I decided to use what Aunt Jo taught me about camouflage. Dad helped me pick out the tree to hide it in."

"And this tree is on your property?" he asks, and I can see the relief in his eyes that we're making progress.

"About a five-minute walk into the woods from the edge of my backyard," I say, and grab my coat off my bed.

"Wait," Ash says.

"Wait for what?" I say. "We need to go find out what's in that tree. Because if I'm wrong, then we need to start looking elsewhere."

"Agreed. But not this moment. Look out your window. We're about to lose the light—" Ash starts.

"I can get to the tree before we do, though," I counter.

"Of course you can if you waltz right out there. But what if there's a Lion in those woods waiting for you to emerge in order to attack you? Or maybe waiting for you to find the message from your dad and *then* attack you?" he says. "Do you really want to fight a well-trained assassin in the woods with no light?"

I want to argue with him. I *need* to know what my dad's message says. But fighting a Strategia sounds awful under any circumstances, much less in the dark. "When are you suggesting we go out there?"

"Just moments before sunrise. We can move across the yard in the dark, and if we're lucky no one will be there. But if we're not and we need to fight, the coming sunrise will at least allow us to see."

I exhale audibly and drop my coat back on my bed. I hate that he's right about this, and as much as I don't want to, I agree—getting that message and finding my dad are more important than rushing. "Fine. I concede. But then we leave with no delay."

"Then we leave," Ash replies, and I wonder how I'll ever make it through the night knowing that there might be something from my dad waiting for me in the woods.

Eight

I STARE OUT the window at the pile of white roses on my front porch, careful to stay crouched down and keep my face to the side of the curtain in case my house is being watched. There are little notes attached to the rose stems with purple satin ribbon, and I don't even attempt to swallow back the lump in my throat.

"I'm so sorry," I whisper to Emily's flowers.

Ash went to bed hours ago and I know that's where I should be, too. It's well after midnight and we need all the sleep we can get before our sunrise mission, especially after our previous night of sedatives and travel. But I can't seem to drag myself away from this window. These past few days I've been twisted with worry and fear over where my dad is and what kind of danger he's in. And all I can think is that Emily has been going through the same distress over *me* for weeks.

What if this is the last time I ever see Pembrook—what if this is the last time I ever see *her*? If I die in Europe, Emily will be left to forever wonder where I went. Her best friend will have just disappeared into thin air.

"Promise me something," Emily says, her hair getting caught in her lip gloss in the warm summer breeze.

"Anything," I say, perching on the fence separating Ben's house from his family's back field, the air thick with humidity and the woods buzzing with crickets.

"Don't say 'anything' when you don't know what I'm going to ask," Emily says, leaning against the fence post.

"Most people would be delighted by that answer," I say, flashing her a big grin. "You could make me promise to kiss one of Ben's cows or streak through the center of town."

She gives me a look like I'm the most ridiculous person she's ever met, a routine we play out so often that the Marco Polo-ness of it is comforting. "By 'most people,' you mean you."

I swat the back of my neck, where I'm pretty sure a mosquito just bit me. "I most certainly do."

"I'm serious," she says, and gives me a warning look.

"Okay, tell me," I say instead of instigating her further, because there is something uncertain in her tone, and Emily's never uncertain, even when she's wrong.

"I saw the UConn brochure in the stack of mail on your table," she says, and she hesitates. "I just . . . I just want you to promise me that if you want to go somewhere else you'll tell me." Her voice is smaller than it usually is and there's worry written in the lines of her forehead.

"I don't understand," I say, now unsure myself, and repeat the familiar phrase we've said in some version since the beginning of ninth grade. "It's close enough to come home on the weekends and far enough to escape the watchful eye of the Christopher. Basically perfect." I study her. We've always said we would go to UConn together. Always.

"No. I know. I mean . . ." She looks momentarily toward the buzzing woods as though they might help her make her point.

And suddenly it dawns on me why she might be asking. "Wait . . . do you want to go somewhere else?" I say, my heart picking up speed, bracing for the possibility that on this lazy mundane summer afternoon, my best friend might tell me she's leaving.

"No!" she says, the word exploding from her mouth. "Don't even think it!"

"You thought it about me," I fire back, and it takes me a moment to rebound from the adrenaline rush.

For a second we're both quiet, breathing in the soupy air, which smells like grass and cows, our chests rising and falling a little faster.

"You're serious," I say. "You're not just randomly asking me a question." I stare at Emily and it's obvious she is. "Something happened, didn't it? What happened, Emily?" I say her name with enough emphasis that she huffs.

"The Christopher," she says like a deflating balloon.

I pull back to look at her, even though I don't need to. "My dad?" I say, my words full of disbelief. "My dad, who always tells us that we're saving him a lot of money because now he won't need to fly to California every weekend to check on us? That dad?"

Emily presses her lips together.

"You know I'm going to get it out of you one way or another," I say, wiping the sweat from my forehead with the back of my forearm. "You might as well just tell me."

Emily shakes her head, but not like she's telling me no, like she's unsure. "I don't know. It was weird. He saw me looking at the brochure and he asked me if it was actually my first choice. I told him of course it was, but he just stood there with one of his all-knowing stares. Then he asked if I would go there even if you weren't here."

My eyebrows push together. Emily has always been a better student than me, likely the best in our entire school. "You know you could if you wanted to . . . go to some fancy school," I say, now uncomfortable that my dad was suggesting she should go somewhere else, that it would be better for her. I've only admitted this out loud once, and it's hard to look at her and know that maybe I'm just being selfish, wanting to keep her here with me. I sheepishly examine the piece of long grass in my hand.

"No," Emily says with so much force that I look back up. "Don't you dare even suggest it, November Adley. I was asking you that question, not the other way around. Now answer me, do you want to go to UConn or not?" she asks, and even though there is fire in her voice, there is relief in her eyes.

And I'm relieved that she's relieved. "One hundred million percent," I say, and we smile at each other, the big goofy kind of smile that makes your eyes squint and your chest feel warm. And just like that the whole conversation drops away, like it never happened in the first place.

The screen door on Ben's back porch swings shut. We both turn, watching Ben balance three glasses of iced lemonade and two bags of chips, and make no attempt to help him.

Did my dad know? Did he know six months ago that I might not be here to go to UConn the way I'd always planned? Questions explode through my mind—questions about Aunt Jo's murder, about our Strategia relatives, and about his and Mom's decision to keep me hidden. But then I spot Emily's loopy handwriting on one of the cards tied to the white roses and my body squeezes tightly around my heart. In this moment, there are so many things outside my control, so many things I don't understand. But the one thing I do understand is that I'm hurting my best friend—my best friend, who I'm supposed to drink my first glass of wine with, go on my first trip to Europe with, the first person I want to tell when I fall in love.

I push my fist into my thigh. *I can't do this to Emily. I won't.* And before I even realize it, I'm slipping into my bedroom and putting on my coat, my heart beating a mile a minute. I know this isn't the smartest thing I've ever done. But I also know that I'll regret it forever if I don't try to see her one last time.

I tiptoe past Ash, who's sleeping on my couch, and into the bathroom. I close the door slowly and hoist the window up, careful not to let the wood whine. I climb onto the sink counter and then out through the window onto a tree branch.

Every one of my senses is on high alert, looking for movement in the shadows and listening for the sound of snapping twigs. I make my way slowly and methodically out of the tree and then slink from one tree to another until I'm far enough from my house and from the risk of being detected that I'm willing to move faster.

I use backyards and patches of trees to stay out of sight as I zigzag my way through the streets that I know as well as my own room. And in my predictably sleepy town, there are only two properties that still have their lights on.

I pause in Emily's backyard and check my surroundings to make sure no one followed me. When I'm satisfied that everything is still, I climb up her porch railing and hoist myself onto her roof. I know she doesn't lock her bedroom window because this definitely isn't the first time I've snuck over here. But I also know that if I make noise and wake her up unexpectedly, she'll most likely scream.

I take off my gloves and hold them between my teeth, sliding her window up so slowly that I wonder if the draft will wake her even though I'm being quiet. The moment that the window's high enough for me to fit, I slide in and push it back down, faster than is cautious.

Emily stirs in her light blue canopied bed and I take a few fast strides across her carpeted floor. She turns over and her eyelids flutter. At a loss for a better option, I press my hand over her mouth. Her eyes snap open at my touch and for a moment she appears terrified and disoriented.

"It's me, Em," I whisper. "I'm sorry for sneaking up on you like a criminal in the night, but just whatever you do, don't scream."

Recognition appears on her face and her sleepiness instantly melts. I lift my hand off her mouth. For a second she's perfectly still.

"*Nova?*" she says, her voice dripping with disbelief, like I might be a hallucination or a dream.

I open my mouth to respond, but before I can get a word out she sits up in her plaid pajamas and wraps her arms around my neck so tightly that I can hardly breathe. She immediately starts sobbing into my hair, her shoulders shaking up and down. Her emotion crashes over me like a wave, pulling me under and tumbling me about, reminding me of everything I've lost and everything I could lose.

A month ago I took Em's love for granted, knew that no

matter what happened in the world I would always have the safe escape of my best friend. Everything felt solid then. The simplicity of my life here in Pembrook was something I could lean on, something that grounded me in the world.

She pulls back and examines me, still clutching my shoulders like I might disappear again. "You're here. Nova, you came back," she says.

The hurt on her face threatens to crush me; I don't know how I'll ever tell her that I'm not staying. "I'm here, Em, and I'm so incredibly sorry. I—"

I don't get my full apology out because she goes from grief to fury in a split second.

"You're *sorry*? That doesn't even begin to cover it. How dare you? *How dare you do that to me*, November Rose Adley!" She practically spits the words at me, her voice shaking. And she pushes me so hard that I have to stand up to avoid falling on the floor.

She stands, too, and she pushes me again. "I don't accept your apology. Do you hear me? I will never forgive you for leaving me like that. You're my *best friend*. Best friends don't . . ." Her words gurgle as she fights back tears.

I want to reach out to her, wrap my arms around her, and tell her that it's over. But I just stand there, struggling to speak. "Aunt Jo was killed," I say. Normally I wouldn't drop information like that so suddenly. But knowing Emily, she'll attack me again before I have a chance to get it out gently in the midst of an apology.

Her tears stop so suddenly that it's like someone zapped her. She takes a step back, her eyes wide with horror. *"What?"*

"She was killed and my dad took me away," I say, knowing

she's never going to accept such a sparse explanation. "He's worried it might have something to do with their old jobs, something—"

"As in their jobs at the *CIA*?" she says, her eyes round.

"Yeah," I lie, careful not to elaborate too much or she will figure out something is off.

She takes a few pacing steps like she's struggling to absorb my words. And I get it. Nothing bad ever happens in Pembrook. Even after my dad told me we were in danger and shipped me off to the Academy, I didn't really believe it until I was face to face with a dead body.

She turns to look at me, her eyebrows pushed together. "I don't even know what . . . No . . . that's just . . . Are you in danger *now*?"

"I'm not sure," I lie again, and follow it up with some truth. "But you know my dad. He's smart and overly cautious." I don't need to sell this; she's been at my house multiple times a week for the past twelve years and she's well aware.

She eyes me, not entirely convinced. "Does he know you're here right now, climbing through my window in the middle of the night?"

I take a step toward her, shaking my head. "But I just had to come to see you. I had to let you know I was okay. And, well, I needed to tell you that I won't be in touch for a little while." My voice is smaller than it was before and it's hard to look at her. I can only imagine how betrayed she must feel. "But you don't have to worry; I'm okay and my dad's okay." As I hear myself speak, I begin to wonder if I made the right choice in coming here and how much of this was actually for me, because I couldn't stand the idea of not seeing her.

91

She wipes her nose. "And whoever hurt your aunt, your dad thinks they might want to hurt you, too?" she asks.

"He doesn't know," I say. "But he wants to be certain before we return. So, Em, you can't say anything about me coming here, not to your parents, not to anyone."

She nods reluctantly, like even though she understands, she doesn't like it one bit.

"I love you, Emily Jane Banks," I say, and she lifts her chin.

"Don't 'I love you' me, Nova. This isn't a goodbye."

I nod, desperately trying to collect myself, because all I can think is: This *is* a goodbye, the hardest one of my life. I've imagined seeing her so many times over these past few weeks, but in my imaginary scenario filled with hugs and crying, I didn't take into consideration how much it would hurt to walk away from her, this time knowing I might never come back.

There is a light tap on the window and my heart jumps into my throat. I whip around, blinking at the silhouette crouched on the roof.

"Ash?" I say in a shocked tone as he lifts the window, letting in the cold December air.

Emily's eyes are so wide that I wonder if they will ever return to normal. "Who the heck is this?" She points at Ash but looks at me.

I don't get a chance to respond because Ash starts talking.

"I'm sorry to interrupt, but we have to go," he says, and I don't know if I'm horrified that he followed me without me knowing it or grateful that he showed up and interrupted this conversation before I broke down in front of Emily.

"Nova?" she says, her hand on her hip, giving me a questioning stare.

Ash looks at Emily. "I'll keep your friend safe. I give you my word."

"I don't want your word," she says, turning toward him. "I don't want any of this."

"We have to go," Ash says again, and there's a warning in his tone, a warning not to linger and let someone other than Ash catch me here.

I approach my best friend, wanting to tell her everything she means to me and that nothing is the same without her, but also not wanting to scare her. So I simply say, "I've missed you, Em," and I hug her. "I'll be back before you know it."

She clings to me. "You better be," she says, insistent, and pulls back to look at me once more. "I'll never forgive you if something happens to you, Nova. I will hold a grudge into the afterlife if I have to." She attempts a smile, but her eyes well up.

I smile back, the weight on my chest almost unbearable. We share a look in the moonlight, one that says what I can't bear to voice—that we need each other. Turning away from her is the single hardest thing I've ever had to do. And as I slip back out the window, I leave a piece of my heart behind.

Nine

ASH AND I move quickly across town. He follows me through backyards and side streets, not attempting to talk to me about what just happened. And even though I don't want to discuss it, I also hate the silence. Every familiar inch of this town does nothing but remind me of Emily and the life I'm giving up. When I was in the Academy all I wanted was to come back here, and now that I'm here I want to shut my eyes, crawl under my covers, and sob. I bite my lip, trying to physically hold back my upset, and I blink away the wetness in the corners of my eyes.

Ash stops when we reach the edge of the forest that leads to my house. He gives me a hard look. I'm certain he's thinking that going to Emily's was a terrible idea. But he doesn't say it; he doesn't have to. We both know.

"We need to retrieve whatever your dad left you in that tree," he says instead.

The shock pulls me out of my thoughts. "Hold on, *now*?"

"Now," he says, and I can tell he's frustrated with me. "We

can't sneak back into your house in the pitch dark, because we'll have no idea if someone is following us. Because you didn't even know that I was following you."

"All of our stuff—"

"I stashed our bags at the edge of the woods. We just need that note and we need to leave." What he doesn't say is "before you cause any more trouble."

"Okay, let me see. . . ." I scan the woods, mentally planning the best route to the tree and twisting my mom's ring on my finger. If I can navigate these woods with a blindfold on, then I can definitely do it with only a little moonlight. "I've got a plan, but it'll require us climbing through a few branches that are much thinner than the ones we practice on at the Academy. You okay with that?"

He nods and I exhale. Sneaking out to go see Emily was one thing, but sneaking into woods that might have a Strategia in them is something else entirely. My pulse is racing and I'm sweating under my winter coat.

I weave us through the familiar forest, going around areas that are overgrown with brush and littered with fallen branches. Even so, our steps aren't completely silent. It's impossible to avoid making noise in the dark when there is so much leaf and plant debris on the ground. And every crunch we make zings through me like a jolt of electricity, making me feel increasingly worse that I put us in this position.

I lead us around a patch of particularly thick brush near my house and our steps get louder. Ash touches my arm and brings his finger to his lips. I stop moving. He scans the forest and my heart pounds so hard in my temples that my vision blurs momentarily. Does he hear something? See something? I desperately want to ask him, but I have no intention of talking, given the possibility of exposure.

I take the most deliberate steps of my life, counting them off as I go, like there is a magic number where this horror ends and we get out safely. We're still a good couple of hundred feet from the cluster of large trees that grow close enough together that we can climb from limb to limb. At least when we're off the ground, our sound and visibility will be reduced. When I count off eighteen steps, a particularly dry leaf crunches under my boot. I freeze, holding my breath.

One excruciating second passes and I scan the trees around me. I cautiously lift my foot, but before I can take a step I hear a faint hum and Ash pushes me to the ground so fast that I barely get my hands under me to break my fall. As I land in a pile of cold leaves, there's a telltale thud as an arrow strikes the tree in front of me. The arrow hits exactly where my chest had been only a half second earlier.

"Run!" Ash says, and we shove ourselves up, my legs moving so quickly that I'm shocked they don't slip out from under me. An arrow flies by my head, so close that I feel its wind on my cheek.

I sprint through the woods, Ash by my side, our boots pounding through dry leaves and snapping twigs with each step. Another arrow hits the tree next to me. By the evenly measured delay between shots, I would guess there's only one archer. And whoever it is has excellent aim in the dark with moving targets. I push my legs harder, demanding that they move faster. I lead us in a zigzagged path behind trees and fallen branches, aware that if I ease up for one second or give the archer a clean shot, one of us will die.

"Up, Ash," I breathe as we run full-speed toward the closely clustered patch of trees I was looking for. My hand-to-hand combat skills are definitely lacking and I've got much better chances of holding my own off the ground.

I grab the tree trunk and hoist myself up onto a familiar branch. I glance over my shoulder, but Ash isn't behind me. Sheer panic squeezes my chest. I scan the trees, looking for signs of him. But the only thing I see is a light-colored bow, and it's pointed directly at me. I immediately jump to a neighboring branch and an arrow hits the trunk. I can't run without knowing where Ash is, but I can't stay here, either.

I yank my gloves off and shove them in my pockets, wiping my now-sweaty hands on my coat. I peek around the trunk, and just as I do, Ash lands a kick, not on our attacker, but on his bow. The wood cracks and splits. The Strategia, who I can now see is a man both taller and broader than Ash, takes a swing before Ash can recover his footing. The impact is so hard that I hear the thunk as the guy's fist connects with Ash's skull. Ash goes flying into the tree behind him, but the guy doesn't stay to fight. Instead, he turns and takes off in my direction.

His black hood flies back as he runs, revealing his brown hair and short beard. His strides are so long that they encompass two of mine. Ash is moving now, too, but he's a good twenty feet behind. I turn and scramble along the branch faster than is safe.

I hear the Strategia's boots scrape along the tree trunk

behind me and hear him grunt as he pulls himself up. Given his speed, I have ten seconds at most before he reaches me. I catch a glimpse of Ash running below us, and if I didn't think I would break something from this height, I would jump down to him. There is no way Ash will make it up here in time to help me fight—if this guy grabs me, I'm done. He moves like a well-trained assassin, and while I'm good in trees, I'm also a student who barely spent a few weeks at the Academy.

I grab a higher branch, pulling myself up quickly enough the bark burns my hands. The guy makes a swipe for my ankle and gets so close that if I were a fraction of a second slower, I would be tumbling to the ground. *Please don't let me die. Please, please don't let this be the end. I won't make this mistake again. Ever. I promise. Just let me make it to my dad in Europe.*

The branch I'm on forks and I take three daring strides and jump to an even thinner one on the next tree.

"Stop, November!" Ash yells, and I'm so surprised that I actually do.

I whip around and the Strategia is running along the branch I was just on.

"Mr. Baines!" Ash shouts.

My mind snaps into focus. *Baines—Old English stemming from the Latin word* ban, *meaning "bones." It likely referred to a thin person. Thin.* I look down at the branch I'm on and it suddenly occurs to me what Ash wants me to do.

The Strategia makes a leap to the branch I'm on. Just as he lands, I jump, grabbing the branch above me, and slam both feet down on the thin one. The branch snaps in half, the sound ringing through the forest, leaving me dangling and leaving the Strategia no time to recover. His arms flail desperately around him and he falls twenty feet, hitting the ground with a dull thud.

I swing my legs back and forth for momentum and get my ankle wrapped around the branch. I pull myself along with my arms and legs until I reach the trunk, then rush down it to help Ash. But the moment my boots hit the ground I can see there's no need. The bearded guy lies perfectly still, his arms and legs splayed out around him, a pool of blood forming below his head where a piece of New England granite sticks out.

For a long second I stare wide-eyed, my feet frozen in place, not able to process what I'm seeing. I blink, but he's still there, unmoving. My stomach turns and my hands fly to either side of my face.

"I didn't know he would . . . Oh my god . . ." My voice is fast, and even in the cold night air, I'm burning up. "I didn't mean to . . . He almost killed you, Ash. I mean, if he'd used a knife instead of a punch . . ." I stare at the man's unmoving face, instantly reminded of all the dead bodies in my dream. "*I did this.* I killed him. I can't believe I killed him." I repeat it because it hasn't fully sunk in, because it's all too awful to be true.

Ash walks right up to me and puts his hands on my shoulders, turning me away from the body. "Look at me, just at me," he says insistently, moving me until the dead man is out of sight. Even in the moonlight I can make out the intensity of Ash's eyes.

Guilt ripples through me. How could I have done this? I'm not a killer . . . I'm not.

"You need to focus, November," Ash says in a demanding

voice. "You need to get the message from your dad. Whatever you're feeling right now will pass; but if you let it consume you, you won't be able to think. You're the only one who can retrieve that message."

I nod at him and break eye contact. It takes every ounce of my determination not to cry. I almost got Ash killed. I killed someone. And I broke my promise to Layla. This isn't the Academy; there aren't teachers and guards, curated challenges and structure. This is real, and it's *deadly*.

"Go," he says, and I do. I jog about fifty feet, focusing all my energy on locating and climbing up the right tree, scrutinizing each detail more than necessary, and trying to push away the image of the blood I fear will be with me forever.

About fifteen feet up, the trunk splits into two parts. I brush aside the leaves in the crevice created by the split and wiggle out a loose piece of bark. Underneath it, exactly where I stashed it four years ago, is a worn square tin a little smaller than my palm. I pull it out of the trunk and pry the top off. Folded inside is a baggie with a piece of paper in it that wasn't part of my original time capsule. *Dad.* I close the tin again and press it to my heart, relieved that I was right and that he didn't disappear without leaving me a message.

"November?" Ash says from under the tree I'm in.

"It's here," I say, and climb down to the ground.

He spots the small tin in my hand. "And your father—"

"There's a new note inside," I say in a hushed voice.

Ash lets out a sigh of relief. "Good," he says. "Let's get out of here, and then we can read it. But first"—he holds up a key with a small wooden horseshoe attached to it—"I found this in the assassin's pocket, practically the only thing he had on him, besides weapons, which I took. Do you know what it's for?"

My thoughts return to the man's bloodied head and I clutch the tin like it's the only thing tethering me to my sanity. Ash holds the key out, and I reluctantly take it.

I tilt the horseshoe to catch a bit of moonlight. "It looks like it goes to a padlock. And if I had to guess I'd say it's for a barn or storage shed," I say, trying to suppress the sick feeling welling in my throat that this not only came off a dead body, but from a person I killed. "There are lots of both around here, especially on the outskirts of town."

Ash nods, like he came to the same conclusion. "Are any of them rentable, possibly a barn someone could pay cash for? Or even better, something someone could use without the owner noticing?"

"Hmmm. It would have to be one of the bigger properties. But I can think of four or five farms that are big enough to have unused barns or sheds," I say, going over a mental map of Pembrook. "Would it need to be walking distance from here?"

"Definitely. And with a direct route through the forest to and from your house that avoids the town and people," he says.

I nod. "Anything else?"

"If I'm right, the building this key belongs to will be in a large open field with no crops or trees," he says.

I hand the key back to Ash like I can't get rid of it quickly enough. "There's a farm about a mile from here, a straight shot through the forest, that has a field tucked way back in the property that pretty much never gets used."

He exhales like he was hoping that was what I would say. "Let's go get our bags and see what we can find."

"But what about . . ." I point behind me.

"There is nothing to hide here," Ash says. "His injuries are consistent with falling out of a tree. Nothing more."

"Won't the arrows be suspicious?" I say, worrying about what the scene will look like to Sheriff Billy. Will he somehow connect it with Dad's and my disappearance?

"Collected them," he says, pointing to a pile of shafts and a broken bow, which I hadn't seen in the dark. "We'll bring them with us and dispose of them."

"But we can't just leave him. I mean—"

"We have to. We have no idea if he was alone, so we need to move out quickly," Ash says, the urgency in his voice intensifying.

I suck in a deep breath. I know he's right. But it all feels wrong—leaving my house without saying goodbye, leaving Emily with lies, leaving a dead Strategia in the woods. This isn't my Pembrook; it's a nightmare.

Ten

ASH AND I emerge from the woods in the back field of Moody Farms. We hug the trees around the perimeter of the open field and a pack of coy-wolves howls in the distance. Old Mr. Moody told me himself that the coyotes in this part of Connecticut are wicked big because they mated with wolves a long time ago, and over time most of the coyote genes got bred out. Who knows if it's true, or if he was just trying to keep us kids from sneaking into his hayloft, with tales of almost-wolves? But it gave me a healthy fear of coming here after dark. I frown at the memory of being scared of such a simple idea, mourning the girl I was before I went to the Academy, before I knew too much.

I look at Ash, following me silently through the dark, our breath billowing out in front of us. There are so many things I want to tell him, things I want to explain. But until we're out of Pembrook and out of the path of the Strategia who are hunting me, neither of us is going to take an easy breath.

I lead Ash to the barn and we slink around it, staying close to the shadows. We do a full lap of the building before he stops at the padlock that holds the wide double doors closed. He taps on the knife secured to my belt loop and I pull it out, my hand unsteady. Ash slips the key into the lock and opens the door about two feet. It's pitch-black in the barn and we remain still and silent, assessing our surroundings. Everything is quiet and there are no signs that anyone else is in the building. The only sound is the wind howling through the bare trees.

Ash strikes a match and my eyes widen.

I almost choke as I take in the large metal frame occupying most of the barn. "A *plane*? I thought if we were lucky we might find a backpack or something with information, but a friggin' *plane*?"

"A private jet," Ash says, smiling for the first time in what seems like forever. "A nice one. Whoever that assassin was in the woods, he must have been important."

Ash passes me the box of matches and I put my knife back in its holster. He blows out his match as it nears his fingers, and I light another. Now with his hands free, Ash starts removing the wooden blocks that stabilize the wheels.

"Hang on. What are you . . . You're not thinking about *taking this thing*?" I say, my words dripping with disbelief.

"Absolutely," he says like it's the most obvious conclusion in the world. "Unless you would rather fly commercial and risk being detected? This is actually best-case scenario."

"But who's going to fly it?" I ask, unable to wrap my mind around this plan, which is galaxies outside my comfort zone.

"We'll just have to wing it," he says, tossing the wooden blocks up into the plane and pulling the barn doors completely open.

"We're definitely *not* winging it," I blurt out.

"Relax, November," Ash says with a good-natured grin. He's suddenly his usual easy self and somehow I've gotten more uptight. "I've been flying planes since I was eight. And with something like this, it practically flies itself."

He heads up the stairs and turns on the lights.

I follow him. "Holy . . . ," I breathe as I look around the small plane in awe. There are two recliners with a big flatscreen TV, a small dining table, and a bed. Maybe Ash was right; maybe this is best-case scenario.

Ash goes right to the cockpit and turns the plane on with ease. While he's pushing buttons he hands me the padlock from his pocket. "I'm going to roll this plane out of the barn, if you wouldn't mind locking up. Just make sure to wipe our prints off."

I nod, taking the cold metal lock and climbing back down the steps. I look up at the old hayloft I used to play in, barely visible in the moonlight, and I sigh, overcome by a pang of sadness. *Goodbye, Em. Goodbye, Pembrook.* I suddenly wish it were light so that I could log the details of it better. But the tail of the plane clears the doors and there is no more time to consider what this moment might one day mean to me. Instead, I pull the barn doors shut and wipe the lock down, careful to erase all signs that we were here.

I jog up to the plane, still struggling to reconcile this experience with my quiet hometown. I climb up the steps, pull the hatch shut, and take the empty seat in the cockpit. I look at Ash, who is confidently pushing controls on the complex dashboard, and I'm undecided if I'm in awe of him or simply overwhelmed.

"Did you find anything else . . ." I swallow, immediately

conjuring the memory of the thud of the Strategia's landing and the blood slowly pooling under his head, dripping down the side of the rock. "Did you find anything else on the Strategia in the woods?" I fasten my seat belt, fighting back the sick feeling that's rising in my throat. "Anything besides the key?"

"I did," Ash says, and glances toward me, pausing for a split second. "He had a Lion tattoo on his shoulder."

I nod, not shocked, but definitely unsettled. If the Lions can find our house in Pembrook, what's to stop them from finding my dad in Europe? I touch the tin box in my coat pocket.

"Are you sensitive to motion?" Ash says, bringing me back into the present. He pushes a couple more buttons and pulls back a lever.

"Not that I know of," I say, but we're already bumping across the dark field, picking up speed, and heading right for the forest. "Oh no . . . ," I whisper to myself.

Ash only smiles as we sail full-speed toward the stand of trees. I grip the arms of my chair and squeeze my eyes shut. *Please don't let me have survived all of this just to die in a plane crash on Moody Farms.* When I manage to open them again, we're in the air and clear of the trees, not impaled on a maple like I feared. It takes my body a beat to catch up to the fact that the immediate danger has passed.

I let my breath out in one audible huff. And as the sky opens up in front of us, the ground dotted with the glow of white lights in the rising dawn, a silence descends. My thoughts drift to the tin in my pocket. I was so desperate to get to the tree to see if my dad left me something, but now that I know he did, I'm equally terrified to read his note.

"Ash, what do you know about the head of the Lions?" I ask, avoiding the inevitable.

"Jag," he says, and I recall Ash telling me in the Academy library about Jag's tyrannical rule before I had any idea that I, too, was a Lion.

"I can't believe I never asked this, but Jag is short for Jaguar, right?" I say, even though I know why I never asked—I still believed that I could walk away from this whole experience and from the Strategia world in general, and I didn't want to think about Jag or my vicious relatives any more than necessary.

Ash nods. "A nickname from his childhood."

Jaguar . . . an obvious play on the big-cat theme in the Lion Family. And if it developed in his childhood, it's always possible it's a reflection on his personality. Jaguars are known for their temperamental nature—solitary, opportunistic creatures that stalk and ambush their prey.

"What do you know about him?" I ask.

"I've never met him, but much of my Family has," Ash says. "They claim that on an average day he's pleasant, but that he has a short fuse and a brutal streak." Ash looks in my direction. "Was there anything in particular you wanted to know about your—" He stops short. "About Jag and the Lion Family? It's a broad topic."

"It's okay," I say. "You can say it: Is there anything in particular I want to know about *my grandfather.*" The certainty of my tone surprises me, considering how rarely I've used that familial term. "Truthfully, I don't even know what I want to know. All of it and none of it at the same time." I pull at my seat belt and Ash looks at me quizzically. "It was just that assassin in the woods . . ." I look out the cockpit window, trying to push away the image of his lifeless body on the forest floor. "Are all Strategia that good?"

"You mean that deadly?" he says, and I nod. "Yes. Some are better." He doesn't bother to elaborate and I suppose I don't want him to. Hearing about the numerous brilliant and talented Strategia across Europe will only further unnerve me at this point. It's enough to know I'm deeply unprepared and that I very nearly got us both killed tonight, a mistake that I hope never to repeat.

"Why is Jag so committed to killing off my family?" I ask. "Is it just ego because my dad chose to be with my mom over staying with his Family?"

Ash shakes his head. "Possibly. I'd always heard that your father was the shining star of the Family, Jag's favorite, who was set to rule in no uncertain terms . . . before Jag told the rest of Strategia that your father was dead, that is. And from what I understand about Jag, he doesn't forgive. He's pathological about rooting out his enemies."

"I know the Bears have pushed back against the Lions in general, but has anyone ever challenged Jag directly?" I ask, trying to grasp the larger framework of Strategia relationships.

"You would think so," Ash says with a hint of annoyance. "You would think that Families would be lining up to fight him. But they don't. Everyone talks about Jag's abuses behind closed doors and among trusted friends, but nothing ever comes of it. Layla and I used to wonder as kids how everything got so unbalanced and how the other Strategia became complacent, but it's something that happened over time, slowly. And at the point when the head Families realized their error, it was too late—Jag's rule was solidified and his power had become far-reaching." Ash sighs. "These days, anyone who opposes him suffers consequences so profound that the fear of him and the Lions is deterrence enough. Even the Bears have come under enormous pressure to soften their stance or risk losing their allies. Thus far they've held their position, but it's on shaky ground, and if they ever backed down completely, the Lions would run roughshod over all of Strategia."

I frown. "So it's essentially a large-scale version of what would have happened if Blackwood had ever stepped down. Conner and Brendan would have won, the Lions would have succeeded in killing the best students from nonsubdued Families, the Bears would be dead or under attack, and the young Strategia would have been forever tilted in the Lions' favor."

"Exactly like that," he says, and hesitates like he's trying to decide if he should tell me something or not. "Layla and I used to talk as kids about opposing the Lions when we took over the leadership in our Family. We only hoped that the situation would remain stable enough until we had the power needed to enact change. But here I am actually doing it, years before I believed it was possible . . . and it's because of you."

I smile. "I'm not sure I can take credit, considering I did what I did mainly to stay alive."

Ash doesn't waver. "No, November. You saw an injustice and you corrected it even though you were uncomfortable and even though it involved sacrifice."

I shift in my seat, not certain I deserve that praise and also not sure I want it. For me this has been about surviving and about finding my dad, not about correcting the Strategia power imbalance.

"You told me once that the Lions don't rule the way other Strategia Families do," I say, bringing the conversation back to Jag.

"The Lions are . . . unique." Ash pauses to think. "Strategia Families typically rely on their leading members to make decisions as a group, on their elders to advise them, and ultimately on the Council of Families when big decisions become too complex. But not the Lions, not since Jag's been in power. He's more of a dictator than part of a Family."

"So he's Henry the Eighth?" I ask.

Ash leans back in his seat like he's hunkering down for a long flight. "You're definitely not the first person to make that comparison."

I stare at the blinking lights below us, a world not yet awake and blissfully unaware that trained strategists and assassins are doing things that may change the course of their lives forever. "I remember you telling me that the Council of Families approved Jag as the leader of the Lions when they shouldn't have, and that by the time they realized there was a problem there was nothing to be done. But I don't understand that. Shouldn't they have tried?"

"They did," he says. "But Jag didn't follow their advice, and in order to oust him they would have had to use force. And the Council of Families never uses force; they are a source of wisdom, a collective of elders who advise and oversee Family politics. The whole system is built on respect."

"Interesting," I say. "*Respect* isn't the first word that comes to mind when I think of Strategia."

Ash looks at me and it seems as though my comment bothers him. "I understand your reservations given your introduction to our society, but there is a lot about Strategia that you haven't experienced. There are power plays and arrogance, certainly, but there are also selfless acts of bravery and loyalty."

His reaction surprises me; a society that kills as frequently as Strategia do is not one I would praise. But I'm not sure that I want to debate that point right now, especially on the heels of what happened in the woods.

"The worst part about the current state of Strategia politics," Ash continues when I don't respond, "is that the Lions have enough resources and power to do a lot of good in the world. But Jag is selfish; he only takes on the missions that serve him politically."

"Don't all Strategia do what serves them politically?" I ask.

"Yes and no," he says. "Yes, we care about power and influence, and yes, we will always choose to support our Family and our Family's territory before others. *But* for a great deal of history we have been team players. We step in when other Families need us, we take on missions that support the greater good, and we compromise when we need to. Jag changed all that. He's not a team player and he doesn't care one bit about the greater good. And what's worse is that he's managed to divide us and pit allied Families against one another through fear and manipulation."

For a moment we sit in silence. And when I don't respond, Ash looks at me.

"It's time, November," he says.

"Time?" I say, but the instant I say the word I realize his meaning—the tin. I touch my coat pocket. "Yeah . . . I . . . are you hungry? Want me to go see if there are snacks in here somewhere?"

"No," he says, and I turn away from him to the big expanse of sky. "We need to know what your father left you because it may very well affect where we land."

I run my teeth over my bottom lip, discovering that it's slightly chapped from the cold, dry air. "Right," I say, not bothering to hide my reluctance.

In my peripheral vision I can see the confusion on Ash's face and I get it, but I don't want to explain that it's not exactly the reading of the message that I'm resisting; it's the thought of finishing it. While it's still in my pocket, untouched, it holds the possibility of being everything I need to hear—an apology for not telling me who I was, an expression of love and regret, an address and a phone number so that I can instantly reach him. And somewhere in my gut, I know I'm going to be disappointed. But even though I would be happy to live with the idealized version a little longer, Ash is right—it's time.

I pull the cold metal tin out of my pocket and stare at it, gathering my resolve. I hook my fingernails under the curved lip of the tin and gently pry the lid off. The baggie containing the note lies on top of a picture of me and Em at thirteen at a carnival with our arms around each other and huge grins on our faces. We had just eaten cotton candy, candy apples, and funnel cakes, fully committed to turning upside down on the Gravitron without puking. My heart aches so profoundly with the memory that I press my palm into my chest.

I take a sip of the nonalcoholic piña colada Aunt Jo made me. "Mmmm," I say, licking my lips and watching the fireflies in my backyard as they blink in and out. I hold out my palm, soaking in the heat from the fire pit. "Where did you learn to make these? They are so good."

Aunt Jo adds some rum to her colada and stirs it with her finger, licking it when she's finished. "I shared these with a very handsome date on a beach in Hawaii last summer. The stars were out and the air was salty and . . . well, let's just say I'll tell you the rest when you're eighteen," she says, grinning at me. "And when I got home I decided they would be my new summer drink. They feel like a celebration, no?"

"Definitely," I say, enthusiastically taking another sip of the coconut goodness. I remember Aunt Jo making that trip, but she never told me about a love interest. "So what happened to your date? Did you ever see him again?"

She adds a log to the fire. "Sadly, no." She brushes a loose brown curl off her forehead with the back of her wrist. "But I will always have these drinks and I will always have my memories," she says, and her expression looks serious, way more serious than her words.

I wait for her to go on, but she just stares at the fire, lost in thought. "Is everything okay?" I ask when she doesn't snap out of it.

She sighs. "It's so easy to take what you have for granted, so damn easy," she says, and looks up at me. "Promise me this, Nova, that you will enjoy every piece of wonderful as it comes along, because you can't go back, not for all the money or effort in the world—sometimes, when something is over, it's over for good."

I stare at her, not sure what to make of the weightiness of her tone. "We're not talking about your date anymore, are we?"

She gives me a small sad smile. "I didn't know when I had coffee with your mother the day she was in the car accident that it would be the last time. No one tells you it's the last time. The air doesn't feel different, your heart doesn't pound, and there are no warning signs. Everything just changes in a single moment."

I twist my glass between my palms. "Do you think about her a lot?" I ask, not meeting her gaze.

"Always," she says. "And I will never stop."

I sigh at the happy memory of me and Em, realizing that Aunt Jo was right—that you must enjoy every piece of wonderful as it comes because you can't go back. I pry the baggie open, pulling out the lined paper, which I instantly recognize as coming from the notepad in my kitchen. I unfold it slowly, like it might crumble in my hand if I'm not careful.

There in the center of the paper, in my dad's handwriting, are three words:

Old Jack's dog

There's no "Dear Nova," no "I know you must be confused right now and upset with me for everything that's happened," and absolutely no contact information.

I turn the note over, my heart thudding and my breath short, but there's nothing more, not a suspicious indentation or even an erased scribble.

Ash waits as I stare at the paper, which I grip too hard, crumpling it a little between my fingers. My mind swings into motion. *Old Jack's dog's name was Angus. And Jack was the Pembrook fire chief for most of my childhood before he retired. He used to sit outside the firehouse every Sunday morning with Angus, the paper, and a hot cup of black coffee. We said hi when we passed, like everyone did, but we didn't know him particularly well. In fact, he was kind of cranky. And what on earth does Angus have to do with any of this?* I run through my memories of Jack and Angus, scanning them for anything that might connect to this situation or might tell me what to do next, but nothing feels right.

I look up at Ash, my face scrunching in concentration. "Does *Old Jack's dog* or the name Angus mean anything to you?"

By the way his eyes brighten, I know his answer before he says it. "Why yes, it does."

Ash knows what this means and I don't. *Again.* The realization hits me like a punch in the stomach—this isn't like the note in the quilt, this one is for *me,* and yet it's not decipherable *by* me. My dad gave me a clue that required someone else to decode. And suddenly I'm angry. What if I didn't have Ash here? Would I be stuck with a nonsense note, left to wonder where my dad is and what happened to him? Not saying anything personal is upsetting enough, but this is so much worse.

"Old. Effing. Jack's. Dog." I say each word under my breath like it's an insult. It *is* an insult.

Ash's gaze lingers on my features in a way that tells me he's reading me, but he doesn't press me to tell him my thoughts. "Angus is one of the older Strategia," he explains. "He's gruff and difficult to deal with, but he's a genius with information. He knows just about everything about everyone."

I nod, not in the best control of my emotions. "And you know where he is?"

"I do," Ash says carefully, probably trying to figure out why a clue is causing me so much grief. "Scotland."

"Right," I say. "*Of course* you know."

"And you wish I didn't?" Ash asks.

"No. I just wish . . ." I shake my head, not ready to vocalize my hurt. "You know what? I'm going to go search the plane, see if that Lion assassin left anything behind."

"Understood," Ash says, and I don't make eye contact with him as I walk away.

✳ ✳ ✳

There is a slight shaking motion and a hand on my arm. I groan.

"November," Ash says.

"Huh?" I open my eyes and sit up so fast that spots form in my vision. "Is everything okay? I was just . . ." I look around the bed where I went through all the items I found on the plane. As usual with Strategia, there was no written information, and there was absolutely nothing identifying the assassin, not even a clue that would tell me the plane belonged to the Lion Family. But at present, the bed is neat and tidy with nothing on it but me. Ash must have cleaned up.

"Sorry, I barely remember closing my eyes," I say, rubbing my hands over my face. "Where are we?"

"The Highlands," Ash says.

I practically fall out of the bed. "*What?* I slept through the landing? I don't even . . ." I pull on my boots and straighten out the blankets.

"I would have let you sleep longer, but we need to go. It's late afternoon here and we have work to do tonight," he says, and I can hear a little distance in his voice. I meant to apologize for putting him in danger in Pembrook after I searched everything last night, but clearly that didn't happen.

"Right. Yeah, of course." I slip on my jacket and grab my duffel bag.

He turns off the plane and I make my way down the steps.

"Another barn?" I say as he follows me out. Although this one looks considerably older than the one we left, hundreds of years older. "Is this a Strategia thing . . . parking planes in barns? Is that why you knew what we'd be looking for with that key back in Pembrook?"

He nods and offers to take my bag with a gesture, but I shake my head.

"For the places we frequent or for important meeting spots, we rent barns or warehouses year-round. And everywhere else we need to travel, we find a location that we can make work. But this particular barn is one my Family uses throughout the year," he says, and walks around the plane to a car that's covered with a tan tarp.

He pulls back the cover to reveal a sleek black Mercedes.

"Whoa. How rich are you guys?" I say, even though I'm sure that's not a polite question. I've just never been around people who kept spare sports cars in other countries for convenience.

Ash laughs for the first time in a long time and I instantly realize how much I've missed our usual banter. These past forty-eight hours have been almost nothing but tense.

"We do okay for ourselves. All Strategia do," he says, and pulls out the keys from under the wheel hood. He pops the trunk with a click and we throw our bags in the back.

"Apparently so," I say. "Remind me to send you my holiday list when this is all over."

Ash opens the passenger door for me and I climb in.

"Where are we going?" I ask.

"The Raven's Nest," he says before he joins me in his James Bond vehicle.

Ash and I drive through the farmland of Scotland with me glued to the window, as I have been for most of the ride; it's undeniably the prettiest place I've ever seen in my life, with rolling hills, villages filled with stone houses that look like they were plucked out of a medieval fairy tale, and lakes surrounded by snow-capped mountains that sparkle in the setting sun. I'm reminded of my aunt Jo and my promise to enjoy every piece of wonderful as it comes along. It's just a bummer that it's not safe to have my phone because I'm dying to take pictures, which I think I've told Ash at least five times by now. But he's mostly been quiet this entire ride. Layla goes quiet when she's thinking, but I've never seen Ash do it before. It's possible this situation requires more contemplating than usual. But it's also possible that he's just annoyed with me.

"I'm still sorry, Ash," I say, and turn to look at him. I attempted to talk to him about this when we got in the car, but he responded briskly and we turned our attention to navigating, filling up the tank, and getting some food for the road. And when I tried to transition the conversation to the Lion Family, he said we would talk about it later.

"Okay," he says, and I get the sense that it's not okay.

It's nearly impossible for me to let things go when I know someone's frustrated with me. I think my insistence causes bigger fights in the end, but I feel incomplete when situations are left unresolved.

"You're mad," I say. "It's fine. I get it. You should be mad. I put us in a shit position back there."

"I'm not mad at you, November," he says, but his tone isn't easy.

"Well, I'm sorry just the same. I know what kind of a risk you took by coming with me. When that guy hit you . . . God, Ash, if it had been a knife instead of a punch," I say again, shuddering as an image of the assassin flashes into my mind.

"But it wasn't."

"No, it wasn't. But still," I say, searching for the words to tell him how much it means to me that he's here, and how much I know that he's taking an unbelievably huge risk. Normally this would be a breeze for me. I've had to apologize to Emily so many times that I consider myself somewhat of an expert. But with Ash it's different. It feels like so much is at stake, not just in our danger-addled situation, but between us personally.

We're silent for a good minute, BBC Radio filling the quiet car.

Suddenly Ash switches it off. "Why do you think I came here with you, November?" He wears the same laser-focused expression his sister uses when she's concentrating on a problem.

My pulse quickens. "Why?"

"Yes, why would I leave my twin sister, my training at the Academy, and risk my life to be here with you?" he asks, and I can see that this answer is important to him.

"Um," I manage. My dad always said I could talk the hind leg off a dog, but right now English seems to have vanished from my brain altogether. Ash waits and I swallow. "Well, you want to stop the Lions, for starters."

"Not the reason I'm getting at."

I've never seen Ash this serious and it's making it harder to think. "You enjoy a good risk?"

"I'm falling for you, November," he says, and my heart pounds so hard that I hold my breath, hoping it will slow down and not reveal how off-kilter those words make me feel. "I realize that might sound trivial to you. I saw those pictures in your room, listened to your stories. And I am certain that you've been surrounded by people who care about you your entire life. But it's new to me. Caring about someone other than my Family wasn't encouraged; in fact it was actively discouraged."

I remember him telling me how attached he was to his best friend and how she was burned alive in her house. I would stop getting attached to people, too.

"You asked me why I decided to come on this mission with you. You listed all the reasons I shouldn't. That is why. The truth. Because being without you felt like a greater sacrifice than all the rest." He steals a look at me and my stomach drops so fast that I reflexively touch it.

For two seconds I just stare at him. I want to tell him that it's not trivial and that I care about him a great deal. But I can't seem to get my thoughts in order or my tongue to work. "I . . ."

"No, you don't need to say anything. I don't expect you to," he says, and before I can respond he continues. "But I do need you to trust me. You didn't say a word to me before you left for Emily's."

I rub my forehead, my cheeks flushing. "I know. I . . . It's just Pembrook. I guess I'm not used to asking someone before I do things there." As the words leave my mouth, I know they aren't even a sliver of what they should be.

Ash laughs, but not like he thinks it's funny, like he thinks it's sad. "I don't want you to ask my *permission*. We're partners. We need to consult each other about decisions that affect the course we're on. We're attempting not only to find your father, but to subvert and potentially attack the most powerful Strategia Family in the world. If we aren't on the exact same page, the Lions will crush us. They might crush us anyway. But if we have a slipup here in the UK like the one we had in Pembrook, we'll end up dead."

I exhale. "You're right. One hundred percent. I didn't tell you because I thought you would convince me not to go. And maybe I shouldn't have gone. It was a selfish decision. I just couldn't stand the thought that I might never see her again. In that moment it felt like I couldn't go on if I didn't at least let her know I was alive. But I didn't think it through. And my carelessness put us both at risk. Again, I'm sorry. I really truly am." I touch the tin with my dad's note in it.

"All is forgiven," he says, and pulls off the highway and onto a dirt road lined with trees.

I stare at my hands for a long moment. He's done nothing but give me the benefit of the doubt since this whole thing began and I've returned the favor with bad decisions and an inability to tell him how I feel.

Ash said he's falling for me. No one I've dated has ever said that to me before. And the truth is, there's no one I would want to hear it from more than him. And I just blew past it with a stutter. I look at Ash. He's just as beautiful in profile as he is straight-on. And as outrageous and daring as he is, he's also got such a good heart. If I could push a rewind button on this whole conversation and approach it differently, I would.

He glances at me, his lips turned up in a small smile. My cheeks deepen their flush and I turn away, staring out the window, searching for the right words. *Get yourself together, November!* The last of the sunlight flickers through the trees, whimsically speckling our path. The sun moves lower in the sky and hugs the horizon, spilling red and orange through the bare winter branches.

Suddenly the trees clear and the dirt road becomes an enormous circle with a well-manicured lawn at its center. On the other side of the green is a giant stone mansion with spires that reach into the darkening sky.

"Raven's Nest Manor," Ash says as I attempt to pick my jaw up off the floor. He drives around the circle toward it, and the closer it gets, the more impressive it gets. "A twelfth-century manor house that was converted into an inn. Home to Raven's Pub, a favorite among locals and a meeting place for Strategia."

"Meeting place . . . but aren't we in Lion territory?" I ask, wondering how worried I should be.

"Technically, yes. But we're on the outskirts. And in ever Family's territory there are places like this, meeting spots th have developed over the past thousand years that all the Far ilies use to trade information and make deals."

Ash stops the car, and before I have a chance to open r door, a butler in white gloves and a long-tailed coat opens for me.

"Thank you," I squeak, looking up at the imposing Gotl manor. There is an oversized wreath on the door and a sin candle in every window, making the whole place feel magi

The butler takes our bags and Ash offers me the crook his arm. If I felt out of my element at Academy Absconditi, nothing compared to this. We take the fanned staircase to front door and Ash opens it for us.

The front foyer is an impressively tall room with orna arched ceilings. The woodwork on the walls is accented gold-framed paintings and garlands of pine and red ber and there is a fifteen-foot Christmas tree that makes the in my town square look plain. I would squeal if I weren't tive Ash would kill me. *Where is my effing camera?!*

Ash leads us to a large antique desk at the far end of room. A man with a neat full beard and a hunter-green t suit sits behind it.

The bearded man smiles. "Nice to see you, Mr. Ashai assuming you'll want your usual suite?" he asks in a Sco accent. He stands and pulls an old-fashioned iron key one of the desk drawers.

"Exactly so, Murray," Ash says, matching the guy's tish accent. I do a double take. I never considered Ash's a with accents, or my lack thereof.

He takes the key. "But no need to see us up. Our bags are light."

Ash lets go of my arm and takes our luggage from the butler who carried it in, giving him a tip. He heads for an impressive curving staircase. Each turn we make, there is some new grandeur, and I'm beginning to seriously wonder about my parents, who gave up this life of luxury and intrigue to live in quiet Pembrook.

Ash opens the door to his family's suite and turns on the lights.

"You're *kidding* me right now," I say, and practically trip over myself getting inside. "It looks like we just entered a Gothic queen's private apartment." There are black velvet couches, tall arched windows and vaulted ceilings, chandeliers, and floor-to-ceiling bookshelves.

"Like it?" he asks with an amused expression.

"Like it? I want to move in," I say, circling the sitting room, running my fingers over ornate furniture that makes me feel like I've stepped back into a fantasy kingdom. "This is really your life. . . . You just keep planes and cars in other countries, and stay in places like this as though it were normal?" There is some amount of awe in my voice.

Ash laughs and gives me a full smile, indicating that whatever tension was there before is now gone. And I smile back.

"We need to get ready to go to the pub. We can eat dinner there while feeling out who might have information about your father," he says, and I look down at my worn jeans.

"Judging by the elegance of the serving staff and that foyer, I'm guessing these jeans aren't going to cut it," I say, but he's

already disappearing with my duffel bag into one of the adjacent rooms.

I follow him into a bedroom with a four-poster wooden bed that has a canopy of sheer black fabric.

"You can stay in Layla's room," he says, and I nod with an open mouth, promising myself despite the imminent danger that I'll enjoy every last detail of this.

He rifles through an armoire and pulls out a floor-length sapphire-blue dress that looks like it belongs to a princess.

"You and Layla are about the same size; this should do," he says, and hands it to me.

Emily would be losing her mind right now, I think. And just like that my moment shatters. Emily is back in Pembrook, worried and scared, my dad is being hunted, and I just inadvertently killed someone in the woods behind my house. Nothing is ever going to be the same. I'm never going to be the same.

Eleven

I SIT AT Layla's vanity, applying smoky eye shadow. I haven't worn makeup since before I left for the Academy, and even though it was never a big thing for me the way it was for Em, I've always enjoyed going through the motions of dressing up. I put on a final touch of cherry-flavored lip gloss, rubbing my lips together, and stand, smoothing my hands over the silky fabric of Layla's blue dress. I smile at myself in the mirror, but my good mood deflates when I catch sight of the tin on the bed behind me in the reflection.

I'm not even trying to convince myself that *Old Jack's dog* holds some sentimental meaning. My dad lied to me, made a deal with the headmaster at the Academy to stop his brother, and then left me a clue that I couldn't decipher myself. It's like the person I've counted on my entire life, the one who's always supported me and made me feel safe, suddenly decided to change his personality. I turn around, glare at the tin, and leave the room, hoping distance will lessen its impact.

Ash's eyes light up when he sees me, and he stands. But

a split second later his smile transforms into a questioning gaze. "Is everything all right?"

"Yes," I say too brusquely.

For a second we just stand there.

I frown. "I just . . . I don't know how my dad . . ."

"Could write you such a sparse note?" he offers.

"Exactly!" I say with a bit too much emphasis.

Ash takes a breath. "It's more than likely he was being cautious, in the event that someone other than you found the note."

I shake my head. "Let's assume you're right that he couldn't leave me an address or a phone number; I can accept that. But what about . . . the rest? He could have said something else. Anything else."

Ash nods like he understands what I'm not saying—that I needed more from my dad, a lot more. It's like Aunt Jo used to say, it's not enough to know you love someone, it's important to let them know it.

"Do you want to talk—"

"No," I say, shelving my hurt because it's only going to make it harder to concentrate on what we have to do. "Not about that. Let's just . . . why don't you tell me about this pub we're going to."

"*Wellll*," Ash says. "It's all very civilized. There's a no-killing rule."

I raise an eyebrow, not convinced by his definition of *civilized*.

"If you attack someone here, you not only get banished from this inn, but from the entire group of properties like this one across Europe," Ash continues. "And as you might imagine, these are something of a favorite among Strategia for trading information and, well, a dalliance here and there."

"Please tell me you didn't just use the word *dalliance* for *hookup*," I say, and my frustration wavers.

"Upset that my vocabulary's excellent and English isn't even my first language?" he says, and grins.

I fight a smile and uncross my arms. "Don't you dare try to be funny when I'm clearly in a mood."

"It's not my fault that you find me irresistibly charming," he says.

Now I do smile. "Is that what you think?"

"That's what I *know*," he says. "Your body language is virtually screaming 'attraction.' You've uncrossed your arms and you're leaning toward me—signs that you're much more open and engaged than you were a minute ago. You've also tilted your head slightly, which suggests interest and makes your pheromones easier to detect. And those are only a couple of the indicators."

My smile widens. "Show-off."

He laughs. "Who ever said modesty was a virtue?"

"Not a Strategia, that's for sure."

"Certainly not," he says, and once again offers me the crook of his arm.

I let out a long exhale and wind my arm in his. "Okay, let's do this." And just like that my mind focuses back on the task at hand. My dad left me one clue, and however cryptically annoying it may be, this is my only chance to figure it out.

Ash and I make our way down the stairs, only we don't

stop at the ground floor; we continue down to a space that I can only describe as a lavish dungeon. The walls are gray stone studded with iron sconces and the furniture is dark wood appointed with red velvet. The bar itself has a wooden canopy over it that is carved into points and spires, mimicking the outside architecture of the manor.

I immediately head for a small table near the fireplace and Ash doesn't object; it provides us with a good view of the room and is far enough from the other tables to allow us to speak without easily being overheard. Plus, the crackling wood masks sounds like white noise.

As I pass through the bar and tables my pulse quickens. The patrons around us are beautifully dressed, seemingly relaxed, and doing nothing more than drinking, eating, and carrying on jovial conversations. Nevertheless, I notice the same subtle and discerning glances as the students in the Academy once gave me. No one looks at us in an obvious way; their movements are deliberate and controlled. And it occurs to me that I no longer see the world the way I once did, that the Strategia part of me is growing.

Ash pulls out a chair at the small table and I move the long skirt of my dress to the side as I sit down. The warmth from the fire momentarily takes the edge off my nerves. Ash situates himself next to me, and as I listen to the hum of conversations in the room, it strikes me that I only hear Scottish accents.

"Oh god," I say, "I don't think I can do a Scottish accent— not believably, anyway."

Ash nods, like he's already considered this. "An American

accent isn't actually a problem," he says with a Scottish accent so perfect it makes me want to groan. "Makes you appear to be a tourist, which is a persona any Strategia might use."

"Good," I say, but I'm not convinced it won't draw unwanted attention. I take a quick glance around the room. "Is he . . . here?" I ask.

"At the bar," Ash says in a controlled tone. "Big beard. The one sitting by himself."

I subtly look up and toward the bar, like I might be considering what I want to drink. There, just as Ash indicated, is a burly older gentleman in a tweed blazer with elbow patches. I let out a sigh of relief. *Angus.*

"It's not luck that we found him here," Ash says, clearly reading me again. "He's *always* here. My parents once told me he's been a fixture in this pub for the past forty years."

I might be halfway across the world, but at least my dad directed me to someone we could easily find. I suppose it could have been worse.

"What do you know about him?" I ask, realizing I should have asked earlier.

"Not a lot," Ash says. "Layla and I have been coming here with my parents since we were little, but I've never spoken with him. Apparently, he has a reputation for being difficult."

I grunt. Difficult for a Strategia classifies as nearly impossible for a normal person.

"And the rest of the room?" I ask, trying to understand how this all works.

"Half Strategia and half locals and travelers," he says, confirming my earlier assessment. "The owners and managerial staff are Strategia, but most of the workers are not. It allows us to hide in plain sight, controlling the bookings and maintaining discretion but still blending in with the surrounding communities. Hence the no-killing rule, which assures these properties remain neutral. You'll find glowing reviews for this place and all the establishments like it online."

He looks amused, but I raise a skeptical eyebrow. I'm not sure I love the idea that while booking a vacation in Europe, there is every possibility of landing in an elegant hotel that's half filled with secret-society assassins.

"But if you study the patrons closely," Ash continues, "you can tell that what looks like casual conversation is actually trading information, planning for missions, and hiring crews."

I focus my attention on the room without being obvious. "What kind of missions?"

"All kinds. Gathering intel, stopping assassinations, planning assassinations, influencing political leaders, protecting people who will never even know we exist," Ash says, reinforcing once again that his "normal" is a universe away from my own.

"So how do these interactions work? Do we just approach Angus and start up a conversation?" I ask.

"You mean you," he says, and it takes me a moment to realize what he's saying.

I stare at him like he has two heads. "Hang on, I'm having this conversation *alone*?"

Ash just looks at me blankly. "Your father left that clue for you. He obviously meant for the conversation to be yours and yours alone."

"A clue that I couldn't decipher without your help," I reply.

But Ash only shakes his head. "Like I said, my family has

been coming here for years; Angus likely knows who I am, what Family I belong to. Me being part of your conversation would upset the whole plan. No one here knows you. Your very best shot at getting the information you need is to talk to him alone."

I hear his words, but I'm having trouble accepting them. It's not like I want Ash to hold my hand, but navigating the European Strategia world by myself with zero experience sounds like a recipe for disaster. The students at the Academy were impossible enough; how am I supposed to handle the adults?

I look up at Angus, who is currently searching his pocket for something, and my worry heightens. Is he looking for his wallet? Is he ready to leave? Because the only thing worse than blindly initiating a conversation with him would be chasing him down in the parking lot in this confining dress.

I stand up before I can talk myself out of it. Ash's eyes widen ever so slightly and I know him well enough by now to tell that I've shocked him by making a move before we could discuss the details. But I can't sit back down, not with all these Strategia watching. They'll immediately know that I'm nervous and that there's something wrong or unusual about my behavior.

So instead, I murmur "Wish me luck," with all the resolve I can muster.

I hold my head high and walk my most confident walk all the way to the bar, sliding onto the empty stool next to Angus. At which point I see what he had been searching his pocket for—a toothpick. He sticks it in his mouth and idly chews.

I momentarily look back at Ash, who is slipping into a seat

at one of the communal tables and joining the conversation like it's the most natural thing in the world. I turn back to the bar to find a bartender standing in front of me.

"Menu, miss?" he says in a Scottish accent.

"Yes, please," I say, happy to have something to focus on besides my nerves. It only takes me a quick glance before I spot what I want. "I'd love some potato and leek soup, creamy mash, and sticky toffee pudding with honeycomb ice cream."

Angus turns slightly and raises a wild eyebrow. "So you're having potatoes with your potatoes?" His voice is raspy and a bit abrasive.

I'm not sure whether I'm relieved or worried that he spoke to me first. For starters, I haven't had time to consider what my strategy will be. But I turn to Angus with my most ladylike expression. "And dessert, of course . . . otherwise it wouldn't be a well-rounded meal."

Only he doesn't react the way most people would, with a polite laugh or a smile or even a return of banter. Instead, his look is hard and his expression is unreadable.

"And to drink?" the bartender asks, and when I don't answer right away he says, "We've got a local cider for the holidays."

"Sounds perfect," I say with a smile.

"What are you having?" I ask Angus, because for the life of me I can't think of a better way to continue our conversation.

"Whisky," he says gruffly, and finishes his glass, clinking it on the bar for a refill, leaving no easy follow-up.

There is a beat of silence and I continue with a lame: "I've never tried whisky."

Angus glances in my direction, his expression unforgiving.

"How long do you intend to keep up the pretense of casual chatting? If you have something to say, get on with it."

My eyes widen. "Says the guy who started talking to me in the first place," I reply, matching his tone of voice.

He grunts, which I suppose is better than silence, but not by much. The pressure of needing to succeed here weighs on me.

The bartender places a mug of hot cider in front of me. I immediately take a sip. It's more sour than our usual holiday cider in Pembrook, but it's warm and comforting and has a stick of cinnamon in it.

"Don't think I didn't notice that Wolf boy sending you over to talk to me. You children are about as subtle as my ninety-year-old aunt after a bottle of wine," Angus says as he sips his whisky, and I have to wonder if he's right. While Ash is well trained and definitely has more experience than me, he's still young.

Now I grunt. "And you've got about as much tact as—"

"Don't have time for tact. Too old," he says.

I take another sip of my cider and decide to attempt a new approach—honesty. "Okay, well, the truth is I was told to find you, but I have no idea why, other than that you have information that I need."

"I have information that most people need; doesn't mean I'm going to give it to you," he says, and now that he's looking directly at me instead of his whisky, I can see that he has sly and assessing Strategia eyes.

My pulse quickens. "I'm looking for information about Christopher, the firstborn son of the Lion Family, who disappeared more than twenty years ago," I say, trying to swallow the fear that comes with saying my dad's name aloud.

The old man's expression turns penetrating and I take a gulp of cider. "What use is information that's twenty years old?"

My hand stiffens around my cider. Is he saying he doesn't know anything about my dad? Or is he just testing me? "I don't want twenty-year-old information," I say, not sure what the protocol is here. I feel like this is the conversational equivalent of tumbling down a mountain, hitting trees as I go.

"Fill 'er up," he says to the bartender, lifting his glass, and he turns away from me without another word.

I wait, but he doesn't show any sign that he's going to continue. "So that's it?" I say. "You're just going to stop talking to me?"

"Precisely," he says without looking in my direction.

I glance at Ash, who's laughing and gesturing while he tells a story. Meanwhile, I'm one sentence into my ask and I've already been told no. And for the life of me, I can't think of a smooth or cunning way to convince Angus to help me. But then again, I'm not sure cunning would even work with him. So I change tactics once again. "Why?"

He pauses for a moment, looking at me like I just said something strange. "Because you're green and sloppy."

"That doesn't mean I don't have information to trade," I say, and my head feels a little odd, like I'm not getting enough air.

"Not interested," he says.

Damn it all. No one would shut me down so completely unless they actually knew something.

I take another big gulp of cider and gather my resolve. "Look, I don't know what the right thing to say here is."

He turns toward me, looking at me like I'm saying wild things, but I know that at the very least, I have his attention.

"I've never tried to trade for information before," I say hurriedly, "so I don't know how it works. And maybe I am sloppy, but you'll deeply regret it if you dismiss me on that point alone."

He rolls his whisky around in his mouth like he's trying to make a decision. He stares at me for such a long time that sweat beads at my temples. "So tell me," he finally says, "what could a young girl, whom I've never seen in society, possibly tell me that I don't already know?"

By his tone, I get the sense that it's his business to know what no one else does, that it's a mark of pride.

"What do you know about Christopher?" I ask again.

"That's not how this works," he says. "You're going to tell me what it is that *you* know, and if I think it's worth a trade, I'll reciprocate. If not, you'll get nothing."

My heart beats faster, making it harder to breathe inside this tight dress. I don't know what's safe to tell him and what isn't. But it's not like I can ask him to wait while I go confer with Ash, either. "Christopher's younger brother was working at Academy Absconditi. He's dead," I say, trying to keep my voice steady and confident.

He sighs, like I'm predictably disappointing. "I'll tell you what I told the last person who came here looking for him. No. Now leave an old man to enjoy his drink without prattling on."

My heart jumps into my throat. Someone else came here

looking for my dad? Brendan's threat about my father rings in my thoughts.

Angus smiles a satisfied smile. "And now I know you were unaware others were following him, which only solidifies my first impression—that you are green and have nothing to offer."

I take a huge gulp of cider, placing the large glass down so hard that it sloshes. "I killed Christopher's brother," I say, even though it's not exactly the truth.

"Right," he says, and half laughs.

"Because I'm Christopher's daughter," I say with force. And as they say in poker, I'm now all in.

The old man stops his drink halfway to his mouth and turns to look at me, dead serious, examining my every feature. His gaze is uncomfortable, but I know breaking eye contact right now would make me appear to be lying.

"You may not know me, sir. But if you knew my mother, Matilde, you know I look like her," I say, gaining confidence and lifting my chin. "Now if you know something about where my dad is, it's time to say it. I think I've more than fulfilled my end of the bargain."

He continues to stare at me for so long that I worry the whisky got the better of him. But whatever he sees on my face must convince him I'm telling the truth, because after a painfully long stare-off he nods and grunts. But when he still doesn't speak, I begin to second-guess myself, convinced that he doesn't believe me and he's just going to shut me out.

"I know—" I start, but he cuts me off with a hard look.

He subtly leans closer, reeking of alcohol. "For those . . . in the know," he says, picking his words carefully, "Jag has placed a bounty on Christopher's head. More if he's alive, but a good healthy sum either way."

It takes all my self-control not to fly off my stool. *Dead or alive.* I grip the bar harder than I should and take another big sip of cider. I've been entirely focused on the Lions as our enemy, but if there's a high-priced bounty on my dad's head, *anyone from any Family* might be after him.

Then it occurs to me that Angus insinuated that people know about my dad. "Wait, what do you mean by 'those in the know'?" I ask. "Are you saying that other Strategia know he's alive?"

"Who's to say?" he answers cryptically.

I open my mouth to ask him a slew of questions but close it again. He already made it a point to tell me I'm sloppy. I force my fingers to relax their hold on the polished bar top and I take a measured sip of my drink. I study him for a few seconds. I haven't played him the way Ash would have or used any of the deception techniques I learned in Professor Gupta's class; I've basically been honest. In fact, I've shown very little Strategia finesse at all. Yet . . .

"You said someone was here looking for my dad," I say, eyeing him. "That information must not be private or you wouldn't have said it in the first place. And considering I've taken a huge risk in telling you who I am, the least you can do is tell me who I'm up against."

He grunts, but his eyes look amused. "Is that so?"

"You know it better than I do," I say. What I don't say is that he told me that *before* he decided to trade with me, which makes me wonder, did he suspect who I was all along? Was he trying to give me a warning or has he been playing me this entire time? I remember Professor Gupta saying in deception class that a good deceiver will make you see a lie where there isn't one and truth when it doesn't exist. Was he just leading me down a path?

"The Ferryman," he says with a neutral expression, watching my reaction.

The Ferryman??? My mind spins. *As in the mythological Greek figure who shuttles dead people across the river? Oh god. That does not . . . I can't even think about . . .*

"If you want to know more, then trade with the blacksmith near Edinburgh," the old man says, interrupting my silent panic, and turns away from me.

"The blacksmith?" I say, and my throat feels unnaturally dry.

"Another." He holds up his glass and it's clear that our negotiation is now over. "And one for the lady."

I try to get my bearings, but everything feels upside down and wrongways. Someone called the Ferryman is after my dad. I still don't have the faintest idea where my dad is besides somewhere in the UK—maybe. And the one clue he left me is now pointing me to some unknown blacksmith? My head feels like it's floating, instead of being properly attached to my body.

I take a sip of my cider and freeze. I stare at my now almost-empty glass. *Oh crap.* I know exactly why the cider tastes different. It isn't sour, it's alcoholic. I know the drinking age here is eighteen instead of twenty-one, but I never assumed when the bartender suggested it to me that he might be offering a real drink.

The bartender puts two whisky shots on the bar in front of us.

"None for me," I say, my voice sounding slightly displaced from my body.

"Nonsense," the old man says. "We did business and now we're drinking. That's what you do when you're on a suicide mission, kid. You enjoy the moments you have."

I hesitate. I have no reason to trust this guy, especially since there is every likelihood he played me. But maybe that's a nonpoint; you can't ever trust Strategia because they will always deceive you . . . enthusiastically. I glance at Ash, who has started up another conversation at the other end of the room. It's December twenty-second, my dad has a bounty on his head, we're all being hunted with no hope for making it home for the holidays or possibly ever. Despite not being able to see any clear path forward, I can't help but think that my aunt Jo would not only agree about enjoying the moments you have—she would actually get a kick out of this guy and his grumpiness.

"Screw it. Let's drink," I say, the world already feeling fuzzy.

"Attagirl!" he says, and slaps me on the back.

"But can you keep a beat?" the old man asks me, and sways.

"Yeeeees. My life is beats," I say, and he looks like he doesn't believe me, but he also doesn't have a better option.

"And you remember your part? 'Cause I won't have you holding up the tune."

I grab the bar to steady myself. "Ring ding diddle iddle I de oh, ring di diddly I oh. Then I repeat the last line you sang," I say emphatically, and hiccup. "Now will you stop blustering at me and grow a pair."

He chuckles. "Right you are. This is shaping up to be a damn fine evening after all." He takes one last shot, which he dedicates to someone named Mike Cross, and offers me his hand as I step down from my barstool. Problem is I'm not sure if he's steadying me or making me sway more.

He lets go of me and sticks two fingers in his mouth, whistling loud and clear. Half the pub turns to look at us. I start clapping my hands in the air to the beat he taught me and he stomps his foot. It only takes a few seconds for some of the other patrons to move our way.

"Well, a Scotsman clad in kilt left the bar one evening fair. And one could tell by how he walked he'd drunk more than his share," he sings in a deep bellowing voice. "He stumbled on until he could no longer keep his feet. Then he staggered off into the grass to sleep beside the street." He nods to me.

"Ring-ding deedle deedle di-de-o Ring di deedle-o dee," we sing together. "He stumbled off into the grass to sleep beside the street."

A crowd gathers around us, some of them clapping with me, which is about the moment that I realize I'm also dancing.

"Later on two young and lovely girls just happened by. And one says to the other with a twinkle in her eye," the old man sings, and there are encouraging whistles from the onlookers. A guy around my age joins us by the bar, dancing and clapping along. "You see yon sleeping Scotsman so strong and handsome built. I wonder if it's true what they don't wear beneath the kilt."

There are bursts of laughter and cheering. I spot Ash pushing his way to the front of the crowd and I grin at him.

"Ring-ding deedle deedle di-do-o Ring di deedle-o dill," the guy who joined us sings with me, and more people from the crowd repeat the last line. "I wonder if it's true what they don't wear beneath the kilt."

The young guy twirls me in a circle and I'm fairly certain a "wheee" escapes my lips.

"They creeped up to the sleeping Scotsman quiet as could be. Lifted up his kilt above the waist so they could see," Angus sings, and the onlookers whistle and cheer. "And there, behold, for them to view beneath his Scottish skirt was nothing but what God had graced him with upon his birth."

The young guy grins at me and we sing, "Ring-ding deedle deedle di-de-o Ring di deedle-o do. Was nothing but what God had graced him with upon his birth."

He twirls me again and dips me with his arm wrapped behind my back. As I stand up, I see that Ash has broken from the group and is walking straight for me. I wave him forward, encouraging him to get involved. But instead of joining in the song, he scoops me into his arms.

The crowd hoots and hollers, but when he begins to walk away with me, objections fly. Ash doesn't respond and he doesn't turn around. He just carries me through the door and out of the pub entirely.

Examining him for the reason he looks so put out, I touch his cheek with my pointer finger, but it slips right down his face. "Did you get jealous that guy was dancing with me?" I say as we go up the steps, and I laugh until a hiccup cuts it short. "I've never seen you jealous before. It's cute. Can Strategia be cute? Isn't it against the rules?"

"I was on the other side of the room for no more than half an hour. How did you manage to bond with old Angus, much less concoct a performance in that time?" Ash says as he continues up the stairs.

"Whisky!" I say, and spread my arms out. "The old man—"

"Angus," Ash offers.

"Angus said it was a solution to . . . well, I don't remember to what, but it made sense at the time," I say.

Even though I can tell he's still concerned, a smile steals across his face. His dark brown eyes focus on me in a way that makes me feel like I'm the only girl in the world he smiles at, even though I know for a fact that's not the case.

"Why are you so attractive?" I say, and his eyes widen. "No, seriously. I want to know. It's weird."

"It's weird?" He tries to maintain a serious expression, but his voice sounds like it's covering a laugh.

"Yeah. Super weird."

"I'm afraid I don't know how to answer that," he says, and puts me down gently in front of the suite, waiting for me to get my footing before he lets go.

I lean against the wall, and as soon as he finishes opening the door, I touch his hand. He intertwines his fingers with mine, and I pull him toward me.

"I'm going to kiss you right now, Ashai, so don't you dare try to object," I say, and the smile he gives me is so knee-weakening that I'm grateful not only for the wall behind me, but for the builder of this wall in particular, and for the inventor of walls in general.

He gently slips his hand behind my neck, and my skin tingles where he touches me. His lips hover above mine. "I would never refuse a kiss from you."

I move my mouth to meet his, and the tingles that started in my neck spread through my entire body. He steps a little closer, and his body meets mine, pressing my back into the wall.

Then suddenly there is the sound of voices on the staircase and we break our embrace. He offers me his arm to walk into the room, but I stumble in just fine on my own.

"We need to get you some water," he says, and I can't help but frown because our kissing didn't immediately resume. "And a charcoal pill. Even so, you're going to feel like ten kinds of hell in the morning."

"Have I shrunk?" I ask.

"Have you what?" Ash says, and half laughs.

"I feel like I'm two feet tall," I say, and touch my head to make sure it's still where it should be. "And my hands feel like flappers."

"Flappers, eh?" Ash says, grinning. "What exactly are flappers?"

"*Flappers*. Flippies. Flappippies." I pause to consider my strange physical predicament, and my lips purse. "Maybe I'm turning into a seal?"

Ash's laughter takes me by surprise and I almost lose my balance.

"Maybe that wasn't whisky I was drinking at all. Maybe it was a magical potion and that old man is really a witch?" I say, giving the situation some hard thought.

"Angus isn't a witch," he says as though my comment warranted a response.

"Did you think I thought . . . no . . . did you thought I think. Shit. You know what I mean," I say.

Ash's grin only grows. "No, I really don't."

"What's a witch anyway by a rose's name that doesn't smell as sweet," I say, and hiccup.

"Glad we cleared that up."

He's having way too much fun at my expense and I'm not sure I like it. I point at him. I just wish he would stop moving, so I wouldn't have to sway to see him. "You said you were falling for me."

"I did," he says.

"How do you even know something like that? I mean, how are you brave enough to say it?" I grab the couch, which has snuck up behind me.

Ash closes the distance between us and brushes back a wisp of my hair. He puts an arm around my waist to keep me standing. "I've always known when things are important. And you, November, are stunning. I don't just mean that you're beautiful, which you certainly are. I mean that you radiate kindness and laughter at the same time that you're besting everyone with your knife skills. You trust people and believe in their goodness, even when everyone around you attacks and betrays you. I've never met anyone like you in my life and I would have to be the most foolish person alive not to tell you so."

"Okay, I knew it . . . or at least I suspected it," I say, getting hung up on the two s's in *suspected*. "You're perrrrfect. Do you really think that's fair to the rest of us? I'm pretty sure I'm going to marry you. Not now. Don't be crazy. But you should just tell your Family that whatever ideas they have about you marrying someone fancy are moot." I wave my hands in the air for emphasis.

Ash laughs. "On that note, I think we should get you to bed."

"On that note," I say, and lean forward, but before I get to his lips, my stomach gurgles. "Oh no." I break away from his arms, taking a fast, dizzying scan of the room, until my eyes land on a beautiful hand-carved wastebin. I drop to my knees and grab either side of it.

Ash pulls back my hair and I throw up until there is nothing left in my stomach. He gets me a wet washcloth and a glass of water. I don't need the morning to arrive to know that I deeply regret my drinking and the defiling of this lovely wastebin.

There is a knock on the door and Ash looks out the peephole before answering it. On the other side is Angus.

"Missed me already," I say from my splayed-out position on the floor. "Did you know that *Angus* comes from Gaelic? And not only that, it means 'one strength.' Cool, huh?" I hiccup.

"Paying homage to the whisky gods, I see," Angus says to me, and hands Ash something. "She forgot her wallet at the bar."

I squint at the brown square and attempt to sit up. "That's not mine." I laugh. "Where would I even put a wallet in this dress? Pssssht." I wave my hand at him like I'm batting a fly.

"Thank you, sir," Ash says, giving the old man a wary eye.

Angus nods at Ash and raises two wild eyebrows at me before he leaves. He seems surprisingly less drunk than I do, which I consider most unfair.

The door closes with a click and Ash opens the brown wallet, pulling out a business card. His eyes widen. "Logan James . . . Blacksmith." He looks at me, his expression turning dead serious.

"Right," I say, and rub my head like it might help clear the fog. "Angus did say something about a blacksmith."

Ash looks at the card like he's concentrating too hard. "Why would he bring you this?"

"Hmmm?" I say.

Ash shakes his head. "There are a lot of whispers about Logan. None of them good."

Some of my memories from my conversation with Angus float into my consciousness and I sit up, suddenly not feeling as carefree as I did a minute ago. "Angus said someone came here looking for my dad. That there's a bounty on his head." I look at Ash. "Have you heard of the Ferryman?"

Ash exhales audibly, the color draining out of his cheeks. "We're leaving at first light."

Twelve

ASH LOADS OUR bags into the back of the car and I notice that mine is significantly fuller than it was when we arrived. I can only guess that he took a few items from Layla's closet or from the room in general before we left, but I didn't actually see him do it because it was all I could do to choke down some bread and butter and orange juice.

I make the mistake of looking toward the sunrise and the bright light feels like it's piercing my skull. If we were doing anything other than looking for my dad, I would run back inside and dive under some pillows for the next two days.

"Feeling any better?" Ash asks, and opens my car door for me.

"I think the charcoal is definitely helping, but I swear I'm never drinking whisky again," I say unhappily as I slide into my seat.

Ash gives me a knowing smile. "Noted," he says, and closes the door.

I wince at the sound of the car door shutting and lean my head back against the seat.

Ash gets into the driver's side and starts the engine. "I'll make sure there's none of it served at our wedding."

I look at him sideways. "Our wedding?" Then it dawns on me—my drunken rambling last night. "Oh god." I put my face in my hands as Ash drives us around the circle and away from the Gothic manor. "Please tell me I didn't say what I think I said."

"I'll admit, I always thought that when a girl finally proposed to me, it would be better choreographed than that. But at the time, I think you may have been a two-foot-tall seal. And it was pretty romantic for a seal."

"This is so not funny," I say.

"Oh, I beg to differ," Ash says as we drive down the empty street shadowed with tree branches in the soft morning light. "That definitely makes my top three best conversations of all time."

"This would be easier if I couldn't remember what I said. Aren't you supposed to forget everything when you're drunk like that? Where art thou, friendly amnesia?" I say, and Ash laughs. "Why don't we talk about something less awful, like how terrifying this blacksmith is."

"I did promise I would tell you more in the morning," Ash says, giving me a way out but still looking far too amused.

"You most certainly did," I say, leaving no room to further discuss me as a marine mammal.

Ash uses his left hand to steer with such ease that I wouldn't be surprised if he'd been driving since he was six. But before he can get a word out, Angus's comment about the Ferryman floods my thoughts.

"The Ferryman," I blurt out, remembering Ash's reaction

last night. "I saw your face when I said his name. You know who he is, don't you?"

His expression shifts to being unreadable, which makes me wonder what he's hiding. "I know of him."

I fight the urge to blabber nervously and instead sit in anxious stillness, hoping he'll tell me the Ferryman is less awful than the hardened killer I imagine.

"He's . . . ," Ash starts, and stops. "He's known by reputation more than anything else. I've never met him."

"What kind of a reputation?" I say, fear seeping into my words.

"Efficient," he says, and my rib cage tightens around me, but Ash doesn't continue.

"Go on," I say, and he turns to me.

"November—"

"No, Ash. Tell me. I know you know more. And if this guy is after my dad, I need to know who he is."

Ash exhales. It's not like him to avoid a direct question. "He's not affiliated with one Family but works with all of them. He rarely takes on missions, but when he does, he completes them. Everyone wants to work with him. He's . . . skilled."

Ash's reserved tone tells me everything I need to know. When Ash says "skilled," what he really means is *a brilliant assassin*.

"What I don't understand is, why did Angus warn me about him?" I say, looking at Ash to make sense of it for me. I was already tipsy when I was trying to reason it out last night and I didn't get very far.

Ash glances at me. "It was part of your negotiation, was

it not?" he says, and there is something akin to worry in his voice.

"Not exactly," I say. "Before he decided to trade information with me, he told me someone had already been there asking about my dad. He wouldn't have said it if he didn't want me to know it, right?"

"No, he wouldn't," Ash says, and his eyebrows dip.

"Do you think Angus knew who I was before I told him?" I ask, my concerns from last night burgeoning into anxiety. "And if he already knew who I was, why would he bother trading with me?"

"I couldn't say for certain," Ash says, and his grip tightens ever so slightly on the steering wheel. "He told you about the bounty and about the Ferryman. Then he pointed you toward the blacksmith, correct? Is there anything I'm missing?"

I shake my head. "Is it possible my dad traded with Angus in order to tell me those things?"

"In order to point you to the blacksmith . . . yes, that could be the case," Ash says. "Angus went so far as to bring you Logan's address—a deliberate and heavy-handed action." Something about the way Ash carefully chooses his words sets me on edge.

"Right, so maybe my dad wanted me to know there was a bounty on his head, which makes sense, and then directed us to the next place we could gather information," I say. "But that doesn't explain why Angus led with the fact that someone was following my dad. If the Ferryman is as good as you say, Angus wouldn't want to cross him by making his plans known, right?" And as I reason it out, my stomach sinks. I feel the color drain from my cheeks. "Oh no. Please tell me that I'm misreading this."

Ash presses his lips together.

"Ash? Did the *Ferryman* want me to know that he's following my dad? Does the Ferryman know I exist?" I say, my temples pulsating.

Ash exhales audibly. "I'm going over what you told me backward and forward, but that is the only possibility I can see."

"Why would the Ferryman want me to know that?" I ask, trying to come up with some reason it's not true. "Letting someone know you're after their dad doesn't fit with the usual Strategia tactics."

"Unless someone is so good at what they do that it's the only way to make it interesting," Ash says, and I feel dizzy. "The Ferryman is a hunter, November. He's letting you know you're a mark."

I stare at Ash, knowing I will regret asking him this question but unable to help myself. "Why do they call him the Ferryman?" My voice is quieter.

Ash doesn't look at me when he answers. "Because when he kills people, he leaves a coin in their hand."

Thirteen

AS WE NEAR Edinburgh, it occurs to me that Ash has been driving this entire time without using the GPS. And I can see on the dashboard that this car is definitely equipped with the technology. I mean, the car knows when it's raining and automatically puts on its wipers. It heats and cools your back and your butt and tells you when other cars and objects are too close. The only thing it doesn't do is provide a solution to having to stop for bathroom breaks. Although I wouldn't be surprised if they figure out how to work that into the seats of the next model.

"How do you know your way around Scotland?" I ask. Since our conversation this morning, we've been carefully avoiding the subject of the Ferryman, because if I let myself focus on it, my thoughts tailspin into doom and gloom.

Ash shrugs. "Just years of driving through Europe, some memorizing of maps, and then when I need to, I look things up in my atlas."

I half laugh. "In a car with a perfectly good navigation system."

"Cell phones, computers, navigation systems all make it

easy for someone to trace where you've been," he says. "We've actually removed some of the microchips in this vehicle, so if someone did know this car belonged to my Family, they wouldn't be able to track us."

"Right," I say. "That makes sense." My weeks at the Academy immersed me in Old World traditional Strategia and I haven't spent much time thinking about what the Families might be able to do with tech.

"Logan isn't Angus, you know," Ash says, and it takes me a second to process the non sequitur.

"The blacksmith," I say, my thoughts edging dangerously close to the Ferryman.

"The blacksmith," Ash repeats. And his sudden subject change makes me think he's been thinking about Logan for a while. "What I mean is, what you did with Angus won't work with Logan. Angus is pretty decent for a Lion, and despite his gruff manner he adheres to traditional diplomacy. Logan, not so much. He's said to be ruthless and a legendary fighter. Some of the people who have tried to negotiate with him have ended up dead. If he weren't the only lead we have, I wouldn't risk it."

Of course Angus is a Lion. I inwardly groan. How could I expect anything other than manipulation and double-dealing? "I thought you've never met Logan," I say.

"I haven't. But his reputation precedes him. Anyone who kills other Strategia during routine trades and then manages to resist numerous retaliation attempts becomes well known," Ash says, and by the tension in his jaw I can tell he's uncomfortable with the situation.

I shift in my seat, turning away from the rolling farmland and forests to get a better look at Ash. "If Logan is so different from Angus, how do we negotiate with him?"

"I'm going to try to entice him with a solid intelligence trade, one that doesn't reveal anything about us personally or our plans," Ash says. "But to be truthful, I'm not sure how well it's going to work. I've only ever made straightforward deals. Someone like Logan would be assigned to a more experienced Family member."

"Right. Of course," I say. Ash is so capable and smart that I forget sometimes that he's still a student at the Academy and doesn't know everything.

"Whatever you do, do *not* tell Logan who you are," Ash continues. "There's a bounty on your father's head. It's not unusual that we would be asking about him. But Logan can't know the real reason. He's not an ally. As far as I know, he's no one's ally."

My stomach flips at the mention of the bounty. Now that my head isn't pounding and I can think more clearly, my anxiety over my father has increased. I exhale, trying to stay focused on the present and not jump to the what-ifs, but of course I can't. "What do I do if he starts questioning me and I don't have answers? Won't he know there's something odd about my lack of Strategia knowledge?"

"Yes," Ash says. "But that doesn't mean you can't play silence to your advantage. Look at Layla. She never says anything she doesn't want to and yet you would never doubt her."

"True," I say, and fidget with the edge of my pink sweater, cursing my previous aversion to black clothing, which would let me blend a little better. Can I really pull off a cool and calm Layla, who is basically the exact opposite of my effusive, over-sharing self?

Ash turns down a single-lane dirt road that runs between two large fields; the car bounces on the uneven surface. "Ready?" he asks, and I realize he's slowing down.

I want to tell him no, that I may never be ready, but I don't have the luxury of saying that, not if I have any hope of finding Dad. "Ready," I say, trying to mask any hint of fear in my voice.

Ash drives us past a classic Tudor-style house, white with a framework of black timbers, and stops in front of a small stone barn with a wooden sign hanging in front. It reads: BLACK-SMITH. The gray stones composing the walls are streaked with soot.

Ash is out of the car and to my door before I realize that I'm just staring and not moving. I would slap myself in the cheek like they do in movies, but if Logan has a view of our car right now, that would be ten kinds of stupid. So instead, I step out into the cold with feigned confidence, and Ash and I walk toward the stone barn. I try to picture the agents in the British spy movies Emily loves and channel their cool composure.

Ash opens one of the large wooden doors and the hinges whine. Inside is a scene plucked from a different century—a fire roaring in a large fireplace, old wooden workbenches, antique iron tools hanging from the walls. In the center of the room a guy with shaggy blond hair and a black apron is striking a red-hot horseshoe with a hammer. For a moment, I'm taken aback. He looks like he's in his late twenties, not at all the swarthy old killer I pictured in my head, and the benign nature of hammering a horseshoe is disorienting.

"Shop's closed," he says without looking up at us, his voice rough between clangs.

Ash doesn't try to explain who we are or why we're here. Instead, he advances with a measured pace and stops about ten feet away from Logan, leaning casually against a workbench, and waits.

After what feels like an excruciating minute, Logan stops hammering and looks up. The moment he lays eyes on me, I want to look away. He's ruggedly handsome but with cruel eyes, like the villain prince in a movie.

"Well?" he says, and there's an unforgiving harshness to his tone. Behind him on the wall I catch sight of a faded wooden sign that reads BAL DES ARDENTS. I only know a handful of French words, but I'm fairly certain *ardents* means "fiery" or something similar, which not only suits smithy work, but also his demeanor.

"We've come to make a trade," Ash says, like he doesn't have a care in the world. Although I know him well enough by now to know it's a front. "A trade for information about Christopher."

"I'm busy," Logan says in an uninterested tone.

"So busy that you'll pass up an opportunity to trade with a Wolf?" Ash says, maintaining his calm. "From what I hear, you don't get many of us out here since you beheaded Charlotte."

I gulp. Ash said Logan killed people, not that he *beheaded* someone from his Family.

Logan grits his teeth and wipes his forehead with the dirty towel draped over his shoulder. He shifts his gaze to me and once again my instinct is to run. "And you?"

Between the coals in the forge and the roaring fire, the barn is warm and I'm overheating in my coat. "If you don't know who I am, then you don't need to know," I say in my best imitation-Layla voice, and I'm actually shocked by how convincing I sound.

Logan grunts. "Leave it to a Bear to be self-righteous."

I stare back at him, neither confirming nor denying his assessment, and I catch the faintest glimmer of approval in Ash's eyes.

"And leave it to a Jackal to try to get information through insults," Ash says, and I take a better look at Logan.

Of course this guy is from the same Family as Aarya—mercurial, dangerous, and probably good at everything.

Logan shrugs. "Let me save you the effort of sweet-talking me, because I couldn't care less about your decorum and rules. I do have information on Christopher, but as you're not the first to ask, there are very few things I'm willing to trade. And I'm not going to stand here listening to you cry about how I didn't accept your terms. I'd rather kill you and use you for fertilizer in my back field."

My pulse picks up. It's obvious by his expression and body language that he's not trying to intimidate us. He means every word.

Ash appears just as relaxed as he did a minute ago, but the look in his eyes has become sharper and more serious. "In that case, I'll trade you everything you know about Christopher in exchange for a drop-off location of Owl-Lion communication."

For a couple of seconds, Logan is silent. He looks from Ash to me and back again. I hold my breath.

Logan drops his hammering tool on the worktable with a loud clang. "Which one?"

I exhale, relieved that he didn't say no.

"The one in Edinburgh," Ash says, and I can hear in his voice that he knows his offer is a good one. But there's also something strained about his eyes, like it physically pains him to give up this information.

Logan grunts. "Convenient."

"Absolutely," Ash says.

Logan grips the worktable in front of him with callused, sooty hands. "This is a trade, not a guessing game. Out with it."

I suppose that's one way to say you accept terms.

The slightest smile appears on Ash's lips. "The drop-off location is just off the Royal Mile."

"Christopher's in London," Logan snaps back, and my chest feels like it might explode. London is huge and finding someone who doesn't want to be found will be more than challenging, but just the same I cling to his words. My dad is *close.*

"Nearby or inside Greyfriars Kirkyard," Ash says.

Logan nods, like so far the information he's getting is acceptable. "Jag's son-in-law was murdered a month ago in Edinburgh," he says in exchange.

"One of the ghost tour guides is an Owl. She facilitates the drop-off," Ash says, and their interaction reminds me of a Ping-Pong match.

"Christopher is suspected of killing him," Logan says, and I fight to keep my eyes from widening in shock.

A month ago? No way. My dad was home in Pembrook . . . My shoulders tense as I remember his quiet behavior, concerned looks, and frequent trips to visit Aunt Jo. *He couldn't be involved. My dad wouldn't kill someone . . . would he?* I relax my body just as Logan glances at me.

"Find the tour guide and you find the drop-off location. She switches the placement of it every time," Ash says, and there is a beat.

I look from Ash to Logan and they are both oddly still, that is until Logan turns to meet my gaze.

Logan wipes the sweat from his forehead with the back of his arm. "I have to say, I think I got a lot more than I gave in that trade."

"Then you should be grateful for your good luck," Ash says, and there's an edge to his tone that wasn't there before.

"See, even that response," Logan says, gesturing at Ash, "makes me wonder . . ."

He and Ash stare at each other, neither of their faces giving anything away.

"If you're part of the head Wolf family," Logan says, suddenly more interested in the conversation, "and I would say you most certainly are a close relative, given your resemblance to your Family members and the access to the information you just traded. If that's the case, you should already know half of what I just told you. But you don't, do you?"

"Now I believe you're wasting *our* time," Ash says, and removes his arm from where he was leaning against the workbench.

"Which means you must be out of society . . . maybe at school?" Logan's eyes brighten. "And what I want to know is, what are two Academy brats doing trading with me?" The strange thing is, he doesn't look at Ash when he speaks, but instead keeps his eyes trained on me. His voice has shifted from its aggressive clip to a smooth cadence; he actually appears to be enjoying himself. His posture has relaxed, and as he flips his shaggy hair out of his eyes, I can almost picture him in clean clothes, schmoozing at a cocktail party. And charming Logan is way more terrifying than disgruntled Logan.

"I wouldn't congratulate yourself for surmising that we're young," Ash says, not missing a beat and seemingly not put off by Logan's prying. "That's nothing a person with average eyesight wouldn't pick up."

"I'm not asking you," Logan says. "I'm asking *her.*" His eyes focus on me so intently that my skin crawls, and I hope he can't tell.

"Ask anything you want," I say with my best Layla-like composure. "Doesn't mean I'm going to answer you."

"Mmmm. Right," Logan says, never moving from the spot where he was working; yet somehow I can't help but feel like he's cornered me. "A Wolf pup and a Bear cub looking for Christopher Shawe. If I were less perceptive I might simply assume you were after the bounty. But no, I don't think that's quite accurate. Is it?" His last words come out with force, like he already knows the answer.

Shawe? A wave of disorientation hits me and I rack my brain. Shawe *is Middle English for someone who lives near the woods or a thicket, which is the exact opposite of our last name—or what I thought was our last name.* Adley *means "clearing." Did my parents choose it on purpose to separate themselves from their Families?*

Ash nods toward the door and I snap back into the moment, taking a few fast steps in the direction of the exit.

Logan whistles long and loud, and before we've made it ten feet, four large Dobermans appear at the barn door. *Oh crap.* I look back at Logan, who's still staring at me.

"This is personal," he says, scanning my face. Logan doesn't bother phrasing his assumption like a question. "And it's not about revenge."

Ash hovers by my side, looking from Logan to the Dobermans and back again. And he sighs like this is all very tedious, which is basically the last response I would expect. "Either make a move or get your dogs out of our way."

I assess the barn in a sweeping glance. Almost everything in it is a potential weapon—knives, swords, tools, oil for quenching steel. And just about every surface is hard and sharp-angled. There's no way to get into a fight here without getting hurt. There's just too much room for error and too many unpredictable factors.

"If this is personal," Logan continues, still focused on me, "then you must know Christopher. And you're too young to know him from his childhood in Europe, so it's only logical to conclude that you know him from his time in hiding."

It's suddenly so hot that I can't catch my breath. He's inching toward the very piece of information Ash said he mustn't discover.

"Right," I say, "because you know everything. Why even bother making trades when you're clearly omniscient?"

Logan's focus doesn't waver. "And then there was your emotional response to consider—fear and concern. Now, why would you be *concerned* for Christopher?" A small smile appears on his lips, but his eyes are just as dangerous as they were when we first walked in. "If you were with him in hiding . . . given your age . . ." He pauses. "Do you know who you look remarkably like?"

Damn it all! I look to Ash for help, and he's already in motion, pulling his jacket sleeve down over his hand and grabbing one of the long metal rods out of the coals. It blazes red-hot at the end. Before I can even take a breath, the dogs start for me, teeth bared.

One of them lunges for my calf, his jaws snapping air, as I throw myself atop a tall worktable just in time. The four dogs circle below me, their lips pulled back, growling.

Logan scoops up his hammer and chucks it toward Ash, who manages to deflect it with the metal rod he's holding. By the time Ash recovers his stance, Logan has grabbed a sword off the wall behind him. It's immediately obvious that Ash's metal rod, which appears to be an unfinished fire iron or a farm tool, won't stand up to Logan's long blade.

I glance at the knife in my boot, but Ash is positioned between me and Logan, leaving me with no clear shot and a good chance of giving up my weapon for no reason. Just then, one of the dogs jumps at the table, its paws scraping the wood as it strains to reach my ankles.

I look down at the table, where there is nothing but an old rag, and then side to side, assessing my surroundings. There's one workstation nearby that has some metal tools on it and a slightly better angle for throwing, but it's definitely not close enough to jump to. And there are a few benches nearby, but they're too low—the dogs would get ahold of me in a second. I frown at the dogs. Defending myself from terrible people is one thing, but defending myself from dogs is a completely different story.

Logan takes a swing at Ash. Ash manages to block the strike, but I can see the strain on his face as he tries to compensate for his inadequate weapon. My heartbeat throbs in my temples and for a moment I just stand there, frozen, trapped, and no solution in sight. Another dog jumps for me, snapping its jaws viciously and slinging a thin streak of saliva onto my boot.

Think, November, think. I look again at the nearby workstation. If I could get to the tools, I might be able to make use of them alongside my knife. Although the way Ash and Logan are positioned, and given their distance from me, I'm not confident it's the right choice. I look up at the ceiling, but there's nothing but bare crossbeams.

My dad's advice about how to surprise someone with my boot dagger rings in my thoughts. *Just because there isn't a clear shot doesn't mean you can't win. There is always a workaround and a way to surprise your opponent. It just takes creativity and a lack of self-imposed boundaries.*

Logan takes another swing, and even though Ash parries, Logan's stronger blade comes only inches from slicing Ash's ribs. I survey my surroundings again—table with metal tools that's too far to jump to, exposed crossbeams above my head, low benches that will leave me in the dogs' reach. My thoughts are fragmented, the pressure of the situation making me indecisive.

Logan swings, forcing Ash backward a step toward the burning-hot furnace. A few more swings like that and Ash will get pushed into the blazing coals. *Blazing coals . . .* And suddenly, an idea dawns on me. I snatch up the old rag near my feet and shove it in my jeans pocket.

I crouch down and jump straight up as hard as I can, reaching for one of the timbers. My right hand gets a grip on the crossbeam, but my left hand doesn't and I drop back down to the table, nearly losing my footing. I glance at the barking dogs, which have surrounded the table, ready for me to misstep so they can rip me to shreds. I take a deep breath, relax my knees, and jump again. *Gotcha.*

I readjust my grip for a better hold and pull myself along the crossbeam as fast as possible, knowing all too well from climbing trees that there's only so long my arms alone will support me. I don't let myself look down, but the growling and the snapping sound of the dogs' jaws are right below me. I shinny all the way to the wall and immediately brace my feet against the stones, relieved to take some of the weight from my strained arms and hands. I study the wall for a path to the nearby crossbeam that leads to the other workbench. My gaze falls on a carved wooden coatrack against the wall. It's a thin foothold and not ideal, but it appears sturdy enough to hold my weight. I reach my leg out toward it, hoping I can grip it with my toes, but it's just out of my reach.

Shit.

If I can't get to the coatrack, there's nothing I can do but climb back to my useless worktable or attempt to fight off the dogs with my boot dagger. From behind me I hear Ash grunt and my forehead beads with sweat. I'm running out of time to make a decision before Logan slices up Ash or I'm forced to give in to the strain of bracing myself against the wall. *I have no choice but to risk jumping,* I tell myself, because it feels better than telling myself *This is a terrible plan that will likely end in me being ripped limb from limb.*

I take a deep breath, make my plea to the climbing gods, and remove my feet from the wall, swinging them like a pendulum. *One shot. I have one shot.*

I build up momentum, my legs reaching farther and farther with each swing until I've hit capacity. *It's now or never,* I think, my arms already starting to ache. I focus on the wooden coatrack secured to the wall. And even though I really don't want to, I let go of the crossbeam. My boot catches the edge of the coatrack, and I use my momentum to launch myself forward toward the next beam. My right hand gets a grip on the rough wood, but once again my left hand slips. For a terrifying second I dangle by four fingers over a sea of snapping jaws.

It takes every ounce of my strength to get my left hand around the beam and pull myself as fast as humanly possible to the other worktable. I drop down onto it, my hands burning and my breathing labored.

Logan swings at Ash, once again forcing him a step backward.

I yank the old rag out of my pocket, stick it in my mouth, and tear it into strips. I snatch up a few of the metal tools and tie a single strip around each one. From my coat, I dig out the box of matches Ash and I used in the Pembrook barn and light one of the cloth strips. I do a three-sixty, scouting all of the potentially flammable materials in the room.

I pull back my arm, aiming for a spare apron draped over a stack of logs, and throw the tool like I would if it were a knife. My aim isn't what it would be with a blade, but it's not terrible, either, and the fiery cloth hits its mark. Next, I aim for a cushioned chair against the far wall, and then for a wooden bucket.

Ash and Logan have their weapons up, pushing against each other. They're about the same size and seem to be evenly matched in strength, but Logan's weapon advantage slides Ash backward again until he's only inches from the flames behind him.

"Thirty more seconds and this whole shop will go up in flames!" I yell to Logan. Ash once told me that Strategia rarely live in rural areas, that they vastly prefer cities where they can blend in, affect politics, and maneuver leaders. So if Logan is living out here making horseshoes, it's by choice. And it doesn't take a genius to look around this carefully arranged shop with its handcrafted ironwork to know that it's his passion.

Two seconds tick by and Logan doesn't react. Have I completely misread him? Ash's foot slides back another inch. I tie the last piece of cloth around the end of a long antique hammer and light it.

"You want to keep doing what you're doing? Fine. This one's going to the dog beds." I pull back my arm and land a clean shot into a pile of straw with a blanket on top. It ignites almost instantly.

Ash and Logan have their weapons up near their throats, pushing against each other. But Logan steals a glance sideways to glimpse what I've done. The flash of anger in his eyes reassures me that I was right when I judged the shop's importance to him. And as Logan turns his head again to more fully assess the flames, Ash takes advantage of Logan's momentary distraction. Ash grabs the hot end of his metal rod with his bare hand, overpowering Logan and burning his cheek. The pain from touching the smoldering metal is obvious in Ash's expression and I cringe right along with him. But it works.

Logan growls and takes two steps backward, breaking their locked stance and allowing Ash to leap away from the furnace. But Logan doesn't touch his face to check the burn like I would expect; instead his eyes flit to a fire extinguisher on the far wall. He looks back at Ash, his jaw locked, and I can see the conflict written all over him. It only takes a beat for him to give up on Ash and dash for the fire extinguisher.

For a split second Ash doesn't move; just like Logan, it seems he doesn't want to walk away from the fight. But his hesitation vanishes when he shifts his focus to me. He scoops up the flaming apron with the tip of the iron rod and waves it forcefully at the dogs. They back up, giving me room to jump down to the floor. And we don't waste a moment weaving a path to the exit. We bolt out of the barn doors and close them behind us, running full-speed for the car. My fingers practically slip off the door handle from the momentum.

We dive into our seats, slamming the car doors. As Ash turns the key and the engine revs to life, the barn door reopens, revealing a wild-looking Logan and a cloud of smoke. The dogs sprint toward the car and Ash slams his foot on the gas pedal, sending us screeching out of the driveway and down the bumpy dirt road so quickly that if I were still feeling sick I would definitely puke.

I look at Ash, who doesn't appear relieved like I would expect.

"You're hurt, Ash," I say, catching sight of an angry red mark on his hand.

He focuses on shifting the gears aggressively, checking his mirrors to see if Logan is chasing us. "Everything we do from this point forward will be known."

"You mean Logan—"

"I mean Logan will make sure that we're followed. He knows we're going to London. He knows what we're after and why. And he may be able to guess the places we might go. We'll be constantly looking over our shoulders," he says, not hiding his frustration.

I cringe, remembering all the information I must have revealed during that conversation. "Ash, look, I know I screwed up—"

Now he does look at me. "Screwed up? November, you just saved us. Without you we'd both be dead. I might be a good fighter, but so was he and he had the weapon advantage. *I* screwed up. I've traded for information before, but never with someone as skilled and vicious as Logan. I should have known things might go south and planned accordingly. This is *my* fault."

"Oh no. Don't you dare," I say. "You're not taking the blame for this. You're here because of me, not because you suddenly got the urge to take on the Lions in some epic strategy battle. And don't try to tell me that the piece of information you gave to Logan wasn't a big deal. He looked like he'd struck gold."

Instead of a rebuttal, a small, amused smile appears on Ash's lips. "You have no idea how angry my Family will be when they find out what I've traded. It took my cousin the better part of a year to get that intel in the first place."

"You had no choice," I say, dropping my intensity to a lighter tone.

The look Ash gives me is surprisingly appreciative. "If only you could give my Family a lesson in forgiveness."

I laugh, surprised. "Forgiveness? That's definitely not what I would call what I'm feeling. Gratitude is more like it."

"Let's just hope things go smoother in Edinburgh," he says, and he flashes me a smile, but I can still see worry lingering in his expression. If I had just held off Logan like he did, I would be feeling wicked proud of myself, not nitpicking my performance. But then I was raised by my dad, who Emily used to joke was my personal cheerleading team, and Ash was not.

I want to smile back at him, but I can't stop remembering what Logan said about my dad. "Ash, who was the guy that my dad is suspected of killing?"

Ash nods, like he knew this question was coming. "Jag's son-in-law," he says, and by his serious tone I know this must be a big deal.

"Yeah. Is that . . . Brendan's dad?" I ask, a heavy feeling in my chest. As much as I dislike Brendan, I would never wish that upon him, and what's more, I can't imagine my dad doing it.

"His stepfather," Ash says. "And the *Regent*."

"And what is a regent exactly?" I ask.

Ash glances at me. "It's still incredible to me how much you don't know about Strategia. You're so much like us, and yet so completely different. What you did with the fire in Logan's smithy . . . I would have thrown a knife, any Strategia with your throwing skills would have."

"Are you saying I should have?" I ask.

"I'm saying what you did was brilliant. You not only assessed how greatly Logan values his smithy, but your attack created a diversion instead of a fight," he says, and I beam at the compliment.

We stop at a red light, and as his eyes linger on me, there is a touch of awe in his expression that surprises me. He glances at my lips and my cheeks grow warm. After a couple of long seconds, the light turns green and his eyes return to the road.

Ash clears his throat. "Regent . . . It's a title borrowed from the old royal court system, denoting the person who would exercise ruling power if Jag were ever absent or incapacitated. It's a holdover from the Middle Ages and it's nothing more than an honorary title in most Families, which are set up to rule by council. But the Lions don't have a council. It's just Jag and the Regent."

"The thing is," I say, "I don't think my dad killed him."

"Are you certain?" Ash says, and I can see that he's not convinced.

"Positive. Unless the Regent was in America?" I say like it's a question.

Ash shakes his head. "Possible, but Logan said he was killed in Edinburgh."

I nod. "Logan also said he died a month ago, but my dad hasn't left our town since early fall. Actually, that's not accurate; he *did* take a handful of day trips to see my aunt before she was murdered, but nothing long enough to make a secret trip to Europe."

"That's odd," Ash says, considering the situation. "Strategia don't often get accused of crimes they didn't commit."

"And why would someone like Logan know that my dad was being accused?" I ask.

Ash frowns in concentration. "I'm not certain. That's not information I'd think he'd have access to, unless the Strategia trackers are whispering about the Ferryman, which I suppose is possible." He falls silent again.

"Tell me what you're thinking," I say, positive there's more he's not saying.

"I'm trying to make sense of and contextualize the accusation," Ash says. "I've never met the Regent. But from everything I've heard, he was nearly as terrible as Jag. The rumor is that Jag strong-armed Brendan's mother into the marriage ten years ago, shortly after which Jag appointed Arlo as Regent, a double insult because the title should have gone to Brendan's mother, who is rumored to be a brilliant strategist. According to my Family, there are plenty of people who would have wanted him dead. But that doesn't explain why the murder was pinned on your father. He isn't an easy target to blame, considering that until very recently no one even knew he was alive."

"Brendan's mother," I repeat, and it occurs to me that after I found out Conner was my uncle, I never thought to ask if my dad had any other siblings. I think I subconsciously didn't want to know.

"Rose," Ash says.

Rose. I swallow and my heart speeds up. "My middle name is Rose," I say, unsure what to make of the fact that I might be named for someone who I not only didn't know existed, but who is part of a Family like the Lions.

Ash must hear the hesitancy in my voice because he glances at me and all he says is: "Hmmm."

"'Hmmm' is right," I say, and we're both silent for a few seconds, trying to untangle this bizarre information.

"And so Jag chose Arlo over his own daughter even though she's a great strategist?" I say, miffed.

"He did," Ash says in a tone that tells me he agrees with my judgment. "The thing that's odd is that no one at the Academy has been talking about Arlo's death. Logan was right when he said we should have already known. The murder of the Lion Regent is big news. *Very* big news."

"It only happened a month ago, though. Isn't communication to the Academy monitored and delayed?" I say.

"It is. But Brendan would have been told, the same way you were told when your aunt was killed," Ash says. "And that is exactly the type of news that spreads quickly. But Brendan protected it, keeping it from the rest of the school."

"Maybe he didn't want everyone gossiping about it?" I suggest, because that's what I would want. But then I remember something Layla said during one of our midnight challenges: *We always expect that people will react the way we do—that when we hit them they'll hit back, or that when we help them they'll be grateful—and when they don't behave the way we think they will, we're surprised.* "No, scratch that. You're right. There must have been a reason he didn't want everyone to know."

"A specific political reason," Ash says. "One that may have an impact on our conflict with the Lion Family, especially if your father was falsely accused."

"You told me earlier that because the Lion attacks on my family have been spread out over the years, something must have instigated this last one. Do you think this is it? Do you think that's why my dad sent me to the Academy, because he knew he was accused and the Lions would be coming for him?" I ask.

"Likely," Ash says, but his voice betrays his doubt.

And again we drop into silence and I stare out the window, analyzing our newfound information.

"There's something else . . . ," I say, turning back toward Ash. "We got information from Logan, but we didn't find out where we were supposed to go next."

"London," Ash says.

"Right, but it doesn't match my dad's previous clues," I say.

Ash glances at me, waiting for me to continue.

I chew on my lip, working my way through the messages we've received thus far. "The first clue we got was in the photo collage in my room . . . and it pointed to an exact spot in the woods," I say. "That message pointed us to Angus—to a *specific* person. And then from Angus we were told to go speak to Logan, which is another specific clue. But from Logan we learned that my dad is accused of killing the Regent and is in London? London isn't specific enough. That doesn't match the pattern of my dad's other clues."

"True," Ash says slowly, like he's considering my words.

"Was there something we missed in there? Something Logan said or didn't say?" I ask.

"I'm playing the conversation back, but there's nothing that I would flag as having a double meaning. Was there anything he said that you noticed, possibly something symbolic or personal?"

I shake my head slowly. "Nothing."

"What about something in the barn?" Ash asks.

"Not really," I say, pausing to re-create the smithy in

my mind. "We have tools at home, but none of them are related to blacksmith work. And the other objects were pretty nonspecific—workbenches, fireplace, swords . . ." My voice trails off and I make eye contact with Ash. "Wait . . . there was that sign in French—"

"*Bal des Ardents*," Ash says. "Ball of the Burning Men. It was a masquerade ball in 1393 hosted by Charles the Fourth where four costumed dancers caught fire and died."

"A masquerade ball," I say quickly, my voice lightening with an excited uptick. "We had one every summer in Pembrook."

"And you think your father might use a masquerade ball as a coded message to you?" Ash asks.

"Maybe," I say. "It matches the other clues in that it wouldn't mean anything to anyone but me." I pause to consider what it all might mean. "The masquerade ball was one of the few town events that we consistently participated in. The balls were always themed and every year for the past eight years or so my dad and I were in charge of decorations. We would build them and the art teacher at my high school would paint them."

The corners of Ash's mouth turn up in a smile.

"What?"

"Nothing. I mean, it isn't anything we haven't said before," he says. "It's just that your upbringing was so wildly different than mine. I can't imagine making dance decorations with my parents, unless we were installing surveillance devices in them. And even then, someone else would make them and we would just supervise."

I smile, too. "It was actually a lot of fun."

"Exactly my point," he says, and we share a look.

I find myself momentarily grateful for all the time I spent with my dad in our sleepy town, even if it makes giving it up more painful. "My question is, how did Dad know Logan had that sign in his smithy?"

"It's entirely possible Logan's had it for a long time," Ash says. "Your father could have made a trip to Scotland in recent years and seen it."

I try to picture my dad negotiating with someone as awful as Logan, and I just can't. "The thing is, my dad almost never left Pembrook, much less traveled abroad," I say. "The only long trips he ever took were with his rock-climbing buddies from college." But the moment the words leave my mouth, I realize how naïve I've been. "Oh god . . . rock-climbing buddies who I've never met, who would take trips to remote state parks and places without cell reception, or so my dad claimed." I look at Ash. "How did I never question any of this before?"

Ash gives me a sympathetic smile, like even though he doesn't fully understand the adjustment I'm going through, he knows it's not easy.

"So the Pembrook masquerade ball," I say, focusing back on the message. "Now we just need to figure out what message he was trying to send."

"Where was your ball held?" Ash asks.

"Stella's Inn, just outside of the center of town," I say. "In a big refurbished barn. All of the town functions were held there. She hosted weddings and school dances and so on."

Ash looks like he's concentrating. "Layla and I have been

to a handful of Strategia events with our parents in London, but none of them were held in barns, I'm afraid."

"How about events held in an inn?" I ask.

"There are a few Strategia hotels that have event spaces in London, but those properties are all Lion-run," Ash says with a worry line in his forehead. "If your father is pointing us toward a Strategia hotel, I'm not sure how we'd find out if they were hosting anything resembling a masquerade ball."

I rub my temple. "What about a trade with someone who might be in the know about Lion events?"

"Maybe . . . ," he says, and his voice trails off. "Although digging for information on Lion-run properties will be tricky. I'm not sure a traditional trade is even possible."

I study him, certain he's running through ideas that he's not saying out loud. "You said a traditional trade won't work . . . is there a nontraditional one?"

Ash glances at me, but he doesn't respond right away.

A few more seconds tick by in silence. *"Ash?"* I press.

"Wellll, that's the thing," Ash says, and I have a feeling I'm not going to like whatever is making him hesitate. "There is a place in London where unallied Strategia socialize."

" 'Unallied'?" I ask.

"They're Strategia who take jobs for hire, who work with multiple Families instead of just one. My Family hires unallied Strategia for missions occasionally. But approaching them is . . . complex," Ash says.

"Complex how?" I ask.

"Because I don't know how to get in touch with them other than to go to their pub . . . which is exactly the type of place someone like the Ferryman might be," he says. "And if not him, then others who may be hunting your father."

I exhale. "When you said these unallied Strategia take jobs for hire, what exactly did you mean?" I ask.

"Let's call them extra hands for special circumstances," he says. "Smugglers. Thieves. But most of them are mercenaries and bounty hunters." By the look on Ash's face, I can tell that even though he doesn't think going to their pub is safe, it's also the only way.

Fourteen

ASH PARKS THE car in an underground car park and we take the stairs up to the street, where Gothic-spired church steeples rise into the sky and stunning medieval buildings house everyday cafés and boutiques. In the setting sun, the city has a moody, ominous vibe that makes me look cautiously at the pedestrians, my awe of its architecture fighting with my fear of encountering other Strategia.

"Welcome to Edinburgh," Ash says. "Just making a quick stop before we head on to London." He told me the same thing a half hour ago, and when I asked what it was, he said in a typical Ash way, "You'll see."

I never really cared much about traveling when I was living in Pembrook, figuring it was something I would get to eventually. But two minutes on a Highland road or two seconds in Edinburgh and it's clear that I was deeply wrong. Why have I been going to soccer camps all these years instead of saving up my money to go to Europe? Not that Dad would have let me go, considering what I now know about our family, but still.

"So that's really how you pronounce it, huh, with a *brah* at the end, Edin-brah?" I ask.

"Yes, like the article of clothing," Ash says, smiling at my reaction.

"I meant like the dude brah, but same same," I reply.

Ash lifts an eyebrow. "Pardon?"

"You've never heard of a brah? Like a bro, but a brah?" I say, even though I'm positive his proper education never included surfer terms.

"Why do I feel like I'm going to regret having this conversation with you?" he asks.

"Hey, Ash," I say in a dramatized surfer voice, "where ya headin', *brah*?" And when he doesn't answer, I say, "Edin-*brah*."

Ash shakes his head and I allow myself a real laugh at his indignation. I slip my hand into his nonbandaged one, mostly because I want to remember walking down this jaw-dropping street with him, but also so I don't walk into anything while I'm craning my neck.

For just an instant, he tenses, and I realize that holding hands probably isn't a Strategia thing. I remember how aggressively Layla reacted the first time I stopped her in the hallway by grabbing her arm. She almost leveled me on the spot. But a half second later, Ash relaxes and his fingers curl around mine, pulling me close by his side.

"You're the perfect tourist," he says with a smile.

"Damn right I am. Remind me to insist that you take me traveling for fun when this is all over," I say.

"Strategia don't typically travel for fun. We travel with purpose," Ash replies, not like he's trying to shut me down, but like he's never really considered the idea before.

"Then you're seriously missing out," I say.

"The more time I spend with you, the more I believe that," Ash says, and there is something genuine in his voice that makes my heart swell. I squeeze his hand. But as sweet as he's being with me, he's equally hawkish in the way he eyes the street and the pedestrians. Then I remember—Ash said most Strategia live in cities. And just like that, my moment of delight is replaced by suspicion.

I immediately question my surroundings: the woman who stares for a second too long from the bakery window. The man walking a poodle—is he holding the dog's leash tighter than necessary? A young guy selling umbrellas, which could easily be used to conceal a thin blade. Ash said that after what happened with Logan, we would be constantly looking over our shoulders; I just didn't realize how literal he was being.

Ash stops in front of an impressive stone building that looks like something that once belonged to an earl or dignitary. Above the door reads CENTRAL LIBRARY and carved into the stone are the words LET THERE BE LIGHT.

I look at Ash, surprised. "A library?"

"This won't take long," he says, and I give him a questioning look. It's strange that he held back telling me we were coming here, but maybe he's suffering from lack of internet access and needs to look something up? Although I'm not sure Strategia actually care about being online; my friends at home would be baffled by the concept.

"About London," I say, now wondering if he omitted any other parts of our itinerary. "Are we stopping anywhere else along the way or are we heading straight there?"

Ash scans the street around us. "I'm thinking we'll drive

for a few hours tonight and stop along a farm road somewhere to sleep, then continue in the morning. Unfortunately, my family doesn't have an apartment in Edinburgh, only in London. Under other circumstances we could stay at the Strategia hotel in Edinburgh, but after our encounter with Logan, I think it would be a categorically stupid idea," he says, keeping his voice low while eyeing the pedestrians passing us to head into the library.

"Maybe we could find an inn or some little place that would be inconspicuous?" I suggest, not thrilled with the idea of sleeping in the car in winter.

Ash shakes his head. "The reason all our Families keep apartments in major cities or stay at Strategia properties is because non-Strategia hotels have security cameras that are easily monitored and staff that are easily bribed. But more importantly, those places don't have a no-killing rule."

"Right," I say, and glance warily at the street for possible onlookers. "So sleeping in the car it is."

He gives me a knowing smile and we walk past a large iron gate and through the heavy wooden doors of the library.

Inside is exactly what you would expect from such a grand building—magnificent domed ceilings and walls lined with dark paneled bookshelves. Ash weaves us through the rooms and along elegant corridors with the ease of someone who knows exactly where he's going. I watch him as I walk. We think differently, were raised differently, and interact with the world differently, yet I have more in common with him than I ever did with the kids in my high school in Pembrook.

Ash stops in a back corner of the library at a counter that has a sign reading REFERENCE DESK. The girl behind it wears all black and has an asymmetrical pixie cut. She leans her elbows on the counter and scrutinizes Ash in a way that instantly tells me she's Strategia.

"Do you have any materials on Cyrus the Great?" Ash asks casually.

To my surprise, I recognize the name from one of Layla's tutoring sessions. Cyrus the Great was the founder of the Achaemenid Persian Empire, which is where the Wolf Family Strategia originated.

"*Audere es facere,*" Ash says under his breath, and it reminds me of the Latin phrase Matteo said to use at the Bear apothecary, which I have yet to tell Ash about.

The girl gives Ash a hard stare and disappears into the room behind her without a word.

I look at Ash, who winks at me, but before I can ask him to explain, the girl returns with a black clothbound book. She plops it onto the counter with a *thunk*.

"Name and date," she says, and pushes a ledger toward him.

Ash writes his name and scoops up the book, and we walk to the other side of the room, where there is a quiet seating area and no people.

I stare at Ash in surprise. "You wrote your name," I say in a hushed voice. "I thought Strategia don't usually keep written records."

"A necessary evil from time to time," Ash says quietly, and flips through the pages of the book. "And a way for Families to keep track of their correspondence."

"Correspondence?" I ask, but there is no need, because Ash lands on a page that has a series of letters circled in pencil.

My eyes widen. I lean over the yellowed pages with him and ogle the letters. By the smudges on the page and the faint eraser marks, it's obvious that the circles have been drawn and redrawn in countless configurations. Secret codes guarded by Strategia in public libraries—another example of how they hide in plain sight.

Ash stares at the page, his forehead wrinkling in concentration, reminding me of his twin sister. And the moment I think of Layla, I realize how much I miss her.

I study the circled letters, attempting to piece them together in some configuration that makes sense. I try them forward, backward, and one letter off in the alphabet, but it's all just gobbledygook. And the longer Ash stares at the page, the more serious his expression becomes.

Finally, he closes the book and stands. "Shall we?" he says in a cheerful tone, which might just be an indication that he's not going to discuss the message here, but for some reason his good mood feels ominous.

I nod and we return to the reference desk. Ash places the book on the counter and the girl stamps the ledger *Returned* like it was nothing more than a commonplace transaction. And then we weave our way out of the library as casually as we came in.

The moment we step outside, I turn to him. "The everydayness of Strategia is eerie," I say.

Ash raises an amused eyebrow. "Is that so?"

"They're just everywhere . . . lurking in libraries and hotels and who knows where else," I say, and Ash laughs.

"You mean *we're* everywhere," he corrects me, and I

realize that even though I know I'm Strategia, I'm still not comfortable identifying as one. While Strategia skill sets are awe-inspiring, the brutality I've seen is stomach-turning. And once again the image of the dead assassin from the woods flashes in my mind.

I shake my head, like the action might somehow erase the memory and the sense of dread that accompanies it. "So that book . . . ," I say. "Families leave messages for each other that way?"

"It's less traceable than emails or phone calls," he says. "Every Family has books and codes in libraries in major cities."

"Is that secure?" I ask, keeping my voice as quiet as possible. "Couldn't other Strategia intercept messages that way?"

"Yes, it's secure, and yes, they could intercept messages," Ash admits, putting on his gloves. "But they don't. It's like the study rooms in the library at the Academy—everyone respects everyone else's privacy because not respecting it would invite retaliation. And if someone was caught breaching another Family's correspondence, not only would that person be punished, but their entire Family would lose the ability to use the libraries. It's not worth it."

I don't know if I'll ever understand the dichotomous nature of Strategia—chaotic and orderly, deceptive and respectful. "And the message you just read?" I say, leaving the question open-ended.

"I'm not sure yet," Ash says, and immediately changes the subject. "Let's grab a coffee and some food before we get back on the road. There's a café on this block where J. K. Rowling used to work on *Harry Potter*. And the view of Edinburgh

Castle isn't bad, either." Ash smiles, but his eyes don't. Which tells me I was right to be suspicious; something is definitely bothering him.

"Okay, Ash, what's going on?"

We cross the street and stop in front of a café with a bright red storefront.

"You mean besides a coffee and a deadly blacksmith stalker?" he says, and pushes the door open for me, temporarily halting our conversation.

Wintry garlands are strewn around chalkboards, and white lights twinkle along the glass displays filled with mouthwatering pastries. Everything smells of cinnamon and nutmeg. Normally I would be soaking in every second of this winter-themed bliss, but all I can think about is what Ash isn't telling me.

I quickly order and we take a seat at a table by the far wall.

I slip out of my coat and lean forward, looking Ash straight in the eye. "Despite the risk of being followed," I say, quietly picking up our conversation, "you randomly took a detour to the library. And now you're doing everything to distract me from hearing what you found other than balancing a seal on your head. While dancing."

He raises an eyebrow at the seal comment, like he doesn't know where I come up with this stuff.

"A desperate need for a coffee or not," I say, "don't tell me it's nothing if it's something. And it's clearly *something*."

Ash sighs. "I'm not avoiding telling you," he says carefully. "It's just that I only got a piece of the message and I'm not sure what it all means yet."

I look at him sideways. "What do you mean, you only got a piece of it?"

Ash sits back in his chair. He gives the other patrons a quick glance, and I can tell by his face that he doesn't find anything out of the ordinary. "The way those codes work is that you only see the latest correspondence but could have missed a long conversation that came before it. It can be hard to interpret out of context."

I frown at him. "Okay, now you're really making me nervous. You never try to qualify things."

He hesitates, not trying to deny it. A waiter brings our food and drinks, setting them down in front of us.

When we're alone again, Ash sips his coffee and studies me. Whatever he sees in my expression must tell him that I'm not going to let this go.

He leans forward with a sigh. "The message said *Harry's dead and there will be retaliation.*"

Instead of me grappling to process some big reveal, my nervousness shifts to confusion. *That's the message he was resisting sharing with me?* "Who's Harry?"

Ash pushes his hair back even though it's perfectly in place and gives the other patrons a scan. "Brendan's cousin. *Your* cousin. Not a first cousin, but a second or possibly a third. He was one of Jag's favorites. Students at the Academy always joked that Harry was the reason Brendan tried so hard to prove he was good at everything. That he was always worried his grandfather would eventually appoint Harry as head of the Family instead of him," he says, keeping his voice down and his body language casual.

I frown, knowing there is a dot I should have connected somewhere but haven't; it's clawing at the edge of my awareness.

Ash rubs the back of his neck. "I didn't recognize him in the woods. It was too dark and the one time I met him was long ago and he didn't have that beard then," he says, and the realization hits me like a slap.

I stare at him, unmoving.

"At first I thought the message must be wrong," Ash continues, "that it couldn't be Harry, because Jag wouldn't send him to America to just sit and wait . . . but then there was that expensive jet that pointed to an important Family member. And it's always possible that if Jag knows about you, he might assume you would go back to Pembrook and therefore prioritized that mission."

"Oh god, Ash," I say, my voice losing its volume and catching in my throat. "You're saying . . . I killed my *cousin*?" I try to swallow the nauseated feeling in my stomach as the image of his limp body and the pool of blood flashes through my mind.

"You survived an attack, November, nothing more," Ash says, and his voice is insistent, like there is no other way to see it.

I shake my head, as though I could somehow unknow this. "Maybe I didn't kill him on purpose, but he's still dead," I say. "And it's my fault."

"There is a world of difference between defending yourself and cold-blooded murder," Ash says, and as much as I want to agree with him, I can't. "Believe me, Harry was doing everything in his power at the time to kill *you*."

I not only have Conner's death on my conscience, but now

Harry's, and what makes it even more terrible is that they were both my relatives.

I sit on my back porch and toss a pebble toward a can that's about twenty feet away from me. It catches the rim and bounces off onto the floorboards. It's raining so hard outside that the forest in my backyard is blurred by sheets of water and the dampness is making my T-shirt stick to me.

"You've been at that for an hour now," my dad says, opening the screen door and joining me on the porch. "What are you doing?"

"Figured I might as well do something useful until this rain stops and I can go to Emily's," I say, tossing another pebble. This one lands cleanly in the can.

"And this is useful?" my dad asks.

"It is if you plan on landing a gumball in someone's soup at lunch," I say.

The look Dad gives me tells me he doesn't approve.

"What?" I say with my most innocent expression.

"You're practicing a skill so that you can splash soup on someone?" he asks.

"Matt Dorsey put his chewed-up gum on my math book cover yesterday! It was gross," I say.

"Your actions matter, Nova," Dad says, and I sigh because he's clearly missing the part about Matt defiling my book. "What other people do is on them, but you're responsible for every single one of your choices."

"Daaad," I say. "It's just a joke."

"Okay," he says. "Well, what if I told you that if you land your next toss, I'll give you twenty bucks?"

My face lights up. "Will you?"

"But if you don't make it," he continues, "you can't hang out with your friends this weekend."

I stare at him, unsure what to say.

"So, are you going to take the shot?" he asks, pressing me.

I hesitate, trying to assess what my chances are. So far, I've made about six in ten. It's not bad odds, but it's not great, either. "No," I huff.

"Why?" my dad asks.

"Because it's not worth it," I say.

"Exactly," my dad says, and I look at him, trying to figure out how this is related to Matt and his stupid gum. "Think about it this way: How would you feel if you splashed soup on him and everyone laughed?"

"I don't know," I say, because I'm actually not sure anymore.

"Well, how would you feel if everyone laughed and then he went home and cried?" my dad says, and my eyes widen.

"Terrible. Really really terrible," I say, flustered. "It was supposed to be a joke. I'm not trying to hurt—"

"I know you're not," my dad says, his voice gentler. "But when you have as many skills as you do, Nova, it's important to use them wisely and with caution. Misuse can lead to consequences you weren't intending, consequences you alone will be responsible for."

I'm gripping my cup of cocoa for warmth when it suddenly occurs to me that I've overlooked the second part of Ash's message.

I examine Ash, my tone serious. "You said the message was *Harry's dead and there will be retaliation.* What does retaliation mean in a situation like this? Retaliation against whom?"

Ash nods, like he couldn't agree more. "That's the part I've been wrestling with. There are a lot of ways the Lions might retaliate for killing a close Family member."

"Let's just say that *was* Harry in the woods by my house. And let's also say that they know or suspect that I killed him. Is the retaliation meant for *me*?" I look Ash square in the eye.

"That would be my guess," he says, and my fear swells.

My thoughts drift to the Academy's eye-for-an-eye punishment system. "How exactly do the Lions retaliate?"

Ash shakes his head. "Let's just hope we don't have to find out," he says, and I hope with all my might right along with him.

Fifteen

THE SUN IS already up as I peel my face off the reclined car seat. I wipe my mouth, grateful there's no drool, especially since Ash is already awake and driving. But judging by the backcountry road we're on and the look of the farms out the window, I'd say we haven't gone very far.

Ash's hair and clothes are somehow pristinely neat, whereas I'm less so, based on a quick assessment in the side mirror, which revealed a wrinkle from the seam of the upholstery running across my cheek.

"Remind me never to go camping with you," I say, adjusting my seat and removing the blanket we bought at a supermarket on our way out of Edinburgh last night. "You're one of those people who mysteriously wakes up looking like they're going to prom."

Ash smiles at me, and in the morning light I can't help but be impressed. "Will coffee help?" he asks.

I spot two steaming cups in the console between us. I didn't hear him stop to get them, but with the lack of sleep we got last night between finding a suitable hiding place and then waking every couple of hours to run the heat, I'm not surprised I slept through it.

"Yes, yes it will," I say, gratefully clasping the warm cup in my hand.

Ash steals a look at me. "I take it prom is a good thing?" he asks.

For a moment I just stare at him, shocked that Ash, who seems to know everything about everything, doesn't know what prom is. But then I realize that of course he doesn't. He never went to a normal school, didn't have normal friends, and probably never watched TV shows. Plus, I think it's mostly an American thing.

"It's a formal dance," I say, taking a small sip of the delightfully hot coffee. "You get all decked out in fancy gowns and tuxes, rent a limo with your friends, and then dance to super-predictable songs in some themed venue. There's always pictures beforehand in someone's backyard with your parents telling you to stand near your date and then there's a rager afterward where someone sneaks in alcohol and at least one person winds up puking in the bushes."

Ash listens, amused by my description. I can't help but think it probably sounds like nonsense to him. "I always wondered what regular school was like," he says, and I give him a questioning look.

"You did?"

"Of course," he says, and takes a sip of his coffee.

It baffles me that this confident, model-esque expert strategist ever gave a second thought to something as mundane as high school. "Mostly it's painfully early classes and a bunch of teens taking their angst out on each other. You're not missing much."

"I've also never been to the movies," he says.

"Never *ever*?" I say with a heaping of dramatic shock.

Ash shakes his head.

"Oh man. Emily would have a field day with you," I say, and realize this is the first conversation in a long time where I feel somewhat like my old self. I look at Ash. "You know what? When this is all over, we're having movie night, and we'll watch *all* the high school classics. When the night is over, you'll know more about American high school than you ever wanted to." I pause. "So you didn't go to the movies and you didn't go to a regular school—what did you do?"

"Mostly Layla and I trained," he says. "Our days and evenings were filled with tutors, and when we weren't training we were shadowing our parents and meeting our foreign contacts. There wasn't time for much else. An occasional shopping trip to pick up supplies or Strategia social functions, sure, but we didn't do what you would probably think of as typical. There were no visits to toy stores or theme parks, and there were definitely no playgrounds. If we exhibited our agility skills in the open, people would have instantly realized there was something different about us."

"Oh," I say, studying him. "That . . ."

He smiles at me. "Don't hold back on my account."

"That sounds like it sucks?" I say, adjusting my tone so the inflection is like a question, not an insult.

But he just laughs. "Sometimes it really did," he says.

"Although I don't think Layla ever felt that way. She was the same as a three-year-old as she is now. Before she could even read she was carrying around books in a little satchel she got in London, like a tiny lawyer." He pauses and I realize this is the first time he's actively shared what his life was like, not just a single memory or an explanation, but more casually, like he trusts me with it.

I lean back in my seat. "So that's what my life would have been like if I'd been raised a Strategia, huh?"

He changes the hand he's driving with. "Yes and no. Not all Strategia have the perfectionist parents that Layla and I do, but there's always some version of training, especially for the kids who are expected to go to the Academy."

"And what would you do if you needed a break? What would you do for fun?" I say, not accepting that it's possible to have a childhood completely devoid of anything silly.

"Set traps for Layla," he says with a mischievous grin. "I once rigged a cake to drop on her head when she entered the dining room. I got in loads of trouble, but it was totally worth it." He sips his coffee. "And if I really needed some quiet time, I would climb up to the roof. There were parts of it that were just decorative, domes with cutout stonework and so on. I would tuck myself up in one nook or another. I'm certain my parents knew where I was, but no one ever bothered me up there. What about you? What was it like being with non-Strategia so often?"

My mouth lifts at the awkwardness of his question, like the word *friend* isn't commonly used in his vocabulary. "I never really thought about it before. But I guess the best word to describe it is *relaxed*. Pembrook is small. My friends all grew up together. There wasn't a lot of trouble to get into, although I definitely did my fair share of digging to find some. And people were . . . happy. I know it probably sounds boring compared to traveling the world and whatnot, but it was kind of perfect for me."

Ash smiles at me like I just told him a secret. "I've never met anyone who was so happy to be exactly who they are."

"What?" I say, nearly choking on my coffee. "Right now I wish I were anyone *but* me."

"No you don't," he says. "You lean into life. Even now, even when you're being hunted by the Lions, you gape at the streets of Edinburgh, light up over the sight of a Christmas tree in a hotel lobby, ask five thousand questions about the Scottish countryside, and plan movie nights with enthusiasm. It's not just about the end goal for you; you look at the everyday world like it's something special, and you make me see it that way, too."

I blink at him, taken aback. But before I can say anything, Ash looks in the rearview mirror, letting his gaze linger.

"Is everything okay?" I ask, resisting the urge to turn around.

He glances at me.

"I mean with whatever is behind us," I clarify.

"Ah, well, I'm not actually sure. Although I *am* sure we're being followed." He doesn't sound nearly as freaked out as I would expect.

I look at the side mirror nervously but can't see anyone behind us. "How can you tell? Do you think it's Logan?"

"A hunch," he says.

I gaze out the window, wondering if he's right, if Logan is angry enough to follow us.

"Logan's precise," Ash says, and his voice takes on the lilt it gets when he's analyzing people. "Did you notice his ironwork? His craftsmanship is exceptional, and he does everything the old-fashioned way, with precision and care, which is not only harder but more time-consuming. If I had to guess, I'd say he's someone who has the patience to be a tracker and prefers the long route. We likely presented ourselves as an interesting challenge. Also, information about you will be worth a hell of a lot right now. So even if I've read him incorrectly and he's not following us, he would have to be an idiot not to sell what he knows. Either way, the likelihood is that we're being followed."

Ash looks in the rearview mirror for the umpteenth time since we entered London. He's been trying to keep things light the entire drive, telling me stories about him and Layla as kids, playing a BBC Radio 2 show where they give hilarious relationship advice, and pointing out landmarks as we go. But our conversation never felt as uninhibited as it did this morning. I don't know what it is about mornings and their ability to make you forget, to give you a little slice of peace before the world descends.

I exhale loudly when Ash says we're nearing the pub where the unallied Strategia socialize. A couple of months ago the most exciting thing going on in my world was the two-for-one cupcake sale at my local bakery.

"Is there anything we can do to make ourselves less conspicuous? Would it help if I dyed my hair or dressed differently?" I ask.

Ash shakes his head. "We will just have to be fast and smart. Although I'm not sure that what we're about to do qualifies as either."

I nod. I know he thinks this is a bad idea, but it's the only lead we have to help us figure out if that sign in Logan's smithy relates to my dad.

"Is there anything I need to know about these unallied Strategia?" I ask.

Ash slows his car down in a bustling neighborhood full of circuitous stone alleys with dim lighting, street vendors, and cobblestoned everything.

"Well," he says, considering the question. "It'll depend on whether or not they are amenable to working with us. If we ask them about the specifics of a Lion event without reaching an understanding first, we could potentially be telling them how to find your father."

I press my lips together. What a mess. "So start with a more general ask, then? About the Lions, maybe?"

"That's what I was thinking," he says. "Like I said, the Strategia in that pub aren't like the ones you've met so far. While they do keep alliances with certain Families, they're more like free agents or . . . specialists. They take big risks and get compensated accordingly."

"So they make their living doing things like capturing people like my dad?" I wait for Ash to deny it, but he doesn't, so I continue. "Back at the Raven's Nest, you seemed to know a few people . . . is anyone you know likely to be here?"

Ash shakes his head. "I'm not sure. I only know this place exists because my cousin used to talk about it. But I've never actually been here or made a trade with a crew like this before."

I scan his face. "So we're winging it?"

"Something like that," he says, keeping his voice confident, but I know him well enough to know he's uncomfortable.

"Should I be worried?"

He focuses back at me. "More like I should be worried that you can read me so well these days."

"These days?" I say with playful bravado to keep the fear from seeping into my voice. "Don't forget that I was the only one who could spot your lie in deception class."

At that, he smiles, big and broad. "I will never forget that."

And for just a split second, the chaos fades and it's just me and Ash smiling at each other.

Then he sighs. "I actually heard something at the Raven's Nest that might be pertinent."

"What kind of something?" I say, looking at him curiously.

"That conversation I joined at the pub? They were talking about a crew based here in London, something about a job gone wrong that resulted in Jag killing the crew leader's brother along with a couple of other members," he says.

"Do you think they're angry enough with Jag that we might be able to convince them to help us?" I say.

"I honestly don't know. It's a long shot."

"But it's worth a try, right?" I say, and at the hopeful uptick in my voice Ash frowns. I've never seen him this worried before and now I wonder if he didn't tell me about this crew because he didn't want to take the risk of coming here.

For once, Ash doesn't try to spin it into a positive. "We'll want to get in and out as fast as possible," he says. "There's no such thing as a no-killing rule here."

For a brief moment I wonder if we're making an awful mistake. But there's no time to stew because he's out of the car and headed for my door. He offers me his hand and helps me out.

I look down at the jeans I changed into at a rest stop. "Will I be okay in this? I'm guessing by the look of this neighborhood that we're not going anywhere fancy."

"More than okay. In fact you might be overdressed," he says, and leads me into a cobblestoned street that's closed to cars. It's lined with small stores ranging from pawnshops to specialty bourbon sellers. I get the sense that a fair amount of the merchandise sold here falls on the illegal-ish line.

We turn down a narrow alley filled with bars that reminds me of a place where pirates and smugglers from a different era might spend their free nights onshore, drinking until they pass out, draped over barrels. I scan the numerous people in the alley, wondering which ones are Strategia, and I pull my coat tighter around my body.

Ash leads me into a tavern called the Dirty Stone, which is aptly named, considering the soles of my boots immediately stick to the floor. We don't stop at the bar or at one of the scuffed wooden tables. We walk straight to the back, through a swinging door, and into a small pungent-smelling kitchen where the foods all appear to be fried.

I give Ash a questioning glance, but he continues through the kitchen like we're doing the most normal thing in the world. Even stranger is that the kitchen staff doesn't look at us. They just go about their business like we aren't there.

Ash opens an unmarked door at the other end of the kitchen, gesturing for me to go through it. I stare at what appears to be a supply closet and consider telling him that I've changed my mind and we should go back to the car. But instead, I take a breath and reluctantly step into a space that smells of lemon and bleach. The door closes behind us, dropping us into blackness, and my heart makes one loud thump. There's a click as Ash pulls a cord to an overhanging light and the bare bulb swings back and forth, casting wild shadows in the tiny space.

"Ash?" I whisper, and he gives me a quick reassuring smile.

He stares at the back wall of the closet and I stare at him. He touches the wall, running his fingers over the wood and concentrating. Then all of a sudden, his face relaxes and he presses a panel. To my surprise and possibly horror, the wall pops open, revealing a door. Boisterous noise spills into the little closet.

"After you," he says, and I slip through the opening, telling myself that whatever helps me find my dad is worth the risk.

As the room comes into view, my heart rate speeds up. *A secret pub!* Only it's vastly different from the one we just walked through. It looks older, plainer—large wooden beams frame its stone walls, the rustic wood furnishings are weathered but neat, and a huge fireplace has a large pot of what appears to be soup hanging over the flames. Iron candelabras with real candles dangle from the ceiling over long communal tables fitted with benches instead of individual chairs.

The men and women are nothing like the students and teachers at the Academy, except for their propensity for black clothing. These Strategia are relaxed and loud and slam their pints onto the tables so hard that liquid sloshes everywhere. The patrons slouch over tables and lean against the bar, shaking their hands and pounding their fists on their knees as they talk. Maybe it's just because they're drunk, but there is none of the Strategia precision and rigidness that I'm used to. Laughter and arguments fill the windowless room and I can't help but be a little awed by the scene.

Ash looks around, and I follow his gaze. I don't know how to identify the crew that took a hit from Jag, but I'm hoping Ash does. Three long seconds tick by before his gaze settles on a table of men and women near the fire. I can tell by the way he lifts his head slightly that he's spotted someone of interest.

"We just might need to be a little faster than I originally thought," he says close to my ear, and I'm not sure if he's reacting to something in particular or if he just realizes, like I do, that there is only one door and no visible windows, making it nearly impossible to get out of here if there's a problem.

Ash and I make our way across the room toward the table near the fireplace, and when we arrive a middle-aged man with a salt-and-pepper beard looks straight at us. "Might as well sit," he says, taking a gulp of beer, "unless you and the missus plan on eyeing us from afar all night. Not that I can say I blame ya, on account of my irresistible beauty and grace, that is." He uses both his hands to fluff his beard. The guy laughs, and even though his tone is lighthearted, I know better. His humor is all calculated.

I scan the room briefly, but no one appears to be paying much attention to us, which I know by now means the opposite—they've all noticed that we're here.

"I don't know anyone who could resist that invitation," I say with a grin before Ash can respond. The man guffaws. I might not be well versed in making Strategia deals, but my gut tells me that keeping up the banter won't do us any harm.

"Now that's the spirit," the bearded man says, and slides over, making room. He pats the bench next to him.

Ash smiles a friendly smile and moves in front of me, taking the first seat and leaving me at the very end of the bench. Considering he has been opening doors and letting me go first this entire trip, I find it hard to believe that he's suddenly changed his MO. He must have another reason, like wanting to put a barrier between me and whoever this man is.

The bearded guy waves his hand in the air and a boy about my age appears, wiping his hands on his apron. "Bring two more pints and a couple more pitchers for the table," the man says. "And a big basket of chips."

The boy nods and sighs, like he's had the same request all night and he's bored out of his mind. I remember Layla once telling me that all Strategia serve their Families, whether that means assassinating people or, apparently, waiting tables.

The bearded man turns to us. "Right . . . now let's see, the skinny one there is Willy," he says, pointing across the table at a man with thin dark hair tied back in a frayed ponytail and a complexion similar to Ash's. "But don't let his appearance fool ya; he's as strong as Eddie over here."

"I could crush him with my pinky, maybe eat him for a snack," says Eddie in a deep baritone voice. He is certifiably one of the more muscled humans I've ever seen. His face and arms are covered in freckles and his hair is the color of spun copper.

"Now, Eddie, let's not," Willy says in a patient, almost tired-sounding voice. "Last time you went down this road, you sulked for days."

Eddie pretends he didn't hear him.

"Mary," the bearded man says, gesturing toward a no-nonsense-looking woman, whose hair is entirely white even though she appears to be younger than my dad. "Best person to have if you get caught out at sea in a nasty storm or cornered in an alley. She's reliably steered our bucking ship and crew through the worst of conditions."

Mary gives us a short, perfunctory nod, and I wonder about these introductions. This is the first time I've ever seen Strategia actively offer information about themselves and others. But Ash did say that these unallied crews make their living doing odd jobs. So maybe this is all part of the process?

"Jenny, our weapons specialist, with the fastest blade in all of Europe; before you even reach for your knife she'll have skewered you," the bearded man says, indicating a young woman with box braids woven into an elegant bun on top of her head. A silver sword earring hangs all the way to her shoulder from her right ear, accompanying her nineties leather jacket and purple lipstick.

"And I'm Hawk," the bearded man says, and wipes some beer foam from his mustache with the back of his hand. "Good at most things, better at some."

Hawk . . . , I think, and immediately start analyzing his name. *Hawks have fierce reputations and great sight. But unlike other Strategia, Hawk isn't a name that has an ancient origin, making me wonder if it's a chosen name rather than a given one. And to that point, all of Hawk's crew's names end with a uniform E sound, giving very little away about where they might be from; but maybe that's the point? Maybe they're all chosen names? They're using British accents, but I know that doesn't mean anything.*

"I hear you're flexible," Ash says, and I look at him, wondering if he heard that at the Raven's Nest, or if he's just testing Hawk. Which begs the question—what kind of flexible does he want Hawk to be?

What's interesting is that Ash didn't tell Hawk our names, real or made up, after that lengthy introduction. And if Ash's cutting to the chase like that, then he wants out of here as fast as possible. I imagine I feel eyes boring into the back of my head and resist the urge to look over my shoulder at the room.

Hawk laughs, giving nothing away. "I do like when a negotiation starts out that way. Means I can charge a hell of a lot more." I look at his crew members to see if I can glean anything, but in typical Strategia fashion, they're impossible to read.

The kid with the apron returns and places two glasses in front of me and Ash, two pitchers of beer in the center of the table, and a basket of piping hot French fries in front of Hawk. Just the smell of alcohol makes my head pound in phantom pain.

"*Salud,*" Mary says in an authoritative tone that feels contradictory to the sentiment. She lifts her beer mug.

We all follow suit and I manage a small sip of the bitter liquid before returning it to the table. Subtle glances from the tables next to us seem to carry an undercurrent of hostility.

It's obvious that we're out of place here, and I'm getting the impression that there are at least a few people in the room who don't appreciate our presence.

"Everyone in town seems to be on the same hunt," Ash says with no fanfare, and I nearly choke. "But we're less interested in the hunted than we are in the hunters."

I look from Ash to Hawk and back again. Oh god, is he outright admitting that we're prying into Lion secrets?

"Ahhh," Hawk says, and grabs a handful of fries. They look so good I snatch a few myself. And he notices. I get the sense that he's intrigued by my casual gesture. "So you're attempting to hire us for a suicide mission, then."

Ash shrugs. "If you think you can't do it—"

"No one said we can't," Hawk says, and his voice is prideful. "But finding myself on the wrong side of Jag is the fastest way to end this life of luxury I've become accustomed to." He holds up his fries as proof. Even though his voice is light, there is a serious undertone to it, a challenge.

Ash appears relaxed, but his eyes are laser-focused. "From what I hear, your crew took a hit from Jag's assassins earlier this year."

Something dark passes over the mood of the table, like Ash just spit in their food.

"You've got a hell of a way of asking for a favor." Mary's tone makes my heart pound, and to make matters worse, the other patrons are openly watching us.

"Not a favor," Ash says, and his voice remains unaffected by the tension at the table. "A deal. Something that benefits us all."

"When people say 'all,' they mean themselves," Mary says, finishing her pint and roughly clanking the glass onto the table.

I wince.

Mary stands up. "I'll be at the bar," she says to Hawk, and doesn't spare us another look.

Hawk frowns after her and I get the sense that losing Mary's approval doesn't bode well. As though someone flipped a switch, the rest of his crew loses interest in us, and they start talking among themselves as though we've already left the table. I glance at Ash and I can tell by the look in his eyes that recovery is unlikely.

"Well, that settles that," Hawk says.

I immediately start to sweat. It can't end like this, not this quickly, not after the risk we took in exposing ourselves by coming here.

"That settles nothing," I say, loud enough for Hawk to hear but not loud enough to carry in the noisy room. It earns me a hard look from Hawk.

Ash picks up right where I left off. "I know that not only are you in desperate need of repairs to your vessel—let's say sixty thousand euros' worth?—but that you're also not the type to forgive and forget." *Way to go, Ash.* I'm not sure how much of this he got from his conversation at the Raven's Nest and how much he's just making up, but either way, Hawk has put down his beer and is giving us a serious look.

"You've got my attention," he says, his joke-laden easiness noticeably absent. "But I'm not sure that's a good thing. Unless I'm wrong in thinking that by just sitting here, you've already compromised us?" He nods toward one of the tables, whose occupants have been watching us like they might eat us for dinner.

In any other situation, I would run for the exit, but this isn't just any situation. So instead I sip my beer like nothing is amiss and take a sweeping glance at the rest of the pub. "Given the thirtyish people in here, I'd say that there are at least five or so who will be reporting to the Lions that you were chatting with us." I have no idea if it's true or not. Hawk might not know exactly who we are, but it's clear he knows we're a problem, so there's no point in trying to deny it.

"Now," Ash continues without missing a beat, "you have a choice. You can either make a deal with us, a solid deal. One where you get your boat repaired and get to take a swing at the Lions. Or you can walk away and take your chances with pissing off the Lions simply because of this conversation; maybe you even get banned from doing business in London."

Hawk leans forward in a threatening way. "That's one idea. Another idea is that I kill you here and now and drop you on Jag's doorstep with a bow tied around your broken necks."

I instinctively glance toward the exit, but there is a group of people standing between us and the door and no clear or fast path out.

"Because you're dying to do Jag a favor?" Ash snaps back.

Something akin to a growl escapes Hawk's mouth and his crew takes notice. "If I have to choose between you and Jag right now—"

"You do," Ash says, and I see Jenny's hand move to her belt, where I'm sure she has any number of weapons stashed. I would slide under the table and melt into the floor if I could.

"Think carefully, now," Ash continues like this isn't all going horribly wrong. "You may never be offered a shot at Jag again, not like this one. As much risk as you'll be assuming, we'll be assuming a lot more."

I look at Ash, who is doubling down on my double-down. We're in as deep as we can go.

Hawk grunts and for a long second he's silent. He looks from Ash to me, staring me down like he's searching my face for something. My heart skips a beat, remembering how Logan figured me out.

"Look," I say carefully and slowly, forcing my face to relax and my hands to unclench under the table. "The way I see it, we've all been forced into one position or another by the Lions, with little or no hope that anything will change. So we all have a choice here. Go forward together and fight. Or roll over like cowards."

A mocking laugh escapes Hawk's lips. "You don't think for a second that some kumbaya speech about togetherness is going to convince us to put our lives on the line for you, do you?"

"I definitely don't think you would do it for us. I think you would do it for yourselves," I say. "Now I'm not going to lie, I don't know the extent of the hit you took, but if you've had even one-tenth of the experience that I've had with Jag, then you can't be dismissing this straight out." I can only hope they hate the Lions more than they fear them.

"More emotional bullshit," Hawk says, and waves his hand dismissively.

"I don't know, boss," Eddie chimes in. "I kinda appreci-ate the heart in it. The old Strategia would have considered this offer."

Willy rolls his eyes. "Oh, great. Here we go with the sentimentality about the good old days." Willy pulls the pitcher of beer farther from Eddie. "I'm cutting you off before you start singing ballads."

"I can't imagine what you mean by that. I have a delightful voice," Eddie says.

An amused look passes over Jenny's face.

Hawk frowns and sets down his beer. "It's time for you to go," he says.

Everything in me sinks. That was it. That was our shot at getting the information we need to find my dad and we blew it. From the corner of my eye, I see Ash watching the table at the end of the room. If he's looking at another table and not at Hawk, it can only be because there is something or someone there of greater importance than this conversation.

"Maybe you didn't hear me," Hawk says, the threat more pronounced.

Ash stands. I don't get up immediately, but by the way Ash looks from me to the back table, I know that if I don't move soon, we're going to have more than just Hawk to contend with.

"And here I thought we were getting along so well," I say to Hawk, plucking up one last French fry and popping it in my mouth. "I even considered asking you to go to the masquerade ball with me." It's as indirect as I can be, as time's up.

Hawk glances from side to side, checking to see if anyone heard me. When he looks back, he's furious. "I'm going to assume that was a rookie mistake, given your tender age." His voice is a growl and he touches the knife hilt on his belt in a menacing way. "But let me be clear, if I see you there, or at any point before, poking around in my business, I will hand you over to Jag with pleasure."

I stand and take a step backward, my heart pounding. Not only has Hawk confirmed there is a masquerade ball, but in the most horrible of coincidences, he is going to be there. I'm not sure if I'm deeply relieved that we figured out part of my dad's clue or terrified that I've just made an enemy of Hawk.

Ash grabs my arm and the moment I look up I know why. Two men from the back table have gotten up and are headed straight for us, and by the way they are zeroed in on us, I'm sure they've figured out who we are.

We don't hesitate. We move full-speed for the exit, weaving around Strategia and between tables. Any relief I had over the masquerade information is now eclipsed by panic.

Ash flings open the door and I run into the dark closet, grab the handle leading to the kitchen, and push it open. I look momentarily for a lock, but of course there is none. At a loss for options, I grab a rolling rack of dishes, and the second Ash clears the doorway, I wedge it between the door and the edge of the counter where a guy is chopping onions.

All at once, everyone in the kitchen turns to look at us, the room dropping into an eerie stillness. The kitchen staff don't try to hide their worried reactions, telling me that at the very least, they're not Strategia.

Behind me, the closet door slams into the dish rack, opening an inch, but the barricade holds. The staff's agitation increases, and a few of them look like they might make a move toward us.

"Run!" Ash says, shoving aside a kitchen worker who steps into our path. And it suddenly occurs to me that even though they're not Strategia, they might have been instructed to intervene if an event like this ever occurred. The instant I have the thought, and before I can move an inch, the guy chopping onions holds up his knife.

Without pause, I grab an empty pot and swing it as hard as I can toward his hand. But instead of lunging forward or swiftly moving out of the way, the guy jumps back and drops the knife, putting his hands in the air. *Definitely not Strategia.*

The door slams into the rack with more force this time, dislodging a few plates and sending them crashing to the floor. Ash and I don't look back, we just run—through the kitchen, across the sticky floor of the pub, and out into the dim alley. The moment the night air hits my face I shudder, not because of the cold but because we were only seconds away from being trapped.

We run through the crowded alley, attracting way more attention than is smart. I look over my shoulder before we turn into the broader cobblestoned street, but the men from the pub haven't emerged yet. I push my legs harder, weaving around the drunk crowds and late-night shoppers.

The instant the car comes into sight, I find an extra burst of energy. Ash clicks the keys and I grab the cold metal handle, but before I can pull the door open, pain suddenly radiates from my shoulder, like a bite from a horsefly or a bee sting.

"Ow," I say, my hand reaching for the burning sensation. My fingers find a thin metal shaft and I look down. There, lodged in my shoulder, is a blow dart. Ash stops dead in his tracks and turns back to me, registering the dart and immediately searching for the attacker. Over his shoulder I catch a glimpse of dirty-blond hair . . . *Logan!* I grab at the car door, but it swims and shimmers in front of me. I try to call out for help, but the words gurgle and drift away from me. My legs wobble and I take one lurching step forward. . . .

"If you even think about using that blade, I will shove one of your horseshoes so far up your . . . ," says a fading voice that I recognize but can't quite place. My vision goes dark and all of a sudden I'm falling.

Sixteen

SLOWLY THE ROOM comes into focus—the cream-colored fabric of the couch underneath my cheek, a coffee table, a fireplace, a faded navy-blue-and-red antique rug on a wood floor, a couple of armchairs, and a heavy writing desk. The simple decor and the medieval-esque antiques remind me of the Academy, but the room is lighter and airier. I push myself up into a seated position and there's a sharp pain in my head, making yesterday's hangover seem like a mild ache.

I rub my forehead and all of a sudden I remember the dart. I stand up fast, looking for Logan, Ash, and anything that will explain where I am. The pain in my head increases tenfold. "Damn it," I breathe through clenched teeth.

"Better sit back down and drink that god-awful concoction Ash made for you."

For a split second I think I'm hallucinating. I thought I heard her voice last night, but the dart knocked me out so quickly I wasn't certain. *"Aarya?"*

"Yeah, yeah. You're surprised to see me. You can't believe

I'm real. I'm your every dream come true, your knight in shining armor." She takes a breath. "Now drink that black sludge so we can get down to business. Logan very nicely laced the sedative on the dart with poison, which is that splitting headache you're feeling. We got you the antidote in time . . . obviously. Or rather *I* did. But clearly there are side effects."

I can only stare at her, frozen in place. She's dressed in simple black clothes, not unlike our school uniforms, with a black utility belt around her waist that's fitted with knives and vials of god knows what. Her hair is tucked behind her ears and she's wearing black eyeliner that I've never seen on her before. She reminds me of the cover art for an assassin movie—totally badass.

When I finally open my mouth, all I can manage is: "Aarya . . . but . . . I don't understand. You're *here*?"

She rolls her eyes. "I forgot how slow you are sometimes. Drink. The. Black. Effing. Sludge."

I sit down on the couch, grateful for the support of the cushions, and take the glass off the coffee table. She wasn't kidding about the sludge part. It tastes like it was made of mud, snail slime, and swamp water. I decide faster is better and gulp it down. The moment I finish it, I clamp my hand over my mouth, fearful that it might come right back up.

Aarya plops into one of the plush chairs across from me and swings her legs up over the arm, like this is all perfectly ordinary.

"Where's—" I start. The drink, while hideous gak, is already starting to clear some of the pain and therefore clear my thoughts.

"Ash?" Aarya says, finishing my sentence. "He'll be back soon."

"But what about—"

Aarya holds up her hand to stop me. "Take a breath, don't puke on my rug, and I'll tell you all about my heroics." She smiles and wags her eyebrows at me. On any other day I would find her delivery annoying, but in this particular moment, I couldn't be happier to see her.

Aarya picks something out of her teeth and takes a deep breath. "Let's see . . . where should I start?" She taps her fingers on the seat cushion. "Ah yes, let's start with me. Now then, after you and Ash left the Academy, everything just got so boring. It was like it was before you came—cliques, subtle manipulations, Family politics playing out in obvious ways. No murder, no blow-ups, and no mystery. Layla was practically singing down the halls she was so happy."

I shake my head. My nightmare was her amusement. "You have to be the only person in the world who thinks chaos is an ideal state of being," I say.

"Well, thank you very much," she says, and makes a purring noise. "Now where was I . . . oh right, *boring*. I was a little peeved, you know, that you and Ash would go to London to take on Jag in a fit of epic stupidity and not even think to invite me." She gives me a look. "So I invited myself. And I must say, you were disappointingly easy to find. You went to Logan's smithy only hours after I agreed to trade with him for information about you if you happened to stop by, which, predictably, you did. I could have found you two in my sleep. You're not even making it interesting."

"Logan—" I say, my thoughts whirling from Aarya's nonchalant delivery.

"My cousin. A *distant* cousin and a total wanker," she says, and I groan at the obviousness of it—of course he's her cousin. "But he's also a wealth of knowledge and a talented tracker."

So Logan knew we'd be showing up. For a brief moment I'm furious. "He tried to *kill* us, you know!"

"Yes," she says with no remorse.

The men from the pub enter my thoughts. "And there were these two guys at the Dirty—"

"The trackers who recognized you?" Aarya says. "Yes, Ash told me about them."

"How much do you wanna bet they were there as a result of Logan, too?" I say.

After a couple of seconds, Aarya laughs. "Yes, that has Logan written all over it," she concedes. "Your escape from the pub deposited you right in his path."

I rub my shoulder where it aches from the dart. "You're right. He is a wanker," I say, but the British expression sounds awkward in my American accent.

"Family," Aarya says like she agrees more than anyone. "But thankfully for you, my fast negotiating skills won out in the end and we got you the antidote to the drug he tipped the dart with and managed to get out of there before the trackers from the pub showed up. At which point Ash fell at my feet groveling, *as he should,* and we dragged you back here to my parents' apartment."

It's hard to know how much of what Aarya says is true and

how much is concocted in her twisted brain, but right now her self-aggrandizing is the least of my concerns.

"Right, so who else did Logan talk to?" I say. "How do you know Logan didn't also trade information to the Lions?" I don't attempt to hide my frustration.

"The truth is, Logan couldn't care less about anything but his smithy and those awful dogs," Aarya says. "All he wants is to make enough money to live his nasty reclusive life without being overly bothered. To that point, he *would* sell information about you to the Lions, but only if he didn't have another way to make money off you; he hates them like everyone else. And while I couldn't guarantee that you would actually show up at his smithy, Logan's an information-monger and I *could* guarantee that he would realize you were a big payday if you did appear. Also, just because Logan had those trackers chase you out of the pub doesn't mean he actually told them your identity; in fact I highly doubt he did. You should be thanking the crap out of me," she says, and I lift an agitated eyebrow.

I stare at Aarya, not sure if she's absolutely brilliant and just saved us or if she took a huge gamble that might have resulted in our capture—or worse.

"But whatever you two did in that pub is another story," she says, and her tone turns more serious. "What in the hell were you thinking going into that place? And then running out like your butts were on fire?" She shakes her head like she's embarrassed for me. "Lucky for you, we can stay in this apartment for the time being. Jackals aren't like the rest of the Strategia—we don't keep lavish flats in prestigious neighborhoods that are easy to find. We're *smart*. We stay in unassuming neighborhoods in unassuming flats, making us much safer here than anywhere else."

My eyes widen at the *we* in her sentence. Why on earth is she here, letting us stay at her Family's apartment? Aarya is a lot of things, not the least of which is surprising, but I never thought her many unexpected traits would include generosity.

"Ash and I got a tip that might lead us to my dad and we were following it up," I say.

"What kind of tip?" Aarya asks, leaning forward.

Before I get a chance to answer her, the door opens. Ash comes through holding a couple of shopping bags and a large pizza. My stomach growls at the sight of it. And right beside him is Ines—with her red braids woven into something that resembles a fashionable Mohawk. I do a double take. It makes sense that Aarya wouldn't come alone, but I'm having a hard time believing that they came here at all.

Ash smiles, and there's something so genuine about his happiness that, despite the lingering pain, I smile back.

"Some Thai, cheesy baked potatoes, and of course . . . pizza," he says, putting the bags and box down on the coffee table.

"Oh man . . . thank you," I say, immediately flipping open the pizza box lid and grabbing a slice. The cheese is still piping hot and stretches as I pull it.

"Americans," Aarya says with an air of judgment, and reaches for the bag with the Thai food in it.

"Ines? You're *here*. How are you here?" I say with a little bit of awe, scarfing the pizza, which ironically is way better than any I've had in America. "Is Felix here, too?"

Ines shakes her head and for a moment anger flashes in Aarya's eyes.

"Felix stayed," Aarya says without any of her usual embellishment, and it's clear by her tone that the topic is now closed.

Ash sits down next to me, scanning me for injury.

"Have you guys heard anything about my dad since you've been in London?" I ask Aarya and Ines, unable to disguise the hope in my voice.

"We've heard about the insanely large bounty on his head," Aarya says, and whistles. "Jag is not messing around about finding him."

Ash gives her a look like she couldn't be more insensitive if she tried.

"Your father hasn't been found," Ines says, and even though I've heard her speak a few times now, the soothing tone of her voice still takes me by surprise. "And with the number of trackers and assassins in London right now, that's saying something. He must be exceptionally strategic and smart."

I smile at her kind reassurance.

"Which also makes him more difficult to find," Aarya says, looking at me and Ash. "I assume that's what we're doing here, right? Finding your father and using his knowledge about his Family to stamp them out like the vile beasts that they are? But what I want to know is what this tip is you and Ash found."

Ash looks at me like he's surprised I would tell Aarya we found anything. "We don't know yet," he says noncommittally.

Aarya huffs. "Tell me that's a joke, Ashai, a bad one befitting your subpar sense of humor. Ines and I left the Academy, manipulated Logan for you, and gave you a safe place to stay . . . so you can't possibly be withholding information from us, can you?"

Ash raises an unconvinced eyebrow. "Magnanimous Aarya isn't one that anyone believes, so don't waste your energy. And don't pretend you did us any favors with Logan. You took a risk in finding us, and what you risked was *us*."

I look back and forth between them, wondering how long I've been passed out and how much they've already argued about this.

"An ingrate is an ugly thing, Ashai," Aarya says as she chews. "You don't agree with him, though, do you, November?"

I don't even know where to begin to answer that. There is no way I'm choosing Aarya over Ash, but it's true that Aarya's shown up for me in crucial ways recently—I'm not ready to dismiss her flat-out. I look at Ines for clues, but she just sits quietly in the other armchair, eating.

Ash seems unaffected by Aarya's blustering. "The better question, Aarya, is *why are you here?*"

"To cut Jag's throat," Aarya says, like it's the most logical thing in the world. "So don't go getting all weepy and sentimental like I'm here for you two out of the kindness of my heart. No one has dared go after Jag like this, and I'll be damned if I'm going to miss it."

"No one thought for the merest of seconds that you were here out of the kindness of your heart," Ash says, and they continue staring at each other.

My pulse races at Aarya's suggestion. I've been so focused on the idea of finding my dad and staying hidden that I haven't fully considered what we're doing in terms of killing people.

"Four Academy students taking on the head of the most powerful and ruthless Family," Aarya says with new enthusiasm. "Can you imagine if we actually pull this off? They'll write ballads about us."

Ash frowns, like he believes her answer but he also believes there is more to it than she's saying.

"Now, about that tip?" Aarya says, and looks at me.

I don't answer right away.

"Unless you think you don't need another two sets of hands?" Aarya presses. "That you and Ash are just so stealthy and skilled that you have this whole thing handled with no need of anyone else."

I groan. She knows we're badly in need of help. And even though Ash doesn't trust Aarya, it has to say something for her that she left the Academy to come here.

"Masquerade ball," I say in a low voice.

"Masquerade ball?" Aarya repeats, considering the idea.

"I mentioned it in the pub," I say, cringing as I remember Hawk's reaction. "In conversation with the crew. And the response was strong. Hawk said if he saw us there he would hand us straight over to Jag."

Aarya whistles. "Great, so not only do we have seventy-two hours or less to prepare for whatever this thing is, but it's being *hosted by Jag* and you two idiots essentially told a crew *who were working it* that you plan to crash it?"

To my complete surprise, Ash smiles. "Not sure you should join us if you're afraid of a challenge, Aarya."

She raises an eyebrow. "If that's your way of saying sorry for screwing up—and I mean *you*—I don't accept."

"No, that's my way of saying if you think you're not good enough, you should stay home," Ash replies.

Ines and I look back and forth between them and it occurs to me that this is the one thing Ash and Aarya have in common: they both love to instigate and take on impossible obstacles.

It also occurs to me that we floated right over something Aarya said. "Hang on, what do you mean, 'seventy-two hours or less'? How do you know when the ball is going to be when you didn't even know there was a ball until a minute ago?"

Aarya looks a little too pleased with herself. "Because no one hires a crew more than a week in advance, with the average being about four days. Anything longer than that compromises security and leaves the crew open to bribes, which is essentially what you two idiots suggested. A crew found accepting a bribe would be executed, so you're just lucky you got out of there without being cut up and added to the stew."

I swallow and look at Ash. No wonder he said not to mention specifics.

"It was a risk worth taking," Ash says, even though I'm not sure he should be defending me in this moment. "Without it, we wouldn't have a lead."

Aarya opens her mouth to respond but Ines cuts her off.

"So a masquerade ball being hosted by Jag is going to take place sometime in the next few days," she says. "The first thing we need to do is figure out where it's being hosted. I can think of at least five properties."

"We know it's something extravagant if Jag has several

crews working it," Ash says, dropping his standoff with Aarya. "It's not your run-of-the-mill Strategia meeting. Plus, the masquerade element suggests a celebration."

"I thought Strategia don't celebrate anything," I say, a little surprised.

Ash leans back on the couch. "We don't celebrate holidays. But we do celebrate weddings, especially when they unite two Families in a political alliance."

"Or someone's ascension to a high office within a Family," Ines says.

"True," Aarya says. "But Jag doesn't keep an advisory council, so there are no offices to fill."

Ash and I immediately turn to each other. "The Regent," we say at the same time.

"The Regent?" Aarya says, now swinging her legs down from the armchair and looking at us more seriously. "What do you mean, 'the Regent'?"

"Supposedly he was killed a month ago," I say. "And my dad's been accused—falsely—of killing him."

Aarya's eyes widen. "The Lion Regent was murdered *a month ago* and I'm just hearing it now?"

"I'm shocked you didn't know, Aarya. It was your *cousin* who told us," Ash says, like he has a bad taste in his mouth.

Aarya frowns. "No. He absolutely did not tell me that. Duplicitous twit. He told me about the Ferryman and nothing more."

I stiffen. "Wait. What did he tell you about the Ferryman?"

"That there's an enormous bounty on your dad's head but that most of the trackers are calling it a wash of a job since the Ferryman has taken an interest in it," Aarya says.

When I don't immediately react, Aarya rolls her eyes like she's talking to a five-year-old. "The Ferryman is a *legend*. He's a god among the crews. He's the one who dismantled the assassination attempt on the British royal family two years ago. And he stopped the attack at the UN a few years before that."

I hear her, but it's hard for me to process. How can someone who did those great things also be hunting my dad? And if the trackers don't want to compete with him, what chance do we stand of finding him before the Ferryman does?

"But back to this Regent business," Aarya says. "First, good on your dad. That guy was a menace."

"He *didn't* do it," I say, even though I'm not sure it matters to Aarya. It does, however, matter to me. "He was in America. I'm sure of it."

Aarya looks momentarily perplexed. "Are you certain? Strategia don't often get accused of things they didn't do," she says, repeating what Ash told me earlier.

"One hundred percent positive," I say, though inside I'm still trying to convince myself that my math is right.

She gives Ash a questioning look, like maybe I've gotten it wrong, but when he doesn't respond, she continues. "Second, if the Regent's dead and has been for a month, then it makes perfect sense that Jag would appoint someone new. And that kind of appointment would be a massive political affair. A masquerade ball is exactly the type of showy arrogance Jag is known for."

"Indeed," Ash says. "And the costumed aspect will allow him to bring in Families who are allied to the Lions without them risking too much exposure. There will be food and entertainment and accommodations for those who are traveling."

"So he'll need a big venue," I say.

"And a lot of rooms," Aarya says, and she, Ash, and Ines share a look.

My heart thuds. "You know, don't you? You know where the ball is going to be held." My tone is optimistic.

"There is a landmark Strategia hotel in central London," Ash says. "It's the fanciest and largest of the Strategia properties in the UK. However, it's also popular with tourists and thus is seldom used for actual Strategia business. But for appointing a new Regent in plain sight . . . it's the logical choice."

I sit back against the pillows on the couch, relieved we're moving forward.

"I wouldn't look so pleased, Ember," Aarya says, bringing back her awful nickname for me. "That location and a Regent appointment are crap news. The place will be swarming with Lions, not to mention crews brought in for extra security, and any secret passage or back entry is sure to be guarded." Ash and Ines nod their agreement.

Aarya pulls out a cell phone and I instinctively swoon.

"You have a *cell phone*?" I say, glancing at Ash like he's been holding out on me.

She looks at me like I'm a toddler getting excited about cake. "It's a burner. No internet, no tracking capacity. Barebones. Did you really think I was that stupid?"

"No, I—" But before I can respond she's crossing the room and pulling out what appears to be a large phone book. I watch as she points to a number on a page and starts dialing.

"Hello, yes, I would like to book a room this weekend," she says in a demanding aristocratic British accent. "Booked up due to a private event? On which night?" She looks at us with a gloating grin. "Well, that is terribly inconvenient." She presses End on the call before saying thanks or goodbye.

Aarya smirks, plopping back down in her plush armchair. "Two days. The masquerade ball is in two days."

My stomach does a fast flip and I frown, trying to understand how my dad, who has always been the most cautious person I know, managed to send me first to Logan's and now into the Lions' den and with only forty-eight hours to prepare. Why this long trail of clues that require so much risk when he could have just given me a date and an address? "What's the endgame here?" I say aloud, hoping someone will say something that will help me understand. "I mean, there are obviously a thousand safer places for my dad to direct me than to a private event hosted by Jag in a hotel overrun by Lions."

Ash shakes his head.

"Ponder the meaning of life another time," Aarya says with a complete absence of sympathy. "This is all we have to work with. And we have a serious lack of time to concoct a plan between now and the ball, not to mention the Ferryman, to contend with."

I understand Aarya's reaction. Strategia live in a world of puzzles. They are used to messy, complicated situations that require you to be unfeeling and get the job done. But I'm not. I've never just followed a path without questioning why it was laid out for me, even when that path was a series of clues leading to my dad.

Ash goes to his bag and digs out his atlas, clearing a spot on the coffee table. "Have you ever been to that hotel?" he asks Aarya and Ines as he flips through the pages, landing on a detailed page of central London. "Layla and I stayed there once with our parents, but it was ages ago and I only vaguely remember the layout."

"I went there for high tea with my mom two years ago," Aarya says, and I take a closer look at her. I can't imagine a world where Aarya goes to high tea. Or has a mother, for that matter.

We crowd around the map, and Ines adds a log to the fire. But I'm still hung up on the why of it all. It's different than anything my dad has ever done, and I hate that I can't rationalize his motives. It feels . . . wrong.

Seventeen

AARYA, INES, ASH, and I sit around a rustic dining room table covered in Indian food that Aarya made from scratch. Not only is it delicious, but she wore an apron while cooking and used all kinds of culinary jargon that I've never heard before as she bossed Ines around the kitchen. I've been side-eyeing her ever since. I really don't know what to make of her and her deeply layered personality. Even Ash seemed impressed.

"You guys are completely useless," Aarya says, and pushes her plate away from her, which I'm assuming means she's done eating and someone else should clear.

"Ah yes, we're the problem," Ash retorts. "Meanwhile you've been spouting utter brilliance all morning."

"I know," Aarya says, and sighs theatrically. "The burdens I must bear."

We're all feeling the pressure of time. We went to bed last night at four a.m. after talking in delirious circles for hours with the hope that everything would make more sense if we slept on it. But here we are at lunch without a complete plan and only one day before the ball.

The only person who looks relaxed is Ines, who's eaten twice as much as the rest of us and is smiling faintly at Aarya's drama.

"Even if we can sneak onto the property, the only way this is going to work," Ash says, leaning forward, "is if we have a way to distract or disorient a couple of guards. Knocking them unconscious is out of the question. Their absence would immediately be noticed and it would be a clear indicator that there were uninvited guests. And imitating them is also out of the question. We run too much risk of being recognized."

"We're talking about well-trained Strategia guards and hired thugs. Anything we do will be spotted for what it is and probably be just as obvious as knocking out a couple of guards," Aarya says. "At least if we take out the guards we buy ourselves ten minutes or so."

"Ten minutes *if* we're lucky," Ash says. "And we don't even know what we're looking for in there. We may go through all the effort of getting in just to have to bolt before we find whatever November's dad wanted her to see."

I shift nervously in my seat at the thought of being this close to my dad but with no clear idea how to get to him.

"And we're back to square effing one," Aarya says, sitting back in her chair, exasperated. "If we keep this up, we're not going to the ball at all."

"Cinderella," I say reflexively.

Aarya grunts. "If only we had a fairy godmother or, I don't know, Professor Hisakawa to brew us up a concoction."

I freeze, her words triggering the memory of a near-forgotten conversation. "Matteo!" I blurt out.

"I have no idea what you mean," Aarya says. "But I'm definitely intrigued by a plan where Matteo is the fairy godmother."

"Actually, he might be," I say, unsure how much I can say and still keep my word to him. "I went to see Matteo before Ash and I left the Academy to ask him—actually, more like implore him—to help in any way he could."

Ash looks at me questioningly.

I don't meet his eyes, feeling guilty that I didn't find a time to tell him. "Matteo gave me the contact info for an apothecary here in London, but—"

Ash opens his mouth, but before he can get a word out, Aarya smacks the table. "Are you *kidding me*? You have a contact for a *Bear apothecary*? Why didn't you lead with this information?"

"Matteo made me give him my word that I wouldn't share the contact with anyone," I say, briefly stealing a look at Ash.

"Extenuating circumstances," Aarya says, like that's a reason. "Besides being able to get us something to sneak into the ball, an apothecary is without a doubt one of the best resources for acquiring something that will kill Jag."

"No, Aarya," I say. "I'm not breaking Matteo's trust and betraying Bear Family secrets."

"First of all, Matteo doesn't even like you," Aarya fires back. "Second, you're not even *really* a Bear. And third, you have no idea how to handle an interaction with an apothecary. They are the secret-holders of the Strategia. They take no shit and they only help who they want to help. If you go by yourself, you won't last five minutes."

Ash frowns, and it's clear by his expression that he doesn't like this situation in the least. "Even if you go in by yourself," he says, "we should know your location and be nearby. As much as I hate to agree with her, Aarya's right that apothecaries are tricky. They are just as likely to hurt you as to help you."

For a second I'm silent. "I get that you're trying to make sure I'm safe, but I gave my word to Matteo and I'm not going back on it."

Aarya starts to talk, but Ines cuts her off. "Aarya, you want to go because apothecaries are rare and a valuable resource. And believe me, I understand the curiosity." She looks momentarily at me and then Ash. "I want to be an apothecary. But taking advantage of Matteo's information will end badly, and will break any chance November has of gaining Matteo's trust in the future—trust she may very much need. And as much trouble as November might have going on her own, it will be nearly impossible with all of us. Do you truly believe that a Bear apothecary will hand out information and poison to a Wolf, a Jackal, and a Fox?"

Aarya grumbles and Ash looks down at his plate, clearly frustrated.

"Besides," Ines says, getting up from the table and crossing the room, "we don't have much time. If November is going to go, she needs to do it today." Ines disappears into the living room and comes back holding the phone book. She drops it on the table in front of me. "Wherever the apothecary is, you should be able to get the address in there."

Ash stands, too.

"And where are *you* going?" Aarya asks, looking put out that she didn't get her way.

"To buy more burner phones," Ash says, heading for his jacket. "November needs a way to reach us."

My stomach does a fast flip. I was so busy thinking about how I couldn't break my word to Matteo that the reality of the situation hadn't hit me—I'm going alone.

I exit the taxi, which looks straight out of the 1940s, and pull my hood up around my face. I know it's absurd, given everything else that's going on, but there was something exhilarating about riding in the backseat of that British cab and paying with British pounds. However, the moment I turn the corner, my thrill fades. Before me is a row of proud old buildings with elegantly decorated shop windows, one of which belongs to an antiques store with a hand-painted sign that reads ARCANE MINDED just like Matteo said it would.

I scan the sidewalk, where people exit a bakery with their freshly baked bread and hot coffees. They move with purpose, securing their scarves tightly around their necks and bending their heads against the wind. But instead of reveling in the enthusiastic shoppers making festive purchases, I study them, assessing each one for a potential threat. If there's an apothecary on this block, there could certainly be other Strategia as well.

I walk quickly to the store and bend my head like the other shoppers, even though what I want to do is scour my surroundings. But if there are other Strategia here, my direct gaze will be a dead giveaway. So instead, I stop in front of the store window, giving it a thoughtful once-over like I'm just here for a browse.

Unlike the antiques store in my town, where everything is piled on top of everything else, these window displays are artful and accented with twinkling white lights for the holidays. I wouldn't be surprised if it's strictly collector's and auction house items—things so fragile and expensive that you would never bring children here for fear they would break something that costs more than your car.

A shopper carrying bulging bags filled with colorfully wrapped presents walks around me and I realize I've been hesitating near the entrance. I take a deep breath, repeat what I need to say in my head one more time, and push the door open.

The inside of the store is full of whimsy and blue. It's not the dark Gothic style of the Wolves, but the precision is the same. To my left is a counter made of rustic wood and decorated with a quill pen, a book of sales receipts, and a bell. Behind it is a thin, pretty guy with shoulder-length hair who looks like he's barely twenty. I frown. The apothecary couldn't be that young, could he? After watching him for a few moments, I turn away and almost walk smack into a middle-aged woman in a floor-length royal-blue dress. Her salt-and-pepper hair is piled high on her head in curls, her posture is impeccable, and her dark eyes are even more penetrating than Ash's.

My stomach drops like I'm free-falling.

She looks from me to the guy behind the counter, and when her eyes settle on me again, I get the sense that she's already formed an opinion. "Can I help you find something?" she says, and her voice is deep and strong like her jawline.

I nod my head and completely forget what I'm supposed

to say. Something about her is hypnotizing and intimidating, knocking me off-kilter.

"Would you like to tell me what it is, or would you like me to show you our recent acquisitions?" the woman says, and there is something hard and dangerous in her look, as if she's daring me to make a wrong move.

My heart thuds and I lick my dry lips, desperately searching for my line. I break eye contact with her, and in my peripheral vision I notice the guy from the counter watching us. I study what I'm guessing is a medieval confessional turned bookshelf, decorated with dried blue flowers and old books. Just a brief break from her intense look and my memory comes flooding back.

"*Aut cum scuto aut in scuto,*" I say quietly, repeating the Latin phrase Matteo gave me, meaning "either with shield or on shield," and it comes out sounding awkward.

"I see," she says after a moment, and her words are clipped.

She stares at me in a way that makes me afraid to move, like if I blink wrong, she'll tell me she can't help me and that I need to leave.

"It's possible we have what you're looking for in the back," she says, and turns around.

My chest deflates with relief, but the moment is fleeting. As she silently weaves her way through the furniture displays, I find myself resisting following her. Something about this woman gives me an unbalanced feeling, like losing a handhold while climbing.

We make our way to the back of the store, where the apothecary takes a ring of old-fashioned keys out of her pocket and unlocks a thick wooden door. I know this is why I came here, to talk to her in private, but I'm not thrilled about disappearing behind a locked door with her.

The apothecary holds the door open and gestures impatiently for me to go through. And I do. I step into a long hallway that's lit by two dim sconces. The walls have wainscoting on the bottom and above that a midnight-blue wallpaper with a patterned velvet overlay, making the dark hallway darker. I instinctively look over my shoulder, just in time to see the apothecary locking the door behind us. I touch the outside of my coat pocket where my phone is and take a breath, reassuring myself that I can text for help if I need to. In fact I can text from inside my pocket, a skill I mastered in school when I wanted to send Emily notes without getting my phone taken away.

"Head straight to the door all the way at the end," the apothecary says, and my self-soothing falls flat the farther I get from the door. It's akin to the feeling I have in dark basements, like I'm being followed and I should probably run.

I turn the cold brass knob on the door the apothecary indicated and the hinges whine as it opens. Intermittent oil lamps made of stained glass hang from the ceiling alongside drying herbs and flowers, some of which I recognize from my plant obsession as a kid. The walls are lined with wrought-iron shelves overflowing with glass vials and jars. A deeply set fireplace blazes and a series of small pots hang within it. Gnarled wooden tables are covered with every type of wonder, from crystals to ornate daggers.

For a brief moment my fear is eclipsed by amazement and

I can absolutely see why Ines would want to learn this trade. But my awe is short-lived because the apothecary brushes past me, her long blue skirt grazing my leg, and that simple contact nearly sends me shooting into the air.

The apothecary moves to one of the tables, which is laden with half-filled glass bottles and piles of herbs. She busies herself with some kind of sorting process and doesn't say a word.

I walk up to the table, standing on the opposite side of it, careful not to touch anything. She looks up, and the moment we make eye contact, I swallow.

"I'd love to purchase a few products from you," I say, and my voice feels out of place in the quiet isolated room.

She doesn't say a word.

"Uh . . . something to disorient, if you have it, and a strong poison," I say, and my tone winds up sounding more like a question than a request.

She doesn't move; in fact she's so still that she appears frozen. I take a breath. Ash, Aarya, and Ines told me to keep it simple, to make my request and to be gracious.

Seconds tick by, and my instinct is to talk, to fill the quiet with anything other than this anxiety-inducing silence.

"I would really appreciate it," I finally say, hoping that the sound of my voice will snap her out of her creepily still posture. But my words seem to disappear into the stillness.

And again, the seconds tick by.

"Is there something you want me to say that I'm not saying?" I ask, and clamp my mouth shut. *What in the heck was that?* It came out before I could even consider it. "I have money. A stupid amount, really, and I was told to give you as much as you want, promise you more if you need it. Speaking of stupid amounts, have you taken a taxi recently? Cool experience, I'll grant you that, but my god is it pricey."

My hand flies to my mouth. Holy hell, what nonsense is spewing from my face? I try to back up, but I stumble, and the floor sloshes below me like it was made of liquid instead of wood.

"Oh no." Panic grips my stomach and I look up at the apothecary. "What did you do to me?" I demand.

A smile appears on her previously unmoving face. "Interesting," she says to herself, and makes her way around the table toward me. I grab at my pocket, my motor control almost nonexistent, and on my third try I manage to get my hand in it. But to my great dismay, nothing is inside. I pull my hand out, examining my empty palm, and there on my wrist is a smear of something oily. *When she brushed past me . . . she must have . . . how did I not notice?* I rub clumsily at the oil, but the swimming feeling only worsens.

I turn toward the door, my balance off, and I stumble into another one of her tables, banging my knee into the leg. I right myself, my head bobbling into an upright position. Between me and the door is the apothecary.

"You're either dim-witted to think you could come to my shop and use a private Family code, or you're desperate. Which one are you? Dim-witted or desperate?" She looks at me like she might eat me.

I grip the table. Matteo told me she might be willing to help me if she thought I was some distant Bear cousin, but that's clearly not the case. She knows I'm an outsider.

"Desperate," I say, my mouth once again moving without my permission. *Why would I tell her that?* "I need your help to find my dad." *Oh god. Oh god. What am I saying? Did she give me some kind of a truth serum?* I look again at the door, considering making a run for it, but I don't know if my legs will carry me, much less if I can maneuver around her to reach the door.

She raises an eyebrow. "I would forget about leaving if I were you. You will be here as long as I so choose—if you leave at all, that is."

My eyes widen, my heart racing. I'm trapped behind two heavy doors at the end of a long hallway, incapacitated and spouting secrets, with no phone. No one is coming to help me because no one knows where I am, and I doubt anyone would hear me if I screamed.

"Now tell me," she says as I struggle to maintain my balance and my hold on the table. "Who is your father?"

I fight as hard as I can, resisting her and the awful drug she's given me.

My dad laughs, which only makes me scowl harder at the ground where he knocked my wooden practice sword out of my hands.

"Want to go again?" he asks.

"Whatever," I grumble under my breath, and pick up my sword with a huff.

My dad gives me a knowing look. "If you don't like losing, then fencing isn't for you. Because you're never going to win all the time. And needing to win is only going to make you unhappy . . . like right now."

"Your sword is bigger than mine," I say, and stab at the leaves.

"You're ten. Of course my sword is bigger," he says matter-of-factly.

"And they're not even real. They're wood," I say, furthering my nonexplanation for why I'm doing so badly.

"Well, that you can be grateful for. You're not ready for a real sword," he says, and my hand tightens around the wooden hilt in frustration.

"I am *ready*," I say defiantly.

"No, you're really not. And from the way you're acting right now, I don't think you're ready for any sword. Even a wooden one."

I roll my eyes and he hits my blade with his, sending it flying again. I open my mouth to protest, but before I can get a word out, he picks up my practice sword and starts walking toward our house.

"Hey!" I call after him, running to catch up. "Give that back!"

"When you're ready," he says in the calm voice that drives me nuts.

"How will I ever be ready if you won't give me my sword?" I say.

He stops and turns to face me. "I'm not referring to your skill. You could have the best fencing skills in the world and your attitude would sink you."

I frown.

"Do you remember two weeks ago when you got into an argument with Emily at school and came home in a rotten mood?" he asks. "You marched off into the woods with your knives. And what happened?"

I eye him warily, not sure where he's going with this. "I threw badly and wound up crying."

"Right," he says, his voice easing a bit. "Not because your

skill suddenly changed, but because your emotions did. You hate to be bad at anything, Nova. And even more so, you hate to lose. But being bad at something and losing aren't awful the way you think they are and they don't mean what you think they mean. They're human. They're how you learn. And most importantly, they give you freedom from always being a perfect winner."

I stare at him, unconvinced. "And being a perfect winner is a bad thing?"

"Actually, it is if you can't not be a perfect winner. It's a trap where you set yourself up to be constantly disappointed. The bravest people I know, the most skilled people I know, all lose and are bad at things. But they own it. And because they can own it, people trust them." He gives me a pointed look. "It's a form of power to be able to embrace yourself in all the ways you are and all the ways you're not."

I strain against the urge to tell her who my dad is. I can't imagine this will end well for me if she finds out he's a Lion.

"My dad is a Lion," I blurt out the moment I think it. "Damn it!" I yell, and smack the table, nearly losing my balance and toppling to the floor.

"A Lion," she says, sucking in air, and there is a dangerous tone in her voice. "You thought I would help a *Lion*." She pulls a slender dagger off her belt.

I take a stumbling step backward, trying to think my way through the disorientation. I now deeply regret not telling Aarya and Ash where I was going. "I can't believe I protected your location." *And now I've just said that out loud.* I'm so frustrated, I could scream.

"Meaning what? That no one knows where you are?" she says, the corners of her mouth pulling up in a terrifying smile.

"Exactly," I respond, getting more upset by the second.

"Come to think of it," she says, looking around her room, "there are ingredients I'm running low on." She gestures at her glass bottles. "You may do nicely in that regard."

For a second, I don't move; I can't even think how to react. My mind wants to reject her words and convince myself that she didn't say she wanted to use me for tinctures or poisons or whatever sick things she makes in here. My eyes flit to the copious jars of dried ingredients on her shelves; I'm suddenly feeling sick to my stomach. I look back at the apothecary, who runs her finger along the edge of her dagger thoughtfully.

Sweat beads along my hairline. "Look," I say, desperately trying to focus on something to say that doesn't reveal my dad. "I get why you're not leaping at the chance to help me."

"I'm *not* helping you," she says, correcting me.

"But you're wrong," I say, and shake my head, angry with myself.

"I find that exceedingly unlikely," she says, taking a step forward.

"Will you stop?" I say. "Will you just stop coming at me with that dagger for one minute? I can't think and I can't tell you what I need to tell you."

"Your not being able to think isn't my problem," she says, unmoved by my ramblings.

I brace myself, trying to navigate my thoughts past my fear. "You're wrong that it's not worth helping me," I repeat, trying to gain my bearings.

"Of that, I am not convinced," she says.

"I'm not who you think I am. I'm a Bear," I say, my brain fighting itself to come up with anything that doesn't sound

242

like it was concocted by a first grader. Whatever she gave me took away my ability to filter and reason.

"Someone who has a Lion father is not a Bear," she says.

"My mom was a Bear. If you look at me closely, you will see that," I say quickly, and immediately redirect my thoughts away from my mom before I reveal anything more.

The apothecary pulls a vial out of a pouch on her belt and uncorks it.

My eyes widen. "And . . . a-and . . . ," I stammer, inching along the table, trying to put distance between us. "What I'm doing is what the Bears have been attempting to do for decades. I'm trying to stop the Lions, stop Jag from using his power to hurt the rest of the Strategia."

She raises an eyebrow.

I grip the table, aware that every second counts, and aware that if it comes to a fight, in my current state I will most certainly lose. "The Latin phrase I said to you, the secret code, is specifically about helping those who are fighting the Lions. It means don't surrender; never give up. With a code like that, I have to believe that stopping the Lions matters to you."

She shakes her head like the conversation is growing tiresome, and she dips the tip of her blade in the bottle. "As it turns out, I'm stopping a Lion right now."

Sweat drips down my temple. *What if she paralyzes me before she cuts me up? What if I'm awake for the whole process?*

"Lions. Jag. Fighting," I say quickly, trying to get my thoughts and my mouth moving in the right direction.

She corks the bottle and puts it back on her belt, returning her focused gaze to me. She takes a step forward, and I once again lose my train of thought.

For a brief second I look around me, searching for a weapon or something to block her path, but even that slight twist of my head makes me wobble. I eye a set of shelves that are ten feet away. If I lunge, I could potentially grab hold of them and pull them down before she reaches me. Of course, I might get pinned beneath them. And even if I could get past the shelves with my stumbling movements, I seriously doubt that I could get through both locked doors and into the store before she reached me and slit my throat.

"I wouldn't if I were you," she says in a harsh tone, following my eyes.

I bite down hard, shaking my head, so frustrated I could cry. I return my gaze to the apothecary, who is steadily approaching. "Fine. Okay. You win. *You win.* I can't think my way out of this and you've made it impossible for me to control my own body. So here I am, stuck with you and that awful dagger. And maybe—"

A small smile appears on her lips. "It's shocking how simple your thoughts are. Base, even. I would expect more from a six-year-old Strategia."

I ignore her insult. "Judge me all you want. But at least I'm not a hypocrite. At least I don't use a code that suggests I'm fighting the Lions when what I'm really doing is getting in the way of those daring enough to try."

Her eyes narrow and she jabs the point of the dagger under my chin.

But I don't back down.

"When I found out I was Strategia, I hated it. The last thing I wanted was to be part of this power-hungry, murderous secret society. But then there was something else, something about Strategia that made me reconsider—that they do everything in their power to stop history from repeating itself and to avoid the types of tragedies they know can happen. And so here I am looking for my dad, when I realize something . . . I can't go back. I can't ever have the life I used to have before I knew I was a Strategia. But I do get to make a choice, a choice about what kind of Strategia I want to be. And even though I don't know much, and even if I'm 'base' like you say, I know that Jag is a tragedy worth stopping. And despite what sentiments some Strategia preach, no one is actively opposing him. But *I am*."

She pauses, her dagger still pressed into my skin, and her expression shifts. For the first time I get the sense that I've said something that caught her attention.

"What makes you think you can stop Jag?" she says. "When you can't even save yourself from me?"

I grip the wood with all my might, trying not to move, lest she decide to slice me open. "Because everything and everyone I love in this world depends on it."

She grunts, and for a long couple of seconds she looks like she's trying to decide something. We stare at each other, each moment stretching out in unbearable silence.

Then suddenly she pulls back the dagger, sheathing it on her belt.

I don't dare speak, for fear that anything additional might make her decide to chop me up for parts.

She pulls a slender vial from a pouch. "Drink this," she says, with no explanation.

I stare at the vial, hesitant.

"I would drink it if I were you, unless you plan on crawling out of here," she says in an impatient tone.

I take a deep breath, cross my fingers, and chug the shot of acidic-tasting liquid. It burns my throat all the way down and I gag and cough like my throat is on fire, wondering if she's really poisoned me this time. But almost instantly I stop feeling so wobbly. My legs stiffen under me and the fog in my brain clears. I no longer feel the urge to blabber my every thought at her.

She crosses the room with swift steps, grabbing a couple of items from her shelves. She places a small glass jar about the size of a lip gloss container on the edge of her worktable. "Drunken Confessions," she says. "The oil I used on you. One dab on the skin should last about an hour."

Suddenly I feel upside down. She's not killing me *and* she's selling me herbs? I nod, instead of speaking, afraid she might change her mind.

The apothecary drops two thin glass vials into a small burlap pouch and ties it. "Two darts tipped with lightning poison." She grabs a glass vial the size of a pill bottle from her worktable, placing it with the other items. "And Angels' Dream. A drop or two in food or on a blade will put a large man to sleep for hours." She slaps my phone down next to the poison.

I'm positive my face reflects my shock. "I . . . th-thank you," I manage, my mind spinning. "How much do I owe you?"

The apothecary levels her gaze at me as I pull out my wallet. "I'm not accepting money."

"I can get you more if you—" I start.

"No," she says, cutting me off.

I stay very still, not sure what she's doing or why she's doing it.

"Bring me Maura's golden bear-claw necklace and we will call it even," she says.

I stare at her, confused. *Maura . . . It's the female form of the Roman name* Maurus, *meaning "dark." But that doesn't tell me anything.* The only thing I can surmise is that this Maura is from the Bear Family and that she must be prominent enough that I would know her by name.

"I don't have time to go to Italy right now," I say, not sure how to navigate this request and confident that it's a bad idea to tell her I don't know who Maura is. I stare at the bottles and frown. I'm so close.

She looks at the clock hanging on her wall. "Well then, lucky for you I happen to know she's dining at La Cucina Della Nonna," she says. "And if you're the Bear you claim to be, doing what you claim to be doing, you should have no problem convincing her that it's a worthy cause."

If she's going so far as to tell me where Maura is, she must want that necklace badly. And if she wants it badly, then it's valuable or important . . . which means it will be nearly impossible to get. I exhale loudly.

"Now get out," she says, and tosses me my phone, and I practically run for the door.

Eighteen

I WALK A full three blocks from the apothecary's shop before I stop and take out my phone. I pull off my gloves with my teeth and start typing a message to Ash, Aarya, and Ines.

Me: *The apothecary will give us what we want . . . something to disorient and lightning poison, but she's demanding a trade.*

It only takes a second before responses pop up on my screen.

Aarya: *LIGHTNING POISON!!! Do whatever it takes to get it. I don't care if you have to sell your right eyeball.*

Ash: *What kind of a trade?*

Me: *Maura's necklace. Who's Maura?*

For a brief second the responses stop, like maybe they're talking among themselves.

Ash: *Matteo's mother.*

I almost drop my phone on the sidewalk. My mom's name was Matilde and Aunt Jo's real name was Magdalene. It wouldn't be surprising if their sister also has an *M* name. For a few moments I stand there frozen, and when I look back down at my screen there are more messages.

Aarya: *Damn it. There's no time to track her down. Will the apothecary accept anything else?*

Aarya: *???*

Me: *No. Maura's here in London. The apothecary told me where she's eating.*

Aarya: *Then why are you texting us instead of finding her???*

Ash: *Restaurants are common fronts for Strategia properties. If the apothecary knows she's at one, then there are likely other Bears there. It's not safe. Come back to the apartment. We'll figure out another way.*

Aarya: *Oh no we won't. We need that poison.*

Ash: *She's not going to a Bear property to steal from a head Bear, Aarya. That's the stupidest thing I've ever heard. Look at how Matteo reacted to her.*

Aarya: *If you wanted to be safe Ash then you should have stayed home. I'll do it if you're too scared. Give me the address.*

I press my chapped lips together and look around me. Two doors down is a bodega, and before I even settle on a decision, I head toward it. I don't want to give Aarya my aunt's location so she can steal from her. I know it doesn't make sense to withhold it, since Aarya would likely be better at getting the necklace. Also, I've never met Maura, and Ash is probably right that it's not safe. But Matteo told me his mom loved her sisters and that matters to me; so if anyone stands a shot at getting the necklace, it's me, and it won't be by stealing. I push the door to the bodega open and walk up to the counter.

"Can I help you?" the old man says.

"Do you have a phone book by any chance?" I ask.

He looks at my phone and then back at me. "No."

"No Wi-Fi," I say, holding up my phone as explanation.

"What are you looking for?" he asks. "Maybe I know."

I hesitate. I've gotten so used to everything being a secret that it takes me a moment to realize that asking where a restaurant is located is completely normal, especially for an American tourist. I scrutinize his face for the telltale sharp look of a Strategia but find none.

"La Cucina Della Nonna," I say, and realize my Italian accent isn't half bad even though I haven't spoken Italian in a long time.

"Ah," he says, and points. "Down the street about five blocks on the right-hand side." And then he adds, "Amazing pasta. Some of the best."

I give him a big thanks, energized by how seamlessly that went, and walk out of the store. I look from side to side. Within ten blocks there are a Bear apothecary and a restaurant where one of the head Bears is eating. Am I in a Bear neighborhood of sorts?

My phone buzzes and interrupts my thoughts.

Aarya: *NOVEMBER? Despite popular belief, patience isn't my strong suit.*

Me: *It's nearby. I'm just going to walk past.*

Aarya: *Address?*

Ash: *Address?*

Ines: *Good luck, November.*

Me: *I'll text you what I find.*

I walk down the street at a brisk pace, counting off the blocks as I go. I know going alone isn't the best idea I've ever had, especially after what just happened to me with the apothecary. But if my mom's sister is at that restaurant, I want to at least get a look at her.

When I'm four blocks down, I spot the sign for La Cucina Della Nonna and slow my pace. *I'll just walk past slowly,* I tell myself. *I'll just peek in the window.* But as I approach, my heart pounds furiously. *Will she look like my mom and Aunt Jo? Will I be able to recognize her? What if she sees me? Will she recognize me?*

I stop five feet from the restaurant window and take out my phone. I pull up Ash's number in case I need to make a run for it and hover my thumb over the Call button. But before I can take a step forward, someone grabs my wrist, knocking my phone right out of my hand. I spin, yanking my wrist against the assailant's thumb to release his grip, and swing with my other arm.

"November," a familiar voice says just as my fist makes contact with his face.

Matteo takes a quick step backward, holding his hands up.

"*Matteo?*" I say, completely shocked.

He rubs his jaw. "What the hell are you doing here?" he demands, clearly annoyed.

I stare at him, like I'm not sure if the apothecary's oil is making me hallucinate. "What am *I* doing here? What are *you* doing here?" I pick my phone up off the sidewalk, slipping it back in my pocket. I look at his jaw where I landed a punch. "Sorry I hit—"

He dismisses my apology and cuts me off. "I followed you from the apothecary," he says, like that's a reasonable explanation.

"You *what?*" I say, trying to make sense of his words.

"Can we just get out of the street for a second?" he says.

I look at the restaurant window. "But—"

"Now, November," Matteo says. "You wait any longer and someone from my Family will see you."

My heart sinks. I want to tell him that it's my Family, too, but I know that answer won't land. Reluctantly I follow him across the street and down a block onto a residential street.

Matteo stops on the sidewalk in front of a row of apartment buildings and turns to face me. "Now tell me: What were you doing at that restaurant?" he says like it's an accusation.

"What were you doing following me?" I reply with just as much frustration.

"I'm not playing this game with you, November," Matteo says with a huff. "Answer my question and I will answer yours."

I stare at him, looking for any sign of deception, but he seems to be telling the truth. "The apothecary . . . ," I say, trying to figure out how to phrase what I need to say.

"What about the apothecary?" Matteo says with frustrated insistence.

"She wants your mom's bear necklace in exchange for the products I need," I say, opting to just use a straightforward approach even though I know it sounds bad.

Matteo frowns. "Are you telling me you were going to steal my mom's necklace?"

"No, no . . . ," I say quickly. "I was going to ask her for it."

Matteo glares at me like I've lost all my good sense. "You were . . . No, November. No. How did you even know she was there?"

"The apothecary told me," I say.

Matteo's frown deepens. "You're definitely not asking my mom for her necklace."

I stare at him, matching his displeasure. "That's not something you get to decide, Matteo. And if someone's going to tell me no, it's going to be your mom, not you. I need to fulfill my bargain with the apothecary. It's important."

"Well, you're not fulfilling it by going to that restaurant," he says forcefully.

For a second we just stare at each other and I wonder if I could outrun him. There are probably a million reasons why that's a bad idea, but all I can think is that my mom's sister—my aunt—is only a couple of blocks away from me, holding something that will help me find my dad.

Before I can respond, Matteo unzips the top of his coat and pulls a necklace out from under his sweater. It has a delicately carved golden bear claw hanging from it.

"*You* have the—"

"We all do," Matteo says. "Me, my mom, my grandfather, your mom, Aunt Jo."

And for a second I remain silent. I never saw those necklaces on my mom and my aunt. Did they hide them from me? And why does Matteo know things about the people closest to me that I don't even know?

"This is what I'll do—I'll give you this necklace if you give me your word that you'll stay away from that restaurant," he says.

I gain an asset needed to find my dad, but I have to give up meeting my aunt. I momentarily break eye contact with him.

"It's an exceptionally good deal," Matteo says, like maybe I didn't hear his offer.

When I don't answer right away, his look turns to confusion. "Am I missing something?"

"No. You're right. It's a good deal," I say, having a hard time meeting his eyes. So I change the subject. "Why does the apothecary want it, anyway?"

Matteo shakes his head. "Maybe because they're impossible to get. Maybe she knows they have a secret compartment for poison. Or maybe she just figured out who you were and decided to meddle. It's hard to know with apothecaries. They're all secrets and deception, but they're so deadly and invaluable that no one interferes with them."

I grunt. "You got the deadly part right," I say, and Matteo gives me a questioning look, but he doesn't ask me what I mean. "Okay, so why were you following me?"

"Layla," he says, but before he can get out another word I react.

"*What?*" I say in shock, looking around the street like maybe she's hiding in an alley somewhere. "*Layla? That's not . . . What?*"

"Not *here*," he says. "But in London, yes."

"But I don't under—" I start.

"I know," he says, cutting me off. "And I can't explain right now; if I don't get to that dinner with my Family, my mom is going to have my head. I was supposed to be there an hour ago."

"How is Layla *here*?" I say more insistently. "And why didn't I know? Does *Ash* know?"

"No, and that's the thing," Matteo says, and his voice sounds like a warning. "You can't tell Ash."

I look at him sideways. "What do you mean, I can't tell Ash? I can't *not* tell Ash."

Matteo holds up his hands, as if to say it's not his fight. "This is all Layla. It certainly wasn't my idea," he says, as though he's reaffirming that he wants nothing to do with me.

"So where am I supposed to tell Ash I got the necklace if I can't tell him about you and Layla?" I say.

He exhales and pinches the bridge of his nose. "Tell me you didn't tell Ash where the restaurant was located."

"I didn't," I say. "I figured it was a Bear Family secret."

For a moment he looks surprised that I would actually care about something like that, and his annoyance dissipates. "Right, well, tell him what happened—that you ran into me on your way to the restaurant and that I gave you the necklace. Nothing more."

I grumble.

He slips his necklace over his head and holds it out to me. "Do I have your word?"

I sigh. "You have my word."

He drops the necklace in my hand.

"But tell me this, why would Layla not want Ash to know she's here?" I say, making a last-ditch effort to get some information.

"Sorry. Can't," he says, and looks behind him in the direction of the restaurant. "You can ask Layla yourself. Meet us at Twelve Clarence Hill Road in Hampstead at four a.m." He takes a step backward.

"Wait," I say, but he just shrugs as he walks backward.

"See you in the morning," he says, and turns away from me.

For a few seconds I stand there, baffled. What the hell is going on here? First Aarya and Ines, now Matteo and Layla?

Why would Layla do this—say goodbye to us at the Academy and then follow us in secret? I can't imagine that she doesn't have a good reason, I just don't know what it could be.

I stare at the little golden necklace in my hand, wishing I didn't have to give it to the apothecary. Did my mom really have one of these?

My phone buzzes in my pocket, and it jerks me out of my thoughts. I open the screen and there are seventeen new messages. But instead of reading them, I just text back: *Got the necklace. Going to make the trade. Will be home soon.*

Nineteen

THE SUN IS setting as I stare out the window of my cab at the quiet London streets, dripping with white lights. And it dawns on me—*today is Christmas*. I missed all the cheer and peppermint hot chocolate. I missed the decorated tree in Pembrook town square, the carolers and the god-awful holiday play our local theater puts on. And I missed Lucille's menorah lighting, where Emily and I routinely eat freshly baked donuts until we feel sick. And most of all I miss *Dad*.

The cab stops at the corner next to Aarya's apartment. I hand the driver some cash and step out onto the street.

I enter the code on the keypad outside her door and make my way up the stairs, my mind spinning with everything that's happened. I knock twice on the apartment door, and before I even pull my hand away, it opens. Ash stands on the other side.

"November," he says, and some tension leaves his shoulders. It's obvious that he's been doing the Ash equivalent of pacing since I left.

I take my coat off, hang it up on the hook, and pull out the bottles and pouch. When I make eye contact with him again, it seems like he wants to say something and isn't sure how to phrase it. But before he gets a word out, Aarya barges into the hall.

Her eyes light up when she sees the bottles. "Well, just look at that! It's a holly jolly Christmas," she says with an enthusiasm that seems out of place with my nerve-racking evening.

Ash gives her a look like he doesn't quite agree as we head into the living room.

Ines sits on the couch, surrounded by masquerade masks and piles of gauze, lace, and various trimmings. "I'm trying to adjust these so that they cover more of our faces," she says, and I'm reminded of all the time she spent with her sketchpad at the Academy.

"Yes, yes, Ines is impressive. Always has been," Aarya says. "But what I want to hear is how in the hell you got that necklace. I never thought you would pull that off in a million years. And what exactly is in those bottles in your hand?" She's practically falling over herself to get to them. It's amazing how Aarya can be both nice and awful all at once.

"Two darts of lightning poison," I say, laying the burlap pouch down on the coffee table.

Aarya snatches it up, clearly delighted. "You must really have done something right."

" 'Doing something right' is not the way I would describe my evening," I say.

"Well, you're wrong. This stuff is exceptionally rare and nearly impossible to procure," Aarya says, and her voice has more pep to it than it's had all day.

I frown at her.

She turns the small vials around, examining them. "Most

poisons take a while to go into effect and most have antidotes. Lightning poison is instantaneous and has no antidote. It's a well-kept secret of Strategia apothecaries." When I don't join in on her excitement, she huffs. "*Jag* is exactly the type of person who probably keeps antidotes on his person just in case. But this is something he can't prepare for."

"Oh," I say, still deeply uncomfortable with the killing talk. I place a small jar on the table. "Also, Drunken Confessions."

Ash picks it up and opens the lid, smelling the oily paste inside.

Aarya stares over Ash's shoulder. "Never heard of it," she says. "Does it need to be ingested?"

"It gets rubbed on the skin," I say. "It disorients you, makes your legs go completely weak, and makes you spout just about anything that comes to mind. It's kind of terrible."

Ash looks up at me, his interest shifting from the ointment to me. "How do you know it's terrible?"

"She used it on me," I say. "First thing when I walked through the door. I honestly didn't think I was going to get out of there alive."

Aarya whistles in surprise.

Ash frowns. "I've heard rumors of apothecaries testing their products on unsuspecting customers, but I've never actually known anyone it happened to. Are you all right? Why didn't you call us?"

But before I can answer, Aarya starts talking.

"She's fine; look at her," she says, brushing off Ash's concern. "The bigger issue is, if she was spouting all her thoughts, what did November *tell* her?"

"She took my phone," I say, answering Ash's question. "And I said nothing about our plan other than that we intend to remove Jag from power."

Aarya lets out a chuckle. "You're telling me you got an unwilling apothecary to change her mind by telling her you were going to take out Jag?" She shakes her head.

"Turns out I'm convincing," I say.

"I'll say," she replies.

"And, well, it helped that I actually meant it. I think that ointment is part truth serum," I say.

Aarya stares at the oily paste like it's chocolate cake. "Fascinating stuff."

"Also, Angels' Dream," I say, putting down the glass bottle. "It's a sedative of some kind."

"A powerful one. It's made with belladonna," Aarya says, and I can hear Hisakawa's voice in my head: *Atropa belladonna, or deadly nightshade. The Gothic siren of any good apothecary.* But instead of bubbling over it like she did with the poison, Aarya looks at Ines, who has visibly stiffened.

Ash picks up the bottle of Angels' Dream. "We'll need some darts for this."

Ines quietly exits the room. Ash notices Ines's reaction, too. We look at Aarya to explain, but she just shrugs.

"Okay, so tell us," Aarya says, changing the subject. "How did you get that necklace?"

"Matteo," I say without a lead-up, because I fear the more details I give, the more likely I am to betray him with my body language.

"*What?*" Ash and Aarya say at the same time.

"Believe me, I was more surprised than you. He stopped

me on the street in front of the restaurant. I actually punched him before I realized who he was."

Aarya lets out a belly laugh. "How did I miss this? And why do you get to have all the fun while I have to babysit Ash?"

"Why is Matteo here?" Ash asks, ignoring Aarya. "In London, of all places?"

I shake my head. I wasn't thinking about the fact that Matteo's in enemy territory; I was too caught up in the necklace trade and the Layla conversation. No wonder Matteo was so adamant that I not tell Ash about the restaurant; a Bear property in Lion territory is something to guard.

"Probably planning some revenge for Stefano's death," Aarya says, and I wonder if she's right, and if that's how Layla convinced him to come.

"Or doing Family business," Ash says. "Considering his mother is also here."

"Or that," Aarya concedes. "But you still haven't explained how you got the necklace."

"That's because you've been talking," I say, which makes Ash smile.

Aarya slashes her fingers at me like they're claws and purrs.

"I told Matteo about the apothecary and it turns out that all the head Bears wear the same necklace. He gave me his," I say, "in exchange for me keeping silent about the restaurant and staying away from him and his Family."

Aarya grins. "He must really despise you."

Ash gives Aarya a hard look. "I'm sure they just have important negotiations going on that they can't risk having disrupted."

Aarya looks like she's not convinced, and I don't blame her. I'm not convinced, either.

Twenty

I CLIMB INTO my makeshift bed of blankets and pillows on Aarya's living room floor. Ines went to bed an hour ago and Aarya's in the bathroom brushing her teeth. We haven't yet agreed on a plan for tomorrow, and we spent most of the evening going in circles about how many guards there would be at the ball and the best way to use the ointment the apothecary gave us. As our conversations wound down, I began stressing over sneaking out to meet Layla and Matteo.

Ash pauses to look at the bathroom door and frowns.

"What?" I ask, although I'm pretty sure I know what he's going to say.

He sits down on an arrangement of pillows and blankets on the rug near mine. "I don't trust her," he says.

I glance at the bathroom door now, too. "She's eccentric and a real pain sometimes, but you have to admit . . . the fact that she's here sort of clears up the trust issue."

"Not even a little," Ash says. "We have no idea why she's here besides wanting to participate in the destruction of Jag, which I grant you is a reason, but not a good enough one for a mission with this much risk."

"I mean, yes, but—" I say.

"And the way she was encouraging you to steal that necklace . . . ," he says, shaking his head, but doesn't finish.

I chew on the inside of my cheek. I hate doubting her. It feels wrong after everything that's happened. And yet I get why Ash is questioning Aarya. He should be.

"Also, Felix isn't with them," Ash says.

"For that, I'm actually grateful. I'm not sure I could pretend to be civil with him after he threw me out of that tree," I say.

"Right," Ash says like I'm agreeing with him, "and Aarya knows that."

I study him for a moment. "Are you saying she left him there on purpose in order to gain our trust?"

"That's exactly what I'm suggesting," Ash says. "There is something they're not telling us, and I intend to figure out what it is."

I nod at him. And for a few seconds we sit there, staring at the fire, both lost in thought. In the quiet, my worries drift back to Layla and Matteo.

"You're stewing about something," Ash says, and I realize I'm staring far too intensely at the fire. "I'm exceedingly familiar with that look because Layla is perpetually in her head about something, and has been ever since she could talk. You wouldn't imagine that a two-year-old could stew, but Layla made it an art form."

I smile, picturing a small and serious Layla. While I can't

tell him what I'm thinking about in this moment, the overall list of things I'm anxious about is *long*. "I'm not clear about the plan."

Ash laughs. "No one is clear about the plan. We'll be lucky if we sort it all out by the time we get to the ball."

"I mean the bigger plan," I say. "We find my dad, and let's say we actually manage to use his knowledge of the Lions to disrupt the current leadership . . . then what?"

Ash looks thoughtful. "You mean, do we go back to the Academy or do we stay in Europe?"

"Yes and no," I say. "I didn't grow up as a Strategia; it's like my whole identity has suddenly changed and I'm not sure what that means going forward or if I'm even okay with it."

"You were always Strategia," Ash says.

"Yeah, but I didn't know that," I say.

"Yes you did." He sounds so confident that I look at him sideways. "You didn't have a word for what you were, but that doesn't mean you didn't know deep down. You've told me multiple times that you always loved knives and swords, that you loved strategy games, that your dad went out of his way to challenge you and teach you survival tactics. You weren't raised with stuffy history tutors like me and Layla and you weren't sent to spar with the estate guards while your parents critiqued you, but you learned what you needed to all the same. You haven't suddenly changed. You've just been given context and a word for your identity. And I get that it must be an adjustment, but you're just as much Strategia as you've always been."

I open my mouth to argue, then close it.

The corners of Ash's mouth turn slightly upward. "See, even you agree."

I smirk. "You think you're so clever."

"That's because I am so clever," he says with a sly grin.

"And humble," I say.

"One of my many winning qualities."

We share a smile.

"The thing is . . . I don't know if I can go back to my old life," I say. "I know you said there was a possibility I could when we were talking in the woods, but I've been over it a thousand times in my head and I just don't see how it's possible. Even if I pull off a visit once a year, that's not the same thing as living there. I never considered a life without Pembrook. But spending time there means putting people I love at risk. How can I ever go back, knowing that?"

"My question is, would you truly *want* to live there?" Ash says. "And not as a nostalgic idea, but in actuality. Would that be fulfilling for you?"

I grip my cup of peppermint hot chocolate, soaking up the heat through my gloved hands as Emily and I leave Lucille's diner.

I wave it under my nose. "Mmmm."

"You act like that drink is your boyfriend," Emily says as we cross the street toward the green in the middle of the town square.

"I don't know what Lucille does to make it so good, but I'm completely addicted," I say.

We take up our usual perch on the bench in the gazebo, which has a clear view of the decorated tree.

"Em, what do you think we're gonna be like as old people?" I ask.

Emily sips her cider and leans back. "Pretty much like this. Only I'll have taken over Lucille's and transformed it into a hip bookstore that serves coffee and champagne. Oh, and dogs."

I laugh. "A bookstore that serves dogs? That sounds like a winner."

"No, idiot. A bookstore where you can bring your dog."

"Okay, and I'll be—"

"A gym teacher," Emily says, cutting me off.

"Um, no. You get to run some hip bookstore and I'm a gym teacher? I didn't know you thought so much of me," I say.

"Wellll," Emily says, grinning. "You'll try to do some extreme-sports-type job, but the only place you'll be able to do it is in Hartford. And inevitably you'll miss me too much and have to move back here, where the only logical job opening will be gym teacher. Of course after a few years of penance for moving away from me, I'll let you work at the bookstore."

I smile. "And eventually we'll be just as cranky as Lucille. Only difference is that we'll be able to blame our farts on the dogs."

She leans her head on my shoulder. "And all will be exactly as it should be."

"I always thought so," I say quietly. But what I don't say is that the real dilemma is Emily—I don't see how it's possible to be Emily's best friend and be Strategia at the same time.

Ash watches me and I get the sense that he knows what I'm thinking.

"The one thing I'm not doing, though," I say, forcing my thoughts away from Emily, "is just killing people all the time."

Ash laughs so suddenly that it surprises even him, and he coughs. "November, no one wants you to kill people all the time. A surprising number of Strategia live peacefully, without ever harming anyone."

"Says you," I say. "But somehow I've killed two people in a month. And I'm just . . . that's not who I am. I'm not going to do that."

"First, you didn't kill Dr. Conner," Ash says. "You stabbed him, but only in self-defense, to save both our lives. Blackwood killed him. And second, I told you to break that branch; so Harry's death is as much my fault as yours. Plus, there was no way to know that fall would kill him. The rock was unforeseeable."

I hesitate, not sure I believe him, but also not sure he's wrong. "And what about the Lions?" I say. "What's the plan there? Because the way Aarya talks about it, it seems like she would take out the entire Family if she could."

Ash sighs. "Let's not forget that Aarya's approach is usually unhinged. That being said—"

"I heard that!" Aarya says from the hallway, and appears in the door.

Ash gives her a scrutinizing look and I can almost see the gears in his head moving, adding eavesdropping to the list of reasons he doesn't trust her.

"And if anyone's approach is demented, it's November's," Aarya says.

"Because I don't like the idea of killing people?" I reply.

"Because Jag killed your mother. He killed your aunt. He effectively killed Felix's dad by sending him after your parents. He killed Stefano by proxy. And at this very moment he's trying to kill you and your father. Not to mention the countless number of other innocent people whose lives he's ruined," Aarya says with feeling.

I stare at her.

"So you go right ahead with your nicey-nicey crap," she says. "But me? If I get any kind of chance, no matter how small, I'm killing him. And I will dance on his grave." Then she turns around without another word and slams her bedroom door behind her.

For a second we're both silent.

"I'm not really sure what to say after that," I confess.

"I don't think anyone knows how to follow that up," Ash agrees. "But what I will say is that the Lions are a special case. Unless Strategia are truly warped, like Jag and Dr. Conner, they only kill when it's necessary or in self-defense. Think about it; it's a million times easier to outsmart or circumvent your opponent than it is to kill them. It's like what Professor Gupta always says: the more you learn in deception class, the less you need to learn in others. You being Strategia doesn't mean you're a career assassin, it means that you have a very special set of skills, skills that can greatly impact the world for the better if you choose to use them properly."

I listen, considering his words. What he's saying makes sense even if it hasn't been my experience as a Strategia thus far, and if I'm honest with myself, Aarya makes a point, too. In fact it was just earlier today that I argued for the destruction of Jag when I was under the influence of that truth serum, calling him a tragedy worth stopping. Maybe I don't know myself the way I always thought I did, or maybe I've been unwilling to embrace who I really am. Either way, there is no road back to my life as I once knew it, and no amount of pining is going to change that. I need to start making decisions about what kind of Strategia I intend to be.

Ash's lips turn up in a subtle smile, like he can hear my thought process. "And not to add fuel to the fire, but you're attempting to upend the most powerful Family in all of Strategia. That combined with your parents' legacies means you will never be anonymous again. In fact, if we manage to pull this off, you may very well become one of the most infamous Strategia in the modern world."

My eyebrows push together, and despite myself, I laugh. "Thanks, Ash. Here I am struggling with this new identity and trying to figure out where my life goes from here and now I also get to be infamous."

He smiles his mischievous smile. "Anytime." But instead of looking away, he holds me in his gaze. "And I'll be there."

I tilt my head questioningly. "Be where?"

"With you," he says, and the affection in his tone envelops me like a hug.

"Oh . . . right, I'd love to . . . I mean, cool, yeah, that'd be great," I say, completely tripping over my words.

Ash's grin widens. "Very smooth, November."

My cheeks flush and I laugh. "Right? Just grace upon grace."

Ash laughs, too, and it feels good to be sitting here with him making light of my romantic ineptitude. So much of our conversation has been about strategy and death recently that it's easy to forget to enjoy the time we have together. And even if I love the idea that he'll be with me, I'm not convinced that wherever my life takes me next is a place Ash would want to be—or where his Family would *let* him be.

"It's one of the first things I noticed about you," Ash says. "Your humor."

"Really?" I say, genuinely surprised. "I always felt like I was so serious at the Academy. It would be different if you met me in Pembrook. Laughing until I cried was kind of my thing. But then maybe you wouldn't have liked me if you met me there." I wag my eyebrows playfully. "To you I would have been a commoner."

Ash shakes his head. "I think you're absolutely wrong, November Adley. I would have known you were perfect anywhere I met you."

"Perfect?" I say. "Okay, now I *know* you're full of it. The last thing I am is perfect."

"Perfect for me," he says with such intensity in his expression that I think I might melt into the floor. And without me noticing it, the space between us has narrowed.

I open my mouth, once again feeling scrambled. "Well . . . I . . . now . . ."

Ash reaches up, running his thumb over my bottom lip and along my jawline to the back of my neck. "That's a response that deserves a kiss if ever I heard one."

This time I don't mumble nonsense at him. I lean closer. "Then what are you waiting for?" I say, our faces only a couple of inches apart.

He closes the distance between us. His lips part as he presses them into mine. His hand drops from my neck to my lower back and he pulls me into him. And for this moment, it's just me and Ash in front of a cozy fireplace in a tangle of blankets.

✳ ✳ ✳

My eyes crack open for the hundredth time and I peer at the clock, which now reads 3:27 a.m. A shot of adrenaline sends me sitting straight up. I stare at Ash sleeping next to me in our makeshift beds, looking for any sign of movement. I listen to his breathing, but it's long and heavy and consistent with a deep sleep.

I carefully peel back the blankets and pull on my socks, glancing at Ash once more before I get up. I tiptoe across the area rug in the living room and test the wood floor for creaky boards before I step on them. I silently lift my coat off the hook, check the pockets for cash, and pick up my boots. Then I open the apartment door with painstaking slowness to make sure it doesn't whine.

The instant it closes behind me, I yank on my boots and throw on my coat. I wait a beat to make sure no one in the apartment follows me and then I'm out of there full-speed down the hallway, down two flights of stairs, and out onto the cold dark street.

It only takes one block to find an idling taxi and fifteen minutes to get across town. I repeatedly glance out the back window, making sure that Ash or one of the others didn't somehow follow me.

The taxicab lets me off on a commercial street filled with

cafés and boutiques that are completely dark at this hour. I double-check the street signs and building numbers for the address Matteo gave me. It's an odd adjustment from always following the map on my phone to suddenly having to use atlases and trust my own navigation skills.

I stand there on the street in the dark staring at the building, which appears to be a run-down Victorian-era shop with boarded-up windows. In faded gold letters the sign reads PASSEMENTERIE. Can this be right—did Matteo really want me to meet him at an abandoned store?

It occurs to me that I never questioned the invitation, not after he mentioned Layla. But Matteo doesn't like me. And now all of a sudden he shows up in London, follows me from the apothecary, tells me to meet him somewhere because Layla is here, and also tells me I can't tell Ash. I frown, tucking my hands under my armpits for more warmth.

For a split second, I think about turning around, grabbing another cab, and sneaking back into bed. I'm an inch away from finding my dad and here I am taking a chance on Matteo—meanwhile no one knows I've left the apartment or where I've gone.

"Damn it," I breathe, and a white cloud billows out in front of me. *No. This is ridiculous. Matteo gave you the apothecary information; he gave you the necklace. Why would he help you just to betray you? Unless he was just trying to lure you into a false sense of confidence so he could make his big move?*

I look down at my boot, where for once I have no knife hidden, and shake my head, annoyed at myself. I take out my cell phone and type a draft of a text to Ash with the address. It's now 3:58 a.m. I lock the phone and walk to the front door of the boarded-up store, grabbing the handle, and to my great dismay, it opens.

"Layla?" I whisper into the darkness. "Matteo?" But no one answers.

I glance behind me at the dark street, realizing that I need to make a decision—inside or outside—and that the longer I linger in the doorway of an abandoned shop, the more likely I am to attract attention. "Dang it," I say, and slip inside the dark building.

My heart pounds so loudly that it makes it harder for me to listen in the darkness. I pull out my phone, lighting up the screen, but all it does is make the area directly around me visible and make it impossible for my eyes to adjust. So I slip it back in my pocket and stand still in the darkness, silently hoping I didn't just make the worst decision of my life.

Then suddenly a candle flame appears at the far end of the room and I jump backward, nearly colliding with the door. But behind the candle, emerging from a staircase, is a girl with a high ponytail and a no-nonsense expression.

"Layla!" I squeal, both relieved that Matteo was telling the truth and genuinely delighted to see her.

"Lock the door," she says in her usual peremptory tone, but even from this distance I can tell she's smiling.

I click the lock into place and walk toward her with enthusiasm. In the light of her candle, I can make out finely carved wood that must once have been painted a crisp white, and glass displays full of lace and frills. Old cloth mannequins are propped up wearing faded Victorian dresses, and broad-brimmed hats lie forgotten on the floor.

Layla follows my gaze. "This place used to be a dress shop

run by one of my relatives in the late eighteen hundreds," she explains. "Ash and I liked to come here when we were little and trying to get away from our parents."

At which point I give her a hug. And when I pull away, she looks slightly embarrassed, like she's not sure why I keep doing that, but she also doesn't tell me to stop.

"I discovered that we owned this property when I was going through some financial records when I was six," she says before I can start badgering her with questions about being in London. "It took us about a year before we had the opportunity to seek it out, but I was delighted when I discovered it was essentially a forgotten building, lost in another time. It became our hideout."

I follow her up a narrow staircase. "Why am I not surprised that you were going through financial records when you were six?" I say, and she looks pleased by my assessment of her.

As we reach the top of the stairs, a large one-room apartment lit by candles comes into view. It has a small kitchen, a couch in front of a fireplace, a canopied bed, an armoire, and a large area rug. Even though it's dusty and smells a little like talcum powder, the room is well decorated in creams and various shades of blue, giving it a cozy feel. I can almost picture the seamstress who lived here, bustling about in her big skirts.

Matteo sits at one of four chairs around a dining table with his arms crossed.

I look from Matteo to Layla, who sits down beside him. "Okay, now what in the heck is going on?" I say. "How are you two here? *Why* are you two here? Why couldn't I tell Ash? You're both the last people I would expect—"

"Have a seat, November," Layla says, cutting me off and gesturing at an empty chair. "Matteo will bring us some tea."

Matteo tilts his head, like he didn't know he was bringing tea but he's willing to adjust. And so I slide into the wooden chair while he makes his way into the tiny kitchen.

I want to rattle off twenty more questions, but Layla's already made it clear that she's not going to respond to that type of approach. So instead, I sit as patiently as I can and wait for her to explain.

"I know you can't stay for long without my brother noticing," she says, and the relief I felt just moments ago shifts to uncertainty. "So I will try to be as succinct as possible. I'm here for exactly the reason you suspect: you and my brother are attempting something that might better Strategia for decades to come, and you will be seriously impeded without me."

I smile slightly because she's right that we're not as good without her, yet her frank delivery is so Layla that it's charming. "I agree. But why didn't you come with us when we left? I mean, you made it seem like there was no way you would ever leave the Academy."

"Make a sound in the east, then strike in the west," Layla says as she sits perfectly straight in her chair.

I pause. "Professor Liu's mind games class?" I ask, remembering the day Liu introduced the Thirty-Six Stratagems by hanging two ropes in the middle of the room with a flag between them.

"The sixth Stratagem says that the element of surprise is an invaluable tool. Once your enemy has focused his troops in one spot, you gain advantage by attacking a weakly defended location," Layla says, like that clears everything up.

I look over at Matteo, hoping for a simpler explanation of how this relates to our particular situation, but he's busy boiling water with his back to us.

"And so you didn't come with us and you don't want me to tell Ash you're here because you plan on attacking us while we're sleeping?" I say.

Matteo grunts a laugh behind me, but Layla doesn't appreciate my joke.

"Don't be ridiculous," Layla says. "We're going to attack *Jag* in his weak spot."

Matteo returns to the table carrying a tray with a full teapot, three cups and saucers, and some biscuits on it. He places it in the middle of the table.

"What is his weak spot?" I ask, and Layla sighs.

"It depends on our strategy," she says. "Think of it this way—Jag's main concern in any conflict is going to be you and your father. He's going to focus all his energy there. He won't anticipate outside help because no one in their right mind would move against him. This gives him a weakness, one that Matteo and I will exploit."

I glance at Matteo as he pours the tea.

"And how does Ash not knowing play into all of this?" I ask.

"There are a few strategic reasons," Layla says. "But the most important one is the same—his energy will be focused on Jag. He'll be forced to plan and act as though he must succeed alone, without the knowledge that he has help. When he falls short, we'll be there."

Having the element of surprise makes good tactical sense,

and even if I don't understand all the details, I trust Layla. She's the smartest person I know.

"Aarya and Ines are with us," I say.

"Interesting," Layla replies, and she and Matteo share a look. But she doesn't seem overly surprised.

"Did you already know that? Did they tell you?" I ask, wondering if there are more layers of secrecy here that I need to sift through.

"No," Layla says. "But we wondered. They left the Academy with Brendan the day after you and Ash."

"*Brendan?*" I say, and nearly choke on my tea. "You're telling me Brendan's in London—" I stop short, looking up at them. No wonder my dungeon threat actually worked on him in the dining hall. I'm sure Brendan wanted to attack me that day and probably would have if he wouldn't also have been risking his own exit. "But why would he leave the Acad—" I pause. "My dad."

"Your dad?" Layla says. "I don't follow."

I put my teacup down. "My dad is suspected of killing the Regent," I say quickly. "Brendan's stepfather, Arlo? There's a big masquerade ball tonight and we're pretty sure it's to celebrate the new appointee. What are the chances that the new appointee is Brendan?" But no one looks surprised.

"Yes," Layla says. "That's exactly what's happening."

For a moment I don't respond. I look from Layla to Matteo and back again. "Wait, you *know* this? We risked our necks multiple times to find it out and you . . ." I laugh, even though it's absolutely not funny. "Of course you know this. You're *Layla.*"

Layla smiles slightly. "While I appreciate your confidence in me, it's Matteo who deserves the credit."

I wait a beat for someone to explain, but Matteo is silent.

Layla sighs. "Matteo?"

He stares a moment longer like he's resigning himself to once again sharing secrets with me. "In the innermost circle of my Family," Matteo says, his voice reserved, "it's been suggested that it was not actually your father who killed the Regent."

"Of course he didn't, but how do they—" I start, but Matteo gives me a look that makes me swallow the rest of my sentence.

"I do not know the exact details, but something about the assassin's style implied that it might have been . . . Jo," Matteo says.

For a second I sit very still, blinking at him, positive I must have misheard. My aunt Jo?

"Which is a possible explanation for her recent demise," Matteo continues, his voice more sympathetic than I would expect.

I try to swallow, but my throat is too dry. "Wait," I manage, trying desperately to unstick myself from this awful moment in time. "You're saying *my aunt Jo* killed the Lion Regent? Is that even possible?"

"You would know better than we would," Layla says, and they both give me a minute to collect my thoughts.

But I don't need a minute. When Logan told me my dad was suspected of the murder, I knew there was something wrong, that it didn't fit. I don't have the same doubts this time. Despite the fact that I've only recently started thinking of my family as being Strategia, I can more easily picture my aunt taking out the Lion Regent, especially if she had a strong motive.

"We know you weren't previously aware of your family's politics," Layla says, slowly easing me back into the conversation. "But do you have any idea why your aunt may have made such a bold move?"

I look up at Layla, realizing my gaze had drifted to my hands. There is only one answer that feels right. "My mom," I say. "Aunt Jo's been furious about her death for the past eleven years, wouldn't let it go. My dad said it was a car accident, but now that I know what I know . . . it's obvious they didn't tell me the whole truth."

"And so you think the Regent was the one who assassinated her?" Layla asks.

I adjust my position in my chair. "I honestly don't know. But what I can say is that if Aunt Jo had a shot at taking out my mom's killer, there is no doubt in my mind that she would take it."

"Hmmm," Layla says, and she and Matteo look at each other.

"What?" I say. "What don't I know here?"

"It's not that you're wrong," Layla says. "It may very well have been the reason she killed him. It's just that taking out another Family's high-ranking officer is the utmost offense."

"That sounds like Aunt Jo," I say, remembering all her tirades about my dad's Family and her penchant for dramatic gestures. To my surprise, a hint of a smile appears on Matteo's face.

"Still," Layla says, "it's never been done."

I look at her sideways. "You mean in the thousands of years Strategia existed, one Family has never assassinated a high-ranking officer in another? Is that even possible?"

"There have been no assassinations of that kind since the Council of Families was established," Layla says with a weighty emphasis that makes me think I haven't been examining the situation with enough gravity. "It's the golden rule of Strategia internal politics—we do not use force to interfere with another Family. Can you imagine the chaos that would ensue if we did, and the *casualties*? We could easily cause irreparable damage to all of Europe and beyond as a result of a civil war among Families."

I listen to her and frown. "So what does it mean, then, if Aunt Jo killed the Regent?"

"Your father has been accused, at least privately," Layla says. "Although I assume even the few Strategia privy to that information probably don't believe it—it's equivalent to accusing a phantom. So that's the first thing to consider, that Jag is already twisting the Regent's death into a narrative that suits his own purposes. And the next thing to consider is the motivation. I know you said your aunt wanted revenge for her sister's death, and while I understand that's a reason, I am skeptical that it was enough."

"Really? Aunt Jo was . . . well, she was a force to be reckoned with, and she wasn't what I would call a rule-follower," I say, and Matteo snorts, only I can't tell if it's in amusement or disdain.

"I don't think you're understanding," Layla says. "Collectively, we have been able to prevent the assassinations of

global leaders, we dismantle terrorist plots before govern-
ments ever know about them, and we circumvent wars. If we
were using our energy to fight each other instead, all these
missions would be abandoned."

I take a sip of my tea, wishing the hot liquid were more
comforting. "You're right. Despite my aunt's hatred for Jag,
she had a huge heart. I can't imagine she would have risked
that without a very good reason."

"Precisely my point," Layla says, sitting back in her chair
with perfect posture. "Which begs the question . . . what is
actually going on here?"

"Point taken," I say, now not sure myself. I look over at
Matteo. "Is that why your Family is in London, because of
Aunt Jo?"

Matteo hesitates. "My Family is here because something
important is clearly happening and the appointment of a new
Regent has far-reaching political ramifications. Beyond that,
it's none of your concern."

"Look, I get it. You don't like me. I probably wouldn't like
me if I were you, either, but if things are as serious as you say,
then I need to know everything I can. This whole thing is hard
enough as it is," I say.

"Tell me," Matteo says. "Are you here to save your father
or to dismantle the Lions and restore balance to Strategia?"

"Both," I say, meeting his intense look.

"And if you had to choose between the two?" he asks, and
my stomach sinks—I don't need to think about it because I
would choose my dad ten out of ten times.

Matteo doesn't wait for my answer. "That's what I thought.

And that's the problem. The consequences of the Regent's death are already in motion. It doesn't actually matter whether it was Aunt Jo or your father who killed him; there is an opportunity here that hasn't existed in decades, one that's shaken the confidence in Jag's previously untouchable power. But you don't understand that because you weren't raised like we were. And even after you saw the damage Dr. Conner inflicted at the Academy, your goals remain self-serving. So why should I give you information when it will only go to help you do what's best for *you*, not for Strategia?"

For a second I'm stunned into silence. First Aarya yelled at me last night and now Matteo, and the weirdest part is that they agree. My cheeks go hot. I want to answer him, but defending myself right now would only reinforce his opinion of me. Not that I should care. So why do I feel this strange need to prove myself to him?

"The masquerade ball," Layla says, changing the topic. "I'm certain that information was not acquired easily. I understand why it's important to the larger political picture, but what role does it play in your finding your father?"

"I'm not exactly sure," I say, glancing at my cell phone, still embarrassed by what Matteo said. It's 4:36 a.m. "But the gist of it is that my dad's been leaving me clues since I left the Academy, and one of them is apparently located at that ball."

Layla looks startled. "And I take it you four have decided it's a good idea to break into a Lion Family event?"

"It's unfortunately unavoidable," I say, because I've been wondering the same thing—why would my dad send me into a Lion event, of all places?

"And the plan?" Layla asks.

"Still working it out," I say vaguely. "But if you have a phone, or some way I can reach you, I can keep you updated."

"I would say so," Layla says like she's not at all pleased by this development. "I'm almost afraid to ask, but is there anything else I should know?"

There is something comforting about her familiar reaction. I wasn't sure I'd ever see her again, and here she is drinking tea and reprimanding me. "The ball is the main thing. And oh," I say. "The Ferryman is hunting my dad."

Once again Layla and Matteo exchange a look.

"We heard." Layla's expression turns sympathetic. "Matteo and I will do what we can to help."

Matteo averts his eyes, dismissing Layla's attempt to smooth things over.

"But the clock is ticking. We need to be efficient and smart," Layla continues, nearly repeating what her twin said word for word.

The mention of a clock prompts me to look at my phone again: 4:43 a.m. Before I can say anything, Layla nods.

"I know. You have to get back," she says. "Give us your number and keep us updated as the plan for tonight develops. I'm certain you will need us in some capacity."

✳ ✳ ✳

I open the door to the apartment carrying hot chocolates, coffees, and a bag full of breakfast pastries and almost walk straight into Aarya. I let out a small yelp of surprise and barely catch the cardboard drink carrier before it crashes to the floor.

"Geez," Aarya grumbles, but her crankiness instantly drops away when she sees what I'm carrying.

"Hot chocolate?" I offer with a smile, and hand her the bag and the drinks, which she gladly accepts. Despite feeling enlivened by Layla and Matteo's help, I can't stop thinking about what Matteo said about my aunt Jo and about me being selfish. I take off my coat and gloves, pulling the Sunday newspaper I picked up at the coffee shop from under my arm. I hang my coat, ready to find a comfy place to read and eat pastries, but Aarya blocks my path to the living room.

"You decided to get up at *five in the morning* and go to the café?" she says with an assessing look.

I shrug. "Couldn't sleep," I say because it's part of the truth, "and I wanted to get an early start." I grab one of the hot chocolates out of the carrier, take a sip, and step around her.

"Hungry?" I say to Ash as Aarya puts the goodies down on the coffee table.

I plop onto the couch with my drink and the paper in hand, momentarily reminded of Sunday mornings with my dad. When I was little he would give me the funnies, but in recent years we would just trade sections back and forth, reading from one end to the other. Of course the news app on my phone is more comprehensive than the paper, but there was something about the ritual of it that we both enjoyed.

Ash rubs his face and reaches for a coffee, but Aarya eyes me warily.

"So what have you come up with?" she asks.

"Huh?" I say, not sure what she's getting at.

"You couldn't sleep and you wanted to get an early start, so you must have been cycling through new ideas. *What are they?*" she asks, and I can only hope the aggression is a holdover from our conversation last night and that she doesn't suspect more.

Ash looks from me to Aarya and frowns, but when he looks back in my direction there's a glimmer of curiosity in his eyes. I'm one lie away from them knowing I'm hiding something.

I take a sip of my warm drink, buying myself a few seconds. "Well," I say, frantically searching for something I can tell them that will both be believable and distract from whatever signals of deception I'm unconsciously giving off. "I was thinking . . . the Lions accused my dad of killing the Regent, right? And while I know that's untrue, I do wonder if he was involved."

Aarya tilts her head and I can tell that at the very least I've caught her interest. "Go on."

"See, not long before my dad sent me to the Academy, he was making frequent trips to see my aunt Jo—my mother's sister—the one the Lion Family killed shortly after I arrived at the Academy," I say. "I never really questioned it before—well, not in this way, anyway—but now I'm wondering, what if my dad didn't commit the act himself but was still involved in the planning?" And now that I've said it, I wonder how I could have previously missed this.

Ash joins me on the couch with his coffee. "Are you suggesting that it was *your aunt* who assassinated the Regent?"

I look at Ash, coming to terms with what I suspect is the truth. "I am. And I think her death was retaliation." I swallow. "The thing is . . . all this time I've been assuming that the Lions were hunting my family and that's what prompted my dad to send me to the Academy. But I don't think that's exactly accurate. If my dad and my aunt were somehow responsible for taking out the Regent, then it had to have been planned. Which means that my trip to the Academy was also planned. Maybe for *years*." What I don't say is that it's just one more item in a long list of lies from my dad.

"This helps," Ash says. "This is a piece of the puzzle that we were missing—the event that started the whole chain reaction. Now we have some context."

"What are you thinking?" I ask.

"Well, for starters it tells us that the clues he left for you aren't the trail of bread crumbs left by a man in hiding; they've been carefully planned and executed," Ash says, and I can almost see the gears in his head turning. "It explains why he knew Logan's sign was there, and also gave him time to make a negotiation that would have Angus point you to it."

"That makes sense," I say, and while I'm happy to have more information, I'm not thrilled with the revelation that my dad had always planned to leave me behind at the Academy and then make it nearly impossible to follow him.

"If he and your aunt had planned to take out the Regent, there is still the question of *why now?*" Ash says. "Something must have prompted the timing."

Aarya nods, wiping a smear of melted chocolate from her croissant off the corner of her mouth.

"While we don't know why he acted now, we do know

your father must have had an alliance within the Lion Family," Ines says as she enters the living room and grabs a coffee. "He would have needed inside information to successfully plan the Regent assassination."

We all sit there for a few seconds, considering the new development.

"Well, one thing is for sure," Aarya says. "We need to get to work. If your dad planned this for what I'm assuming is *years*, and part of his plan is for us to go to the Lion ball, then we damn well better deliver." She stands. "I'm going to make us a frittata, and then we'll get to it."

Ash sips his coffee, lost in thought, and I unfold the newspaper with a snap, looking for something comforting and familiar more than feeling any desire to read the news. I straighten out the pages, but before I even read the top headline I sit straight up, nearly spilling my drink down my shirt. There on the bottom left-hand side of the page is a photo with a caption under it that reads: *Displaced lions confuse zoo workers.*

"Uh, guys . . . ," I say, and spread the page out on the coffee table in front of me.

Ash immediately moves closer.

"'London Zoo Lion Family Mysteriously Found in the Wrong Habitat,'" I say, reading the headline.

Aarya reappears in the doorway.

I continue reading out loud. "'The much-adored pride of lions at the London Zoo were discovered at eight a.m. on Christmas Day as having swapped habitats with the antelopes. What is baffling the local authorities is that based on footprints, the swap seems to have been orchestrated by a single individual. "One man or woman moving four lions and six antelope alone without injury or incident is nothing if not astounding," says the zoo director. "Even our best animal curator couldn't accomplish such a feat." The local police have reviewed the security cameras but have no clear images of this magical intruder. The animals have been returned to their rightful cages and are healthy and happy, the zoo director assures us, and then jokes that "It's an odd day indeed when the prey supplants the predator."'"

Aarya leans over the coffee table, casting a shadow on the paper, and to my surprise, she starts laughing. "Oh my god, that's brilliant. Tell me that was your father."

I look up, not sure if I find this amusing or further disorienting. "Has to be, right?" I say, figuring if it were Layla and Matteo, they would have said something earlier. "It was timed so the story would run in the Sunday paper, which my dad and I always read together. But what does it mean?"

"Are you kidding? It's a blatant warning to the Lions," Aarya says.

"Obviously," I say. "But what else?"

"The timing," Ash says. "Your father killed the Regent and timed this to coincide with Jag's new appointment."

Brendan, I think, but I don't say it.

I stare at the article. "So then he's trying to provoke Jag."

"Definitely," Aarya agrees. "And clearly he wants it to be public. Well, not *public* public, but Strategia public. He's taking a shot at Jag's reputation, making the point that he's not as untouchable as we all think. Your dad has flair."

Does he, though? It's not that I disagree with Aarya's

assessment, but the person she's describing doesn't sound like my dad.

I reread the short article, looking for some other meaning or something that makes sense to me. But I find nothing and am left once again feeling like the person I thought was my dad is a lie.

Twenty-One

ASH, AARYA, INES, and I sit in the cab silently. I lean against the window, watching the lit-up London streets as we go. I slip my hands in my sweatshirt pockets, still bummed we couldn't bring our coats. Aarya insisted we'd have no place to stash them after sneaking into the hotel—no place we could guarantee that we'd get them back, anyway. I slowly press the buttons on my cell phone in my pocket, typing *On way* into a text message to Layla and Matteo.

I've been updating them all day, piece by piece as the planning came together, an action I initially imagined would be reassuring. But Layla only proceeded to find fault with every strategy. And the whole thing felt odd, like I was a double agent of sorts, erasing all evidence of our texts and not telling Ash, Aarya, and Ines what I was doing.

I keep my hand on the phone, but I can't tell if they've replied because I set it to silent. I chew on the inside of my cheek, and my thoughts drift back to what Matteo said about me being selfish. I want to push against it, denying that it could be true, given the countless risks I've taken in the past month. But I'm also not sure I can argue that my actions had a higher purpose beyond staying alive and protecting my dad.

The cab stops, interrupting my train of thought. We pile out about five blocks from the hotel and I can feel the reassuring pressure of the knife stashed in my boot as I step onto the sidewalk. I gently touch the rope tied to my belt and readjust the backpack on my shoulder, which is full but light, stuffed with my ball gown and mask. The air is unusually biting, given our lack of layers, but no one seems to notice.

Ines and I walk behind Ash and Aarya down the busy London sidewalk populated by a fashionable late-night dinner crowd and upscale bar patrons. Spirits are running high and holiday lights are everywhere. Ever since we exited the cab Ash and Aarya have been arguing about what route to take, which is impressive, considering it already took us an hour to agree on one earlier.

Ines walks casually, like she doesn't have a care in the world, but her eyes are so alert, I wouldn't be surprised if she could describe the last fifty people we've passed from memory. I, too, scan the crowd, looking for the signature hawkish Strategia eyes that are out of place in otherwise relaxed behavior.

It occurs to me how markedly different my life is in this moment. I must have walked down the street with a group of friends a thousand times in Pembrook, laughing and talking. And here I am now, walking with another group of friends, but on my way to sneak into a ball in London where the penalty for getting caught crashing is certain death.

Now only one building away from the hotel on the opposite side of the street, I can see two men dressed as security guards outside the front entrance. One is unusually large, with copper hair, and the other is slender, with a ponytail.

Hawk's crew!

I glance at Ash, who I can tell shares my concern by the worry line in his forehead. As if it wasn't going to be hard enough to sneak into a huge, well-lit, well-guarded property, now we have people who will not only recognize us but threatened that they would hand us over to Jag.

I pull my hoodie up, better shadowing my face, and we cross the street right at the corner of the hotel and far too close to the guards for comfort. Eddie and Willy scan the sidewalk in front of them, taking note of every person nearing the door. Eddie looks in our direction. I loop my arm through Ines's and lean my face on her shoulder, laughing—a casual pose Emily and I often assumed and one that is typically un-Strategia. Eddie looks right past us and we continue down the street running along the side of the hotel, slipping out of his line of sight. I stand up straight once more and Ines gives me a curious nod of approval. And even though I'm fairly certain we went unnoticed, I do a quick glance over my shoulder just to be sure.

The hotel property is sprawling and takes up an entire city block, but the building itself is only about four stories tall. We circle down the side of it, around the back where the hotel presses up against a park with gardens and tall trees, and continue past it and around the other side. All the entrances save the main one are closed, with signs that redirect patrons to the front of the building. For a moment I think maybe we've had a stroke of luck and that there will be fewer guards to navigate around.

"Unfortunate," Ash says. "With Hawk's crew at a singular entrance, it will make it nearly impossible to get out if something goes wrong."

Aarya stares at Ash from under lowered eyebrows. "*That* was Hawk's crew? I guess this is what I get for pairing up with you two against my better judgment."

I slip my hand in my pocket.

Me: *All entrances blocked but front. Need distraction for guards in case we have to run for it.*

And the second I type it, I'm exceedingly grateful Layla decided to follow us.

"I still say it would be simpler to pick one of the locks on the side doors instead of counting on November's climbing skills," Aarya continues, keeping her voice down and giving me a wary look.

Ash shakes his head. "And risk coming face to face with a security guard who is likely guarding the inside of that door? No thanks."

"A guard we could easily knock out with Angels' Dream," Aarya says, bringing up one of the many options we disagreed on earlier.

"Aarya, we already decided," Ines says calmly, the same way you might remind a child to pick up their toys.

Aarya frowns at Ines. "No loyalty, I swear."

And so we retrace our steps to the back of the building where it adjoins the park.

"Well, let's just hope November doesn't screw this up," Aarya adds, but no one responds.

We walk close to the hotel wall, stopping under a balcony leading to a second-story room. From what I can tell from the ground, the lights are out and the curtains are drawn. We take a quick scan of the park to make sure no one is nearby. We all look at each other in silent agreement that this one will do.

"Ready?" Ash says, and I nod.

Ines faces the park, scanning for possible onlookers, and Aarya stands with her arms crossed and a sour expression. She's been resisting me all day, and I have no idea why. Maybe she never got over her suspicion about me being out so early this morning, or maybe she's still pissed that I don't want to rip Jag's head off with my teeth. It's hard to tell.

I grab the white stone of the wall and hoist myself up. There is a fair amount of decorative work and the grooves around each stone are deep enough that climbing the wall is no problem; I could grip these handholds in my sleep.

I wedge my boots on a small ledge, pushing up, and grab the second-floor railing. I get a good hold with both hands and swing my legs over the side, landing silently on the stone balcony. I sweep my eyes over the park below. A group of four twentysomethings, all wearing Santa hats and talking too loudly, walk along one of the park paths. I look below and my friends have shifted to casual poses and appear to be chatting.

The instant the loud group passes, I grab the rope off my belt, tie it securely around the railing with a tight double knot, and drop it down to them. Ash is the first one up and he winks at me.

"Brilliant work," he whispers, and I smile back at him. It feels kind of exhilarating, getting to use my climbing abilities.

Ash pulls out his lock-picking tools, and by the time Aarya and Ines climb up, he's got the door open.

Ines unties the rope from the railing and we all step inside, locking the door behind us. Even in the dark, I can tell that the room is luxurious. There are heavy drapes on the windows, a king-sized bed with a high headboard and a chaise lounge at the foot of it, and an open door leading to an equally lavish sitting room. Suitcases lie open on wooden luggage racks, and in one of them I spot the corner of a masquerade mask. My pulse quickens at the sight of it. *We're in a Strategia's room.* I creep to the door leading into the sitting room and peek through. All is silent, but for how long?

Aarya eyes the suitcase. "Let's get on with it and get the hell out of here," she whispers, and I know she must see the mask, too.

Ash ducks into the sitting room and I head into the bathroom, shutting the door behind me. I take off my backpack and unzip it. The black-and-white tulle skirt explodes out of the opening—I had quite the time compressing it earlier this evening. I pull out the dress and yank off my sweatshirt, tying it securely around my waist. I tuck my gloves into my jean pockets and my hat into my left boot, so as not to crowd the knife in my right boot. I slip the dress over my head and wiggle into the form-fitting black bodice. The tulle is so puffy that it completely conceals my jeans and my tied sweatshirt below.

I grab my phone and unlock it. There is a message from Layla waiting for me.

Layla: *We have you covered. Waiting nearby.*

Me: *In. Won't be able to read responses here on out. Wish us luck.*

It only takes a moment for her to reply.

Layla: *Understood. And it's not luck; it's skill.*

I smile at the text before erasing the thread and shove

the phone into a hidden pocket in my skirt—something Ines added for us to conceal our weapons and the ointment, and a lucky break for me.

I exit the bathroom just as Aarya is helping Ines smooth a wig over her signature red hair. In a matter of minutes, we're all in formal wear, save our boots, and I tie on my black-and-white mask. It covers my entire face except the underside of my nose and my mouth.

Ash returns from the living room wearing a long velvet cape pushed back over one shoulder and a mask that appears to be sculpted out of gold leaf. I stare at him in awe while he collects our backpacks and steps out onto the balcony, tossing them down into a nearby bush.

He closes the sliding balcony door, and the moment the lock clicks into place, muffled voices come from the hallway. Ines runs to the hallway door with fast silent steps. She peers through the peephole and we all stand poised to flee—although climbing down this building covered in copious amounts of tulle would be a good way to break a bone.

Ines turns around. "It's clear," she whispers, and I let out a huge sigh of relief.

She looks back out the peephole and cracks the door. She peers through the opening, looking in both directions. I count to five in my head. Ines turns, nods, and then steps into the hallway. We waste no time in following her. But the moment the door clicks shut behind us, my stomach flips. There's no turning back. We're in a Lion-run Strategia hotel, uninvited, and all the exits are potentially blocked by guards.

We walk down the long hallway at a steady pace, my heart

beating so loudly that I'm surprised Aarya hasn't scolded me for it. Ahead of us is a grand curving staircase, and the closer we get to it, the more I wonder about my dad's clues. Each one has been aimed at me but has ultimately been useless without my Strategia friends to help decode it. Was he trying to protect me by not letting me do this alone? But then again, if he wanted to protect me, wouldn't he just tell me where he was and protect me himself?

We make our way down the stairs toward a large elegant lobby that has a comfortable seating area, a bar, and the entrance to a restaurant. Scattered throughout are masked Strategia in gowns and tuxedos. I want to lift my skirt on the stairs, but I can't risk revealing my boots or, god forbid, the edge of my jeans.

We head toward the bar, scoping out the room as we go. On the far side is a red velvet rope. And in front of the rope is Hawk. I suck in a quick breath and hold it for a few seconds. Even though I'm wearing a mask and know it would be nearly impossible for him to recognize me across the room, I'm unnerved. Ash and I share a glance and I can tell he's thinking what I'm thinking—bad effing luck.

"What?" Aarya hisses as she grabs a spot at the far end of the bar where the drinks come out.

I sit down next to Aarya, but Ines and Ash remain standing.

"The crew leader is at the rope," I say, keeping my voice down.

Hawk greets two guests as they arrive, and they lift their masks. He takes a good look at them while a server offers them a glass of champagne. He gives a quick nod and moves on to ask the next guest to lift her mask.

Aarya stares daggers at Ash. "Care to do anything else to make this harder than it already is? Maybe you want to streak across the room . . . or light a curtain on fire?"

Ash winks at her and leans lazily against the bar. "We knew the crew would be a problem. I'm shocked that you're shocked."

Aarya gives him a withering look.

While some Strategia go straight to the velvet rope, others appear to be in no rush, casually chatting on couches and drinking at tables. And thankfully, there are also some clusters of non-Strategia to use as marks.

I slip my hand in my pocket, searching out the keys on my phone, and type to Layla.

Me: *Entrance problems. Will update when in motion.*

"Far right, four-top," Ash says, and I follow his eyes.

Four non-Strategia men seem to be engrossed in conversation and drinking something of the whisky variety. There are enough empty glasses on the table to indicate they have been consuming a fair amount.

"Agreed," I say. "It'll seem like they naturally drank too much."

Ines nods.

And we wait, scoping out the room for other possible marks to create our diversion. But despite my best efforts, my eyes keep drifting to Hawk, and while I can't hear what he's saying, I'm certain he's memorized the guest list, making him far more organized and savvy than I originally gave him credit for. I eye the champagne server standing next to him. From his uninterested expression and the fact that he keeps checking the clock on the far wall, my bet is that he's not Strategia and is merely a hotel employee.

"What about the champagne guy?" I say, and look at Ash.

"I considered him, but spilling drinks isn't enough to distract someone like Hawk," Ash says.

"It might work if it was part of our larger distraction," Aarya says. "But we would have to get uncomfortably close. How sure are you that he won't recognize you behind those masks?"

"Look," I say. "He's speaking to each person individually. If we arrange it so that you and Ines are in front of us, it might work."

"My vote is yes," Ines says, and we all turn to her. "I can unbalance the server if November can push the drinks toward Aarya."

"No problem," I say. "And if our distraction doesn't work, you can create a stink, Aarya, storm off to the bathroom, and we can regroup."

Aarya smiles. "Creating a stink is what I do best."

"So then we're agreed," Ash says, and we're all quiet, the nervous kind of quiet that happens right before you step onstage or run a race.

Next to Ash, the bartender preps a tray with four glasses and fills them with the same amber-colored alcohol the men at the four-top are drinking.

Me: *Get ready.*

I clasp Ash's hand, passing him the small jar of Drunken Confessions ointment. Ines fluidly shifts her position so that she blocks him from the view of the rest of the room. Ash pulls a toothpick out of his pocket, unscrews the jar lid, and scoops out some of the clear goo. When the bartender turns to replace the alcohol bottle on the shelf, Ash swipes the toothpick along the bottom of the drinks where the glass is thicker and will hide the smudge. I'm assuming it'll also make it less likely for the server to accidentally touch the ointment.

Not a minute passes and a middle-aged woman dressed identically to the champagne server collects the tray with the four drinks. And just as we hoped, she delivers them to the table of non-Strategia men.

We wait while the server removes the plethora of empties. I count the seconds off. Five seconds until the first man grabs his tumbler. Two more seconds before the next does the same. And four seconds after that until the last two join in. At which point the first man leans forward, bracing the table and drooping his head. *Hole in one.* The second man, also losing control over his movements, overgesticulates and knocks the leaning man's glass right off the table. It lands with a loud crash, shattering on the shiny stone floor.

The lobby crowd turns to look, including Hawk, and the server rushes to get something to clean it up with.

The first man tries to stand, clearly annoyed with the second, but he only makes it halfway out of his chair before he grabs the table awkwardly. His weight tips it, sending the remaining glasses sliding into him, and everything crashes to the floor.

"Now," Ines whispers, and we walk at a casual pace toward the velvet rope, pausing briefly to observe the chaos in order to blend with the rest of the room.

We approach the rope, Ines and Aarya side by side and Ash and I behind them. I force myself to relax with each step we take toward Hawk, unclenching my hands and lowering my shoulders.

The table of men has two servers at it, nervously trying to clean up the mess. I hear one of them tell the men that they're cut off, and everyone involved is getting increasingly loud.

"If you'll only follow us . . . ," the male server says.

"I will not!" one of the men replies indignantly. "I'm not done here."

"I'm afraid you are done," says the female server.

In my pocket I type *Now* into my phone and press Send, only hoping that Layla and Matteo succeed in distracting Eddie and Willy out front.

We stop near Hawk, who gives Aarya a quick glance. "Welcome," Hawk says in his scratchy voice, momentarily looking toward the drunken argument. "Please remove your masks and help yourself to a glass of champagne."

"Do you know who I am? Do you know how much money I spend in this hotel?" says one of the men in a booming voice. "You can't kick me out. *I'm not leaving.*" I hear what I think is a chair crash behind me.

Well, there's the truth serum part of the ointment.

"Take your hands off me!" exclaims the man.

Hawk turns his attention back to the altercation, frowning.

Ines reaches for a glass of champagne, pulling it forward quickly and into the lip on the edge of the tray hard enough to unbalance it. The champagne server isn't looking at Ines, he's staring at the stumbling men like everyone else.

"Watch out," Ines says to the server, who immediately attempts to readjust the wobbly tray.

I reach out in the same moment as though I'm trying to help, stepping forward and directly into his path. He trips over my ankle and I reach up, sending the almost-steadied tray flying, crashing into Hawk and soaking him and the hem of Aarya's skirt.

Hawk growls at the server like he might eat him.

"I'm sorry. I don't know what . . . Sorry," the server says, trying to pick broken glasses off the floor.

"Look at my dress!" Aarya says with annoyance, and my heart sinks. She must think we have no chance of getting past this rope.

Hawk takes a handful of fast steps away from us. I hold my breath in hopeful anticipation as he grabs some cloth napkins from an empty table, but as he turns back in our direction, my chest deflates. *Damn it.* Before he can return, though, the argument at the table escalates. I look just in time to see one of the men lose his balance and crash into the male server, knocking them both to the floor.

Hawk pulls his walkie-talkie off his belt. "Eddie," he growls into it. He waits a beat, tries again, but there's no immediate response. And in that moment I'm grateful to Layla. But I also feel a sense of pride, like maybe I'm better at being a Strategia than I originally thought.

"Shit," Hawk says under his breath, and my body tenses. I'm afraid to blink. Hawk turns toward the champagne server. "Leave that and go get one of the security guards from the front entrance."

The young guy stands and for a second I think Hawk is

going to walk back to us. But he doesn't; he heads toward the altercation. We don't waste a second. We step around the rope and slip through the door.

The ballroom is brimming with Strategia. I gulp. There must be more than three hundred people here. First thing I do is search for alternate exits. But unfortunately there is only one other door, above which is a small sign that reads WC in fancy script. I'm fairly certain it stands for water closet, which I'm guessing means it leads to the bathrooms, not an exit; to top it off, it's guarded from the inside. And the windows are the large picture kind that don't open, which means being discovered or causing a scene here would be disastrous.

"How can I help?" Ash asks, breaking my train of thought.

"I'm not sure yet," I say, quickly taking in the details of the room, which is decorated in a winter wonderland theme.

The high ceilings are strewn with white lights, looping into the center and hanging down like sparkly snow. Along the walls there are twinkling white artificial trees; the tables are laid out in all white with silver candelabras and fragile china, and a live band plays Christmas music.

As we walk through the crowd and tables, a platform becomes visible with a single table on it. Perched behind that table like it's a royal court sit three people in matching red-and-gold masks—an old man with silver hair that reaches his shoulders, who I can only assume is Jag; a woman with strawberry-blond hair in an elaborate braid, who must be Rose; and a young guy with a shock of white-blond hair.

I look at Ash, giving him my best expression of shock from behind my mask, and his eyes reflect my surprise. I'm just glad most of my face is covered, because he doesn't seem to realize that I already knew Brendan was here.

"You've got to be kidding me," Aarya says, noticing him, too, and I can't tell if she's happy that she might get a chance to take him out or if she's annoyed to have another obstacle.

As they begin to discuss this development, I look away from my Lion relatives and force myself to study the room.

"Okay, let's see," I say, more to myself than to anyone else. "My dad and I made decorations every year for the masquerade ball. So if I had to guess, whatever we're looking for is connected to the decor."

"Was there a common theme for the decorations you made?" Ash asks, and the conversation about Brendan dies down.

I shake my head. "It changed every year."

"Is there anything here that feels personal or like a coded message?" Aarya asks.

"Maybe the trees," I say. "I mean, I grew up next to a forest and we spent a lot of time in the woods, but there have to be at least forty trees in here and they are pretty uniform. So I'm not sure that's it."

I scour the room, starting at one end and moving strategically to the other, looking for anything that sparks a memory or stands out. But like the trees, most of the decorations aren't unique, just one of many scattered throughout the room. We weave in and out of the tables and I stop at one to get a closer look. The centerpiece for each table is a glass vase filled with white twigs, white flowers, and a branch of pinecones with white-painted tips. And surrounding the glass vase are tea lights and, at this table, a card with the number 32 written on it in calligraphy.

They all stop with me as I stare at the decorations.

"It's not that there aren't things here that are personal," I say. "In fact, there are a ton of things. The fake snow—every single year my dad and I would get hot cocoa and sit outside on the first snowfall of the year. The pinecones—I decorated some in school when I was in third grade with glitter and googly eyes to look like me and my parents. And the trees, like I already said."

They all stare at me.

"Gross," Aarya says, and Ines elbows her. "What?" she says to Ines. "It's ridiculous how sentimental she is."

"I think it's beautiful," Ines says, and there is something almost wistful in her voice.

"Could the message be like your collages?" Ash asks me. "Some combination of all those stories?"

I consider the idea. "My instinct is no," I say. "Those pictures combined in a really specific way. These don't. Not to mention that each of the decorations is replicated all over this room. This is table thirty-two and I would bet there are close to fifty in here with the exact same arrangement. It doesn't make sense that my dad would have us go through fifty tables or trees just to hunt something down."

The band finishes playing their song, but instead of starting another one, they fall silent, and so does the room. Jag stands from behind the table on the platform, lifting his glass of champagne.

"Family and friends," he says in a deep voice. "We are

so pleased you could join us on this special day." His tone is confident and warm and he has a relaxed air about him that makes him easy to watch. I stop momentarily. How can someone so awful be so charismatic?

Jag's mask isn't as concealing as ours, leaving half of his face visible. He has a strong jaw like my dad and the same even hairline. The similarities are unnerving.

My dad places a grilled cheese sandwich and tomato soup on the coffee table in front of me where I sit on the living room floor, surrounded by library books detailing the origins of names by country and mythology, Latin root words, and linguistics.

"Take a break and eat before your food gets cold," he says, sitting down on the couch with a book of his own.

"Mmm-hmm," I say in agreement.

"The name books will be there when you're done," he says, but I can hear the smile in his voice. He's always encouraged me to immerse myself in new subjects, not merely to learn them but to dig deep and pull them apart piece by piece like a mechanic rebuilding an engine.

"It's just so interesting," I say, shoving a bite of soup-dipped grilled cheese in my mouth and keeping my eyes on my book. "They all mean something—last names, first names. All of them. And once you get the hang of it, they're pretty easy to decipher. Ask me a name, any name." But before he can give me one, I start talking again. "Like for instance, your name is English, but it stems from the late Greek Christophoros *and it means 'to bear' or 'to carry,' which makes sense because you've always had a lot of responsibility. People's names tell you something about them."*

My dad puts down his book and listens; he always listens.

"What if people don't know the meaning of their own name—do you think the meaning ceases to be relevant, or does the meaning hold whether they know it or not?" he asks, and I look up from my reading to consider his question.

"I'd have to say"—I pause, reviewing the names I know and the qualities of the people who have them—"they hold. Whether people know it or not, their name says something. Sort of like the difference between the words cinnamon and stink. Cinnamon just sounds happy and brings up an image of something pleasant, whereas stink just . . . stinks." I down a spoonful of tomato soup. "So go ahead, ask me a name."

My dad thinks for a few seconds. "Hamilton," he finally says.

"Hamilton?" I say. "Like American history Alexander Hamilton?"

"Like my father," he says, and for a moment I'm taken aback. He never talks about his family. He told me once that his parents died before I was born and that he was never close with them. When I asked for more information, he just said there was nothing more to tell. I didn't even know that was his dad's name.

"Your dad was named Hamilton?" I ask, curious. "Boy, are you lucky you got Christopher. You could have been Hamilton Junior."

"You have no idea how lucky," he says, and even though he matches my smile, I can tell his heart isn't in it.

"Okay, Hamilton," I repeat. "It's derived from Old English, and hamel in Old English means 'crooked.'"

"Interesting," he says.

"Right?" I say, wholeheartedly agreeing.

Jag sweeps his eyes across the room. "The appointment to Regent is not only a great honor but a great responsibility.

Brendan is young but strong, like I was at his age," he says. Brendan smiles at the praise, but not in the cocky self-confident way he would have at the Academy. This Brendan seems to be more reserved, almost shy.

We all glance at one another, silently confirming the unfortunate reality that Brendan is being appointed. I remember Ash telling me that Jag took over as head of the Family when he was only a teenager, and that everything went sideways from there. I can't imagine that power will look any better on Brendan.

"Of course this appointment comes with a heavy heart after the untimely passing of his stepfather," Jag says, like it's a great tragedy. "But as I always say, one must not lose oneself in sorrow at a time like this, but rely on logic and strategy. . . ."

People around the room nod and Jag clocks their agreement.

"Strategic planning to apprehend the perpetrator of this unforgivable attack, who we believe further insulted our Family by removing a lion from its rightful habitat," Jag says, and the crowd hangs on his every word.

I look at Ash to see if he's thinking what I'm thinking, that my dad intentionally provoked Jag with the zoo prank because he knew Jag wouldn't let it pass without saying something.

"Whoever the criminal is, I assure you that he will be not only eliminated, but made an example of," Jag continues. "We are employing all available resources. And in addition to our own skilled trackers, we've contracted the Ferryman in this sensitive matter."

There are approving murmurs throughout the room. While this is information I already have, it somehow sounds more ominous coming from Jag.

Jag waits for the crowd. "And I am pleased to report that the updates have been most promising. In fact"—he pauses for effect—"we may very well have the culprit in hand *before the end of the evening.*"

Surprise ripples through the room and I find myself frozen. The masked Strategia begin to whisper to one another.

Aarya looks at me with worry in her eyes. If Aarya's worried, it means that wasn't Jag's bravado—my dad is in real and immediate danger.

"Now," Jag says, "let's not spend any more time on this unpleasantness. This is, after all, a celebration." He lifts his champagne glass. "To my grandson, Brendan."

"To Brendan," the crowd echoes, and Jag returns to his seat.

I glance at Ash, my pulse racing, but he's not looking at me, he's looking at the crowd. The band once again starts playing and the room explodes with excited conversation.

"November," Aarya says with insistence, and I turn toward her. "Now. You need to find that message from your father *now.*" She nods in the direction of the door. Hawk stands inside it, scouring the party guests like he's looking for something. And I'm willing to bet the something he's looking for is me.

My breath comes fast and my mind spins, making it harder to concentrate. I scan the decorations again, searching for anything that might spark recognition. But they appear as uniform as they did a few minutes ago. I want to cry out of frustration. Everywhere I look is a dead end. The crowd thins a bit behind us, and Aarya pushes us farther into the center of the room and away from Hawk.

"November," Aarya says again with emphasis.

"I know," I say, matching her urgency, trying to clear my thoughts of panic.

"Well, whether you know or not, we need to get out of here," she says.

"Enough, Aarya. You're not helping," Ash says.

"Helping? I'm trying to *keep us alive*," Aarya says.

"Don't focus on the room, focus on what you know," Ines says, and I turn to her. "You told us you used to make party decorations with your father, no? What exactly did you do?"

I consider Ines's question, forcing myself not to look at the surrounding threats. "We built them from scratch. We'd go to the art supply store and a hardware store and spend a good couple of weeks during the summer constructing them," I say.

"Let's start with that. Most of these decorations aren't handmade," Ines says, and I realize she's right. "Arguably nothing in this room was crafted except the centerpieces on the tables."

Ash nods his agreement. "And in those centerpieces, the most handcrafted item is the branch with the pinecones— the tips were painted white and they had to be glued onto the branch," he offers, and before he even finishes speaking, I'm looking at the centerpieces, hopeful.

"So, okay, sentimental pinecones," Aarya says with urgency, telling me we're just about out of time. "Let's start looking."

We weave in and out of the tables, subtly inspecting the pinecones in each vase as we go. But each table has decorations like the one before it—one branch, four pinecones, and no message. My stomach twists and my chest tightens. My eyes flit nervously to Hawk. If we're wrong about these pinecones, there's no time to make a second guess.

Once again the band stops, only this time it's Rose who stands. "If everyone will please take their seats, the serving staff will bring in dinner," she says, and her delivery is cold, lacking the charisma that came so easily to her father. "Your invitation included your seating assignment. However, if you are unsure which table number is yours, please consult the gentleman at the entrance." She gestures toward Hawk. "Enjoy."

"Oh, shit," I say, and we all share a look. We are about to become blaringly obvious the moment people sit down.

"If we're lucky there will be openings at one or more of the tables," Ash says, and I can hear the apology in his voice. "But getting into them without being noticed is unlikely. I'm sorry, November, it's time for us to go."

I fight back panic. "The Ferryman is closing in on my dad—*tonight*. There's no way I can leave when we're this close."

"Finding the message isn't worth being killed," Ash says when I don't move.

I hesitate for a moment longer, searching for any argument that we should stay. But as much as I hate it, I know Ash is right—there's no finding my dad if Jag gets ahold of us.

Aarya eyes Hawk. "We're not getting back through that door, not without creating a scene."

"We'll have to risk the bathrooms," Ash says, and Ines nods her agreement, but I don't ask them what they mean because all my concentration is still on the pinecones.

Aarya leads the way to the door with the WC sign above it and the large security guard. We pass tables twenty-two and twenty-three, which I scour with unabashed hope. But like all the other centerpieces, there is nothing unique about the pinecones. I feel like screaming, I'm so mad at myself, at my dad, and at the situation in general.

Every step we take toward the door feels like a failure.

"November," Ash says when I lag by a step.

"Fifty tables, Ash, and we only looked at fifteen of them," I say. "Why on earth would my dad leave us that many tables to search? He could have at least left me the table number in the last clue." And as soon as I say it, I stop walking and look up at Ash with new determination. "Ash, when was the date of that historic ball from Logan's sign? The *Bal des Ardents.*" My words are fast.

Ash stops, too, and his eyebrows momentarily dip. "The year was 1393." He pauses. "I want to say January?"

"We will never exit this room," Aarya says, like maybe we don't understand the gravity of getting caught, "if we don't *walk toward the door.*"

"Ines, what was the date of *Bal des Ardents*?" Ash says, ignoring Aarya.

"January twenty-eighth, 1393," Ines replies, and recognition of the missing clue sparks in her eyes.

"So table twenty-eight," Ash says.

"Or table one," I say, "for January," and as the words leave my mouth, I realize my mistake. "Go. I'll catch up."

I turn, immediately walking toward the tables, not asking them to come with me—with more than half the crowd seated, it's a risk I don't expect them to take.

If one is for January, then eleven is for November.

But as I near the tables, it occurs to me that I can't inspect the pinecones in front of the dinner crowd. And I don't have

312

a plan for taking the pinecone branch out of the arrangement. I'm going to look like a complete nutter or like I'm up to something. I press my nails into my palm. *Think, November, this is your only shot.*

I'm so focused on getting to table eleven that I accidentally bump into a Strategia woman holding a glass of champagne, almost knocking it out of her hand.

"Pardon," I say in my best imitation of a proper Layla, and I wobble my step as I move away from her. "I think I've had a few too many glasses myself," I say with a smile, quickly explaining away my un-Strategia-like clumsiness.

"That's quite all right," she says, like she doesn't mean it, and before she can scrutinize me too closely, I turn and zigzag through the tables.

And it occurs to me, if that woman will accept a claim of drunkenness, maybe others will, too. After all, this is a celebration and there appear to be copious amounts of alcohol. I stop abruptly in front of table eleven, which is already three-quarters full.

"Good ol' table twenty-one," I say, hiccupping and plopping sloppily down in a chair that has a woman's scarf on it.

The man next to me frowns disapprovingly. "This is table eleven," he says. "And you're in my wife's seat."

"Oh my goodness gracious," I say, ignoring him. "Have you ever seen such a lovely centerpiece?" I flick a decorative branch with my pointer finger. "It's just"—another hiccup escapes in what I consider a damn good impression of myself drinking whisky—"beaufitul, beautitul, feautibul."

"Please do forgive us," Ash's voice says behind me, and I

lean back, nearly falling out of my chair. I grab the table for support. "We went to the bar a little too early this evening," he says, taking my arm to help me stand.

I wobble and swipe the branch with the pinecones. "You're not getting away from me that easily, gorgeous," I say to the branch, and pause as though it's speaking back to me. "No! You flirt!" I pause again. "Oh, all right, but *only one . . .* ," and then I press the pinecone into the man's cheek and make a kissing sound. His face looks so shocked that I don't need to concoct a laugh. The one that erupts from my mouth is real.

Ash immediately escorts me away, shooting an apologetic look over his shoulder, and I make a show of stumbling as I hug my pinecone branch. I resist looking up at Brendan or back at Hawk. Each step we take through the tables feels like it could be our last.

A few people take note of us, and I hiccup as I pass, leaning my weight on Ash as we go. *Just let us get out of this room. Twenty more feet and we're in the clear.* As we reach the end of the tables, I get a good look at Aarya and Ines. They haven't left, but they are standing awfully close to the exit.

As we approach, I realize Aarya isn't looking at us but past us and across the room, and I can tell by her expression that she doesn't like what she sees.

"Hawk's looking this way," she says, and it takes all my self-control not to make a run for it.

Instead, we walk at a reasonable pace to the door, me wobbling and laughing.

"I'm correct in assuming this is the way to the loo?" Ines says to the guard as though she owned the place, and the confidence in her voice surprises me.

He nods, examining each one of us and pausing when he gets to me and the branch I'm clutching. He tilts his head, unsure, like he might tell me to leave it behind. My heart pounds against my ribs and I do the only thing I can think of in that moment. I lick it. I lick the branch from bottom to top, because even children know that no one wants to touch something someone else licked.

The guard narrows his eyes and Ash steadies me as I wobble.

"Are you going to open the door?" Aarya says, impatient, daring the guard to object. "Or are you merely decorative, in which case, *step aside.*"

The guard grumbles under his breath at Aarya's rudeness, but her challenge works and he opens the door.

Ines nods a thank-you and Ash helps me out of the room. The minute the door closes behind us, we pause for a fraction of a second to examine the empty hall ending in two doors. There are no turns leading back to the lobby, no windows to climb out of; there is *no way out.*

I look at Ash, my eyes widening. "Please tell me we didn't just trap ourselves."

But he's not looking at me, he's walking and so are the others. "Not sure yet."

I grip the branch a bit tighter, as though I were protecting it from an unseen threat, and follow them to the end of the hall.

Aarya opens the door to the women's room and Ines and I follow her. She quickly bends down, checking underneath the stalls, and opens the door again, beckoning Ash in. He locks it behind him.

He looks at the bathroom like he's planning a battle. "No windows."

"Not a one," Aarya says. "And despite my applause-worthy work with that guard, I'd say we have about ten minutes before he comes back here looking for us."

I scan the room, my eyes falling on a vent near the ceiling. "Don't commercial buildings have huge heating and cooling vents? Could we maybe—"

"That only works in the movies," Aarya says.

"While some HVACs might be large enough to fit us, if we attempted to crawl through it, we would make an untold amount of noise," Ash explains.

"So what exactly are we—" I start, but stop as I realize they're now staring up. I would stammer about how we're not actually going to climb through the ceiling, but of course we are. It makes more sense than any other route right now. And suddenly I'm reminded of something Professor Basurto said during my first tree-climbing class. *There's my favorite use of trees—evasion. They are the perfect escape route because they offer unpredictable terrain.* While this isn't a tree, it follows the same basic principle of evasion by using the things around you in unusual ways.

Ash carries over a fancy garbage can that has a small hole in the top and a wide lip. He climbs on top of it and pushes aside one of the ceiling tiles.

He sticks his head up into the ceiling. "It's wide enough," he says, and the moment he says so, Aarya and Ines start unzipping their dresses.

"Unless you want your skirt to get caught on some wiring

and potentially plummet through the ceiling, I suggest you change *now,*" Aarya says, and I don't waste a moment.

Ash pulls off his black-and-gold cape and tosses it into the ceiling with a light thud, climbing up after it. I yank my skirt over my head, and as it hits the floor, Aarya scoops it up, climbs onto the garbage can, and hands all three of our dresses and masks up to Ash. I can hear them hit the bathroom ceiling in various places as he throws them, which I suppose makes more sense than trying to drag them behind us.

I readjust my sweatshirt, placing my phone in my pocket and checking my boot dagger. Ines glances nervously at the door and it occurs to me that it's not only the guard we have to worry about, it's the other Strategia.

Aarya pulls herself up into the ceiling and Ash pops his head down. "Ines, you next, since November is the tallest."

The idea of being the last one in the bathroom hits me like a jolt of electricity. Ines quickly climbs the garbage can and I look over my shoulder at the door like it might bite me. She reaches out to take the pinecone branch and I reluctantly hand it over.

"Replace the garbage can in its original position," Ash says, speaking quickly, and the instant Ines's legs lift off it I pull it back by the wall.

"Now unlock the door and check the hall," Ash continues, and the urgency in his voice tells me he dislikes me being the last one in the bathroom more than I do. "If all is clear, leave it unlocked and come over to me." Ash positions himself so that his arms hang down into the room. "With a good jump, I should be able to pull you—" Ash stops talking and gives me a sharp look.

Women's voices spill into the outside hallway, and there's the muffled sound of a door closing behind them.

"Leave it locked," Ash says.

"Don't you dare leave it locked," Aarya snaps back.

"Now, November, *jump now*," Ash says in a commanding whisper, but I'm already running for the bathroom door.

Aarya's right. Ash is trying to protect me, but if I leave it locked, the women will instantly know something's wrong, and the guards will be after us in a minute, completely ruining our head start. I turn the lock and sprint toward Ash, launching myself into the air and grabbing his arms above his elbows.

He pulls me hard, sliding me into the narrow space along a metal beam so fast that I scrape my stomach. I yank my legs up, lightly kicking a ceiling tile, before finding a beam to brace myself on. The door cracks and Aarya slides the missing ceiling tile back into place, dropping it the last half inch so slowly that I hold my breath. And we all fall into complete silence. Ash continues to hold one of my hands as I balance on my stomach on the thin support beam. He pulls out his phone and uses the faint glow from the screen to show me the structure of the dropped ceiling.

The metal beams form a grid of two-foot squares, and there are only a handful of inches of clearance above my head, making the only option for forward motion an army crawl on my stomach. To my far left is a wide metal tube used for heating and cooling that is probably the reason we have as much space as we do. And there are tangles of wires running alongside it.

Ash points forward in the soft glow of his phone, which to my relief has us moving away from the ballroom and not over it. Aarya gives him a thumbs-up and we slowly and methodically crawl in the direction of Ash's dim phone screen.

My elbows and knees press into the metal as we scooch along and I'm certain we're all going to have bruises tomorrow. We move as fast as we can while still remaining silent, and I look over at Ines, who is carrying the pinecone branch in her teeth. We're only a short distance along when Ash holds up his hand, telling us to pause. He lifts the corner of a tile and peers beneath it for a split second. He points to his right, slightly changing our direction, and we follow along behind him.

Ash pauses again, lifting up the corner of another tile, and this time I hear a group of adults recapping their evening at a gala and laughing. Ash waits, continuing to peer down through the sliver of space. I hear the ding of an elevator, and as the doors close, the chatter is abruptly cut off. Ash holds up his fingers, counting off—*three, two, one.* The instant his last finger falls he pushes the tile aside, grabs the metal support beam, and swings himself down. I'm next, and by the time my feet hit the ground Ash is already three doors down and pressing the button for the elevator.

Ines drops with Aarya right behind her. The elevator doors open and we fly inside the empty space. Ash pushes the second-floor button, and as the doors close behind us, Ines offers me the branch, which I gladly accept. The air between us is tense with the fear that the guard has likely checked for us by now and found us missing. None of us says a word as the elevator climbs and the doors reopen.

We step out, do a fast look both ways down the hall, check

the room numbers, and reorient ourselves. No one has to tell us to hurry, we all just start running, taking a corner faster than is safe, down the hall and to the room we changed in. Aarya does a quick knock on the door. She presses her ear up against it and, after three grueling seconds, concludes that no one is inside. Ash whips out his lock-picking tools, and the instant it clicks open, we pile in.

We run through the living room and bedroom and out onto the balcony. Ash relocks the balcony door, using his tools, and I tie the rope. One by one they climb down. As soon as Ines lands on the ground, I toss the branch gently down to her and untie the rope. I swing my legs over the balcony and waste no time grabbing hold of the decorative masonry. I work myself three-quarters of the way down and jump the last few feet into the grass.

Ash hands me my backpack, which he retrieved from the bushes, and I shove the branch into it as we all book it out of the park. When we're three blocks away without any obvious pursuers, Aarya looks at me and her serious expression melts into a smirk.

"You're absolutely mental, you know that? The way you licked that branch . . ." She laughs. "I always thought you had some quirk, but that was brilliant."

"You didn't see her make the pinecone kiss the man at the table. . . . I'll never forget his look of utter shock and horror," Ash says with a grin.

And now that we're on the sidewalk hailing a taxi with the branch in my hand and no Hawk staring us down, I allow myself a laugh, too.

Twenty-Two

WE ALL SIT in Aarya's living room and I unzip my backpack, pulling out the branch. I run my fingers over it, humming with anxious anticipation. It has four pinecones, all identical and all superglued to the branch. I take my knife from my boot and begin to cut the glue, easily popping off the first cone.

I examine the bottom of it, pulling at the remaining glue. I inspect each of the scales for anomalies and look at the branch, but there is nothing there but pinecone and wood. So I start on the next one, which proves much the same.

"Anything?" Aarya asks impatiently.

I shake my head, removing the third pinecone and examining it carefully. But once again, there is nothing special about it, and no message from my dad. *What if I got it wrong? What if it wasn't table number eleven, or if it was, but the clue wasn't the pinecones?* I hold the fourth cone in my hand, knife poised to cut it off.

"I would move faster if I were you," Aarya says. "Or the Ferryman might very well kill your father while you're being precious about those pinecones."

Ash gives Aarya a sharp look and Ines shakes her head.

"What? I'm only stating the obvious," Aarya continues.

"If it's obvious, then you don't need to state it," Ash says.

But Aarya only shrugs. "Testy, testy."

I cut the fourth pinecone off, turning it over. The wood beneath it is smooth and normal. But as I pull off the superglue on the base of the cone, my face lights up. The bottom of the pinecone is hollowed out and inside is a small rolled-up piece of paper.

I tip it into my palm and immediately unroll it. Written on the paper in my dad's handwriting is a message. I read aloud:

> We're taking to the street in treason
> Welcome to the first Death Season
> It's time to make a change, and we've picked a day
> The head Lion we will slay

My mind races. "A rhyme?" I say, confused.

I'm silent for a beat and Aarya taps her fingers on the armchair. "Out loud, November, say what you're thinking *out loud*."

I shake my head. "I'm just . . . I've never heard my dad recite a rhyme in my life, much less write one."

Ash looks at the paper with me.

"Your nonrhyming father aside, we need to decipher the meaning," Aarya says, and leans forward with a curious look, like she would take the paper from my hand if she could. "It's a threat to Jag, that's for certain. But clearly that's not all. If it matches the other clues he's left, then you should be able to understand it."

"November?" Ash says.

I stare at the paper, hyperaware of the small time window and the insurmountable pressure. Nothing immediately jumps out at me, and so I read it again, but the words just swim on the page like nonsense. I huff. "Why is he making me chase clues about him over two damn continents?" I say, more to myself than to them. "Here I am trying to understand some absurd rhyme when I should be warning him that the Ferryman is closing in."

Aarya grunts. "Are you kidding? If it were my dad, it would have been five continents, only to end up back where I started . . . annoyed."

"My dad isn't like most Strategia," I say reflexively.

"Are you sure?" Aarya says in a tone that tells me she has her doubts. "Because testing children in frustrating and uncomfortable ways is about as Strategia-like as a parent gets. And I'm sorry to burst your rosy bubble, but he sent you to a Lion property and into a celebration hosted by *Jag*, of all people. He's not exactly trying to keep you safe."

I open my mouth to argue with her, angry that she would even suggest such a thing. The choices my dad's made my entire life have been about keeping me safe. He loves me. He's doing this *for me*. But given the recent chain of events, I'm also not sure she's wrong.

"Let's just go out on a limb here and suppose that November knows her father better than you do, Aarya, and give her a minute to digest the message," Ash says.

"Oooh, please don't use *sarcasm* on me, Ashai," Aarya says with overblown drama. "How will I ever go on?"

"With the same psychotic clown routine you've been using for years," Ash says.

"Rawwwrr," she says, and slashes her fingers at him like a large cat.

But I'm barely listening because I'm staring at the message, reading it repeatedly, not absorbing the words and my mind drawing a giant blank. I exhale in frustration. *Stop it. Get control of yourself. It's just like learning to fence. The more emotional you get, the more ineffectual you'll be.*

I elongate my breaths, slowing my heart rate and rolling back my shoulders. And I look at the message again. I'll break it down in pieces, translate it, write it backward—whatever I need to in order to make sense of it.

"Okay," I say. "What I've been doing so far isn't working, so I'm going to think this through out loud. Jump in if you notice anything, 'cause right now I'm just spinning my wheels."

Aarya puts her hand on her chest, looking aghast. "As if you thought I would keep my opinions to myself and deprive you all of my musings."

I look from the paper to Ash, ignoring Aarya. "What we know is that every clue so far has required both me and Ash to decode, so I don't imagine that this one is any different. There are probably things in here that you all will know and I won't." I clear my throat. "Let's see . . . the first bit reads: *We're taking to the street in treason.*" I pause. "On this part, I've got nothing. That doesn't even sound like something my dad would say, to be honest." I look up at them to see if they have any input, but no one says a word. "Then he writes: *Welcome to the first Death Season.* What's weird about this is that he did say 'death season' to me once and only once, when I was six."

"Would he expect you to remember that?" Ash says.

"Actually, yeah," I reply. "It's part of a story we've told

dozens of times. And . . . hang on . . . you know what?" I say, feeling a glimmer of hope. "*It's time to make a change, and we've picked a day* could also be a variation of that story." I read the next line. "But *The head Lion we will slay* has no meaning to me beyond the obvious killing-Jag connotations."

"A code based on personal experiences," Ash says. "That fits the pattern."

"It definitely does," I agree.

"So let's hear it, Ember," Aarya says. "When did your dad say those things to you?"

I raise a wary eyebrow at the nickname. "Okay, so, my mom died in October the year I turned six," I say. "By the time early December rolled around, there was none of our usual cheer. Everything felt . . . wrong."

Ines gives me a sympathetic look, but Aarya looks like she wishes I would get on with it.

"Then one evening," I continue, "my dad came into my room with a pile of those holiday magazines . . . did you have those? The ones where everyone is wearing terrible Christmas sweaters and looking pristine while ice-skating?"

Ines shakes her head.

"Well, anyway, he came in and dumped the magazines onto my bed and told me to sit up. He said that winter was always our family's favorite season and that he was going to be damned if it was going to transform from one of the happiest times of year to the death season. He said we were going to treat that winter as the first winter."

"So the 'death season' could translate to winter," Ash says.

"Right," I say, feeling more confident. "He said we would treat it as the first winter and that it was time to make a change.

He told me to pick a day, any day in December, and we would start a new tradition, something that was just ours, that had nothing to do with the years before. So I chose the twentieth."

"Hmmm," Aarya says, like she's considering the whole thing. "Winter and December twentieth."

"The weird part is that it's five days past that date," I say. "And December twentieth is obviously in winter, so why the redundancy?"

"Unless the December part isn't necessary," Ines says, and I look at her.

"How so?" I say.

"Your story said to pick a day, right? And you picked the twentieth. So what if it's winter and the number twenty?" she says. "Like in, for instance, an address."

My eyes widen. Could this really be the clue I've been waiting for all along? "Ines, I think you might be a genius."

Ash grabs the atlas of the UK and spreads it out on the table. He flips to a map of London and we all crowd around it.

It only takes a few seconds before Ash plunks his finger down. "Found it. Winter Street."

"And Winter Avenue," Aarya says, pointing to the complete opposite side of the city.

For a brief second we're quiet.

"*We're taking to the* street *in treason*," Ash and I both say at the same time.

"Well then," Aarya says, grinning. "Twenty Winter Street it is."

"Or One Winter Street," I say, "considering the rhyme says *first Death Season*. It could be One Winter Street, apartment number twenty, for instance."

Aarya gives me a look that almost appears to be respect. "Yes, yes it could."

"But what about the last line?" I ask.

"If I had to take a guess," Ash says before Aarya can jump in, "it was designed to look like a threat, in case anyone else found it. It's actually a brilliant code."

"An address," I repeat, and stand, itching to get to it. I need to tell Layla.

Aarya is already up, checking the weapons in her boots and on her belt. "While I understand that we have a seriously limited time constraint to find your dad, I just want to say that it's a terrible idea to go to an address that the Ferryman may or may not know about without staking it out first."

"If you wanted to be safe, Aarya, you should have stayed home," Ash says, repeating her comment from our text conversation.

I grab my coat and gloves and toss Ash his. And in less than a minute we're out the door.

Ash drives through the streets of London, and I sit up front with him, tapping on my knee, silently repeating my hopes that we'll find my dad and that this isn't just the location of yet another clue. Here we are racing to beat the Ferryman, and I can't even be certain we're headed toward my dad. If I don't see another clue for ten years it will be too soon.

Ash looks over at me, periodically reading my face. "Something we should know?" he asks.

I shake my head. "Not exactly. It's just . . . that message

from my dad . . . it . . ." I look over at Ash. "It was a rhyme. My dad doesn't rhyme," I say, repeating my objection from earlier.

"Apparently he does," Aarya says from the backseat.

"Are you thinking the message was altered? That it wasn't from him?" Ash asks, ignoring Aarya.

"No. It was his handwriting," I say. "And it follows the patterns of the other clues he's left us. It's just that all of a sudden, after *seventeen years* of raising me in a small town away from Strategia, talking to me in non-Strategia ways, and teaching me non-Strategia values, he suddenly does a one-eighty."

"Didn't your dad also lie to you your whole life?" Aarya says, which earns her a disapproving look from Ash through the rearview mirror.

"He did," I say. "And I'm learning to accept that, even though I don't like it. But sending me to Logan's and to that Lion ball is different. Why would he willingly put me in danger . . . to what, test me? Everything in me tells me he wouldn't do that, yet here we are with an address that he could easily have hidden in the tree outside my house instead of in a Lion event. What kind of a parent would do something like that to their child?"

"Mine," Ash and Aarya say at the same time, and it puts the kibosh on my rant.

"I'm sorry," I say. "I didn't mean—"

"You did and it's fine," Ash says. "You're right that Strategia parents aren't as warm or cuddly as other people's parents. But they have a level of responsibility that other parents don't. They know their children will grow up to stop disasters, to thwart attacks, to sidestep wars—and they do what they need to in order to get us prepared. When you're looking out for everyone, there are always personal sacrifices. Strategia aren't perfect."

"Speak for yourself," Aarya says.

I nod because I'm not sure what to say. Ash's point is absolutely fair, and from a nonemotional standpoint that logic makes perfect sense. But I'm not coming from a nonemotional standpoint and I don't want to. I want my dad—the one I've always had, the one who loves me so much he would risk everything to keep me safe.

Ash slows and I spot the sign for Winter Street. We pass a restaurant cleaning up for the night and a closed chocolatier's with the number 6 on the awning. And the instant Ash puts the car in park, I'm out the door.

I walk quickly to a brick apartment building with white trim, bay windows, and a bronze number 1. It only takes a few seconds for Ash, Aarya, and Ines to join me. We don't discuss it; we just casually walk up to the door, and Ash pulls out his lock-picking tools as though they were keys. I stand next to him, blocking him from the view of any pedestrians, and in a couple of seconds we're inside.

The lobby is modest but clean, with mailboxes near the entrance and a flight of stairs with a polished wooden railing. We walk toward the staircase at an easy pace, avoiding any movements that might signal we're out of place here. And we make our way steadily up two flights, where the apartment numbers begin with twos.

Three doors down is apartment number twenty and my heart pounds furiously as we close the short distance. I take a hopeful breath, raise my hand, and knock. Four seconds pass. I knock again. Still nothing.

Please let my dad be here. Please.

I look at Ash and he pulls out his lock-picking tools,

slipping them into the keyhole. There is the familiar click, and he cracks the door an inch. He peers through the opening, but instead of taking his time assessing the inside like I would have imagined, he opens the door wide.

For a split second I try to convince myself that it's because he sees my dad, but in my gut I know that's wrong. And the instant I lay eyes on the room, I panic. The living room is a mess—furniture overturned, glass on the floor, and *blood*.

I rush into the room. "Dad!" I call out, but there's no answer.

Beside me, Ash has his knife drawn and Ines is clutching a blow dart. But I can't think about weapons right now. All I can think is that there is blood on the floor that belongs to someone, and I hope more than anything that someone isn't my dad.

I race into the bedroom, which is disconcertingly tidy, with a quilt folded at the bottom of the bed and my dad's plaid duffel bag, which matches my own, sitting on the floor next to an armoire. My heart sinks. "No," I say, backing out of the room.

Ash touches my arm. "November—"

But I pull away. "I'm not . . . This is not . . . No," I say, trying to unknow this horror.

I walk back toward the living room, but Ash blocks my path. "Why are you . . . move, Ash," I say.

"I need you to listen to me," he says, his voice demanding my attention. "Whatever happened here happened not long ago."

I stare at him, trying to take meaning from what he's saying, but all I can think about is the blood splatter in the living room.

"Which means that we may not have very much time here,"

he continues, and his look is hard and serious, not soft and comforting like a non-Strategia's would be. "The Lions will be coming back to scrub this place clean and go through your father's things. This is our only chance to search the apartment ourselves and we need your help. You're the only one who would know if your dad left you something."

The instant Ash suggests it, some of the emotional fog clears.

"Right," I say, my voice tight. "I understand."

Ash steps out of my way after giving me an assessing look and we move back into the living room.

Ines is bending down near the floor, inspecting a few drops of blood on the wood. "I would say this happened no more than an hour ago," she says. "The blood is still fresh."

"No wonder Jag gave that speech," Aarya says, walking around the room, taking in all of the toppled furniture. "The Ferryman was probably en route as he spoke." She turns from one side to the next and chops her hand in the air, like she's simulating the altercation. "If I had to guess, though, the Ferryman wasn't alone. I would say that there were three or four people in this fight, based on the wreckage and the locations of the blood."

Ines nods her agreement.

I walk through the living room, fighting the urge to break down, and scour it for anything that might be personal or that my dad might have left for me to find. There are a coffee table and a couch with a charcoal-gray throw in front of a fireplace, two overturned chairs and a broken table next to the window, and a bookshelf with books scattered on the floor. The problem is that everything in the room is bland; there's nothing that reminds me of Pembrook or that feels personal in any way.

Aarya and Ines systematically inspect the apartment, flipping through the pages of the books and checking the kitchen drawers for false bottoms. Ash stands by the window, peering beyond the curtains down the street. I can only assume he's keeping watch for Lion assassins.

"Anything?" he asks after a couple of minutes.

"A big fat nothing," Aarya says, and I nod in agreement.

"I'm going to check the bedroom," I say as I move toward it, remembering the day at my house when I was certain Ash wouldn't find anything in there. And to my surprise, Ines follows me in.

"How can I help?" she says.

"The quilt," I say. "At my house there was a message in one of the seams."

And she immediately goes to work. I pick up my dad's duffel bag. *Plaid blanket, plaid duffel bag—it feels like an obvious association. Plus, no one but me would know that we have matching bags.*

I go over the outside of the duffel bag with my fingers, checking the seams and the fabric for any possible bumps, but find nothing. I open the bag and it's empty, with only the faintest whiff of my dad's peppermint aftershave remaining. I press my lips together and shake my head, forcing myself to focus. And then I see it—inside the side pocket is my dad's favorite whittling knife with the handle shaped like a wolf.

I pull it out and flip it open, but there's nothing there but the blade. My heart sinks—what if he didn't have time to leave me a message? I slip the blade into my boot, unwilling to leave it behind for the Lions to find, and I move to the armoire. I pull the doors open and inside hang simple black and dark gray clothes, exactly what you would expect from a Strategia wardrobe. I flip through the shirts and pants, running my hands over the pockets and the cuffs, looking for anything that might be out of place.

I pull the last pair of pants aside and on the final hanger is my dad's gray wool scarf—actually two of my dad's gray wool scarves. I frown. He's worn this scarf through my entire childhood and now I come to find out that it's not even special—there are two. I grab the fabric of the first one, running my fingers along it. At the very bottom is a frayed edge. I instantly have a flashback to the game my mom used to play with me—the one where she would make me distinguish between two seemingly identical objects.

"November?" Ines says, now staring at me.

"I think"—my throat is suddenly parched—"this is my mom's." I pull it off the hanger, holding it close to my body. "I just don't know why it would be . . ." I stop, my fingers finding the tag and a small bump inside the fabric.

I separate the tag fabric and sure enough, folded inside is a small piece of paper with my dad's handwriting.

"Got it!" I say, and Ines smiles.

She quickly folds the blanket exactly as it was when we came in. I wrap my mom's scarf around my neck and slip the note in my pocket. I close the armoire doors and zip the duffel bag, placing it where I found it. In a flash we're all out the door, down the stairs, and walking to the car.

I stick my hand in my pocket to text Layla.

Me: *Dad captured. Found note.*

We jump in the car and Ash pulls away from the curb.

"Okay, let's hear it," Aarya says from the backseat.

I take the small piece of paper out of my pocket, unfolding it. Unlike the other notes where the handwriting is neat, this one appears to have been written quickly. Did my dad know he was in trouble when he wrote it?

I read aloud:

The tall bouncer at the pub also guards the Lion estate.
He goes there directly after his shift at 2 a.m.
I love you, my sweet girl.

I stare at the last line. While I know it's not the important part of the message, I read it over and over, swallowing back the emotion that threatens to come.

Aarya whistles. "I don't know whether this is cause for celebration or the worst thing I've ever heard."

"The Lion estate," I say. "That's Jag's house, right?"

"Yes," Ash says, stopping at a light. "But a Family estate is more than a house. A number of Family members live there in addition to the head family, guards, and staff. The properties are large, with meeting rooms, a great hall, and a dungeon."

My heart races. *A dungeon.* "And the Lion estate is where you think the Ferryman took my dad?" I ask.

"Without a doubt," Aarya says. "But a Family estate isn't just something you sneak into. We could spend weeks planning to break into one with a large crew and it still might not be enough time to do it properly."

I nod. "I don't expect you to come with—"

"I'm coming," Ines says, and I turn to her in surprise. "It's half past midnight. If we head to the pub now, we'll arrive in time to track that bouncer."

"You want to go *tonight*?" Aarya says in disbelief, staring at Ines like she's completely lost it. "You're not even giving us *one day* to think this through? We might as well just hand ourselves over to Jag."

"Do as you wish," Ines says. "But please don't distract us. Every minute here counts."

Aarya's mouth drops open, but Ines doesn't seem put off in the least.

"Where's this pub?" I ask.

"The London Market," Ash says, and I can hear by the tightness in his voice that it's not a good thing.

"So central London?" I say.

"Under," Ash says.

I stare at him. "Under what?"

"Under central London," Ash says, and I instantly understand Aarya's objection. "It's a Strategia market in the middle of an underground labyrinth."

My stomach drops. "As in the only people in this market are Strategia?" I say. "And because this is London, those Strategia are disproportionately Lions?"

"By golly, I think she's got it," Aarya says, clearly not happy with the situation.

"The pub is called the Lions' Den," Ash says like it's all the explanation that's necessary. He hits the gas pedal. "We're going to need more weapons."

I immediately text Layla.

Twenty-Three

ASH, AARYA, INES, and I move through Aarya's apartment, quickly stocking weapons and assessing the ones we have for easy access. I stash my dad's whittling knife and my mom's scarf in my duffel bag for safekeeping and triple-check the position of my favorite boot dagger.

I step into the bathroom and pull out my phone.

Layla: *When you go underground you'll lose reception. I'll take my own route down and follow you once you locate the bouncer.*

Me: *Ash thinks he and Aarya are recognizable. So Ines and I will track the bouncer and they'll wait near the edge of the Market. Hoping you know what that means so you don't accidentally run into them.*

Layla: *Understood.*

I flush the toilet and slip out of the bathroom, joining my friends in the living room.

Ash stands over the coffee table tying small burlap pouches. He hands one to each of us. "There are ten darts in each, predipped in Angels' Dream," he says.

Aarya pulls out something wrapped in linen from her

bag. "Here," she says, unfolding the fabric and handing me a wooden blowpipe. "I know Ash gave you his spare, but this one is much better."

I take the blowpipe, tucking it into my coat pocket. "Thanks, Aarya," I say, and Ash looks like he's not entirely comfortable with the gesture.

"Also," Aarya says, "about the lightning poison . . ."

Ash's eyebrows rise, as if he knew something like this was coming.

"Do we really think it's a good idea for November to have both of those darts?" Aarya shifts her gaze to me. "What if you get incapacitated? It's just poor logic."

"Let me guess," Ash says, like he's gearing up to argue. "You think *you* should have one of them?"

"Not me," Aarya replies with feigned innocence. "And not you, either, since we all know that if November gets taken out, you're likely to be right behind her doing some inadvisable thing to save her life. I just don't think we should take any chances, considering we only have two darts of the lightning poison, which is why I'm suggesting we give one to Ines."

Ash looks at her suspiciously.

"I actually agree," I say, responding before he can. I know Ash doesn't trust Aarya, but Ines is a different story. "It's too risky to have both darts in the same place. We need a contingency plan." I pull one of the small glass vials out of my coat pocket and hand it to Ines.

"Great," Aarya says, but from the look on Ash's face, it's clear he doesn't agree.

"Is there anything else I need to know about the Market?" I ask, putting on my coat.

"Just keep your hood up and stare ahead confidently. Strategia can smell weakness," Ash says, pulling on his gloves. "The good news is that no one in the Market is particularly trying to attract attention; most people are conducting business or restocking supplies and don't appreciate others being overly watchful."

And just like that the conversation is over and we're headed for the door. With every step my thoughts race with hopes that my dad is okay and fears that he's not. *Hang on, Dad; we're coming.*

Ash and Aarya lead the way into a narrow cobblestoned alley that runs between a fancy Italian restaurant and a bookstore with colorful window displays. Even though the lights on the main street are bright, the farther we go down the alley, the darker it gets.

Me: *Almost to Market.*

Near the end of the alley, Aarya stops in front of an old wooden door and pulls a set of lock-picking tools out of her jacket. There's a faint click and it swings open. We all slip quietly inside. Ash takes a fast survey of the alley and closes the door behind us.

For a second we're in complete darkness. Then a match strikes and lights Aarya's face up like a spotlight. She moves the flame toward the wall, illuminating two oil lamps, and pulls one down to light the wick inside.

Instantly the room brightens, revealing bookshelves of boxes and merchandise that suggest we're in the storage room of the bookstore. Aarya leads us to the back wall, which I can now see is paneled entirely in dark wood, with electric sconces.

Aarya presses a piece of decorative metal on the side of a sconce and one of the wall panels swings open, revealing a door. Secret doors, secret pubs, coded messages in books at the library, private Gothic inns—it's like finding out that all of your childhood suspicions that you could step through your closet into another world are turning out to be true.

Aarya pulls the panel fully open and Ash walks through, offering me his hand. I intertwine my fingers with his and join him on a stone staircase. The steps are worn unevenly, reminiscent of the ones in the Academy. Above our heads the stone arches, and I can't see very far in front of me. The temperature reminds me of a cave, which Dad always claimed stays pretty consistently around fifty degrees no matter the season.

Ash and I stop at the bottom of the staircase and the oil lamp Aarya carries illuminates a portion of the straight stone passageway. I turn in both directions, but there doesn't seem to be a distinguishable difference.

"The labyrinth," Ash whispers near my ear, and I swallow.

I eye the passage warily as we follow Aarya down it and through a doorway into a large rectangular stone room. I look at Ash for an explanation.

"A medieval apartment," Ash whispers, and points. "You can tell by the hearth in the wall."

My eyes widen. "People *lived* underground?" I say, and even though I'm not cold, the hair on my arms stands up.

He shakes his head. "This wasn't always underground. In fact the passageway we just came from used to be a street.

And this was a ground-floor apartment. Over time this city has changed dramatically, and in an effort to level out some of the streets, parts of the buildings, markets, and houses got cut off and paved over. Sections of the city just got trapped down here."

I shudder at the spookiness of it all. And in the way that darkness can sometimes invite gruesome thoughts, I immediately picture someone afflicted with the plague being attended to by a doctor with one of those ghoulish beaked masks.

We exit through the far end of the room and find ourselves on another underground street. We zigzag like that for the next fifteen minutes or so. And even though I'm not scared of the dark, I feel the impulse to scrutinize shadows and corners for monsters. I can't imagine the nerve it would take to navigate this alone with nothing more than an oil lamp.

Then, suddenly, we come to a stone door and Ines leans back, using her body weight to push against it. We follow her through and Ash pulls it shut behind us. They've silenced their steps and I do the same. Unlike the small homes, streets, and shops that we've been moving through, we're now in what appears to be an endless room of high-ceilinged arches and stone columns.

Ash whispers next to my ear. "Catacombs of an old church."

As pretty as the stonework is, the idea that we're walking over people's graves is giving me the willies.

Aarya stops by a seemingly solid wall, which I know by now should not be taken for granted, and frowns at me. "Get yourself together, November. We're about to enter the outskirts of the Market and I swear you look like you just got chased by a mummy."

I close my eyes for a couple of seconds, focusing on all the places I'm holding tension. When I open them again, Ash nods his approval.

Ines glances at each of us, almost like she's wishing us good luck. *"In omnia paratus,"* she says, which I think roughly means "ready for anything," and presses hard on a stone in the wall about the height of her shoulder. Sure enough, another secret door opens, this one with jagged edges formed by the outline of the stones.

Aarya turns off the oil lamp, casting us into near darkness, and leaves the lamp in the catacomb. She's the first one through the door with Ines by her side, and Ash and me right on their heels. Ash clicks the door shut in one fluid motion.

Aarya and Ines don't speed-walk, but they do keep a brisk pace. And they've dropped the casual demeanor they were using on the surface streets of London for more deliberate movements and a focused stare. Next to me Ash wears the same look he did when I first met him—penetrating eyes with a dash of bravado. I lift my chest and neutralize my own expression, pulling my hood down a little farther to shadow my face in the dim torchlight.

The first turn we take, the streets are eerily empty. However, the farther along we get, the more I hear the buzzing of conversation and the promise of a crowd. As we turn a second corner, Ash reaches out, squeezing my fingers. He meets my eyes momentarily, giving me an encouraging nod; then he and Aarya break off from our group. My stomach churns uneasily the farther away he gets.

Ines walks by my side as we turn away from our friends and emerge through an archway into a big courtyard made of stone. The ceiling looms high above us in a series of domed arches, and the courtyard is bustling with vendors and shoppers from all over the world. Wooden stalls display everything from rare daggers to deadly poisons. And shop windows are lit with oil lamps and candelabras. It's the medieval assassin's version of my town square.

I concentrate on keeping my face unreadable, but everywhere I look there's a potential threat. I move with purpose like Ash suggested, but even so, I fear that every Strategia we pass knows I don't belong here.

Our pace doesn't slow as we weave through the busy central square and onto a cobblestoned side street that's much broader than the ones we were previously navigating. It's well lit with torches and oil lamps and is an Old World version of the lively London streets aboveground. We pass several restaurants and an antique sword dealer before stopping in front of a pub.

Ines pushes the door open and I quickly scan the room. It's exactly what I think of when I picture a tavern—cozy and boisterous, with a handful of wooden tables and a lively bar. The place is sparsely lit by torches, which works to our advantage because of the shadows they cast. I immediately head for a small table in the corner near the window that doesn't leave us exposed to the other customers, careful to avoid eye contact with anyone as I pass.

I choose a chair that gives me a view of the pub across the street, which seems to be much bigger and fancier than the place we're in. Above the entrance to the pub there's a big wooden sign with the name THE LIONS' DEN painted in gold letters. And outside the door are two serious-looking men, one of whom I would guess is nearly seven feet tall. I gulp. My dad was right when he described the guy as tall.

I peek at my phone in my pocket for messages from Layla that came in before I lost reception.

Layla: *Be safe. See you in the Lion estate.*

I erase Layla's text as Ines sits down across from me. She doesn't say a word and neither do I; we just tilt our heads down, covertly keeping track of that bouncer like our lives depend on it.

Seconds turn into minutes and I'm sweating so badly that if anyone could see my face they'd probably wonder if I was ill. *Please go. Just go already.* I plead and scream silently at the tall bouncer to leave his post and head for the Lion estate, but to no avail. He just stands outside the pub with his arms crossed. So I start counting, which is the only thing I can think to do that will keep me grounded.

When I've counted to exactly one hundred and thirty-eight I hear chairs scrape against the floor directly behind us. From the sound of it, six or so people are sitting down. And at one hundred and forty a familiar voice booms behind me. I stop counting.

Hawk. Of all the places he would go after the ball, it had to be this tavern?

"Scooped him right up—never stood a chance." He's bragging, and I can almost see him gesturing at his crew. "Mary and Jenny were part of organizing it from the start. And it's not the first time we've worked with the Ferryman, neither."

"Is that so?" says a voice I don't recognize. "That must have been quite the golden calf. I'm not sure we could pay as much as all that."

"Then we might not be the right crew for you," Hawk says, and it's clear by his tone that he loves to negotiate.

I sit bolt upright and Ines kicks me under the table. *The Ferryman? Mary and Jenny? Scooped him right up?* Anger swirls inside me, clenching my fists and tightening my jaw. With great effort, I exhale the tension, writing Hawk an IOU in my head. And suddenly my desire flip-flops—I now want that bouncer to stay exactly where he is until Hawk moves so I don't have to walk past him.

As though the universe is conspiring against me, I glance outside at the bouncers, and sure enough, two men have arrived to take their place. My muscles tighten, bracing for our exit. *No, no, no.* I've been waiting for what feels like years for them to change shifts and it happens the moment Hawk sits down behind me and says he played a part in capturing my dad? This can't be happening.

Ines slides her chair back from the table. Reluctantly I stand, careful to keep my head down as I turn around. The bad news is that Hawk's whole crew is at the table, plus a middle-aged bald man I've never seen before. The good news is that Hawk is fully engaged in his conversation, pandering to the bald man the way he once did with me and Ash. But with six crowded around a table meant for four, they've practically boxed us in. Even Ines, who's slighter than me and perfectly graceful, has a hard time maneuvering between them and the window.

And then it happens: Hawk laughs and leans back, tilting his chair on two legs and colliding with Ines as she walks past. She barely stumbles, but the space is tight and the forward motion causes her to knock into the bald man, spilling his pint of beer all over his lap. As if on cue, Hawk and his crew all turn to look at Ines and me. *No!*

The bald man growls and grabs Ines by the wrist. Her free hand immediately moves to her belt under her coat, where I know she has multiple knives.

"I hope you're reaching for your wallet, darlin', otherwise you're going to sorely regret it," the bald man says to Ines in a way that tells me he's used to people backing down from him.

Anger flashes in Ines's eyes and I get the distinct impression that in any other circumstances she would take her chances and fight this guy. But I can't think about how to help her because Hawk is staring at me and I at him. And it's instantly clear that he recognizes me. My eyes flit to Mary, the no-nonsense woman who dismissed us angrily when Ash and I tried to hire them, and her expression is as hardened as ever.

"I'll get you another," Ines says through clenched teeth, and yanks her wrist out of the bald man's grasp. And for a moment I can't believe she's forcing civility. Is she waiting to see what Hawk will do, or does she know something I don't about unallied crews?

"*Tsk, tsk, tsk,*" the bald man says, and I'm reminded of what Aarya said about Strategia smelling weakness. "I'm not sure I like that tone of yours. Not very, uh, apologetic."

Jenny, the weapons specialist with the long sword earring and the leather jacket, clenches her jaw. But no one else at the table so much as tweaks an eyebrow. Time slows to a near halt, everyone calculating what move they're going to make without having arrived at a firm decision.

"Run along now," the bald man says to Ines, pushing his chair out farther and completely cutting me off from the exit. "We'll just keep your friend here company until you return."

I glare at the bald man. My possible escape routes are absolute garbage—I can either jump on the table and hope I can get off the other side without one of Hawk's crew cutting me down or I can try to force my way past this jerk, which will probably end the same way.

The bald man turns to me, wiping his lips with the back of his hand—a hand cluttered with rings, one of which is a big silver owl. My thoughts immediately go to Nyx—*the Owl Family*. And in that instant time speeds up again.

Before I can react to being cornered, Ines grabs the bald man's mostly empty pint and clobbers him in the head with it. *Oh god. Shit. We're dead.* I would expect something rash like that from Aarya, but not in a million years did I think Ines would lose her cool.

I reach for my knife and the table of four men next to us stands up, posturing for a fight. They look from the bald man to me and Ines, and I realize they must be friends with him, or work for him. Even if Ines and I had a chance of fighting Hawk's crew of five, we have no chance of fighting ten.

To my utter shock, Mary stands, too. Only she doesn't turn on us; she faces off with the four men. "If you want those pretty faces of yours to stay pretty," she tells them, "I would *sit back down*."

I stare at her, mouth open. Maybe she didn't like the bald man to begin with or maybe she realizes how young we are, but whatever the reason, it's working to our advantage.

The rest of Hawk's crew stands, too, in solidarity with

Mary. Mary cracks her knuckles. The four men don't back down and she throws a side kick at the one closest to her, connecting with his ribs and sending him smashing into the table behind him. And like a scene out of a Western movie, a brawl erupts between Hawk's crew and the bald man's crew.

The whole bar turns to watch the fight, taking the spotlight off me and Ines.

"You owe us for this job you just cost us," Hawk growls, nodding at the bald man, and I get a sense that unallied Strategia are just that—unallied. They didn't work with Ash and me because the risk was too high, and likewise they would have turned us over at the ball because that was their job, but the moment the ball ended, they were independent agents once again.

Before I can reply, Hawk pulls one of the bald man's friends off Eddie's back and punches the guy square in the jaw. Ines offers me her hand and I take it, climbing over the unconscious bald man. We slip out the door and into the alley as the bar begins to attract a crowd. But my relief is short-lived, because as I glance at the Lions' Den, I realize we have a bigger problem—the tall bouncer has already left.

Twenty-Four

INES AND I stand still for a fraction of a second, surveying the street in front of the Lions' Den, before she starts walking purposefully toward the center of the Market. But I still don't see the bouncer, and considering he stands a good half foot taller than most people here, I'm not convinced I'm missing something.

"Do you know he went this way?" I ask, keeping my voice low.

"No," she says, but doesn't look at me.

"So you're *guessing*?"

"I'm guessing," she says, and panic grips me once again.

We emerge into the domed Market and I scan the crowd. But the bouncer's nowhere to be found. I glance at Ines, and even though her expression is unreadable, I can feel the anxiety radiating off her. If we lose him, that's it. Game over. We will never find the Lion estate or my dad in time.

I keep scanning the crowd, aware that each moment my eyes aren't down I risk discovery. Every muscle in my body is tense and I take a forceful breath, willing my posture to relax.

There at the opposite side of the square, the tall guard emerges from a shop. The relief I feel is so intense that my eyes water. I know Ines sees him, too, because she picks up her pace.

The tall bouncer exits the Market through an archway, but instead of heading straight for him, Ines leads us through an alternate archway to the left. The moment we exit, the noise diminishes and so does the light. The couple of torches that illuminate the street cast large patches of shadow. About a hundred feet ahead of us the bouncer turns left and we silence our steps. Then, without warning, something grazes my sleeve.

I whip around, my hand reaching for my knife, only to find Ash, with Aarya just a few steps behind. Even from a quick look I can tell there's tension between them. I didn't hear them approach and I have no idea what direction they came from; it gives me an unsettled feeling. We're all so good at sneaking up on one another that you never know who's following you.

As we near the turn where the bouncer disappeared, we slow our pace. Ines peeks around the doorway and Ash surveys the street behind us. They nod at each other and we turn into an abandoned apartment, weaving around a broken table and some chairs. At the far door, Ines peers out, looking both ways and pointing to her right. And so we follow the bouncer, transitioning from the torchlit streets to the pitch-black ones, where he must have stashed an oil lamp, because all of a sudden there is a beacon of light ahead of us. Ash finds my hand with his and I'm grateful for the comforting gesture.

The guard turns through another doorway, and before Ines can catch up, the light disappears, casting us into complete darkness. Ash pulls me to a stop and we all stand silently still for a couple of awful seconds.

"I'll follow," Ash breathes in a way that suggests we should stay put. He lets go of my hand.

I don't dare speak, but as his body heat disappears, my anxiety heightens. I reach out, finding Aarya's coat sleeve, and grip it like an anchor. But she's having none of it. She grabs my hand and yanks me forward, placing my palm firmly on the cold stone wall, as if to say "Hold this," and moves away from me. I want to ask Ash what he's found, but before I work up the nerve, light reappears inside the archway.

Ines cautiously peers around the doorway and Aarya pulls out a knife. But whatever Ines sees must be nonthreatening because she walks through with confidence. Aarya and I follow her into what appears to be an abandoned shoemaker's shop. There are workbenches littered with shoe-shaping tools and shelves showcasing boot designs that I can only guess are hundreds of years old. Ash stands in the center of the forgotten room holding a lit candle, scanning everything with purpose, and it instantly becomes clear why—there is no exit other than the one we just came through, so unless the bouncer vanished into thin air, he must have used a secret door.

Ines pulls a candle out of her jacket pocket and lights it. It never occurred to me to keep a candle on me, but it's now obvious that was an oversight—the light from real flame is superior to that from a flashlight and you never have to worry about the batteries failing you at a critical moment.

In the light provided by the two candles I take closer inventory of the edges of the room, searching for signs of a door.

On the far wall Aarya inspects tools that hang from iron hooks, Ines moves to the fireplace, and Ash kneels down, running his finger across the ground.

"This place is spotless," he whispers. "Not a boot print on the ground or dust on a bench." It hadn't occurred to me, but now that he mentions it, it makes the room seem off. It has none of the grime that the other stores and apartments did. I'm assuming it's purposeful, that it keeps other Strategia from being able to track the path to the secret door, like footprints in snow.

"Let's just hope we can find that door before a Lion pops out of it," Aarya says, and even though it hadn't crossed my mind, I'm now very much aware of that threat.

"I'm surprised you don't already know where the door is," Ash says under his breath without so much as glancing at her.

If I wasn't sure something was going on between them before, I am now. I head for one end of the shelves of shoes to inspect it while Ash heads for the other end.

Aarya turns around, eyes wide with offense. *"Excusez-moi?* I risk my life ten times over to help you two, and this is how you thank me?" she replies, and part of me agrees with her. Why on earth is Ash picking a fight with her right now, of all moments?

But Ash doesn't let up. "If you're going to lie, Aarya, at least try something original. I know you're better than that rote response."

Even in the dim light I can see her cheeks flush, and I'm fairly certain some of her anger comes from being called unoriginal.

"Fascinating accusation from someone who was working

not long ago with Dr. Conner to *kill* November," Aarya says, and by the way Ash's face tenses, I can tell she's struck a nerve.

He turns away from the shelf to face her. "Where did you go, Aarya? When November and Ines were in the Market, where were *you*?"

"Exactly where I said I would be," she says, only her voice has lost a little bit of its oomph.

"No, you most certainly were not," Ash retorts. "Try again, Aarya. I checked the east side of the Market and you weren't there."

As much as I try to ignore them, I can't. I glance at Ines, who returns my worried expression.

Aarya licks her lips, leaning into the fight. "You always think you know what's going on, that you're *so* good at reading everyone. Then tell me this, if you're such an expert on my tells, why did November understand me better after two weeks at the Academy than you did after two and a half years?"

"Are you two really having this fight right now?" I ask, anxiety lacing my words. If there was ever a time that we needed solidarity, it's now.

"Yes," Ash says with assurance. "We're about to do the most dangerous thing any of us has ever done, and I want to be sure that walking into the Lion estate with Aarya doesn't mean we're walking into a trap."

Anger flashes in Aarya's eyes and this time she doesn't bother to hide it. Ines must see it, too, because before Aarya can open her mouth and spew the vitriol we all know is coming, Ines jumps in.

"Enough," she says with force. "We most assuredly do not have time for this." They both open their mouths to respond, but Ines cuts them off. "I don't care how right you both think you are. All I care about at present is not dying in the labyrinth before we even get to take a shot at Jag." She gives them a warning look. "Aarya, Ash has every right to question you, because you know as well as all of us that your behavior at times has been suspicious. I'm not saying you need to justify your actions, but you can at least not fan the fire."

Aarya stares at her, shocked, and so do I.

"And, Ash," Ines continues, "you know Aarya never played by the rules, so why on earth do you expect her to now? Just because she isn't straightforward like Layla doesn't mean you should attack her character." She pauses and no one even tries to speak. "So go ahead, Ash, ask what you really want to know, and then both of you get over yourselves and get back to work."

A stunned silence falls over the room.

And after a few moments of considering her offer, Ash says, "Why are you two *really* here?"

Ines sighs, like she knew this was coming. "I can only answer for myself—"

"Ines, you don't have to—" Aarya starts, clearly feeling guilty that Ines is revealing something personal because of her.

"I do," Ines says to Aarya, before turning to me and Ash. "My parents had a high standing in the Fox Family; they did a great deal of advising for the head family and helped them govern. And they hated Jag—they believed he was single-handedly dishonoring the legacy of Strategia, tarnishing the good we had done over the centuries. For years they spoke out against him, trying to get the Foxes to take a stand like the Bears had." She nods in my direction. "But their warnings were ignored. Then the Lions began targeting talented members of other Families, and my parents fought harder; they had foresight—they argued that the Lions' actions would eventually spill over onto the children, and onto the *Academy*." She takes a breath. "But as you all know, Jag seeks vengeance on those who speak against him, and my family, even with their high standing, were no exception."

My chest tightens with worry at this all-too-familiar story.

"I was seven years old at the time," Ines continues, "and they drugged me with Angels' Dream." She glances at me for a brief second. "When I woke up in the morning, my parents and older sister had been murdered in their beds. The Lions kept me alive as a reminder to my Family of what happens when you speak out against Jag."

Angels' Dream—no wonder she reacted when she saw it. My heart breaks for her. I know too well the pain of losing family members to the Lions, but I cannot imagine the terror she must have gone through that morning.

"My Family didn't disown me, but they might as well have," Ines says. "They wanted me to go away so they wouldn't have to act, claiming there was no evidence the attack came from the Lions. And I wanted to go away, too; I couldn't stand the sight of them and their cowardly avoidance. But instead of me living with second cousins on the coast like they planned, I left Spain altogether. And a year later I was lucky enough to find another family that suited me better. I haven't been back since."

"By another family, she means *my* family," Aarya says.

"Ines came to live with me and my terrible siblings and my lackluster parents."

I can see the shock in Ash's eyes.

Aarya stares at him. "Now are you satisfied, Ashai? Or do you want us to sign a pact in blood?"

Suddenly it all makes sense, Aarya and Ines's closeness, and the way that Aarya is always trying to protect her, even though Ines is the better fighter.

Ash looks at Ines. "I am truly sorry," he says.

I never would have suspected that might be the reason Aarya was here, to right a wrong done to Ines, but now I'm looking at her in a new light.

"I'm sorry I doubted you, Aarya," Ash says, and I can tell he means it.

Aarya looks surprised by Ash's admission and maybe a little embarrassed that we now know she's not as unfeeling as she wants everyone to believe. "Well . . . right. Fine. I mean, you should be. Let's just get back to searching for this door."

And we do. Ash and I return to opposite ends of the bookshelf. We spend the next fifteen minutes going over every inch of the wall—twice. I even use the little step stool to look on top of the shelves, but I don't find anything, not a suspicious crack or a hollow-sounding part of the plaster.

"Nothing," I say.

"Nothing over here, either," Aarya replies, and Ines, too, walks away from the fireplace.

"Let's switch spots," I suggest. "Maybe fresh eyes will help."

"If I didn't find anything over here, you're not going to,

either," Aarya says, and even though Ash and Ines don't say it out loud, it's obvious they are thinking the same thing.

"Then what would you suggest, Aarya?" I say, frustrated by the dead end.

"That the bouncer is freaking magical," she says, frowning.

I turn in a circle, staring at all the little odds and ends that make this room unlike the other stores and apartments I've seen down here. And then it suddenly occurs to me that we missed something.

"You guys," I say. "There's no dust in here, right?"

Ash stops what he's doing. "Right."

"And the fact that there's no dust means the Lions altered this space. So now I'm wondering what else might have been altered. For instance, was this furniture originally here, or was it staged by the Lions?" I ask, walking around the room, examining the things in the middle of it that I initially thought were irrelevant.

"Debatable," Ash says. "Occasionally there are furnished stores or houses in the labyrinth, but that doesn't mean the Lions didn't add items to this particular room."

"Exactly, which means we could have dismissed something as old and discarded that is actually a clue," I say, and we all go back to searching the room again.

I start at the workbench, examining the shoe-shaping tools, but before I get very far Ash starts talking again. "The step stool," he says with an excited lilt to his voice that makes us all leave what we're doing. He picks it up and moves it. "See how the floor underneath is scratched?"

We all look up at the same time, immediately realizing our mistake.

"It's not that we missed something where we were look-ing . . . ," Ash says.

". . . it's that we were looking in the wrong places," I say, finishing his sentence.

Ash moves the stool back to its original position and stands on it, reaching above his head. "It's hard to find a door in a wall when it's actually in the ceiling." He runs his hands along the wood and stops suddenly at the edge of a crossbeam. He smiles down at us. "Got it."

Twenty-Five

ASH STICKS HIS fingers up under the edge of the crossbeam on the ceiling, gently lowering a hatch. When he has it about halfway down, a rope ladder falls to the floor. We all look at one another and it's one of those moments when everything comes into sharp focus; one wrong move and we're dead.

"Everyone do a quick check for your knives and for your blow darts. And hand over your phones," Aarya whispers, and we do. "No mistakes, no fumbles."

Ash and Aarya grind our SIM cards into the floor and snap our phones in half before stashing them in some old boots. The four of us share a look, affirming that everything is in order. Ash places his lit candle between his teeth and climbs upward, while Ines snuffs hers out, slipping it back into her jacket pocket.

I follow Ash up the rope ladder with Aarya and Ines right behind me. As soon as I reach the ceiling, I pull myself up into a small circular room about the size of a walk-in closet that has nothing in it except a stone staircase. Ash waits with the candle while Aarya and Ines hoist themselves into the room, and after closing the hatch, the four of us start up the steep staircase together.

The stone steps are worn, suggesting that the Lion estate is an old building—possibly a medieval castle or manor house. I run my fingers along the uneven stone wall, sending a silent plea that the braided lock of hair Layla gave me will bring us luck.

Ash stops in front of an arched door. He loads a dart tipped with Angels' Dream into a blowpipe and we follow suit. When we're all ready and braced, he grabs the door latch and snuffs out his candle. For two seconds we're cast into complete darkness, a circumstance that caused me to panic an hour ago but that now feels a million times safer than whatever is on the other side of that door.

Ash cracks the door ever so slowly and a small sliver of light appears. Without hesitation he sticks the wooden pipe through the half inch of space and blows on it. He throws the door open and in one fluid motion runs for the stumbling guard, catching him right before he hits the ground. The three of us emerge from the staircase and I help Ash lower the guard silently to the floor.

We scan what appears to be an extensive wine cellar, blowpipes in hand. There are no other guards in sight, which strikes me as odd. Why only one guard? Are the Lions so confident that no one would have the guts to break in, or that their door is so well hidden that most people wouldn't find it? Ash and I make eye contact and I can tell he's wondering the same thing.

We move methodically across the room between the rows of wine barrels, pausing intermittently to listen, but the cellar is unnervingly quiet. I keep hoping I'll spot a pathway that will lead us to another part of the basement and to the dungeon itself, but no such luck. There are only wine, stone walls, and one flight of stairs. Ines takes the lead, creeping upward with grace.

She stops at the door at the top of the stairs, crouching on the ground to peer under it. Four seconds pass and she stands back up, holding up two fingers, which I'm assuming means there are two guards. She taps her blowpipe and points to her right, then she taps Aarya's and points to her left, mapping out a plan of execution.

She lifts the latch slowly, careful not to let the metal creak. The instant the latch unhooks, she throws the door open. Ines and Aarya bolt through and a half second later I hear the whizzing sound of two darts. Ash and I are right behind them and we each run for a guard. I barely get ahold of mine, swaying under his weight, and place him silently on the floor. My pulse pounds in my head and my temples throb.

We pause once again to assess our surroundings. We're in what I would consider an antiquated version of a mudroom. There are iron hooks on the wall with hooded cloaks hanging from them, wooden shelves containing gloves and hats, and winter boots lined up against the wall in varied sizes. Everything is black and matches the Strategia aesthetic. I gulp. The number of items in this room suggests a large household and I'm willing to bet that this isn't the only entrance or the only mudroom in this place.

Aarya quickly makes her way to the archway leading into the estate. She peers around the stone and, after a beat, waves to us to follow her. And we do, but not before I take another look at the passed-out guards. With all these cloaks, why aren't we seeing more of them? This feels too easy.

I follow my friends into a wide corridor lit by sconces and hung with oversized paintings of serious-looking men and women posed with lions. The ceilings are so high that the paintings loom above us, requiring us to strain our necks if we want to look at them. But maybe that's the point—grandeur and intimidation.

Aarya slows as we approach a tall archway. She judiciously peers around it, waits a beat, and gestures for us to follow. I look through the archway into what appears to be an empty study with a fireplace and a large desk. And we keep moving past a sitting room, two hallways, a music room, and three closed doors. I know it's the middle of the night, but the emptiness seems out of place and it's starting to give me a sinking feeling.

Aarya pauses again before another archway with an open door, this one bigger than the ones before it. She peers inside and once again waves us on. I peek inside on my way past and my heart nearly stops—it's a large room not unlike the dining hall at the Academy, with fancy tapestries and portraits on the stone walls. The realization creeps up on me slowly, like a spider you didn't know was on your arm. *My dream! This reminds me of the room from my dream with all the dead bodies—the dead bodies of my dead friends.* I immediately break out in a sweat. I want to call out to them, to tell them we have to turn around, but I just stand there unable to form the words. Ash grabs my hand, pulling me forward. I open my mouth to warn him, but he shakes his head as we move toward Aarya and the door she's standing next to at the end of the corridor.

Unlike the other doors we've seen so far, this one has large iron brackets on either side, the kind you would put a wooden bar through. And it has a keyhole. These extra security

361

measures spark a flutter of hope in my chest. There are very few rooms that would require security, and one of them is definitely a dungeon. By the look on Ash's face, I can tell he, too, thinks we may have found it.

Despite the progress we're making, I can't shake off the image of the room from my dream. "My nightmare, Ash, I saw—" I breathe, but Aarya gives me a death stare.

"One more word and I'll knock you out with a blow dart," she whispers back, and looks through the keyhole.

And I believe her. I shut my mouth and glance over my shoulder, certain there is some great danger lurking there. Aarya stands and makes eye contact with each one of us, as if to make sure we're ready. Ash gives her a nod and she turns back around. She presses on the latch with painstaking slowness, moving it only a millimeter at a time, her face scrunched in concentration.

The latch unhooks. Only Aarya doesn't crack the door like Ash did, she pulls it fully open. On the other side a guard is whipping around to face us. I strike him with a dart in the neck and Aarya grabs him by his shirt. But he's big, and as his legs go out, Aarya stumbles forward under his weight. I lunge, grabbing his arm, and together we lean him against the wall.

Aarya winks at me. I don't understand how she could possibly be relaxed enough to have a wink in her. We slink down the stairs side by side, blowpipes in hand and ready for more guards.

At the bottom of the stairs there's a narrow hallway and at the end of it is another door with a metal grate that forms a crude window, and *no door handle*. We crouch low and move toward the door as fast as possible.

Ash cautiously looks through the grate and drops back down to face us. He and Aarya start gesturing and pointing. It takes me a couple of seconds before I realize they're speaking in sign language, or arguing, from the looks of it. And by the way they point, I'm fairly certain it has to do with the no-door-handle issue and how the heck we're going to open it. But whatever the conflict, it resolves quickly and Ash pulls out a metal hook tied to a piece of black cord.

Ash counts down on his fingers—*three, two, one.* And Aarya pops up from her crouch. She sticks her blowpipe through the window and I hear the familiar whizzing sound of her dart. Two seconds later there's a thud. Ash stands in the same instant, slipping the hook and cord through the iron grate. He jiggles it for a moment and pulls. Metal clicks and the door unlatches.

Ash pulls it open and we cautiously go through. We step onto the dirty stone floor, and the smell nearly knocks me over—damp rot, urine, and hay. I gag silently and inspect the cells on either side of me. We pass two that are empty and one that contains a skeleton hunched in the corner. Bones protrude from the person's torn clothing and iron shackles hang loosely around the wrists. I turn away, wishing I had never looked in the first place. *Dad, where are you?*

We reach the end of the corridor and there are two archways to choose from. Ash and Aarya negotiate with sign language once more, resulting in me and Ash taking the archway on the right and Aarya and Ines taking the one on the left.

Ash and I creep along the filthy stone, and once again the absence of more guards is unnerving. My dad's supposed to be some big prize for Jag, and yet this dungeon is practically empty. Wouldn't Jag have this place on lockdown?

We approach a large cell on our right and my breath catches in my throat. On the far side, slumped on the floor with his arms and legs in chains and his head hanging, is my dad. I run to the cell door, gripping the wrought iron and fighting back a sob. My dad's face and clothes are streaked with blood.

Ash slips his lock-picking tools into the lock, making the faintest clicking sound, and my dad's head whips up. The moment he sees me, his eyes widen like he can't believe I'm here. He left me that note; did he not think I would come? But the look of surprise and panic on his face is unmistakable.

My dad shakes his head. "Run!" he mouths without making a sound.

Ash puts away his tools and slowly pulls on the cell door; even at his glacial pace, the metal whines.

And then we hear it—a girl's scream.

Ash abandons his attempt to be quiet, throwing open the cell door.

"Run!" my dad commands, this time aloud, but before he can get out another word and before Ash and I can set foot in his cell, ten guards rush into the passageway, surrounding us.

Ash and I lift our blowpipes and I grab the lightning poison from my belt.

"I would reconsider if I were you," says a man's voice.

The guards part in front of us, making way for an older man with shoulder-length silver hair. *Jag.* He has the same jaw and nose as my father. His movements are neat and precise, like his black clothes, and he appears to be in no particular rush.

Behind Jag are seven more guards, including the tall bouncer from the pub, who has Ines's limp body slung over his shoulder. Meanwhile a short, stocky guard holds a knife to Aarya's throat.

"You look surprised, granddaughter, although I don't know how you could be," Jag says, and the word *granddaughter* hits me like a punch to the gut. His boisterous demeanor from the ball is missing, replaced by a more conservative, almost professorial air. But his charisma is still present—he is a natural leader who doesn't need to shout but can command you with a mere look. "Did you think I wouldn't be waiting?"

Suddenly it all makes sense, the lack of guards at the entrance, the clear path to the dungeon. I scan the passageway. We are so vastly outnumbered that fighting isn't an option; even if Ash and I could hold our own, they would kill Aarya and Ines before we could do anything about it.

"Just kill him, November," Aarya spits, her anger in sharp contrast to Jag's comfortable confidence. But even if I were willing to let her and Ines die to attempt it, there's no good path forward. Throwing my knife isn't an option. The guards would cut me down before it left my hand.

Jag frowns at Aarya like he's disappointed. "And I thought we were getting along so nicely these past few days."

I'm looking from Jag to Aarya, trying to decipher the meaning of his words, when I hear the faint clicking of boots on stone. Around the corner comes Logan, his unkempt dirty-blond hair falling around his face, a healing burn on his cheek, and a satisfied smile on his lips. My eyes widen.

"You treacherous little—" Aarya seethes, but Jag cuts her off.

"Enough, Aarya," Jag says without raising his voice. "It only stands to reason that someone who would readily betray their friends deserves betrayal in return." It's a simple statement, one made without fanfare or overenunciated words, as though he were discussing nothing more than the weather, but it bowls us all over like a tidal wave.

Aarya's mouth hangs open and we all stare at her. Has Aarya been speaking to Jag—has she been planning this with Logan from the start? Was Ash right about her all along? The force of the realization nearly knocks the wind out of me.

"How effing dare you!" Aarya manages, and looks like she might fight him, regardless of the knife pressed to her throat.

Logan watches her struggle.

Aarya's face turns bright red, and she slams her boot into the shin of the guard who's restraining her. Jag flicks his hand and the guard knocks her so hard in the head that she slumps in his arms. I glance at Ash, who looks like his worst fears are coming true.

Jag returns his gaze to me, examining my frozen stance, with the vial of lightning poison in one hand and a blowpipe in the other. "I think it's time you put those down, don't you?" he says, like I'm a child who brought my slingshot to the breakfast table. "Or are you going to fight to the death here and now?"

I look over my shoulder at my dad, who's watching every word and every movement but hasn't interjected. His eyes are full of frustration, and somehow I understand him. Jag would probably use Dad's concern as an invitation to hurt me.

"He can't help you, November," Jag says.

I look back at Jag, whose placid expression hasn't wavered, and as I meet his eyes, I feel as though I've shrunk.

"I'll put down my weapons if you'll let the rest of them go," I say, forcing myself to maintain eye contact.

Jag sighs. "A compromise is essentially a loss. I never barter," he says, and pauses. "And tell me, what is it that you're threatening me with in that tiny vial?"

My eyes flit to the poison, terrified of handing it over to Jag.

"It seems I've made a very simple request that you are unable to fulfill. Maybe we should just use it on the small one to give you incentive to move things along?" He gestures to Ines and my heart jumps into my throat.

"Angels' Dream," I lie.

Jag tilts his head, reading me, and it's obvious by the way Logan smirks that they both know I'm lying.

I drop the vial and blowpipe, but to my dismay the small vial stays intact. Ash follows my lead and drops his blowpipe and his knife. And in a last act of defiance, I stamp on the glass, smashing the poison and grinding it into the damp floor.

Jag looks me in the eye, and for just a moment his calm expression turns threatening. Then he sighs, like he's thought better of it. "I'm surprised your father never taught you that an undisciplined mind only leads to suffering."

"I hope he burns you alive," Logan murmurs, clearly still bitter about the fire I started in his smithy.

Before I can open my mouth to respond, there is a sharp pain near my temple and the world goes black.

Twenty-Six

MY EYES FLUTTER, and before I can bring my surroundings into focus, the rank smell of the dungeon sends me into a coughing fit. I attempt to put my hand to my mouth, but my arm is met with the resistance of cold metal. I follow the line of my arm above my head and find that my wrists are spread in a wide V and shackled to the wall. *Shackles, dungeon . . . Dad.* The events of the past twenty-four hours flood my thoughts and my eyes widen with a jolt. Shackled on my left are Ines and Aarya. Ines is still passed out, but Aarya is alert. To my right Ash is frowning in concentration. But my dad is nowhere to be seen.

"Ash?" I say, and my voice cracks. "Where is he? Where's my dad?"

Ash shakes his head, but before he can answer, Aarya starts talking.

"Lower your voice," she scolds, and I can tell she's in a particularly foul mood. "Do what Ash and I have been doing—seethe in silence."

Ash snaps back at her. "We're shackled to a wall in a dungeon, Aarya. Sneaking around is a moot point."

"Which I'm sure you blame *me* for," she says, her tone increasingly acerbic.

Ash doesn't answer right away, and I can't tell if it's because he's angry or concentrating. Aarya scowls.

"No, actually I don't," he finally replies, and we both turn to him in surprise. Ash doesn't think Aarya betrayed us—how is that possible?

"However suspicious I find your behavior, and however foolish it was to make a deal with Logan," Ash says, "I can't ignore the fact that Jag was lying. He doesn't give off normal tells; in fact he displays the opposite of normal indicators. He shows pleasure every time he lies. But a lie is a lie."

"My bargain with Logan was meant to pay him off and prevent him from going to the Lions, not cause him to," Aarya says, indignant.

"Also not lost on me," Ash says. "It was obvious how much Logan was enjoying outwitting you."

"Sociopath," Aarya grumbles, but some of her frustration drops away. As much as she tries to hide it, I think our opinion of her really matters, even Ash's, and even in this moment when we're chained to a wall in the Lion Family dungeon.

"Pitting us against each other is just another way to manipulate and dominate us," Ash says. "And Jag is clearly a master manipulator."

"My dad," I say again, and this time it's Aarya who answers.

"We're in the opposite corridor," she says, and my heart sinks. "The one Ines and I were ambushed in."

I look up at my shackles, pulling at the cold metal, but they're secured tightly around my wrists with almost no wiggle room. I pull again, anger surging in my chest—anger that we're shackled to a wall like criminals in the Dark Ages, anger that I was ripped away from my dad the moment I found him, anger that my aunt was murdered and my mother before her. Just anger. I yank harder, the metal grating against my skin, and let out a frustrated grunt.

"Although we did manage to take out three of the guards before they restrained us. I noticed you didn't take down a single one of yours," Aarya says. Most people wouldn't be keeping a petty tally over fighting skills, given her screw-up with Logan. But then again, Aarya isn't most people.

"For someone who doesn't want other people to talk, you certainly do a lot of it," Ash says, giving Aarya the side eye.

"Well, in case you were wondering, I still don't like you, either, Ashai," she says, but her voice betrays her.

"How did Jag know?" I ask in a huff, and they both turn to me.

"How did Jag know what?" Aarya says.

"That Ash didn't trust you?" I ask. "If Ash is right that Jag is manipulating us, how did he know that might work, that we might believe you sold us out to Logan?"

"I'm a Jackal," Aarya says like it explains everything. "The rest of Strategia aren't fond of the fact that we don't play by their rules. And we get blamed for all kinds of things we didn't do. Instigating World War One, for instance."

I frown. I actually do remember Layla telling me that at the Academy.

"It doesn't help that your Family is always up to something," Ash says.

"That, too," Aarya concedes, making it sound like a good

thing. "And rat-faced, two-timing jerk-offs like Logan don't do us any favors, either."

I frown, remembering what Logan said about burning us alive. I'm certain that even if Aarya is responsible for Logan tracking us, I share in the blame because I antagonized him with that fire. "Do you think it's possible that Logan told Jag?" I ask, and Ash and Aarya look at me. "Ash, you said Logan was a skilled tracker, right? What if he followed us through the Market? He could have easily waited outside that shop, listening to us. I mean, you two had an argument about trust." But the moment I say it, a wave of anxiety hits me. Layla was supposed to follow us. What if Logan found her? I look at our restraints. We're still here, shackled to a wall with Layla nowhere in sight. What if he hurt her? What if he *killed* her? Ash didn't even know she was here; he has no idea anything is wrong.

"Possible," Ash concedes. "In fact, likely. Logan is exactly the type to pass along that information. But it's why Jag used it that worries me."

Ash's agreement only sinks me further into my anxiety.

"You think there's a reason besides Jag wanting to kill us and win?" Aarya says.

"I do," Ash says. "I think Jag's playing a more complex game than we thought and I want to know what it is."

"Well, lucky for you, you'll probably find out before you die," Aarya says, but no one is in the mood for her morbid sense of humor. I'm barely even listening, my fear for Layla and my dad eclipsing everything else.

I glance at Ash, feeling torn over telling him about Layla—if

I panic him I could throw him off focus and take away any chance, however slight, of him getting out of here alive. But is this secret really one I can keep to myself?

"Ash?" I start, but when he looks at me I change my mind. "What do we need to do to pick these locks?" I say instead.

He shakes his head. "I haven't been able to figure that out. They stripped us of everything that could potentially be useful."

I examine my zippers and the metal accents on my boots, but none of them would work. I scan the communal cell, taking a proper look for the first time. The floors are filthy with grime. There are a couple of crude beds made of hay, and a variety of unpleasant restraints. Plus, there is a pot in the corner that I hope like hell I won't have to use. But nothing that even resembles metal for lock picking, not that we could reach it if there were.

I look again at my jeans and my hoodie and frown. My coat's gone and so are my weapons, even the ones stashed in my boots.

"How long have I been asleep?" Ines asks in a groggy voice as she blinks at us.

"We're not sure," Aarya says. "My best guess is that they used some of our darts on us—knocked us out for a few hours."

"Agreed," Ash says. "Which would make it sometime in the early morning, but given the lack of windows it's impossible to know."

Ines looks up at her arms spread out on either side of her head. "Well, that's a problem."

"Ya think?" Aarya says.

"I have a pin tucked into my hair," Ines says, and we all

turn to look at her like she just proposed. "I've carried one ever since Blackwood nearly suffocated you with that locked mask, Aarya."

Aarya's expression softens with a sweetness that's completely out of keeping with our current situation, and completely out of keeping with Aarya in general.

"And the lightning poison dart," Ines adds, and I could cry from relief.

Aarya leans forward to give Ash a vindicated look.

"But with my arms spread like this," Ines says, "I can't actually reach either." Ines turns first to Aarya, then to me. "So the only way we'll be able to retrieve them is if you two work together."

For a split second I'm not sure what she means. But when I examine our positioning, it clicks—there is only one way we could possibly finagle a pin out of her hair. "Our feet?"

"Toes, to be precise," Aarya says, kicking off her left boot. "Where's the pin, Ines?"

"In my right braid," Ines says. "A few inches back from my temple."

"I think I see where you mean," I say.

Aarya nods. "If you can grab the braid and hold it in place, Ember, I'll push the pin out from my side." She steps on her sock with her right boot and pulls her left foot out of it, wiggling her toes.

I stare at my boots, which are laced up tightly and not easily removable. And with my hands splayed out like this, they are nearly impossible to reach.

"If you put your foot by mine, I can untie it with—" Ash offers, but I cut him off.

"They're double-knotted," I say.

"You double-knot your laces?" Ash asks like he might be amused by this discovery if we were in any other situation than this one.

"I didn't know anyone over the age of ten did that," Aarya says.

"People who don't want their laces to come untied do it," I reply, frowning at my feet.

"Clearly," Aarya says.

"Can you get your boot up to your hand?" Ash asks.

"Honestly, I don't know if I can fold my body like that," I say, doubtful. "But I'll give it a try."

I shinny my back straight against the wall and brace my arms to give me some leverage. Then I raise my straightened right leg up and to the side. Unfortunately, I'm not quite flexible enough and I'm struggling to get my boot to my fingers. I strain for all I'm worth, pushing it closer inch by inch. I manage to grasp a loop of my laces with the tips of my fingers. However, I lose my grip and my leg falls back to the floor with a thud.

I take a frustrated breath and give it another go. Only this time Ines kicks her leg over, pushing it against the back of mine and propping it up. And it does the trick. With my laces now in reach, I grab the center knot and pull it out. But before I can yank on the loops, Jag appears on the other side of the bars with four guards behind him, one of whom is the tall bouncer from the pub.

I drop my leg to the floor, but it's too late. Jag's already taken note of my positioning and Aarya's bare foot.

"Oh no, don't stop on my account," Jag says as the bouncer unlocks the cell door.

The sound of his voice chills me.

"I had come down here to make you aware of the festivities," he says like we're guests and not prisoners. "But I see you're already playing a game of your own."

None of us moves or attempts to speak.

Jag steps into the cell. His silver hair is neatly arranged around his face, his black clothes are impeccable, and the cloak he wears around his shoulders is lined with deep red velvet.

Jag positions himself in front of Ines. "Now let's see what we have here." He eyes Aarya's bare foot and my partially untied laces. "Given your bare feet, I assume Ines has something she can't reach, something useful, perhaps something she might . . . pick a lock with?" The way he uses our names like we're all familiar to him is unnerving. He waits a beat. "Yes, I believe that's exactly right. The question is, where is this mysterious item, and how shall we find it?"

When no one answers, he concentrates on Ines. "Not in your boots, I imagine, or you would just have taken them off. And my guards searched your clothes."

Aarya looks like she wants to murder him.

"No," Jag says. "I think whatever you've hidden must be somewhere in . . . your hair." His assessment is that of an expert strategist, with a reasoned tone to match, yet his words cut like a knife. "I think we'd better check, don't you?"

Two of his guards approach Ines, and as they do, Aarya kicks the one closest to her in the knee. The guard grunts, and before she can pull her leg back a second time, he backhands her so hard her lip splits.

Aarya spits the blood on the floor, confirming what I

imagined the grime in here might consist of. "Lion guards who let a chained prisoner get a kick in," she says. "*Tsk, tsk.*"

The blood drains from my face. *Damn it, Aarya, why are you egging them on?* But the moment I think the question, I know the answer—to distract them from Ines. And I respect her for it, no matter how risky and incendiary it might be. She's fearlessly standing up for her friend—sister, really. Jag must realize why she's doing it, too, or maybe he just realizes Aarya loves a reaction, because he doesn't bother responding to her; he doesn't even spare her a look.

Instead, he focuses all his energy on Ines. The guards unshackle her and drag her forward, pushing her to her knees. They undo her braids and the lightning poison falls to the floor.

Jag picks it up, turning it curiously in his fingers. "Well," he says, clearly pleased. "This looks remarkably like the vial you smashed on the floor last night, November. Interesting how things work out sometimes, isn't it?"

He looks me in the eye, and even though his expression remains unchanged, I can't shake the feeling that maybe they did search our hair—that they searched it and he knew what was there, choosing instead to intimidate us. His warning rings in my head: *an undisciplined mind only leads to suffering.*

"While I'm intrigued by a substance that is so precious you would destroy it rather than give it to me, I don't imagine that poison will aid you in your current situation," he says, pulling out his knife and lifting Ines's chin with it. "So I think it only prudent that we search a little further."

My whole body tenses and I steal a fearful glance at Aarya.

"I remember you," Jag says to Ines, his tone unwaveringly

calm and sure. "You're that little Fox girl whom I let live, aren't you?"

Ines's expression remains neutral, but her eyes burn with hatred. I know Jag sees it, too, because he nods at her.

"Such a shame," he says as though she disappoints him. "I remember receiving a report that your family went down rather easily. I would have thought them harder to kill." Anger sparks in my chest. His tone is polite and his cruelty is effortless.

My wrists throb, and I realize I'm straining against my shackles, like maybe I could break them off the wall by force. And instantly I realize Aarya was right; Jag is a monster that needs to be removed from power by any means necessary.

"But enough reminiscing," Jag says. "We've got a little problem-solving to do." Without warning, he grabs a handful of Ines's hair and slices cleanly through it near her scalp.

I gasp before I can stop myself, frantically searching for a way to keep him from hurting Ines. "It must be difficult to be so lacking in the, uh . . . manhood department," I say.

Aarya chuckles.

"I mean, this is *a lot* of effort to go through just to show us that you're tough," I continue. "Maybe next time you should try something other than giving a girl a haircut while two guards hold her down?"

Jag looks me square in the eye. "You do know your emotions show on your face? That I *know* this distresses you, that *I* distress you," he says, and slices off another chunk of Ines's hair. "It's a disappointment, really. I was hoping that if I had a granddaughter who was clever enough to sneak in here, she might also be good at deception. But then again, it's better not to get attached to toys you can't keep." He slices at Ines's hair again, and he must nick her scalp this time because a dribble of blood runs down her temple. "Oh dear. It seems you've distracted me and I'm not looking where I'm cutting," he says, slicing off the last remaining section.

He drops the red locks on the floor in front of her. Jag nods to the guards to put Ines back in her shackles, and this time Aarya doesn't take a swing at them. We all remain perfectly silent.

"Take the hair," he orders the guard with the mustache. "Find whatever they were hiding."

The man scoops up Ines's hair and exits the cell. My stomach churns. Is this my fault? If I hadn't smashed that vial, would Jag have done this?

Jag paces in front of us, tapping his knife on his palm. "You see, November, I had intended on simply asking you a question. But after seeing how deeply you feel for your friends here, I'm thinking it makes good sense to give you some motivation to answer it."

Fear grips my chest, and my heart pounds. How could I have been so loose with my emotions? I should have remained silent. Guilt wraps around me like a noose.

"The only choice we need to make now is which of your friends will provide the best motivation," Jag says, stopping in front of Aarya. "The Jackal? The Fox?" He points his knife at them and pauses to read my reaction. "Or the Wolf?" The moment he points to Ash, Jag's eyes brighten with recognition, and I curse myself—my emotions clearly showed on my face.

"The Wolf it is," Jag says happily, like he's choosing a ripe melon at the supermarket.

The same two guards who unlocked Ines's shackles pull Ash from his. They stand him up, restraining his arms, while the tall bouncer cracks his knuckles and waits. Ash looks at me, as if to tell me it's okay, but I don't believe him; I'm in full-blown panic.

"Let's see here," Jag says, assessing Ash.

I brace myself, waiting for his question. But before Jag even asks one, he gestures toward Ash and the bouncer punches Ash in the face, splitting his lip open and sending a line of blood down his chin. I want to scream, but I know it will only make things worse.

Jag clears his throat. "Now, I want you to think carefully about how you answer me, granddaughter, because a wrong answer will have unfavorable consequences."

I hate that he calls me granddaughter. And I'm certain that's why he keeps doing it.

Jag nods, seeing that I understand. "So . . . I know you killed the five guards on your way in, but what I don't know is who killed the two in the main hall?"

For a second I just stare at him in complete shock. "What are you talking about?"

"Strike one," Jag says, and smiles. "A terrible sport, baseball, but it's an American expression I've always been fond of." He gestures again and this time the bouncer knees Ash in the stomach. Ash grunts and sucks in air, wheezing.

My mind whirls. We didn't hurt those guards; we only knocked them unconscious. And then it dawns on me . . . *Layla.* Could it be Layla who killed the guards? I don't pursue that line of thought, however, because right now my best chance is to appear confused and distraught, and that's actually perfect, because I am. My emotions are finally a tool, not a hindrance.

"Okay, okay, wait," I say quickly, spreading my palms open as if to appear nonthreatening. "I'm just as confused as you are."

Jag lifts his eyebrow.

"We put those guards to sleep using Angels' Dream," I say, choosing my words carefully. "And then we came directly down to the dungeon. We didn't kill them."

Before I can continue, Jag looks at the bouncer and he punches Ash so hard in the face that Ash's head flies back. My eyes well at the sight of Ash in pain.

"Strike two," Jag says. "I didn't ask you *if* you killed the guards, I asked you *who* killed the guards in the main hall. Be careful, now. Three strikes and you're out."

The bouncer pulls his knife from its sheath.

My breath hitches in my throat. "It's not that we didn't try to get people to help us," I say with emphasis, quickly crafting an answer that is not only believable but is also the truth. "*But no one would.* So if there is someone killing your guards, it doesn't have anything to do with us."

Jag stares at me, and I'm hyperaware that he's reading my features, looking for a crack in my answer and an excuse to slit Ash's throat. I don't dare blink, afraid that any movement will turn out for the worst.

Just then the metal door behind us whines on its hinges. I release my breath and Jag turns around. A middle-aged woman enters the cell. She's dressed similarly to Jag, with strawberry-blond hair and the same blue eyes as Brendan. *Rose.*

"We've had another"—Rose hesitates—"*incident,* this time in the gatehouse."

Jag listens, his face unreadable.

"I think we should delay," Rose continues.

"We're not delaying," Jag states simply, showing no upset but also leaving no room for argument. "I told everyone to be here this morning and be here they will."

By "everyone," I can only imagine he means his guests from the ball last night.

Rose frowns. "With all these people arriving, our risk—"

"I can't imagine how repeating yourself will change my mind," Jag says, shutting her down matter-of-factly, and her face takes on a neutral expression that reminds me of my dad's in his cell last night.

"Bring them upstairs in half an hour," Jag says to the guards, and brushes his hands together as though we got him dirty, leaving the cell as confident as he entered it.

I stare at Ash, who has a bloody lip, but he's not looking at me, he's looking at Rose. And he has the strangest expression on his face, like he's asking her a silent question. The guards lock Ash back up in his restraints.

Rose makes eye contact with me, and I freeze. Despite her dainty, elflike features, there is nothing soft about her. She follows her father out of the cell with the guards and the bouncer.

We remain quiet until their footsteps fade and we're certain we're alone again. I look from a bleeding Ash to Ines, whose hair is raggedly shorn off but who holds her chin high and wears a proud expression.

"I'm so incredibly s—" I start.

"I'm not," Ines says. "All I am is determined."

"But last night," I start. "If I hadn't smashed that vial—" I stop, the lump in my throat growing.

Ines turns to me, her proud expression unchanging. "November, don't you dare," she says, and my eyes widen at her uncharacteristically forceful tone. "My hair is just hair. Ash's lip will heal. Complicit Strategia are the backbone of Jag's rule. *Always be defiant.* Always, always."

And her energy uplifts me. "Dance on his grave," I say.

"Dance on his grave," Ash echoes, and we all fall into silence, Jag's order to bring us upstairs looming over our heads.

As the seconds tick by, bringing us closer to whatever Jag has in store for us, my dream comes flashing back to me—all my friends dead on the floor and me holding the poison that killed them. "I have to tell you guys something, something I probably should have mentioned before," I say, and they turn to look at me. "Right before we left the Academy I had this dream, and I think it foretold our deaths—"

"Lucky for you it was a dream and you're not a goddamn fortune-teller," Aarya replies.

"It felt real, so real," I say. "And that big room upstairs—"

"Are we really spending our final moments analyzing your *dream*?" Aarya says with a bit of amazement. But after a second of thought, she shrugs. "I guess there are worse topics. Go ahead, Ember, dazzle us with your weird brain."

"I'm serious," I say, not able to shake the feeling that I owe them so much more than an apology. "The big room upstairs was in my dream, and you were all lying on the ground choking on poison, poison I was holding in my hand. And . . . I know this is my fault. That you've all come here because of me and now Jag will kill you because of me."

Aarya cocks her head. "By 'big room' you mean the great hall? The one that looks remarkably like the dining hall at the Academy, which your subconscious could have plucked it from? And by 'poison,' do you mean something similar to what Dr. Conner used on Ash to traumatize you only days earlier?"

"You didn't make anyone come here—to the UK or to this estate," Ash says, picking up where Aarya left off. "We all knew exactly what we were doing when we left the Academy. We wanted to be here. And if we all go out together fighting Jag, so be it. It's no fault of yours and it certainly doesn't have anything to do with some ominous dream."

Ash's and Aarya's words hit me hard. Even now, chained in a dungeon, they don't blame me. They're not the cuddly feel-good type of friends I was used to in Pembrook, but they are every bit as dependable and supportive.

"Don't spoil my fun," Aarya says. "I'm enjoying watching her grovel because she's had one very obvious vision that told her we would be in danger and now feels like she's psychic."

Ines laughs and for a moment I just stare at her. But then Aarya laughs, too.

"Continue, Ember. We all need a good chuckle before Jag cuts us up into little pieces or feeds us to his crocodiles," Aarya says. "What other nonsense would you like to spew at us?"

"I . . ." I look at each of them and find that despite this being the lowest point in my entire life, I, too, am smiling. "Thanks, Aarya. I actually really needed that. You're a good friend."

Aarya brushes off my comment, but I can tell by her slightly startled expression that the acknowledgment means something to her.

"She used to help me through my bad dreams when I first

came to live with her," Ines says, smiling at the memory. "No matter how bad they got, she always found a way to make me laugh."

Aarya looks increasingly flustered. "Ines, that's private—"

"Wow, Aarya, who knew you had such a big heart?" Ash says, now wearing a smile as well.

Aarya's mouth opens. "I have *no such thing*. Don't you dare even suggest it."

"No sense in hiding it," Ines says. "Might as well just come out and admit the truth."

Aarya's face turns bright red. "I can't wait until Jag kills us all. Then I won't have to listen to this crap for a second longer."

Even though it's a morbid joke, we all laugh at her absurdity. And for just the briefest of moments, we're not four Strategia in a dungeon awaiting death, we're four friends sharing our lives with one another. As I look at each one of them, I realize how much they gave up to be Strategia, how they probably never got the summer nights lying on a blanket under the stars telling jokes and eating junk food, never got told to keep it down while playing Truth or Dare at a sleepover, and never suffered the amazingly awkward moment of slow dancing at a school dance. They're always focused, always strategizing, always guarded. I sigh, fervently clinging to the hope that I get more time with them.

Twenty-Seven

THE BOUNCER UNLOCKS the door of our cell, trailing eight guards behind him, and everything in me sinks. *This can't be happening now. I need more time. I need* . . . Then it occurs to me: Layla's not here. She didn't break us out of the dungeon, she didn't even give us a sign that she was going to try. I swallow, the blood draining from my cheeks. *What if I was wrong about her being the one who killed those guards, or worse, what if she's been captured, too?*

Two guards approach each of us, and as they lower my arms out of the shackles, I realize how sore I am from holding them above my head. All my struggling produced a couple of angry red welts on my wrists. But I don't get time to inspect them because the guards yank my arms behind my back with force and tie my wrists with a knot of rope.

They escort us out of the cell in a line with me at the very back, Ash at the front, and Ines and Aarya in between. A guard holds each of my arms with a steel grip that I'm certain is going to leave bruises.

"I guess it takes eight Lion guards and one giant to handle

four Academy kids," Aarya says flippantly in front of me, and the guards next to her stiffen. "I'm also guessing you want to smash me into something right now?" she continues when they don't respond. "Go ahead. I'll wait."

I tense, waiting for them to throw her into the bars on the cells we're passing. But the guards don't respond.

"Ahhh, I see," Aarya continues. "Jag doesn't let you think for yourselves. That's probably a good thing, though. And that big one, geez," she says loudly enough for the bouncer to hear her in the front of the procession. "Good thing brute strength is an asset."

In a way, I understand Aarya; she's getting in her punches where she can, even if they're verbal. The guards lead us out of the dungeon and up the flight of stairs we snuck down last night. The wide corridor with the looming portraits is now populated with Strategia, who stare at us uncomfortably. And it gives me hope to know that while Jag may be willing to torture Academy kids in his dungeon, other Strategia don't find it as palatable.

The guards lead us into the great hall. It's a huge rectangular room with vaulted ceilings. At the far end there is an elevated platform, upon which Jag sits in a thronelike chair that's trimmed in gold, with a red velvet seat. Rose stands next to him with a stony expression and next to her is Brendan, who doesn't look victorious the way I thought he would, but ghostly pale and uncertain.

A large crowd is gathered, speaking in hushed voices that hum with anticipation. Heavy wooden doors close behind us, and the crowd parts as the bouncer approaches, creating a pathway for us to be brought to Jag.

And that's when I see him. *Dad*. His hands and chest are bound with rope and he's on his knees in front of Jag, surrounded by four guards. There is blood on his face and I see cuts on his arms. He makes eye contact with me, and despite his banged-up appearance, his eyes have the same steady look they always do. A sob rises in my throat.

Jag leans back in his throne, exuding self-assurance as the guards line us up in a neat row. He's the picture of poise, transformed from his unassuming private persona to his showy public one. I glance around the room, searching for some sign that Layla is safe, but find none. There are twelve guards standing with us, thirteen if you count the bouncer. Plus two with Jag and two more at the entrance we came through, which is the only way in or out of this room. There is no place to hide in here, nowhere Layla could be.

Jag clears his throat and the room falls eerily silent. "Welcome, Family and friends," he says, and his tone is easy and imbued with his usual charisma.

I scan the crowd, wondering how many different Families are here, but it's impossible to tell based on appearance alone.

"Today we meet under unusual circumstances." Jag takes his time getting up from his throne and moving between us and the crowd. "As I told you all last night, the Ferryman apprehended the man who not only killed our former Regent but made a mockery of our Family. A worthy capture, one that is a testament to our Family's strength and dominance, and one that will be remembered for decades to come. *This* is the man who appears before you." Jag gestures at my dad. "While I knew the criminal would be cunning, and I knew he would be resourceful, what I did not imagine, could not imagine, was that he would also be someone I once knew better than my own self. This man, who has committed unspeakable acts of betrayal, of cold-blooded cruelty, this man . . . is my son, Christopher." Jag pauses, letting the information sink in.

There are low murmurs from the crowd and people look at one another, unsure. I hear my dad's name being whispered.

"Like you, I was led to believe that Christopher was murdered as a young man," Jag says. "Like you, I trusted my son, believed that he was unshakably loyal to this Family."

I look at my dad, but he just stares forward at the crowd, unflinching. And it becomes clear why Jag invited all these people—this public display is meant to show his Family and all of Strategia what happens if you challenge him. He's spinning fear behind the façade of justice.

"Under markedly different circumstances, this would be a happy occasion," Jag continues, momentarily lowering his head as though the whole ordeal has taken a toll on him. "But unfortunately, that is not this day. Instead of the bright, capable boy who was meant to lead this Family, the man who has returned to me is a traitor." His expression is somber. "Not only was he captured after making an attempt on my life, but he passed his twisted ways on to his daughter, who admits without remorse to recruiting fellow Strategia to move against me. She killed our very own Harry." There are uncomfortable whispers in the crowd and people lean over each other to get a look at me.

"Unfortunately, there is no hope for my son and his daughter," Jag says as though this is a difficult decision for him. "They have been thoroughly corrupted . . ."—he pauses, making sure he has everyone's attention—"by the Bear Family."

My eyes widen, and I'm not the only one who's shocked. The room hums with tension.

Jag sweeps his eyes across the crowd. "Our sources show that these two have been working with the Bears for many years now in an attempt to destroy this Family. They have gone against everything we Strategia stand for, undermining our value system and threatening our way of life with their flippant disregard for our rules."

I glance nervously at the crowd. I remember Ash telling me that leaving Strategia was forbidden, that it was punishable by death. And from the nodding among the onlookers, it's obvious they think we're guilty of that and much, much more.

Jag clasps his hands behind his back. "It's a sad day when a father has to pass sentence on his own son and granddaughter. I can see that you agree I would be remiss not to. But the burden that is weighing heavily on me this day is not restricted to these treacherous Family members. It extends to the Bears who supported them—the head family that hides in London as we speak and the apothecary who provided these traitors with poison intended to kill me, to name just a few transgressions." Jag's knowing gaze falls on me for the briefest of seconds, a look of victory in his eyes; my stomach does a fast unnerving flip. "I fear the time has come for me to right this wrong. The Bears have been taking liberties for years now, and if the Council of Families won't move to correct their offenses, it leaves me no choice but to take action myself."

I flit my eyes to Ash, but he's watching Jag, his expression laced with worry. Suddenly this public display makes sense. This was never about us; he could have killed me and my dad in his dungeon and no one would have been the wiser. Jag is using us to *start a war with the Bears*. And if he succeeds, Jag will go uncontested, free to abuse his power and dominate the rest of the Strategia. This is what Ash meant when he said he wanted to know what Jag was up to, that he thought Jag had an ulterior motive.

Without warning I hear my dad laugh, and I'm so surprised that I flinch. "Bravo," my dad says to Jag in a big booming voice. "Wonderful performance. You should take a bow."

Jag frowns at the sound of his voice and gives my dad a warning look before returning his attention to the crowd. "I will make no exceptions for my son and granddaughter; they will receive the same treatment I would afford any traitor who abandoned Strategia, compromised our secrecy, and attacked their own Family: execution."

Jag snaps his fingers and one of the guards opens the door, letting through a man dressed entirely in black and holding a double-sided axe. His tunic has a wide hood that comes down over his face in a blackout mask. Sweat drips down my temple and I try to get my dad's attention.

But my dad isn't looking at me; he's still looking at Jag. "Do you honestly imagine anyone believes that you're starting a war with the Bears because of *me*?" he says in a clear voice. "Certainly not. For years you've been looking for a reason to make the Bears bow to your depraved rule; I am merely an excuse."

People in the audience shift, looking from Jag to my dad and back again.

Jag's expression remains unfazed, but he looks at the crowd as if gauging their reaction to my dad's words. "It is impossible to argue with the facts," he replies, and straightens his tunic, an easy, unconcerned gesture.

"If you were relaying facts, you wouldn't be hosting a private execution. Careful now," my dad says. "Or people might think you're doing this for personal reasons."

In any other situation, I would be cheering on my dad for getting under Jag's skin, but not with an executioner in the room.

Then I see it: Jag's eye twitches. "You might find it judicious to spend the last minutes of your life more wisely, like saying your goodbyes. But no matter, it's easy enough to gag you. Guards," he says, and once again scans the room, like he's looking for some unseen threat.

One of my dad's guards shoves a cloth in his mouth, stopping him before he can reply.

"Now bring him up here," Jag says, his voice perfectly controlled.

The bouncer places a large wooden block on the ground in front of us. It's covered in dark marks that I can only assume are bloodstains. I feel the color drain from my face, my heartbeat pulsing furiously in my temples. And as the guards drag my dad forward, I struggle.

"Are you all really going to let this happen?" I say angrily to the crowd, in a last-ditch effort to buy time, for Layla to show up, something. "Are you really going to let him kill his son and granddaughter without question? Maybe you will, maybe you'll stand there, justifying our execution as punishment for breaking some archaic rule. Maybe you'll ignore your misgivings about why the firstborn son of the Lion Family suddenly disappeared as a teenager, and the fact that he left because his own father put a hit on him. And even if you can make peace with all the things that don't add up, how will you possibly explain away my friends? Is it right that Jag murder a group of Academy students without their Families, without the permission of the Council? A Jackal, a Fox, and *the head Wolf's son*."

Once again shock rolls through the crowd in the form of hushed conversations and worried looks.

"Enough!" Jag says, only it's not the quiet tone he used to silence Aarya last night; it's forceful, signaling a small crack in his composure.

But I keep talking, Ines's words about defiance ringing in my head. "Ask yourselves this: Are you comfortable letting someone who would murder children rise to be the head of all Strategia? Strategia have rules; we have order. Jag breaks all those rules and yet he still runs this Family. How can this be? How can he be allowed to kill off the most talented students *at the Academy*, of all places, a time-honored institution where the child of every Family is an equal?" When I stop speaking, my dad is staring at me, proud.

There are a couple of gasps in the crowd. I can tell Jag wants to muzzle me, too, but is too prideful to let it look like the only way he can control the situation is by gagging everyone.

"The ramblings of a guilty child," Jag says like it's all very sad that I'm so desperate, but his eyes are angry.

"If you don't believe me, ask them." I nod at my friends, speaking as fast as I can, hoping my words are connecting. "Ask *Brendan*. He's not a good enough liar to hide it. And then ask yourselves: What if your children, cousins, brothers, sisters are next because they disagree with Jag? Because the Lions are not the problem here. I refuse to believe it's the Lions. My dad's a Lion. I'm a Lion. The person who is abusing his rule, the person who is killing other Strategia without cause, is *Jag*."

Jag's face tightens, but instead of addressing me, he gestures at the block, redirecting everyone's attention to my dad and the executioner.

My dad's guards force his head down onto the bloodstained wood.

"No!" I scream, and the sound is guttural, ripped straight out of my heart. I struggle against my guards with wild movements, but however I thrash, I can't break their hold on my arms.

Jag's eyes twinkle as he walks up to me on his way back to his throne. He leans in, speaking just loud enough for me to hear. "You will die last, watching your father and every one of your friends go before you."

For a heart-stopping second, I remember the coded message Ash was reluctant to give me—*Harry's dead and there will be retaliation*—Jag's setting a trap for us in his dungeon, hurting my friends, this. After soaking in the expression of horror on my face, Jag calmly walks back to his throne, confident once more.

In desperation, I struggle harder against my guards. "Dad!" I yell as the executioner takes his position.

I throw my shoulders backward and kick my legs up in the air, as though I were doing a backflip. The guards manage to support my body weight, but I lean so far back that I'm practically inverted, giving me enough momentum to kick the guard on my right in the face. There is a crunching sound and blood comes pouring out of his nose. He drops me, causing the other guard to lose his footing, and I hit the ground hard on my side. But before I can right myself, the stumbling guard regains his grip and yanks me to my knees by my hair.

"Raise your blade!" Jag commands the executioner, victory ringing in his voice.

The executioner lifts his axe with both hands, the blade hovering over him for a split second, and the entire room seems to pause with it. Then he drops his arms, the blade whipping through the air so fast and with so much force that no one has time to react as it changes direction—slicing the bouncer's head right off.

A scream stops in my throat so abruptly that I choke. Blood sprays outward and the crowd lurches back. It's so quiet that when the bouncer's head and body hit the floor, the noise echoes, like the sound is being broadcast through a loudspeaker.

I stare unblinkingly at my dad.

Then everything happens at once. The guards throw open the door to yell for backup and half the room looks toward the exit, not like they're scared, just like they want no part of this fight. The executioner doesn't waste a moment. He swings his axe again, taking down one of the guards holding my dad.

"*Kill them!*" Jag orders behind me, his usual calm replaced by anger. All I can think is that he sees his mistake in inviting members of other Families to watch the execution—people who might need him politically but also have no interest in risking their lives to save his.

The guard whose nose I broke unsheathes his knife while the other one yanks my head back, exposing my throat.

"Nova!" my dad yells, but he and the executioner are outnumbered, fighting four guards.

Ash, too, calls out for me, but his hands are still bound. He whips his head to the side, smashing it into the face of the guard on his right.

My guard steps toward me, his fingers tightening around his knife handle. I attempt to go backward, but the other guard's grip on my hair makes it impossible to move. I keep my eyes open, looking straight at my oncoming killer.

"Do you think you'll remember this?" I ask. "The day you killed an innocent seventeen-year-old? Or will it just be another day working for Jag?"

For a split second, he hesitates. Instead of softening, though, his expression hardens and he closes the distance between us. Just as his blade comes toward me, there's a buzzing sound and the guard grunts like the wind was knocked out of him. Then his eyes widen and he steps uncertainly to the side, dropping his blade. A wooden shaft sticks out of his back. *An arrow?*

My eyes sweep the room, but before I can locate the archer, there's another buzzing sound and I duck reflexively. The guard holding my hair sways, loses his grip on me, and drops to the floor. I look from him to the crowd, where I see Layla, bow in hand, which she reloads to take out one of Ash's guards. I search for Matteo, but he isn't with her, and I'm not exactly surprised. I was shocked he came to London in the first place. I could hardly expect he would risk coming to the Lion estate.

"Layla?" Ash says in disbelief. But before Layla can get another arrow out of her quiver, one of Jag's men is on her, throwing a kick that splits her bow in half. Ash jabs his elbow into his remaining guard's throat, and as the man chokes, Ash breaks free of his restraints and moves toward his sister.

I bend down fast, grabbing a knife from the dead guard's belt and sawing through the rope that's tied around my wrists. I turn toward my dad, who's fighting two guards alongside the executioner. But before I can get to him, another Lion guard collides with my shoulder, sending me back a step. The moment he makes eye contact with me, he swings, connecting with my jaw before I can find my balance. My mouth fills with blood.

I regain my footing and lunge forward, slashing at his torso. He nimbly jumps backward, my blade cutting nothing but the air in front of him. He yanks two knives from the sheaths on either side of his belt. I readjust my stance, watching his hands and his eyes, hoping he's not as good with knives as I fear he might be. He begins to lift his blades, and I brace for his advance, but it doesn't come. Instead, his eyes widen and his back arches unnaturally. I stare at him in confusion as a wet patch appears on the front of his black shirt. *Blood.*

The guard falls to his knees, dropping his blades, and there standing behind him is Ash.

"November," Ash says with relief, immediately scanning me for injury.

Then Layla is at his side, and with their matching expressions they look unmistakably like twins.

The room is in complete chaos. Everywhere I look people are fighting to the death. Ines drops one guard with a kick to the throat and punches another. She moves with grace and self-assurance, like a petite ninja. And her shorn hair doesn't diminish her flair; if anything she looks more badass than ever. Aarya's no slouch, either. She's got two knives and is slashing them through the air with remarkable speed.

Jag is watching them as well, his face twisting into a grimace. He grabs a knife from his belt and pulls his arm back, aiming it at Aarya. Ash follows my line of sight as I scream, "Aarya!"

Jag's hand is extended, the knife already flying through the air. But Ines has seen him, too, and dives in front of her friend.

A look of horror washes over Aarya's face as she realizes what's happening. "No!" she screams. But it's too late; Jag's knife has lodged in Ines's chest, a clean shot, a kill shot.

Ines slams back against Aarya, who wraps her arms around her friend, and together they slump to the ground. Ines's face contorts with shock and pain.

Aarya rips off the sleeve of her own shirt, pressing the fabric around the knife wound. But there is so much blood that it's soaked in seconds. Aarya stares at her fingers, covered in red, continuing to put pressure on the wound.

"I'm getting you out of here," Aarya says, sliding an arm under Ines's neck.

"No, Aarya," Ines responds in a self-assured voice.

Aarya grips Ines firmly, lifting her slightly.

"Stop," Ines commands, her voice strained, and Aarya does.

For a moment they just stare at each other. Aarya bites back tears, and Ines places a shaking hand over Aarya's, squeezing her friend's fingers as if to tell her not to worry.

"I . . . th-thank you," Ines says, but her voice comes out gargled and her eyes struggle to stay focused.

"Don't you dare thank me, Ines. You're not dying," Aarya says stubbornly.

But Ines's breathing is getting progressively more labored. "Thank you . . . for being my sister."

Aarya opens her mouth to respond, but Ines's eyes flutter and close, her body going limp in Aarya's arms.

Aarya touches Ines's face. "Ines?" she breathes. "Ines?" But Ines is gone, and by the way Aarya's face crumbles, she knows it. She folds over her friend, squeezing Ines into her body, her pain so visceral that I feel it in my own chest.

I pull at my shirt, like I can't get air, like it was all sucked out of the room, my breath fast and stilted. But deep down inside, anger is forming, small and tight and hot, like a red coal from a dying fire. My hand clenches around my knife and before I can even form the thought, I'm looking for Jag, ready to avenge my friend, to guarantee he never hurts anyone ever again. But when I look back toward the throne, he's gone, and not only him, but Rose and Brendan as well. I do a fast scan of the room, scared I won't find him and scared of what I might be capable of when I do.

"There," Layla says, and points. Jag is already halfway across the room, heading for the door.

My dad drops the guard he's fighting with a fast kick and immediately turns to me. He follows my sight line to Jag just as Jag slips out of the great hall.

"Nova—" my dad starts, but looks again after Jag. "Stay here. Stay safe." And with a heavy expression, he leaves me to hunt down his father. I know he has to follow him, that he can't let Jag slip away, but I can't, either.

"I'm coming with you," Ash says, his eyes strained with the same conflict of chasing Jag or staying to fight with Layla and Aarya.

"No, just me," I say. "We can't leave Aarya by herself."

"Go, November. You'll lose them if you don't," Layla insists, and I do.

Twenty-Eight

I RUN AFTER Jag and my dad, weaving around fighting Strategia and dead bodies. The heavy door is half open and the guards previously stationed at it are either missing or dead. I run out of the great hall into a mostly bare foyer hung with tapestries. Luckily there is only one hallway to choose from. But before I can run for it, I hear boots pounding straight for me. And out of the shadows at the end of the hall charges a man dressed all in black. He locks eyes with me and I recognize him as the guard who held the knife to Aarya's throat last night in the dungeon. He unsheathes a sword.

I hold up my knife and ready my stance as he barrels toward me, aware that my weapon is no match for his. As he gets closer his movements become more deliberate and his face more focused. He slashes at me with so much force that the air moves. I barely manage to jump out of the way, avoiding his blade with just inches to spare.

As he raises his arm again the distinctive hum of a bowstring comes from behind him. But before he can turn, I hear the thud of metal hitting flesh. His eyes bulge and he stumbles, dropping face-first to the floor, an arrow sticking out of his back.

I peer down the hallway, and from the shadows comes a tall guy with broad shoulders and a serious expression.

"*Matteo?*" I say in disbelief. He has a half-empty quiver of arrows slung over one shoulder and a longbow in his hand.

"November," he says, and we share an awkward nod, neither of us knowing what to say, and no time to say it if we did. For the briefest moment there's a glimmer of understanding between us, but then we're both moving again, him into the great hall and me chasing after my dad and Jag.

I pick up speed, not stopping to assess my surroundings the way I normally would. Instead, I race down the hallway, through the door at the end, and into an empty banquet hall. But the only person in the room is a dead guard with an arrow sticking out of his back that matches the arrows in Layla's and Matteo's quivers.

I move as fast as my legs will carry me around tables set with fine china, push through another door at the far end of the room, and burst into an enormous kitchen. The staff doesn't jump, but there is a general air of nervous tension that tells me something happened here. And what's more, they look from me to the side door, as though someone just passed through that way and they expect me to do the same.

I fly across the kitchen and through the door, stopping short as my boots hit grass and the cold air pricks my sweaty skin. There in the middle of the open courtyard is a small crowd of Strategia, and all eyes are turned to my dad and Jag.

On the ground, not far from the side door, are two dead guards. By the way Jag glances at them disappointedly, it's clear he came this way because he thought they would be here. Both of them were shot with arrows. *Thank you, Layla and Matteo.*

My dad stands in front of his father with a knife in his hand and his back to me. Jag lifts his own blade. I want to let my dad know I'm here, but I don't dare call out his name for fear I'll distract him.

"Your guards are dead," my dad says to Jag, "and there's no one left to do your killing."

"Is that what you think?" Jag says, adeptly slashing his knife at my dad. "One simple command and everyone here will tear you limb from limb."

My dad fends off Jag's blade with his own, and it's immediately obvious that they are well matched. I anxiously scan the onlookers to see what effect Jag's words had on them. I recognize a few of their faces from inside the great hall but have no way of knowing what Families they belong to.

Jag lifts his chin, his stance prideful. "The person who kills my son will be rewarded with my absolute loyalty and an enormous sum of money. You and your Family will be favored in *all* deals and *all* agreements. You will be fully supported by the Lions and be envied by all other Strategia."

Jag throws a kick at my dad, who dodges.

My pulse races and my muscles tense the way they do before a fight. I'm positive an offer like that isn't easily passed up, not with the money and influence Jag presumably has. I raise my knife, moving closer to my dad. But he catches sight of me and puts his hand out, indicating I should stop. And I do, bracing for the inevitable onslaught.

My dad slashes his knife at Jag, who leans out of the

way. But Jag is fast, and he returns with a kick that connects squarely with my dad's ribs, sending him staggering back a few feet. I take another anxious step forward, and again my dad gestures for me to stay where I am.

As though they heard my silent plea for help, Ash, Layla, Matteo, and Aarya come flying through the kitchen door. I can only assume the battle in the great hall is over and that it went in our favor, but none of that will matter if Jag wins this fight. My friends look from me to my dad and Jag, assessing the situation and moving closer, weapons in hand. But even with four more fighters, if this crowd turns, we're outnumbered by at least ten.

Jag runs at my dad, getting so close that his knife tears through my dad's shirt. Before my dad can recover, Jag advances again, this time nicking my dad's shoulder and sending a line of blood down his arm. My dad returns with a punch, connecting with Jag's jaw and splitting his lip.

Jag spits blood onto the grass. "Did you hear me?" he says in a commanding voice, glancing at the crowd. "I said *kill him!*"

Three seconds tick by and the onlookers stare at one another as though they expect someone else to make the first move. But no one draws a weapon; no one jumps to his aid. My dad advances with a punch and Jag blocks, but my dad nicks Jag in the cheek with his knife, not enough to do any real damage, but enough to make him bleed. Jag reaches his fingers to his face, incredulous.

A snarl escapes Jag and he slashes his knife through the air in two fast swings, but unlike his previously precise movements, these are furious and out of control. And just like when I was a kid and my emotions got the better of me, my dad moves, waits for his moment, and delivers a perfect hit. He catches Jag's knife midswing and sends it flying through the grass.

For a second everyone is perfectly still. Jag eyes his weapon, but it's too far away for him to retrieve.

"Your reign is over," my dad says, his voice confident. He takes a step toward Jag. "I want to be perfectly clear with you what that means: you're not only done leading"—as my dad continues, his voice booms in the stillness—"you're done being Strategia."

"They'll never follow you," Jag says, not backing down. "You're *weak*."

"I disagree," my dad replies, and for a second, I think I misheard him. *Leading? As in leading the Lion Family? But he doesn't . . . he couldn't . . . could he?*

"You're an embarrassment to this Family," Jag says in a condescending tone. "You rejected Strategia; you shirked your duties, you have no place here."

"I never rejected Strategia. I rejected *you*. And while you're correct that I didn't build a reputation among Strategia as your son, I didn't disappear from society. The Strategia know me by a different name." He pauses. "The Ferryman."

There are gasps in the crowd and the confident expression drains from Jag's face as he realizes he publicly announced that the Lions hired the Ferryman to . . . capture himself. I'm so shocked I nearly drop my knife. And suddenly the missing pieces fall into place. Hawk said Mary and Jenny helped the Ferryman capture my dad. Which means that while the blood in the apartment was real, the scene must have been staged. Hawk was also at the ball. I couldn't understand why my dad sent me into such a dangerous situation without a net, but

Hawk was the net; Hawk wasn't hunting me, he was keeping an eye on me. I stare at my dad in awe.

Jag's expression hardens. "Rose—" he begins, but my dad cuts him off.

"Rose will lead with me," my dad says, and I can't believe what I'm hearing. My dad is going to lead with *Brendan's mom*?

Jag puts one of his hands to his heart as though he's going to say something, while the other drops by his side. But it drops unnaturally fast. For a second I can't decide if his wrist flicked slightly or if I just imagined it. Then I see it—a small glass vial in the palm of his hand. *The lightning poison!* And from where my dad is standing, I know it's not visible.

And once again I see a flash from my dream—the great hall filled with dead bodies, Jag holding poison. While Aarya and Ash were right that it was just a dream, I realize that it wasn't the death that scared me; it was the fear that I wouldn't be able to do what I needed to in order to stop Jag.

There is no time to warn my dad, so instead I ready my knife and yell the one thing I can think of that will affect them both.

"Hamilton!" I scream.

Jag's eyes flit to me just as I had hoped, and I can tell my dad has registered my meaning—Jag is being crooked. And as Jag raises a blowpipe to his mouth, I don't hesitate. I pull back my knife and throw.

My aim is true and my knife lodges deep in Jag's chest. But to my utter surprise, a dozen more knives and an arrow strike him as well. Not only did my dad and I react in time, but my friends and some of the crowd did, too.

Jag falls to his knees, gasps for one last breath, and slumps to the ground. We're all still for a beat, everyone absorbing what just happened and braced for backlash. But no one defends Jag. No one even looks upset he's gone. After it becomes obvious that the conflict is over, my friends lower their weapons and everyone starts talking, astonished voices filling the courtyard.

My dad turns to me, but I don't move. It feels like I'm frozen in place, stuck between my moment of terror and my relief.

"I hope his last words were the desire to look like a pincushion, because if so, he got his wish," Aarya says. Even in the midst of her grief, Aarya can't help being Aarya.

But I'm not looking at my friends because I'm running full-speed to my dad.

"Dad?" I manage, my voice cracking.

He opens his arms, pulling me into a big hug. My dad, who I love more than anything, is *here,* hugging me, not lost in Europe or chained in a dungeon. I wrap my arms around him, burying my face in his shoulder. His familiar scent brings tears to my eyes and he rests his cheek against my head.

"My girl," he says gently, and I soak up his reassuring voice like it was sunshine.

For a few long seconds, I just hold on to my dad, nothing needing to be said, nothing needing to be done.

But my moment of peace is short-lived. I pull back, staring at him. "You *left* me," I say, and there's hurt in my voice, but also an accusation. "You made me chase you all over the UK! And, and, Logan, and that ball. *How could you?*" All the feelings I've suppressed over the last month are bubbling to the surface.

My dad examines my face, taking careful note of my upset. "I owe you an explanation, Nova. You have every right to be upset with me. We will talk at length and I'll answer all your questions. Just not here," he says, and glances around the courtyard. "Let's get you kids inside."

We follow my dad down a long hall and he opens a door to a cozy sitting room. There are an oversized wine-colored couch with two armchairs and a coffee table, a set of bookshelves, a few old trunks, and a lit fireplace. He holds the door open and Layla and Matteo file in, with Ash and me behind them. Aarya is last, and before she comes through the door, my dad quietly talks to her.

"Aarya," he says with a heaviness in his voice, "I cannot tell you how sorry I am."

For a moment, Aarya looks surprised, like she's not used to adults showing concern over her. But as I register the grief on her face, I realize that my own frustration with my dad is a luxury, that I can only be mad because he's here, that while I might not like what he did, I have everything to be grateful for.

Aarya shakes her head as if to downplay her sadness. "Ines was proud to fight here today. She would have made the same choice one hundred times over."

My dad watches Aarya thoughtfully, reading her expression and her reaction to his tone. "I don't know what your plans are going forward, if you intend to return to the Academy, but if you need time, you're welcome to stay here with us."

For an instant, Aarya seems shocked by the offer, and I'm reminded that my dad isn't like the other Strategia parents, that his time in Pembrook changed him. Or maybe being raised by Jag made him choose a different direction, a direction that involved being a loving and affectionate parent. Whatever the case, it's clear that Aarya isn't sure how to react.

"I . . . well . . . I should really . . . ," she starts, and it's the first time I've ever seen her at a loss for words. She sighs. "Thank you. Maybe I will."

My dad closes the door behind Aarya and gestures for us to sit.

"Layla and Ashai," he says. "Zareen's kids. Your mother and I were once good friends when we were studying at the Academy."

I look from my dad to Ash and Layla, trying to make sense of his words. Their mother went to the Academy with my dad? Is that why Layla and I were paired as roommates? And then it occurs to me that my dad's favorite whittling knife has a wolf handle. He told me his best friend gave it to him when they were teenagers.

"She always spoke highly of her days with you as well, sir," Layla says, but Ash matches my look of shock. I could groan. No matter what is happening, Layla always manages to know more than the rest of us.

"Matteo," my dad continues, his voice taking on a meaningful tone. "You and Layla were invaluable today. Your strategy and skill were advanced far beyond your years."

Matteo seems almost embarrassed under my dad's prideful

look. "It was an honor to be a part of it," he says with polite and almost shy formality.

"There have never been Academy students who have taken so much risk or accomplished so much as you all," my dad says, and I feel my cheeks get warm at the dadness of his gushing. "Because of what you did here today, the power balance will not only be restored among Strategia, but the world at large will be safer. Of course this adjustment will take time and it will take work, work that will involve the Council of Families and all of your respective Families." He pauses. "Now, I'm certain you all have questions," he continues, "and if I can answer them, I will."

"Did you know that Jag intended to start a war with the Bears?" Layla asks, wasting no time, and I look from her to my dad.

"I did," he says. "But by the time November's aunt and I realized what was going on, the Regent and Jag were already planning their attack. If we didn't act immediately, the other Families would be forced to take sides and Strategia as we know it would be forever changed."

I reflexively look at Ash and he meets my gaze, an understanding passing between us. This is the reason Ash had been searching for. This is the reason everything happened when it did.

"November's aunt took care of the Regent," my dad says, confirming what I already suspected. "We sent November to the Academy to protect her and to keep Conner from killing Matteo, and I came here to stop Jag."

They all look at me, but I'm just as surprised about Matteo as they are.

Aarya chuckles. "Boy, Matteo, I bet you feel like a jerk for punching her."

Matteo's eyebrows dip and he looks like he wants to say something to her, but he stops himself and closes his mouth. Maybe he's going easy on her because she's in grief or maybe he's just more mature than she is. But whatever the reason, I'm not paying attention to Aarya's needling, I'm staring at Matteo.

"The punch . . . ," I say, my voice trailing off. "It was Blackwood, wasn't it? Blackwood told you to punch me." My thoughts race as I connect the dots. "So everyone would believe we were enemies, completely disguising the reason I was there." The best poisons are psychological and emotional, Professor Hisakawa taught us. "And Conner redirected his energy to me." I look at my dad. "Oh my god. You knew Conner would want to kill me more than he wanted to kill Matteo." The question I don't ask, though, is how did my dad know Conner wouldn't succeed?

"Truthfully, it was more than the Lions' attack on Matteo that we needed to prevent," my dad says. "If Conner's actions remained hidden, the Lions would have succeeded in systematically killing the best students from noncompliant Families, and the surviving young Strategia would have been forever tilted in the Lions' favor. Either because they were fearful or because they were loyal, the remaining Strategia would have grown up pledged to Jag. Change the young, change the world. My father knew this, hence beginning his attack at the Academy. What you did in that school is every bit as important as what we accomplished out here."

We're all silent for a moment.

"When Rose realized what her father was planning at the Academy, we all decided it was time to take action," my dad continues, but I cut him off.

"Rose? You were talking to Rose?" I say. Ines surmised he needed a contact in the Lion Family to pull off the Regent murder, but it never occurred to me it was Rose.

My dad nods. "We've been in contact for some years now."

"Angus," Ash says, shifting gears. "He mentioned the Ferryman to November. Did he know it was you?"

My dad nods. "Angus is an old friend," he says. "He's known me since I was a boy. And the tip you acquired about Hawk's crew being vulnerable, while true, was also orchestrated by him."

Ash raises an eyebrow, clearly impressed by my father.

"Logan was another story, however," my dad says. "There was no avoiding him, but there was also no controlling him."

"Exactly what I said!" Aarya says, and gives Ash a vindicated look.

"And Hawk's crew," Ash says. "They were in your employ the entire time?"

"They were," my dad replies. "They kept track of you all for me and were meant to run interference at the ball if things went wrong. If you were looking closely, you would have seen that under that executioner's mask was Eddie."

I stare at my dad, baffled by the scope of what he did here and the skill it took to pull it off.

"And the note," I say. "The one you left for us in the apartment telling us to come to the dungeon. You acted surprised to see us. But you knew we were coming the whole time, didn't you?"

My dad takes a heavy breath, a weight appearing to rest on his shoulders. "I never wanted you all to come to the dungeon. It was never my intention. But Jag found out you were in London shortly before the ball and he was preparing to send his assassins with instructions to kill everyone but Nova, whom he planned to execute publicly."

Aarya blanches.

"With no better alternative, I slipped information to Logan, giving him a chance to make more money, win Jag's favor, and outwit you. Then Rose convinced Jag that he should let you all come to him, to sneak into his dungeon, that it would be impactful for all of Strategia to see the far reaches of his power."

We're all quiet for a beat and I look at Ash and Aarya. Would they still be here if Jag's assassins had come for us? I shiver involuntarily.

Matteo, who has been mostly silent, clears his throat and glances toward the door. "Forgive me, I don't mean to interrupt, but I can't stay. My Family is expecting me."

My dad nods, understanding. "Tell Maura I'll be in touch shortly," he says without further explanation.

"I will," Matteo says, and stands, but turns toward me before he leaves. "Also . . . I just wanted to say, November, that my mom's in town for another few days." He pauses. "And well, if you want to meet her, I think she would really like that." The tension that's usually between us is noticeably absent.

My eyes widen and warmth spreads deep in my chest at the idea that my mom and Aunt Jo's sister wants to see me. "I'd love to," I say, my delight seeping through my words, and with a friendly nod he turns. "And, Matteo," I say, calling after him. "Sorry I punched you in the face the other day."

He shrugs. "I guess that's just our thing."

We share a smile and he walks out the door, closing it behind him.

I turn back to my dad, to find him watching me, and realize how different we both are since the last time we saw each other. But my moment of reflection is short-lived because it suddenly occurs to me that Matteo is leaving but we aren't.

"Why aren't we leaving?" I blurt out. "I mean, why are we still here, at the Lion estate?"

They all look at me, then at my dad.

His expression reminds me of the day he told me I was going to the Academy; it's reassuring and sympathetic, with the recognition that he's delivering difficult news. "We're staying here."

"*Staying* here?" I say in disbelief. "Do you mean for the next few hours, or—"

"For the foreseeable future," he says, and my eyes nearly bug out of my head.

I swallow. "You can't be serious. You want me to *live* here, in the *Lion estate* with *Brendan*."

Aarya chuckles. "Just think, if you need to kill him, at least you'll know where he is." Even Aarya's optimism is twisted.

"Dad?" I say.

My dad looks thoughtful. "We need to be here during the transition," he says. "There will be some discord as a result of Jag's death and it's important that we get the Lions organized and cohesive as soon as possible." He pauses. "But after all our affairs are in order, I'm not opposed to looking for a new location for the estate."

I press my lips together. It's not lost on me that I'm being

413

selfish in requesting that a huge household of people shift because I don't like the building, and if I'm being honest with myself, it's actually not the estate that I don't like—the estate is just a fancy manor house—it's the idea of it that I'm resisting. But his response makes it easier; I'm calmed by the thought that I'm not trapped here, that my dad is listening, and that he cares how I feel.

I've never seen such utter shock in my friends, though, who like all Strategia tend to mute their expressions but are not doing so presently. They just keep glancing from my dad to me and back again, like we're a puzzle they can't solve.

Aarya looks like she might faint. "If my parents loved me that much, I'd never leave home," she says. "Not for the Academy or any reason."

I look at Aarya. That is by far the most vulnerable thing she's ever said in front of me, no jokes, no sarcasm, just awe. And I realize that while I might be in a difficult situation right now, my dad truly loves me, and so I let it go, whatever frustration I was harboring. In that moment it disappears.

Twenty-Nine

DAD SITS ON the end of my four-poster bed. The room is decorated in pastel blues and whites, with a large fireplace and a chaise lounge. The cheery decor feels out of place with the ominous events that just transpired here, but right now I couldn't be more grateful for it. If this room were drab and cold I would feel even more disoriented than I already do. Not to mention, now that it's bedtime, I'm fairly convinced someone is going to spring out of a secret door and cut me open.

"It's going to take some time to find our rhythm in this new world," my dad says, clearly recognizing my hesitancy. "And it's going to be challenging. But I will be here with you every step of the way."

"And you're absolutely positive that Brendan isn't going to come after me with a knife while I'm sleeping?" I say.

My dad smiles. "Rose took him away for a few days. It's going to be a hard adjustment for him—for all of us, really—but one that is worth making."

I snort. I remember provoking Brendan at the Academy,

asking him if the fact that we're cousins meant I'm also a contender for the throne. But when I said those words, I wouldn't have guessed in my wildest dreams that I would have to live with him, much less lead a Family with him. I never wanted to lead a Family in the first place.

"I know your introduction into Strategia hasn't been an easy one, and I know that Brendan has made it harder than it needed to be," my dad says like he can read my thoughts. "But I assure you, there is a great deal of good here, even if it's not immediately obvious. And given some time and space away from Jag, Brendan will have an opportunity to make choices that are his own. I know too well what it means to be raised by that man."

I frown, frustrated by the possible truth of that answer. "Fine," I say.

"Fine?" my dad repeats, and the corners of his mouth turn up ever so slightly.

I fidget with the edge of the white comforter. "As much as I hate to admit it, I saw what Conner did to good people like Ash. I can only imagine what it must have been like for Brendan with Jag."

Now my dad does smile. "I truly wish your mother were here to see the amazing person you've become." His voice softens.

"Dad . . . ," I begin, not sure what I want to say.

He watches me and waits, his expression relaxed and open, inviting my questions.

I sigh, letting my worries go for right now. There's been enough turmoil for one day and I'm utterly exhausted by it. "Tell me about Mom."

He gets the faraway look he's adopted over the years whenever he talks about her. "What do you want to know?"

"Everything. All of it," I say.

He laughs. "That could take a while. How about I just start at the beginning, and eventually, sometime over the next couple of years, I will finish telling you what a remarkable woman she was."

I smile. "Deal."

He sighs, looking up briefly. "Your mom was the most brilliantly strategic student the Academy had ever seen, that *I* had ever seen. The first time we spoke, we'd only been there a week and she walked right up to me in the dining hall and said 'I don't hate people because of their Family. I certainly have a few members in my own that I would rather not claim. I hate them because of their character. Let's hope yours doesn't suck.' And as much as I wanted to convince myself that I didn't like her and that her opinion didn't matter to me, it was impossible. Everyone cared what she thought; she was one of those magnetic people who smiled and turned perfectly composed assassins into babbling mush. So of course I tried to impress her." He winks at me.

"Did it work?" I ask, finding myself leaning into his happy memory.

"Not even a little," he says. "Took me two years before I got her to smile at me and another six months before I convinced her to sneak out of her room and spend time with me." He looks at the fireplace, remembering. "People always assumed that we were enemies who eventually fell for each other. But the truth is, I was head over heels from the beginning."

"Dad, why didn't you ever tell me any of this? Why did you keep it from me?"

My dad nods like he's been waiting for this question. "It was the single hardest thing I've ever done, sending you off to the Academy without telling you about Strategia, without telling you that everything was going to be okay. But if I had told you then, it would have confused and hurt you, putting you in danger and damaging your ability to complete your mission."

While I'm not sure he's wrong, I still don't like it. "Okay, so maybe telling me right before would have been a mess, but why didn't you tell me before that? You had *seventeen years.*"

He takes a breath. "Telling you was something your mom, Aunt Jo, and I debated many times. We needed to train you, to give you the tools you would eventually need to integrate into Strategia society. But we also recognized that you had a unique opportunity growing up in Pembrook, one that would make you a better person and a more compassionate Strategia. You got to be a kid, without the Lions and the Bears and the political discord. You got to be best friends with Emily, and do countless other things Strategia kids don't get to do because they know too much and because their responsibility is too great. Tell me, would you trade that time if you got to do it all over again?"

I chew the inside of my cheek, trying to concoct an argument that would have let me have both the truth and my life in Pembrook. But he's right. I could never have known and had a normal childhood.

My shoulders drop slightly. "No, I wouldn't have traded it for the world, not even with the pain of giving it up."

My dad looks relieved, like he had assumed so but he's happy to hear me say it.

"When I found out who you guys really were, I thought that you and Mom and Aunt Jo had been in hiding, that you were completely divorced from Strategia. But that's not true, is it?" I ask, trying to understand some of the missing pieces.

"We never wanted to leave Strategia. It was just the best choice in a bad situation." He pauses. "You see, when your mom and I were young, we believed we could make Strategia the powerhouse for good that it had the potential to be. But it quickly became apparent that we couldn't do that through uniting our Families, that we needed to find another way." He takes a long look at me.

"By becoming the Ferryman?" I say, still a little mystified by the idea.

"That was part of it," he says. "Your mom, Aunt Jo, and I didn't want to stop our work, but we also couldn't do our work under our own names. To tell you the truth, we had no intention of creating that alias; it just happened gradually, and over time we saw how useful it could be."

I'm instantly reminded of Hisakawa's last poisons class, where she said: Capitalize on what is already in your environment. *Blend.*

"So you were planning this Lion takeover my whole life?" I say, a little startled.

"Not exactly," he says. "But as Jag aged, he became more vicious, and it became apparent that he couldn't remain in power."

"And Aunt Jo?" I ask.

For a brief moment pain appears in his expression. "There was an opportunity, one we couldn't pass up—"

"To kill the Regent?" I ask.

"Right," my dad says, rubbing a callus on his left palm. His expression is heavy and he waits a beat, thinking something over. "Jo called me shortly before she died," he says, and my heart nearly stops. "She said that no matter what happens, she didn't regret what she did, that she got the bastard who killed your mother and that was enough."

My eyes widen. So it was the Regent who killed my mom.

"And she told me that if something did happen to her, to tell you she loved you," my dad continues, and I study my fingers, suddenly feeling very raw. "That she loved you and that in this whole dark world you were her bright star. She said she'd see you on the other side. She'd be the one in the red dress with the fabulous hair." He smiles a sad smile at the memory of my feisty aunt.

And the grief I was suppressing, the grief that was too big to deal with at the Academy, backs up on me. It starts low in my chest, making my throat tighten and the bridge of my nose tingle, and when I look up at my dad, I lose control of it. My chin trembles and my eyes water. He reaches out to me and I bury myself in his arms, crying quietly against his shoulder. Tears for Aunt Jo, my mom, and Ines, for the fear that I would lose him, and for the countless deaths in these last few weeks. All of it pours out of me, hot and messy and unbridled, onto my dad's shirt. And he strokes my hair and my back, telling me over and over that it's going to be okay, that he loved her, too, that he's sorry.

We're like that for a long while, me curled against him like

I used to when I was a little girl, safe in the confines of his hug. He doesn't try to move away or get me to talk. He just waits. He waits until my breath slows and my chest stops heaving. I wipe at my face, suddenly exhausted, but also with a lightness I haven't felt since before the Academy.

I exhale and sit up. "I want to be on board with this, I really do, especially if it's something that you and Mom and Aunt Jo fought for. I just . . . It's going to take me some time," I admit, turning my mom's ring on my finger.

"That's entirely fair," he says, his tone acknowledging the fact that I'm struggling with this. "You have lots of time to choose who you want to be. Even if you decide you never want to lead, that's okay, too. I'm incredibly proud of the girl you already are."

I soak in his words. Because right now, I can't make sense of a grandiose plan to save Strategia and fix the Lions. It's enough that we're together again and that he's proud of me.

I smile at him, and it's a real smile.

And he smiles back. "I know we missed December twentieth," he says. "So I'd like to make it up to you. What do you say to you, me, and a day of winter fun?"

A warmth seeps through my body, one I didn't realize was missing, but one it now feels like I can't live without. "That would be amazing, but"—I pause—"do you think we could bring my friends? After seeing you with them today, I think they need a little dad therapy even more than I do, especially Aarya."

"Sure thing," he says, and it suddenly occurs to me that, for the first time since I was five, when I said *friends*, I didn't mean Emily.

"And, Dad?" I say. "I want to see Emily."

For a moment he hesitates, then nods. "We'll figure out a way. I promise."

There is a knock on the door, and from behind the wood Ash says my name.

"Come in!" I say, and my dad gives me a knowing look.

"I'll let you kids talk," he says as Ash enters.

Dad kisses me on the head, like he has before bed for the past seventeen years, and I smile my good-night as he leaves the room.

Ash sits down next to me on the bed. "Everything okay?" he asks.

"Yes and no," I say, not sure words can properly express the jumble of emotions I'm experiencing. "My whole life just took a one-eighty. It's going to take me a little while to catch up. But I'm working on it."

He nods, his expression understanding, and suddenly it dawns on me—*it's over.* The running is over, the hiding is over, but also the twenty-four-seven time with Ash. I look at him, more conflicted than ever—part of me thrilled to be done with that chapter of my life, and the other part dreading giving him up.

"Go ahead," he says, reading my face. "Ask."

The words stick in my throat, hard to form. "You're leaving, aren't you—"

"No," he says definitively.

My chest flutters with hope, but I'm scared to get excited before I'm sure. "Not leaving tomorrow or not leaving for a while?"

"I'm not leaving until you kick me out."

"But what about your family?" I start.

"Layla will go home and explain it all to them," he says with a satisfied smile.

"Won't they be mad?" I ask.

"I don't know," he says. "Layla's pretty persuasive. I think she's going to sell it as a political boon, a way to repair our Family's relationship with the Lions."

I would say that's smart, but everything Layla does is smart. "And the Academy?"

He shakes his head.

I look at Ash for a long moment. I owe him so much, more than so much. "Thank you for being here, Ash, thank you for all of it, for . . . I don't know how to tell you what it means to me." I stop, because it's not actually what I want to say.

But before I can continue, Ash replies, "Thank you for trusting me."

"No. No," I say to stop him so I can come up with the words to express how I feel. The last time we had a conversation like this I got tongue-tied and wound up saying nothing. I can't let that happen again.

Ash looks amused. "No, you do not accept my thank-you?"

"You're not supposed to be thanking me. . . ." I wave my hand at him. "I'm the one doing the thanking."

His amusement reaches his eyes. "No thank-yous. Got it. I'll add it to the list of unkissable offenses."

I give him a look, and he raises his hands in surrender.

I take a breath, trying to keep my flustered feeling from interfering with my honesty. "You told me once that you truly cared for me," I say, slowly refocusing. "When most people say that, they're talking about their emotions, about some fluttery feeling. But you showed me, and not just because you took unparalleled risks, but because you kept me grounded and made me laugh even in my darkest moments. And what I wanted to tell you is that I truly care for you, too."

"That's a good thing, November, because I'm certain that I'm in love with you," he says. "And it would be awful at this point to find out that you were indifferent."

I laugh, my cheeks getting warm. "I say the most emotional thing I've ever said to a guy and somehow you manage to one-up me," I reply, grinning at him and secretly wishing he'd say it again.

He gives me a mischievous look. "Then I'll strive to one-up you in love for as long as you let me. I can't imagine that anyone will ever love someone more than I love you. So please, give it a try. But be prepared to lose."

I laugh again. "I'll take that challenge."

He leans close, pressing his lips into mine. And in this moment, even though I have no idea what tomorrow will bring, I know that my dad is safe and that Ash loves me, and that everything is going to be okay.

Acknowledgments

I usually write long acknowledgments because, as it turns out, it takes a giant collective of creative smarties to craft my books. See that sentence? I guarantee someone is going to have to fix it. And all the ones after it. But this time around, I'm going to simply say that without your help ("your" referring to Boss Agent Extraordinaire Ro, Editor Genius Mel, Team Awesomeness at Random House, Mom of Love, Husband of Devotion, Baby of Mind-Blowing Everythingness, Family/Chosen Family and Friends of My Heart, Brilliant CPs and Writer Buds, FAMB Lovelies and Readers), I would be a complete and utter mess.

You all bring a level of joy to my life that is just plain giggly. You cheer me on, uplift me, and you make my writing and my world shine. There will never be enough words or exclamation points to describe the gratitude I feel when I wake up in the morning and realize that I get to do something I love, with people I love. So please accept this babble as a small token of the enormous, indescribable feels I get from knowing you all are there. Thank you. THANK YOU.